The
Winter
Charlatan

ISBN: 978-1-7365164-2-3 (Digital)
ISBN: 978-1-7365164-0-9 (Paperback)

Any references to historical events, real people, or real places are used fictitiously. Names, characters, and places are products of the author's imagination.

Front cover image by Victoria McCombs

First printing edition 2021

To my Oma,
Thank you for everything

Chapter One

AFTER FROST BITES YOUR fingertips, you have two hours until it circulates to your heart, freezing it forever; that's what the cave mages say. That, and that belliberries make the best pies.

I believed them when I was younger, until a treacherous snowstorm caught our family on the outskirts of the Wandering Mountains with little protection from the unrelenting snow that surrounded us through the bleak night. Though my fingers froze, my heart didn't, and I never believed the cave mages again.

Except about the belliberries. Those pies were divine.

Still, frozen heart or not, I pulled my parka closer around my neck and nuzzled into the thick fur as a harsh wind lashed across my nose.

It was the strongest winter we'd had in ages, though they say that every year. Elenvérs hadn't seen the heat of summer in hundreds of years since the kingdom moved to the ice palace nestled between the calm Northern Mountains and the enchanting Wandering Mountains. While the snow lessened during half the year, the ice never melted and the flowers never bloomed. We lived too far north for heat to find us now, and the court that once overlooked autumn colors now saw nothing but white mountaintops and endless icicles, until those who remembered warmth were gone and replaced by those who knew no heat besides that of a cave mages' magic.

The snow whipped up from banks along the rocks, swirling in the air and funneling through trees before settling back on the ground as the wind traveled to find a new playmate. Crystals draped from frosted trees, casting the glow of the morning sun into tiny fragments around me. White flakes rested on green pines that grew along the mountainside, and the occasional cluster of snow fell from the trees with a soft sound as wind interrupted their slumber.

For a moment, the beauty captivated me.

The Wandering Mountains might carry a fair amount of uncertainty, but they were far more beautiful than the predictable Northern Mountains. The frosted trees dripping with winter charm. The calm snow resting underfoot. The frozen lakes beautiful enough to be a painting. The peaceful air that was too far away from civilization to carry any noise other than whispering winds.

Focus.

It'd be easy to get lost in these mountains, but I had to stay alert. This was my one chance, and if it didn't work, I didn't have another plan. This was already a long shot.

My mind banished the doubt. I had to break the curse.

The White Bear only revealed itself to the pure of soul, and I'd washed my soul in the spring of refinement three times this morning to be certain the tricky creature showed itself to me. My plan was foolproof.

With my bow and arrow, I'd bring down the bear. An anxious finger rested on the relaxed string, rubbing nervously against the fletching while Elis gave my hand a sideways glance.

"Stop your fidgeting. You're making me nervous."

I peeked to my side. Elis looked anything but nervous—though I hardly knew what nervous looked like on her. Wolf's fur lined her sharp face while subtle snowflakes rested against her brown hair and the tip of her eyelashes. She crouched behind the low hanging branches of a pine tree to hide herself from sight. True to training, she'd mapped out a path for us up the tree if we needed to hide quickly, putting a lot of faith in my ability as an archer to protect us once stuck there.

No one should pass by. The only ones who traveled into these frozen woods were aspiring knights looking for the White Bear to prove their value to their king.

"It's just a bear, we'll be fine," my voice came as a whisper.

Elis whispered back, "I don't think you understand what a bear is."

A grunt escaped my lips. "I've seen some of the knights who bring back the bear's paw, and I'm just as strong as them. It can't be that ferocious."

When Elis didn't reply, I glanced in her direction, but her hazel eyes remained fixated on our surroundings as she scanned the area. The large pine trees made it difficult to see, but I appreciated the change in color that would provide an easier background to spot the White Bear.

We'd traveled out early this morning before the sun peaked over the mountain tops. I'd always valued Elis for her reliability as a sister, but I'd never loved her more than when she agreed to join me this morning with no questions asked. Even still, as we'd hid in the snow for hours seeking out the mysterious White Bear, she didn't ask what I planned to do once we acquired its paw. Her unwavering loyalty amazed me, and I ranked it as one of her highest attributes.

I didn't tell her that enough. "I really appreciate you being here."

She glanced my direction. "Your nose is the same color as your hair. You look terrible."

Her candor was another one of her attributes that I enjoyed. Still, the corner of her mouth twitched upward while she repositioned herself. Her own nose carried a tint of redness to it as she sniffed.

Red was good. Red was not blue. We might come out of this with frostbite, but we were not frozen. Not yet.

I'd stay here until I froze beyond thawing if it meant I caught that bear. I needed this.

I took a moment to bury my nose into the hood of my parka as the frosted fibers rubbed against my skin, providing little relief from the chill. This had already taken longer than predicted, and my stomach complained of hunger while my skin complained of the crippling cold. *Where was that blasted bear?*

"Are you certain Briggs said he came here?" I asked Elis, whose suitor, Briggs, told her where he found the White Bear on his quest to become a knight. After retrieving the bear's paw, he snuck past King Olin's personal guards to hide it under the king's pillow. The queen wasn't amused but King Olin was impressed. Briggs was knighted the next day and began pursuing Elis a week later.

His instructions to the bear sounded clear. Travel east from the caves of the people, down the Lost Man Trail to the edge of the Wandering Mountains. Go to the second mountain on the left, then travel halfway until you find a stream—free flowing despite the frozen temperature. Follow the stream to the source. The bear will be nearby. It always comes, as if it knows it's being called upon.

Besides the stream, there was little to distinguish this part of the Wandering Mountains from the rest of the range. Every inch of the rocks was coated in the same layer of snow and ice. If it weren't for the stream that flowed with clear water while the rest of the mountain stood frozen, I wouldn't know this valley from the next.

Travelers often got lost here, and it was easy to see why. It wasn't marked with mines and civilization like the Northern Mountains were. The Wandering Mountains were large and uncharted and lifeless. Mostly lifeless.

"We're lost," I said, digging my fingertip into my palm to stimulate blood flow.

Elis sighed, and her visible breath coiled around her nose. "It will come."

She held more hope than I did.

Searching another mountain would take too much time, and we must return to Elenvér's castle before anyone questioned our absence. It wasn't unusual for Elis and me to take off for a week at a time, but whenever we left, trouble usually found us. After a few days, the king would send a few knights looking for us. It was his way of showing he cared.

Elis gave me one of her famous sighs. "Of course I'm not certain, but I'm fairly sure. Why are we here anyway?"

Ah, she finally asked. I wasn't ready to share the answer. "Mmm," I mumbled in reply, and she frowned.

Customarily, these parts of the Wandering Mountains were only ventured into by brave men and women aspiring to knighthood, which could be achieved if they found the White Bear, cut off its paw, and returned it to the king. The way the paw was given mattered. King Olin didn't see aspiring knights on request, so instead they had to find a unique and clever way to present the paw to him before he'd grant knighthood.

I enjoyed seeing the different ways knights offered the paw, like when Briggs snuck it into the king's chambers, but my favorite was under the silver platter at dinner one evening. Even the cook was surprised.

It was a tradition that continued from before I was born, and the idea behind the ritual hadn't changed. Knights proved their soul's purity by their ability to spot the White Bear, then proved their skill by acquiring the beast's paw, then their cleverness in how they got the paw before their king.

Pure, skilled, and clever. The three markings of an Elenvérs knight. As far as I knew, no one ever sought out the bear unless aspiring for knighthood.

My legs tingled, and I shifted my crouched position from my feet to my knees. "I'm going to freeze," I complained.

"You wanted the paw," Elis whispered back. "We are getting the paw. Where is that bear? Do you suppose we can't see it?"

That would make matters worse. I took a few breaths before replying, "Just keep looking."

The White Bear only revealed itself to the pure of soul. Any others can't see it. I'd never heard of an aspiring knight who didn't see the bear. If there was one, they must have fled the kingdom in shame. A magical beast, the White Bear served one purpose—to reveal itself to those who sought it if they were worthy. He still put up a fight, as if he knew the trainees needed to prove their skill, but he never failed to show to the deserving seekers.

Unease snaked through me and I shifted again to rest fully on my legs. This new position made it difficult to move quickly if needed, but it didn't look like we'd be going anywhere any time soon. The snow started melting into the layers of my thick pants, and I instantly regretted the change in posture. I was about to shift back when Elis let out a sharp gasp.

My head sprang up, looking for the White Bear. My fingers pulled back the bow string slightly, ready to fire.

I saw nothing.

To my side, Elis aimed her bow through the tree with a steady hand. "Finally," she whispered. She slid her foot down and moved her knee up, giving her a balanced base to shoot from.

The trees must be blocking my sight. With as much stealth as I could muster, I tipped slightly to my left to find the same angle as Elis, whose eyes remained straight on the opening in the trees several meters ahead. Her arrow tracked some hidden movement.

From my new position, I could see more than before. The mouth of the stream burst from the heart of the mountain to let the water flow down the rocks as they carved their path into a stream. Sunlight gleamed off the endless snow and reflected with a blinding white.

I saw it all.

There was no bear.

"You're a better shot, you shoot." I barely heard her voice. My own ears rang.

The White Bear was not a well-known creature. Whether it was the same bear who showed himself each time, resurrected through the magic that kept him alive, no one knew. I believed it to be. Others thought it was a clan of bears that lived in these mountains and a different one was seen each time. Same bear or different one, two things were known: the bear was always alive and with all four paws, so if it was the same bear, he comes back to life and regrows his paw.

And the bear only showed himself to the pure of heart.

But I didn't see the bear.

To hide my embarrassment, I dropped the arrow and cursed lightly. "You better shoot now before he gets away." Jealousy filled me as I played with my arrow, pretending to stumble as I tried to notch it again while Elis focused on her shot.

I didn't consider myself to be a bad person. I definitely didn't consider myself to be any less pure hearted than Elis. Why could she see the bear when I could not?

Perhaps jealousy was one of the reasons the White Bear didn't show itself to me. I had plenty to be jealous of.

Elis released her shot. It struck against something on the side of the stream where the tip turned invisible while the rest stayed suspended in the air. Hoping, I fired my arrow at the same spot.

Just as my arrow hit, the bear came into view. He stood by the side of the stream with his muzzle wet and dripping. The clearest shade of white adorned his coat of fur, paired with the striking blue of his eyes. He was larger than I thought he would be, especially as he stood up and let out a mighty roar, releasing a vibration through the trees.

The roar sent me into motion. I notched another arrow and fired right for the vulnerable spot under his front arm. He came crashing down in time for my arrow to whiz past his shoulder.

The White Bear charged.

Together, my sister and I dropped our bows and drew our swords. She'd gotten a second arrow in his side, but the wound didn't appear to bother him as he clambered at us in full speed.

Elis ran around her side of the tree while I barreled through the snow in the opposite direction, drawing the bear my way. His eyes remained on me, not once flickering to Elis as she rounded the tree and came at him from the side.

She let out a battle cry. If he didn't see her before, he heard her now.

His head swung in her direction as she whooped but he remained on his course for me. Not to be outmatched in gusto, I let out a loud shout and attacked the bear head on.

The broadsword was one of my strengths but facing a charging bear was much different than facing Cassian in the battle arena. As similar to a bear as he was, fighting this creature would be more difficult. One thing I knew though: it'd be foolish to attack a beast of this size head on. At the last moment I rolled out of the way, allowing him to run past me. Snow flicked up into my face as his grunts grew louder. I was on my feet before he turned back around, brushing the snow off my parka. Elis gave me a nod. Her feet planted into the snow as she narrowed her eyes. Her hand twitched over the hilt of her sharpened sword.

The beast eyed us before bolting again for me. Together, from our opposite angles, Elis and I charged him.

He stood on two feet and swung with a great paw. My mind told me to aim for his sharp paws that clawed in my direction—after all, the paw was all we needed. But before I could bring my blade down, the bear gnarled at us, revealing a mouth full of sharp teeth.

Those teeth. I shouldn't have looked at the teeth. Sweat formed on my brow despite the chill in the air.

The claws were the closer, more immediate threat, so I planted my boots in the deep snow and brought the weight of my blade down on them. Unfortunately, I angled my sword outward too far, so as the White Bear curled his mighty arm, his paw struck the broadside of my sword. The tip plummeted into the snow.

He brought his paw back around, striking me with the back side. The force knocked me to my knees. My jaw popped and cheekbone throbbed. I was lucky the claws hadn't met my tender skin.

I was luckier that Elis was faster in her attack. She aimed her sword for his paw and swung with all her might, slicing into his arm.

The White Bear dropped to three of his paws and let out a roar. Before he could move further, I scrambled to twist my hand around my sword and drove it across his wound. The paw separated from the rest of his body.

Crimson mixed with the white terrain. Our swords stayed tight in our hands as we watched to see what he would do next.

The White Bear seemed to understand what we'd come for. He backed up with his head held low. I dropped my arms to my knees and released the tight grip on my blade. I'd been prepared for a much worse fight. My heart raced, and I left small puffs of breath floating through the air as I breathed.

The stub where his paw once was had stopped bleeding, confirming that the bear held magical properties of some sort. When he'd gone a short distance, the White Bear turned back and fixed his eyes on us. He lowered himself into a deep bow, as if congratulating us on the easy victory. His gaze lingered on me, and something flowed through my veins.

Fear. He knew I hadn't seen him. He knew I wasn't worthy.

He can't know that. He's just a bear.

Still, his eyes studied me for a few moments before he turned and hobbled off back across the mountain, taking my secret with him.

Elis had already pulled out a cloth and picked up the paw to wrap it. "Why didn't you shoot first?"

I clumped snow in my hand to draw across my blade, cleaning the bit of blood from the steel. "I dropped my arrow."

She peeked up at me. "You saw him, right?" The accusation was clear in her voice.

I feigned an innocent face. "Of course I saw him. Did you not see me fighting alongside you?" My voice came out slightly strained. I didn't need to share my failure with her or have her question why I hadn't seen the bear at first. Perhaps it was a fluke in the magic that surrounds him. Or perhaps it was the jealousy in my heart.

I'll do better. I'll be better.

She fastened twine around the cloth and tossed me the paw. "Alright, now tell me what you plan to do with that. You aren't planning to become a knight, are you? I doubt your father would approve of his daughter being a knight."

Ah, my father. I recoiled at the word. It was meaningless to our relationship. "Unless the king wishes to claim his daughter in front of the court, he couldn't protest as my father, and he has no grounds to protest as my king."

Elis was my sister, but not by blood. After my mother gave birth to me, she took advantage of her close friendship with Elis's mother by asking her to do something no mother should have to do. The queen traded me to Elis's parents in return for their newly born son to claim as her own. That boy, Cassian, was raised as the royal heir, a secret which was guarded behind icy walls.

I wondered if my first cries had even stopped echoing in the halls before she decided to give me away.

King Olin and Queen Marigold would never publicly claim me as their daughter, and they had valid reason not to. I never should have been born. My existence would prove detrimental to the kingdom.

And we all knew the affairs of Elenvérs come first.

"So that's it, then? You plan to be a knight? That's how you want to spend the last of your days?"

"For the record, I'd make a great knight," I said. "But no." I fished our tent from where we'd buried it in the snow and clasped it to my back.

I waited until Elis finished refastening the belt with her broadsword on her hip so I could see the expression on her face. At last, she glanced up to find me grinning.

"Now we travel to Witch Marlogne's home to offer the paw and demand she remove this blasted curse that holds me."

Elis's word choice was as strong as the mountains surrounding us, and her glare bit deeper than any frost.

Chapter Two

THE FROZEN MOUNTAIN TERRAIN stretched ahead as we trudged onward. The sky offered small flurries of snowflakes that swirled about. I drew my parka closer to my numb chin. A light gray hue settled over the sky, bringing clouds close enough to the mountain that I could almost touch them. Wind hissed through the air, breaking up the bitter silence that settled between us.

"You're a fool," she said.

I said nothing in return.

Every once and again Elis offered another harsh comment about my choices, but my resolve wouldn't waver. Not even for her. At last Elis quieted, but she remained fuming with her arms crossed over her chest.

I ignored her and kept my focus ahead.

Because I grew up in the ice palace between the Northern Mountains and the Wandering Mountains, I should know how to tell the difference between the snow-covered rocks, but the Wandering Mountains were foreign to me.

There had been no need to venture into these mountains before today, but now I wished I'd explored them more freely in my childhood.

I knew why I hadn't. Parents tell children frightening tales about how people get lost in these mountains and are left to the mercy of magical beings. Those tales were meaningless to me now. I wasn't a naïve child anymore, and those magical beings might be my only hope.

It took me months to track down someone to give me directions to Witch Marlogne's home, and I'd traded a beautiful rug for a copy of the scrap of paper they called a map. I fished the paper out now, squinting at it as if I hadn't already memorized every inch. In vain, I attempted to match it to the scene before me, desperate for validation that I was on the right path. No such validation came.

We traveled low in the mountains, moving north in search of the mysterious witch. The trees grew taller here, and the snow stacked heavier, slowing our movements. A large stream sat idle at the foothill of the mountains at our side, the water frozen in place, mirroring the dull gray of the sky. A clump of snow dropped near Elis's head and she cursed at it. Her smile turned sourer by the minute.

She'd come around soon. She always did.

My stomach curled within me, letting out a low vibration of protest. We packed light for our journey with no more than a sack of dried meat, glazed bread, and root vegetables to last us the week. If we reached the witch tonight, it would take three days to return home, and we'd need every last crumb from the bag to keep up our strength.

Perhaps we should have killed the bear and eaten to fill our bellies.

The desire to eat a magic bear might be the sort of thing that made my soul unworthy, and the thought made me fret again. What made the bear the official measurer of our soul's purity? My soul was just as good as any others.

Elis had seen the bear. My frown deepened. If Elis saw it, then I should have seen it too, for despite not being blood sisters, we were as similar as two beings could be. We both carried the same ambition to make something of ourselves, we both had the same opinions of the politics of the land, and we both carried the same sweet tooth that led us on many escapades through to the kitchens at night.

We were the same—and yet, Elis had seen the bear while I had not.

"You should have told me where we were going." Elis broke the silence with a sharp tone.

I kept my face ahead. "Would it have changed your mind?"

"It certainly would, I don't care to die by the hands of magical beasts," she shouted.

I laughed, but the sound carried no joy. "You've been fed too many tall tales, sister."

"We've heard the same tales, *sister*." She spat the word. "Did you forget about Corbin Galloway?"

I flinched at the name of the man who died at the witch's hand a few months back. The plan relied on her generosity, so news of Corbin Galloway's death was worrisome, but I'd met Corbin and never found him to be a pleasant fellow in the first place. Perhaps Witch Marlogne felt the same way.

"He didn't bring the paw as a gift, and his left knee was always weak. He didn't stand a chance in the fight. We do. Did you forget about how we defeated that dragon?"

A patch of clouds thinned out, revealing a hint of sunlight behind them. I imagined the sun wanted to come out to watch us quarrel. Our fights were always a spectacle, but they never lasted long.

Elis caught up with me just so I could watch as she continued stomping by my side. Her nose looked redder now, and her hair didn't move as she turned her head. Frozen in place. She huffed as she spoke, casting her breath through the air. "That *baby* dragon. And we were alone with him for no more than a few seconds before knights caught up to us and defeated him while we waved our swords around in the air."

I turned so she couldn't see my grin. She usually backed off sooner if she thought me in a bad mood. "That's not how the story went when we snuck out to tell it at the tavern that night."

"We got in trouble for that, if I recall right."

"We get in trouble for everything. We will likely get in trouble for this."

She stopped. "Then let's not go."

I turned and planted my feet firmly in the ground. "That's not an option for me."

She looked me over, frozen as still as the seracs climbing into the sky behind her. I searched for understanding in her eye, but only found disappointment. "I need to try," I said, pulling a twig from an overhanging branch and snapping it.

"Would you die to break the curse?" she asked. In all our years, she'd never asked that.

"I'll die anyway," I said without hesitation.

Six months. That's how long I had. Six months until I was destined to prick my finger and fall asleep for a hundred years, just as my mother had and her mother before her. Six months until everyone I knew vanished and I woke up in a world I didn't belong. Six months until my kingdom fell from my grasp and Cassian took over on a throne that was not his. Six months to break the curse that has never been broken.

I'd be willing to do anything to stop the sleep from taking me.

Elis couldn't understand. I'd been wrong, we weren't as similar as two beings could be, because she didn't have this curse over her, and this curse—it defined me.

She'd been with me through all my previous attempts to break this curse and listened to me cry at night when we failed every time. My pain was visible to her, and while she kindly ignored my tears, I knew she didn't forget them.

She knew. More than anyone, she knew.

Yet she didn't see that I'd rather die in this lifetime than wake up in one where I've been forgotten.

My mother hadn't realized she carried the curse in her, so she couldn't try to break it. My grandmother, from what I learned, hadn't been willing to die to break this curse. I was. I would die for this, and that relentless determination would be the thing that freed me from my bonds.

Witch Marlogne would be the key.

A tricky witch to pin down who never stayed in one place for long. That's why when news reached Elenvérs that she settled in the Northern Mountains, I'd devoted everything to getting to her house and asking her to help break the curse. First, I identified what object she would find valuable enough to barter for. Then I tracked down the map. And now finally, I'd gotten the paw. All there was to do now was pray she hadn't moved on already.

This had to work. It's my last chance.

"I'd rather you be asleep than dead." Elis's soft voice interrupted my thoughts. She pulled back her hood as the snow and wind had died down, and the tips of her ears poked out from her hair, pink as lady's slippers. One hand gripped the bag slung over her shoulder, while the other rested on her sword. The anger in her eyes was subdued. "After waking, you'll still have so much life to live. Eventually you'll forget about us."

The corners of my mouth drew down. The possibility of forgetting them isn't what worried me; that could never happen. But they might forget about me.

"Let's just focus on finding that witch," I said.

Beside me, Elis sucked in her breath and drew to a halt, pointing her arm across the way. "I think we found her."

She saw everything first.

Around the bend of the foot of the mountain sat a little hut nestled against the rocks and snow. The hut was built with wood and a swooping roof that made way to icicles hanging off the sides, each one the exact same shape as the others, looking more like decoration than reality. It mirrored something from a drawing book, and I had no trouble believing this house belonged to some special creature. The rest of the hut looked immaculate, too. The door curved at the top, with a handle painted dark red. The color's resemblance to blood was not lost on me, and once I spotted the red, I found other flashes of the same color built into the hut. Red along the window frame. Red in the rug by the door. Red in the paneling on the walls.

My steps faltered, sudden nerves catching up to me. Infuriatingly, Elis carried on, as if she hadn't been worried about the witch moments before. I wouldn't be outbraved by her. I quickened my pace and reached the door before her.

Once there, all other emotions melted away— my frustration with Elis, my confusion at not seeing the bear, my fears about the curse—it all disappeared to be replaced with jittery anticipation for what stood inside.

Elis and I took a deep breath almost in unison. Her eyes found mine, and we drew bravery from each other's glance before we willingly put ourselves at the mercy of the witch.

Elis really didn't get enough credit as a reliable sister. I would never be able to repay her for joining me today, and she would never ask me to.

I held my hand steady as I knocked, so the first image the witch got of us was one of strength. Then, we clasped in front of us, notably away from our swords, as we waited for an answer.

Creak, creak, tap. Someone moved inside. My hand itched for my blade, but I held it at bay against all instincts, certain this exchange would go better if I started it off without a weapon in my hand.

Elis's breath tripped beside me.

I watched the window, but if the witch peeked out, she did so without being spotted. The knob turned sharply, and the door yanked open. I jolted.

Witch Marlogne stood in the doorway. She was half as wide as the door itself and just as short as she was plump. Her purple dress fell past her knees exposing thick ankles, and her dark skin suggested she originated from the western countries. Black coated her eyes in darkness, but after a second look I saw streaks of brown running through them. Two wrinkles spread by the corners of each eye, but the rest of her skin remained smooth. Her hair was braided down her back and curled back up into her dress pocket. I stared at it, the length easily twice the length of any hair I'd seen before.

A small dragon with beady red eyes sat at the tip of one of her silver shoes.

This wasn't what I expected a witch to look like. Where were the warts, or the horrendous smell? The black caldron with slimy green potions? As far as I could see, she had no warts, and the only smell was of cinnamon mixed with apples that wafted through the air, greeting us pleasantly and giving me the feel of home. Calm. The feeling of calm oozed from her house. I urged my senses to be on guard for trickery.

Witch Marlogne examined us as we studied her. When she spoke, her voice sounded like rocks striking against each other. "You are not the children I ordered to eat. Ahh well, I suppose I'll save you for dinner." She wagged a plump finger at Elis, who impressively didn't waver.

I kept my voice neutral. "Witch Marlogne," I started, unsure of the proper way to address a traveling witch. "We are Rowan and Elis Trelluse, and we have brought a gift in exchange for your assistance." I held up the cloth containing the bear's paw, which she eyed.

She made a humming noise within her throat and tapped her fingers against her chin in a quick manner before she shrugged. "Perhaps I kill you now and take the paw for myself, hmm?"

She must hold a fair amount of magic to have known a paw lay within the folds of the cloth. I snatched it back behind me and out of her sight before she could reach for it. "If you try to harm us, I'm afraid I'll have to kill you first."

Elis nudged me. We hadn't spoken of how we would attempt to woo Witch Marlogne into assistance, but I was aware that threatening her was probably not the smartest move I could make. I'd have to push past my instinct to find a pleasanter tone, if not for my sake, then for Elis's, who had nothing to gain from this trip, but plenty to lose. That fact warranted more caution from my side.

Witch Marlogne chuckled and held the door open wider. "I was merely teasing you, girl. This will be fun. Come, come inside." She turned and waddled in, leaving the door open behind her as she chuckled again.

Before I could step in, Elis put a hand on my arm. "Kill her? Are you sure that's how you wanted to play that? Is angering her wise?" She eyed the cottage warily.

I brushed off her arm. "I got us in, didn't I?"

I ignored her tight lips while I unlatched my sword and set it outside the door. Then I entered into the dim light of the home. Elis did the same, though more hesitant to relinquish her sword before joining me inside just as the door slammed behind us with a crack that vibrated our bones.

Both of our heads whirled back while a slow smile came from the witch, each white tooth glittering in what light remained from outside the windows.

From the back, her voice crawled out to meet us. "Welcome to my home."

Chapter Three

THE COTTAGE INTERIOR LOOKED normal at first glance, but as I continued observing, I spotted strange variances from usual homes. A painting of a boat that sailed slowly across the sea visibly moved as I watched it. A small flame burned inside a closed jar, though there was no kindling. A couch was covered in toad skin.

It was fascinating.

Thick magenta fabric hung across six windows, three from each side. A fireplace crackled in the corner, along with the fire in a glass jar. The curling flames brought a mystical aura to the room, and shadows danced among the sparks.

It was a bookshelf that interested me the most. The shelves were lined with books and knickknacks of all sorts. A small pouch here, a vial there, little wooden trinkets on the bottom shelf. I understood none of them. A glass cage in the middle held tiny animal skulls, most likely rodents. But what made this bookshelf different was how it wrapped up to the ceiling and back down without ever stopping. How did none of the objects fall? How did she reach her books?

Elis nudged me and nodded back toward the fireplace. A small dragon lay within the flames, his red, scaly back rising and falling with content breathing.

That was enough to remind me of the danger here, and I cursed under my breath. I hadn't thought this through; magic was not a foe I could conquer.

"So, tell me again who you are." Witch Marlogne stood over a table chopping lettuce with her bushy brows set low and face relaxed, patiently waiting as we'd devoured the details of her home.

"I am Lady Rowan Trelluse, and this is Lady Elis Trelluse, daughters of Weston and Corrin Trelluse."

At my words, she slammed the knife down into the table, driving the blade into the thick, dark wood. Her skirts flared as she spun toward me dramatically. "You dare come into my house and lie to me?"

My throat went dry.

She waved her wrinkled hand over us, flicking her fingers. "Again. Who are you?" With a small grunt, she plucked the knife out of the table and returned to chopping lettuce as if she hadn't just stabbed the table a moment before.

I let my breath out as I exchanged a glance with Elis. She shook her head.

How could Witch Marlogne know? She couldn't.

"We are Rowan and Elis Trelluse, raised by Weston and Corrin Trelluse from the kingdom of Elenvérs." Honest, but just enough.

Witch Marlogne's laugh crackled through the room. Her belly shook with her shoulders. "You think you can trick me?" She pointed a big finger toward Elis. "You. You are Elis Trelluse, daughter of Weston and Corrin Trelluse." Her finger slid to hover over me. "But you? Tell me who you are. For is that not the very reason you've come to me?"

My stomach turned within me. I'd hoped to ask her to remove the curse without telling her how I'd gotten it. My life had been spent hiding my parentage, and I'd never given away that secret. I'd remained true to my word, as my parents had. We'd all kept it for the sake of the kingdom. But Witch Marlogne knew who I was despite that.

My shoulders slumped. "I wasn't expecting you to know. The cave mages don't. You must be keener than them." Perhaps flattery would help me here.

She laughed again as she piled the lettuce into three bowls. "Or more honest."

For a second, the blood froze in my body. The possibility of the cave mages seeing my true identity and not revealing it hadn't occurred to me.

"But yes," Witch Marlogne said as she arranged the salad. "I am much smarter. Prettier, too."

Elis's arms hadn't uncrossed since entering the cottage. Her nostrils flared. "Listen witch, we aren't here to play games. If you know why we've come, then can you help us or not?"

Now I was the one signaling Elis to ease up, but she ignored me, staring into Witch Marlogne as if her eyes could pierce her.

The witch didn't seem to mind. "I can't help if she isn't honest. Tell me who you are."

I'd spoken my true name many times, most often in front of mirrors as I pretended it was the moment that I revealed myself to the kingdom. My curse would be broken, and I would take my place next to my parents to claim my title. I hadn't pictured it being like this.

If I wanted to break the curse, I must trust her. She already knew the truth anyhow.

"I am Princess Rowan Sordwill, daughter of King Olin and Queen Marigold, rightful heir to the Elenvérs throne." Far less fanfare than I'd expected. It was hard not to feel disappointed with the moment.

Witch Marlogne made a bubbling noise within her throat before she coughed and brought two bowls toward us. "Eat. You're both hungry."

Though uncertain about how much we could trust her or the food she prepared, the idea of nourishment was too good to pass up. I'd preferred something heartier than vegetables, but I'd take what I could get. Elis snarled at the bowl, but I eagerly grabbed it.

"It won't hurt you, dear." Witch Marlogne waved the second bowl under Elis's nose, who finally took it with a huff. I slid my parka off my back and settled into the couch with the bowl on my lap, keeping one eye firmly on the witch as she made herself a bowl and sat across from us.

"So, you wish to break your grandmother's curse?"

The comment seemed obvious. I couldn't imagine not wishing to break the curse that holds me. "Clearly I do."

My tone came out sharper than intended, and she stabbed into her lettuce as reply. "There's no need for unpleasantness, lass. What makes you think you can when your mother and grandmother couldn't?"

Beside me Elis hadn't taken a bite yet but inspected every piece of vegetation thoroughly. I shrugged my shoulders as I prepared another bite. The bowls and forks were made of dull wood which made it difficult to pierce the lettuce. "I'm more strong-willed than my grandmother and—"

"That's an arrogant thing to assume when you've never met her."

I squinted at the witch's stoic expression. I couldn't tell if she was mocking me or not. "I've heard stories."

"Reliable." This time the mocking tone couldn't be mistaken for anything else. I'd take mocking over threatening. Corbin must have done something rash to infuriate her enough to kill. Besides the brief moment when she attacked the table with her knife, I hadn't seen a hint of aggression from her.

I took a bite of butter lettuce and sliced carrots. "Anyway, she couldn't break it and my mother never even tried."

Though she must have known this, Witch Marlogne put down her fork. "And does that hurt you, that she's never tried to break her daughter's curse? That she's leaving you to your doom?"

I hadn't meant that. I meant that my mother never tried to break her own curse, because she hadn't known she carried it. But while she can't be blamed for her lack of attempt before the curse took hold, she knew that I held the curse. She knew and had never done a thing to break it. Instead, both she and King Olin prepared me for a life without them by handing me off to be raised by another family while they took that family's son as their own. A son in place of a daughter who never should have been born.

"They believe it can't be broken, so they think it's better that I live the life that I have without fighting it."

"And when they saw you chose to fight anyway, they still chose not to fight alongside you?"

Elis shoved her untouched bowl away. "Enough. Can you help her or not?"

Witch Marlogne sighed and brought her empty bowl to her bookshelf to set it down. Then she moved along the bookshelf, looking through her items. Finally, her hand settled on a small chest with golden lining. When she opened it, a small glow came from inside.

I allowed hope to curl within me. This could be it. She would help me break the curse and I would be free. I'd march back into Elenvérs and remove Cassian from my position, claim my rightful place as the heir of Elenvérs, and lead this mighty country that I love with glory.

I wouldn't fall asleep and fade from forgetful minds.

My hand reached for Elis's, and I squeezed tight, waiting for whatever the witch held in that chest. She turned around with the glow radiating from between her closed fingers.

"I cannot remove the curse. It is not within my power." When she spoke, her voice dripped with pity.

With the release of my hope came a surge of anger, drawing me to my feet where I tried to walk out the frustration. My hands ran through my mass of hair as the emotions overwhelmed me. Disappointment. Frustration. Hopelessness. I'd allowed myself to believe this could work, but in the end the witch turned out to be another failed idea.

I'd given up my best rug for this. I'd cut off a perfectly nice bear's paw for this. I'd frozen my lips for this. I had placed all my hopes on the witch.

"Come on," Elis picked up our bags. "If we leave now, we can make good progress before nightfall. Maybe return to Elenvérs by tomorrow night." Her eyes held a sliver of pity for me. I attempted a smile in return.

The witch's crooked hand waved at us. "Now wait just a minute, I can't break the curse, but maybe I can help."

Curiosity made us pause, and in our hesitation, the witch released the grip on her fingers, exposing a small, glowing, golden orb in the palm of her hand. I leaned forward.

"These are very rare. If people hear that you have it, many will try to take it from you."

"What is it?"

"A wish. It has its limits, but it's still a wish. It should be strong enough to help you."

I eyed the orb. I'd heard of wish granters like this. "Could I wish for my curse to be voided?"

"No. Even wishes have limits," she repeated.

"Then what good is that for her?" Elis asked.

The witch sneered at Elis. "She's a smart lass. She can think of something."

The wish called to me, tempting me with its abilities. I stared at it in her hand, so small but so powerful.

"What are the limits?"

"Can't wish for more wishes, can't break curses, can't give you any sort of power." She ticked off on her fingers as she listed. "It's a one request only sort of thing, nothing ongoing, nothing too vague. And no future requests. The future is unstable. Your wish has to be something that can be fulfilled right then and there."

"Can it bring someone back to life?"

She thought before answering. "No. But I don't know how that would help you."

"Can it turn back time?" I asked this with more hope. If I held onto it, I could wait out my curse, then wish to go back a hundred years. My curse would be fulfilled, but I wouldn't be gone, not really.

"No. It can't play with time. It's not that powerful."

Her words crushed me.

Elis looked to me. "We have no use of the paw, at least this could help you."

She was right. The paw did nothing for us, but the wish could prove useful. Just when I was about to fish the bear paw from my bag, the witch crackled.

"I wouldn't trade it for the paw alone. I could use this to wish for a paw."

This paw was useless to us now, where just hours before I'd clung to it as my only hope. Now, I let it fall to the floor.

Elis shook her head and groaned, grabbing her bag again and making for the door. I didn't follow her, my eye glued to the wish. "What else do you want?"

She raised her chin. "Simple. I want to know what gifts the fairies gave you at birth."

She knew an uncomfortable amount of information about me. "Why?"

"Because I know everything else but that, and I'm a curious lady. Tell me." She licked her lips. "What gifts did they give you?"

Elis shook her head, but I chewed on my lip. There's no harm in her knowing the seven gifts given to me, and we'd come all this way, enduring the cold and the hunger to bring the bear's paw to the witch so she could help us. It didn't feel right to leave with nothing.

"The first fairy gave me gracefulness," I started. Witch Marlogne lowered herself into her seat with a relaxed grin and her eyes half shut, as if I was reading her a soothing bedtime story.

"The second fairy gave me wisdom. The third gave me skill with the sword."

She peeked open an eye. "Linda?"

I nodded, then waited to see if she would say more. She didn't, so I continued. "The next fairy, Giselle, gave me the gift of memory, so that I would be able to remember every moment spent with my family during the short time that we were together."

Witch Marlogne laughed, leading perfectly into my next gift.

"Thistle gave me the gift of laughter, so that I would be able to face my sad story with joy."

She opened her eye again and raised an eyebrow. I flustered, "At least, that's what it was supposed to be for. In truth, the gift of laughter surfaces at unfortunate times."

She shook her head. "Thistle. Such Thistle."

Elis tapped her fingertips along the door handle. I spoke faster. "Nully gave me the gift of the voice of an angel."

"She always does." Witch Marlogne interrupted again. "And let me guess, Bluebell gave you beauty?"

I shook my head. "No, my mother didn't want me to stand out among others."

"Well, with that hair you'd stand out, pretty or not!"

I flushed at the slight implication that I wasn't pretty without a gift. Elis tapped on the door, reminding me that she wanted to leave. I took out the bear paw and set it on the table in front of the witch.

"Still one more gift."

I couldn't forget. The last gift was one never bestowed upon a newborn before me, though I couldn't feel blessed by it. "The last fairy took away my ability to ever bear a child." The grin fell from her face, and I looked away from the pity that replaced it. Thanks to the gift of memory, I'd never forget how my mother put her hand over her chest and tears filled her eyes as the fairy gave me this gift. King Olin wrapped his arms around her, but she wasn't upset. She looked the fairy in the eyes as a tear slid down her cheek.

"Thank you," my mother had whispered. "Thank you. She'll never have this pain that's inside me."

"This curse will not carry on after your daughter. It will die with her." I mimicked the fairy's words.

The gift was meant to bring peace. After me, no more daughters of my bloodline will be cursed to sleep for a hundred years. The kingdom won't know that though— they think the royal blood lives on in their treasured Cassian, the boy who has what should be mine. The boy who was given both my title and my kingdom to protect the people from the uncertainty of a cursed princess. Cassian was the safe option; no curse lingered over him. The throne would pass seamlessly.

It wouldn't matter for long. I'd use this wish to make things right.

Witch Marlogne's bones creaked as she straightened her bent body and waddled toward me, wrapping her hands around mine and dropping the wish into my palm. It tingled in my palm with a gentle warmth. "Take the wish and use it wisely."

The light faded outside the doorway that Elis stepped through without saying goodbye. I followed her before realizing I'd left my bag behind. As I turned, Witch Marlogne held it out for me.

Before I could thank her, she spoke. "You didn't see the White Bear, did you?"

My fingers froze outstretched. Her calculating smile told me she knew the answer, and she made that noise in her throat again. "Interesting. I'm very curious how your story will play out."

I'd almost forgotten about the blasted bear. "It must have been a mistake. I saw it after a moment," I explained as I headed for the door, checking to be certain Elis hadn't heard the witch's speculation.

"Do you want the paw?" She held up the folded cloth. "You could present it to your king, gain knighthood before you sleep."

My lips tightened. "It'll do me no good. Knighthood won't save me." I turned away from the paw.

"One more thing," the witch stopped me. I paused beside the threshold. "The wish has limits, but I believe it can break your curse. You'll just have to be clever enough."

"How?" I asked. Elis was several paces away, kicking up snow in her hurry to leave.

Witch Marlogne's eyes sparkled. "Clever," she repeated. "Wishes such as this have saved many from trouble in the past. Use it well."

The door shut in my face before I could thank her. I rolled the wish in my hand as I turned to follow Elis, still nursing my disappointed heart that dared to believe I could break my curse so easily.

Chapter Four

THE WITCH'S WORDS CLUNG to me like a cloud through the week, even as we returned to Elenvérs and settled back into our routine. It only drifted from my mind as a proposal for attack was brought forward among the advisors of Elenvérs. My thoughts cleared as I focused on the words to be certain I'd heard them right.

If I were sitting with them, instead of spying, I wouldn't have to strain so hard to hear.

The speaker restated his declaration for the others in the meeting room who'd quieted. "I say we regain control of the land," he said.

Thick curtains surrounded me, hiding me from the advisors' sight as I spied on them during their monthly gathering. My fingers pinched the dark blue fabric by my nose to peel it back slightly as I peered through the slit to the figures around the table. Seven people, always seven. The king, his heir, and his five lords. Seven leaders to rule Elenvérs, each with a heart that sought justice, truth, and wisdom.

That's what Elenvérs was known for. Justice. Truth. Wisdom. Elenvérs never attacked unless they found the cause to be worthy enough to lose lives over, and they never fought unless there was no other option. Most disputes were settled in the king's court where the advisors worked together to deliver a peaceful resolution. When they deemed fighting was necessary, they went to war, marching under the banner that spread fear among the other countries, because those countries knew that when the Elenvérs knights fought, they did so with their whole hearts.

It was our virtue that won us many allies, securing trading treaties with countries at a much lower price than our neighboring kingdom. In these frozen mountains of eternal winter, trade was vital to survival.

I once thought my heart was a perfect match to those in this room—honorable and virtuous.

But instead, I was nothing more than a girl hiding behind the curtain who couldn't even see the White Bear.

"Technically, we do control the land." Rivers leaned against her hands on the table as she looked over the map. The hilt of her sheathed knife caught the light and cast red fractals on the wall behind her. That small blade had taken down many foes. Legend said the blade whispers the weakness of her enemy into Rivers's ear, and while I suspected the story to be a fable created by Rivers, I wouldn't want to be caught on the other end of that dagger.

"Technically, they don't respect our ownership." Irritation rolled like an avalanche from Annon's voice.

"I'm just pointing out," Rivers said through gritted teeth, "that riding in pompously to remind them that they submit to us might not win them back to our side."

King Olin stood behind the head of the table, patiently letting the advisors discuss the situation. Cassian stood at his side, though he shifted on his feet and glanced at the nearby chair more than once. He'd never sit in the presence of the judgmental advisors.

The other three advisors—Carlene, Tristian, and Ebony—sat in the tall-backed chairs inspecting the map. The small town of Harrowhut, hardly more than a hundred caves, refused to participate in the king's tax this year, as they had done the previous two years.

Elenvérs, once wealthy from minerals found in the Northern Mountains, hadn't required the standard tax on the people. While other countries taxed as often as once a month, Elenvérs only taxed once a year and spent all the money collected giving back to the people by fortifying their caves or building more paths to spring waters. But our once plentiful mines were growing bare, and our wealth was running out.

It wasn't common knowledge that our resources were thinning, but people would know soon enough.

When Harrowhut refused the king's tax three years ago, King Olin pardoned them. But then the next year came, and now this year, and it became apparent that Harrowhut wanted nothing to do with Elenvérs, denying us not only taxes but their presence at the Full Moon Feasts and End Year Celebrations.

Then, last month, when a large mountain cat raided their homes, they called to ThornHigh for help, sending a clear message that they aligned with a new kingdom. ThornHigh didn't send help, claiming the cat would leave soon. It did, and Harrowhut praised ThornHigh's wisdom.

"We don't need Harrowhut," Rivers said. "Peace is more important than one small town."

"But do we want to lose them to ThornHigh?" Carlene scratched a finger along ThornHigh's name on the map. "They belong on our side of the border. They'd give ThornHigh a foothold in our lands."

"If we try to reclaim Harrowhut, ThornHigh will fight for them," Ebony said.

"They aren't worth us fighting over. It's a handful of families," Cassian leaned his hands against the table.

"Our people," Annon said as he slammed fist against the map, "are always worth fighting for."

Cassian blushed and ducked his head, but King Olin put an arm over him. Standing so close together, it was difficult to imagine how anyone believed them to be related. Though they both had similar body frames that came from years of battle practice, Cassian had curly brown hair while King Olin's hair, now gray, was once golden. My mother's hair was a strawberry blonde, which was how I got my red hair, but they claim Cassian got his coloring from King Olin's parents and brother, Annon.

There were other traits that set them apart. My family's rounded nose to Cassian's sharp one. The slight upward tilt of our eyes compared to the straight eyes of Cassian. Our full bottom lip paired with a thin top lip, compared to Cassian's evenly shaped mouth.

To me, it was clear that I was the heir. I held the look of the monarch. Though Cassian owned my title, he was obviously nothing more than a common lord's son.

King Olin cleared his throat, and all eyes turned to him. "If Harrowhut wishes to align with ThornHigh, I don't think it's wise to stop them, no matter the message it sends to the rest of the towns."

"No other towns would consider leaving, especially not for ThornHigh." Rivers hissed the name of our enemy's kingdom.

Annon looked displeased. When it came to protecting the Elenvérs name, Annon and Rivers saw the justice in fighting, but the other three advisors erred on the side of caution, and they usually won out, which crafted Elenvérs' peaceful reputation.

We should've forced Harrowhut to decide if they were part of this kingdom or not, so they couldn't reap the benefits without the work. It wouldn't have been wise to allow Harrowhut to remain within our protection only when they needed it and to receive the generosity of the cave mages while not participating in the king's taxes.

Almost as soon as I thought it, Ebony spoke up. "It's not a good enough reason to fight. I say we send a paper offering release, so they can't come back looking for help if things go wrong for them. They are either fully in or fully out."

I always liked Ebony best. She would be my lead advisor one day, along with King Olin. While the king wasn't the best father, he was a wise and just ruler.

Annon looked irate, which only fueled my opinion in the matter. When I ruled, I would remove Annon from advisory, even if he was my blood uncle. His ambition wasn't good for our country. He'd lead us to ruin with his love for the sword.

The list of reasons I had for disliking my uncle was a long one, going far beyond his unsettling personality. It didn't matter if he was one of the greatest warriors we'd had in centuries. Elenvérs was not at war, so his strength and strategic mind were worthless.

"I want to be there for them if they need help, whether they stand with us or not," King Olin said. His heart for his people wouldn't allow him to turn any away.

"I agree." Cassian nodded.

"You're being foolish." Annon's knuckles whitened as he bore his fist into the table.

He looked like he might say more, but King Olin interrupted with gritted teeth. "That will be all for today. Thank you for your council." The king always listened before he offered a response, but with his brother he allowed a harsher tone, just as Annon took one with him.

No further arguments came. When the king dismissed them, they were done. Slowly, heads bowed while chairs creaked across the floor and feet shuffled.

That's when I felt it.

The slow itching made its way up through my throat into my nose.

I was going to sneeze.

Please walk faster. They needed to leave the room before I gave myself away. My fists clenched in an attempt to fight off the sneeze and I buried my head into my chest, careful to not move the curtain too much with the gesture. They shouldn't be looking my way anyhow.

What would the advisors do if they caught me sneaking in on their meetings?

One. Two. Three. They were almost all out. I watched, willing them to move faster. King Olin and Cassian stayed back at the table to gather the map and inconspicuously wait for me, while Annon took his time leaving. Once the four other advisors had left, Annon turned back around.

It couldn't be held off any longer. I sneezed. I closed the back of my throat and scrunched my nose, so the noise wasn't more than a small snort. My back pressed into the ice wall where the cold trickled through my layers, but my heart was already frozen.

"Is there something there?" Annon spoke, his voice followed by footsteps. Each footstep made my chest sink deeper. I was caught.

I'd be dragged before the advisors and made to explain myself. My father wouldn't offer the truth about my right to be here. Cassian would never say anything. I'd either give up my secret and condemn Elenvérs or I'd be thrown out for spying.

The floor swayed beneath my feet. I counted down the seconds to my doom.

"Lord Annon," King Olin called. "We need to speak." The footsteps halted. "You need to remember that we are a peaceful country, and a people who do not fight battles for the glory of it. Your eagerness for your sword will land you in trouble, and that attitude has no place at my court."

Annon didn't waste a moment before replying. "My skill with the blade acquired you this court."

"My queen acquired me the court."

Though relieved for the distraction from me, my mouth opened a little in surprise that King Olin would go so far as to throw that in Annon's face. After a moment of bitter silence where I envisioned the two brothers staring at each other while Cassian cowered, Annon scoffed and stomped from the room.

Though the younger of the two brothers, King Olin came to the throne after his kiss awoke my mother from her long slumber. He was a prince of Elenvérs at the time, the kingdom that kept my mother protected while she slept. Then, exactly a hundred years after she fell asleep, my father woke her with a kiss. The kingdom which should have been Annon's—the man who fought for his country and spent his childhood studying for the role while my father idly spent his days in ease—instead went to King Olin when the kingdom fell in love with my mother. She restored the rightful line to the throne after her brother had died without a child during his time.

Annon resented my mother since the moment she opened her eyes. He'd tried to wake her first.

I might have felt bad for him, but I couldn't bring myself to care for him.

Lord Annon had a right to be bitter, and many pitied him. Many countries aligned with Elenvérs because of Annon's strategic mind, and we owed him much.

But I could do nothing but hate the man. I hated him for what he'd done to me.

The memory of it still burned, even after thirteen years, and I thought of it every time I looked at his face. The smallest sting rose in my finger all over again as if he had pricked it only the moment before.

Thanks to the fairy's gift of memory, I remembered every moment of what took place when I was three years old.

I'd gone with Cassian and Elis's parents to the Full Moon Feast, where my mother met us in the library to give me a hug. Not knowing we were there, King Olin and Annon had come in.

Annon took one look at me and my mother together and figured it all out right then. I doubted he needed his brilliant mind to put it together. Looking at us hiding there together, anyone would have guessed. He turned to his brother with shock. "The cave mage promised you'd bear a son if you got pregnant, but you had a daughter, didn't you? The only heir to Elenvérs is going to sleep for a hundred years."

My parents denied it, but Annon wasn't relenting. He sent a maid running for something, and when she came back, he held up the object proudly.

"Prove it." In his hand, he held a spindle.

My mother clutched me, furthering Annon's resolve, but King Olin's eyes went cold.

"Prove it. If she is your daughter, she is destined to prick her finger on this." He held up the spindle. "And fall asleep for a hundred years. Let that time start now. If she isn't your daughter, this won't hurt her."

Elis's mother, Lady Trelluse, held Elis in her arms as she watched me without the ability to form coherent sentences. Her eyes flickered to my parents. They'd asked too much of her when they told her to give up her son in place for me and keep such a secret. She'd done it because she loved my mother, and my mother loved me.

That was the first time I'd ever seen a spindle, and I clung to my mother's hand while I stared at it in fear. Annon saw the fear in my eyes, and he smiled victoriously.

Cassian stood in the corner sucking on his sleeve and hiding behind King Olin, unable to understand what was going on.

"Annon, this isn't necessary," King Olin tried to talk him down.

"Did you really think you could switch the heir to the country with some other child and not be caught? The stability of the kingdom is at stake and you'd play with it like that?"

"You're not pricking my daughter's finger with that thing." Lady Trelluse finally spoke up in attempt to maintain the lie, and Lord Trelluse tried to take me from my mother, but she held tight.

Annon just smiled. It was the look of pure evil, but it was King Olin who sent a chill through my spine colder than anything I'd felt in the mountains.

"Do it," he said. "Prick her finger. You'll see that Cassian is my son."

He nodded at my mother and spoke with his eyes. Though her fingers trembled, my mother released me into Lord Trelluse's arms who held tight as Annon approached us and lifted my hand into his, gently pressing the spindle to my finger.

I didn't fall asleep. I did cry.

Annon looked unconvinced—disappointed even—and almost ready to prick me again, but he shoved the spindle in his pocket and left without another word. King Olin picked up Cassian and followed behind.

That day taught me two important things. I learned the curse likely wouldn't take place until the last day of my eighteenth year, as it had for my mother and her mother before her. Any accidental poking before that wouldn't result in deep sleep.

I could be grateful for that. It allowed me and my mother to breathe a little easier.

Second, I learned that any love my real father might have for me was masked in comparison to his love for Elenvérs. In the visits my mother made during the next couple of years, she came alone, and my time with my father was reduced to polite passings in busy castle corridors.

It was that day that bitterness took root in my heart, an ugly quality that I couldn't shake, but only grew as the years went by. Every time I saw my father with Cassian, every time I was overlooked or unseen by the court, every time I was told to accept my curse as if no one cared that they would one day lose me, the bitterness grew within. With all my might I struggled against it, but it wouldn't budge.

How could I not be bitter, when I was so alone?

Perhaps there was a third thing I learned that day as well as I watched King Olin walk away with Cassian in hand, not giving his daughter another glance. Throughout the years, he devoted countless hours to Cassian, not once fighting to break the curse on his daughter or seeking me out.

It was a harsh lesson, but I learned it well.

I knew my father's love for Cassian would always be greater than his love for me.

Chapter Five

"YOU NEED TO BE more careful," Cassian said as I stepped from my place behind the curtains.

I didn't want his advice, nor the way he looked down on me. "I shouldn't need to hide in the first place."

King Olin barely glanced up. "Cassian's right, you can't be caught."

I'd been hiding there without the advisors' knowledge my entire life and never once been caught. I'd continue hiding until I retook my place as queen.

King Olin humored me in allowing me to sit in on these meetings in case the curse was ever broken. I'd once asked him if he'd make me queen if that time came, and he'd said yes, but in the years that followed I hadn't raised the question again for fear of a new answer. I'd seen how fond he was of Cassian.

I hoped, when it came to it, he stayed by his word. I couldn't wait to see Cassian's face when he did. He wouldn't dismiss me so easily then.

I could show them the wish now and tell them how I would beat the curse. But I didn't trust Cassian enough to not steal it from me.

"What do you think about all this?" King Olin waved his hand over the map and then brought it back to stroke his thick beard that used to tickle me when he kissed my cheeks as a baby.

I took my time looking over the map, but I already had my answer. "I'd let them go, but I'd make them sign an official release so they can't come back if they need us. It's not fair for us to be used like that."

"So, you agree with Ebony?"

I nodded, biting my tongue against claiming I'd had the idea before Ebony spoke it.

Now alone, King Olin sat himself down in one of the chairs, and a relieved Cassian did the same. "What would you do if ThornHigh goes after any of our other towns?" King Olin asked.

"Fight," I hurried to answer.

"You say that almost as often as Annon," Cassian said.

I despised the comparison. "We can't let them into our beautiful country."

"You wouldn't be strong enough to fight."

My brow creased. "What do you mean by that?"

He shrugged as he leaned back in the seat with his hands crossed. "You couldn't give the order to send the knights into battle, knowing some would die. You aren't strong enough. You don't have what it takes to shed blood if it comes to it."

"I could kill someone if Elenvérs needed."

Cassian was already shaking his head. "No, you can't. You can't even hurt me in battle practice."

"That's because we aren't supposed to, so stop it."

"Cassian, what would you do?" King Olin stepped in before the situation escalated.

It took him a moment to reply. "I'd fight, but only for the town. Leading them myself, I'd march the soldiers into the town and push any of ThornHigh's men out, showing the town that we fight for our people while not declaring war on ThornHigh itself. If ThornHigh wishes to retaliate for us protecting our own town by declaring war, then the war is on them and our souls remain pure from the bloodshed."

The mention of a pure soul cast a shadow over my eyes as I remembered the White Bear. The wish given to me from Witch Marlogne weighed down my pocket, and I slipped a hand inside to feel it tucked among the thick fur. Touching the wish made me feel strong because it reminded me that I had power.

If this worked as the witch said it would, I should be safe. I just had to figure out how to use it.

King Olin nodded to Cassian. "Very wise. Battle is not something to be ridden into lightly. Let's pray these people never know the pain of war."

Cassian stood from the table to tuck his gray training shirt beneath his leather belt. His thumb brushed over the embossed sigil of Elenvérs on his wrist strap. I had a matching band, but I kept it around my ankle to differentiate myself from Cassian. The king had given it as a gift to me for my tenth birthday, and my joy over the present had been immense until I saw Cassian with an identical one the next day.

Cassian's eyes remained on the map. "And as for the other matter at Brisburn? Will you send a small squad to investigate?"

The king closed his eyes for a moment and ran his hand across his forehead, taking a moment to rub the bridge of his nose. It was easy to forget his age when he dressed in regality. He was strong. He was healthy. And sometimes, it looked like he had the strength to go on ruling forever.

46

Our paths rarely crossed outside of professional settings, so I hardly saw him as anything but my reigning king.

But occasionally, in moments like this, I caught a glimpse of the exhaustion that rested behind his eyes. Over the past few years, wrinkles had overtaken his face and gray had begun to infiltrate the blonde in his hair, dulling the color the same way that ruling had dimmed his eyes. I sometimes wondered if he regretted taking the throne from his brother when he hadn't been prepared for this life. I wondered if he would have preferred a simpler life where he and my mother lived together in one of the caves and where he wouldn't have to pretend that I wasn't his daughter.

One where the kingdom didn't come first, but his family did.

A deep sigh filled his chest. "Three people have gone missing in the middle of the night. I think that warrants an investigation. Let's pray this gets resolved quickly."

Cassian bowed, as if King Olin had personally chosen him to lead the squad. Cassian's training wasn't complete. He had a few years before he served with the Elenvérs knights, and years beyond that before taking his place as king.

I'd be rightfully titled crown heir before that happened.

When Cassian straightened, he nodded to me before turning on his heel to leave the room through a side door different than the one the other advisors had taken. I'd see him later at battle lessons.

For a strange moment, I was left alone with King Olin, and I almost told him everything involving the White Bear and Witch Marlogne. I almost told him about how the witch had asked to know the gifts from the fairies, and if he knew why she'd care. I almost told him about the strange bookshelf in her house that stretched across the ceiling and the wish that she gave me. He might know what I should do with it.

For a moment, so small that I almost missed it, I thought of what it'd be like to confide in my father. I could tell him about how I didn't see the White Bear and ask why my soul wasn't worthy. I'd ask him how to be rid of this jealousy and bitterness in my heart.

But the moment passed as he stood up and mumbled a goodbye to me. I lowered my head in a small nod and crossed the room to the back door.

My heart was mine alone to heal, and my faults were mine alone to fix.

I closed the door behind me. The narrow hallway glowed blue from the sunlight shining through the ice encrusted stained-glass windows.

Ice. So much ice.

The entire palace was made of ice—from the floors, to the walls, to the knobs of the doors—all ice. As the sun peeked over the frosty mountain tips, it hit the walls and sent the rays scattering in snowflake designs across the room, tiny fragments of lights that hung in the air as fairy dust would, beautiful enough to dance in like a childhood fairytale. All of Elenvérs had danced in that light many times before. Those were some of my favorite memories of the palace.

While the sunlight was beautiful, the moon cast its own brilliant glow through the ice. As much as we loved the day, night was when Elenvérs shined.

At night, the palace glowed while the snowflakes came to the surface, each showcasing their individual beauty along the walls of the castle, like winter's fine tapestry. Above us, the sky turned dark blue and the stars came out, a brilliant white against their dark backdrop. The moon hung in the sky, close enough that if you reached up, just a little, you could almost touch it. I longed to touch the golden moon as a child.

It was a quiet sort of beauty, more like a sleeping power, soft and majestic.

The cave mages' magic kept the palace warm. Outside the palace walls, the mountain air sharply bit our cheeks, reminding us that the world remained a cold place.

But here, within the beauty of Elenvérs, we were safe.

As I left the advisors' room behind me, Annon stepped out from the shadows, the smile on his face glowing as the ice around us.

His voice sent a chill across my skin. "And what were you doing in the throne room?" The way he asked it didn't sound like a question—it was an accusation. One hand gripped the front of his blue jacket—the same one he wore the day he mercilessly pricked my tiny finger—while the other hand hid behind his back. His lips curved slyly.

He thought he'd caught me.

He might have.

My breath stuttered in my throat, but I attempted to make my face look natural. "Good evening, Lord Annon. I'm simply looking for Cassian. He's late for battle lessons."

Lessons didn't start for another several hours, but I was betting on Annon not knowing that. The inside of his eyebrow drew in as he watched me move past him. For a moment, I thought he wouldn't say anything else, but just as I'd taken my first step past him, he cleared his throat.

"I found something the other day that I think you'll find quite interesting."

As I'd moved past him, he'd turned, so his back remained concealed to me. Now, he pulled his arm from behind him, revealing a flat, rectangular object in his hand. A small painting. The edges were beaten up and the color faded, giving it an antique look. Just as I was about to ask what it was, he flipped it over.

The oil painting stared back at me through familiar faces that I'd seen many times before. I used to stare at those faces and wonder about the people who I'd never get the chance to meet.

I couldn't guess how Annon came across this. They were supposed to be hidden.

My mother's face aligned in the center of the photo, and the other figures circled around her. Her parents at the top, King Habazzek and Queen Freya. Next to them, my mother's three brothers— Mathias, Shallen, and Ortheo.

Shallen was my mother's favorite. He was also an almost identical reflection of me.

I kept emotion from my face as I stared at the painting, avidly aware of Annon's twitching eye on me, and while I didn't give anything away with my eyes, I took too long to answer. "Her Majesty's family. I haven't seen her younger brothers before."

Annon snatched back the picture, holding it up to admire it for himself. "No? I think you see them every time you look in the mirror."

I gave a tiny laugh. "They do have red hair like mine. I get it from my uncle and grandfather." I listed two men that he had never met, so he couldn't know if I told the truth. Even if his ambition led him to seek them out, both men's hair had turned gray by now, masking their once brown hair.

Annon's lips stretched to the sides of his pointed jaw. This was a game to him. There was almost a laugh in the shadows of his words. "You must be afraid to know that you'll soon fall asleep for a hundred years. The last day of your eighteenth year. What are you now? You look eighteen already. How long do you have left?"

His eyes roamed over me, and I took a step back. This conniving man wouldn't tear apart what my family had worked so hard to protect. Once my curse took hold there'd be questions when I suddenly went missing and wasn't heard of again. Though I hoped to break the curse, everyone around me had only ever planned for what would happen when I didn't. They'd gone over every detail, sometimes talking about me as if I were already gone.

We'd prepared, but we hadn't prepared for this. As the years had passed, we'd fallen into a comfortable rhythm of naivety, believing that we'd pulled off the switch, and that no one would start questioning until I was already asleep.

But the questions had come.

Annon held his chin up, and his smile deepened. Unease curled within my fast-beating heart. "Lord Annon, I don't know what ideas you have, but I guarantee you that you're wrong. In five years, I will still be right here to watch Cassian take his rightful place. Now, if you'll excuse me—"

I turned to leave. Over the click of my heels, Annon's voice came, a slight laugh creeping into his tone. "I know who you are. And I know that the king is harboring a fraud in your place. And when I show the kingdom, they'll take a proper look at who should be their king."

Every instinct in my body said to run.

Quiet as a whisper, his voice found me. "Let the games begin."

Chapter six

I COULDN'T BREATHE.

Cassian didn't care. His fingers adjusted along the polearm before thrusting it back into my chest, driving me into the ground. If the polearm had a weapon attached to the end, as they most often do, I'd be dead. As it was, the blunt end crushed me against the dirt. Cassian gloated.

I wanted to stay there, but if I didn't get up, he'd hit again. Harder.

With great effort, I rolled to the side in time to dodge his next advance. He had some nerve, striking at an opponent who obviously couldn't defend themselves. That was Cassian's style: aggressive with no sign of mercy.

It was usually mine too, against everyone but Cassian. With him I had to be defensive to stay alive. Though it made my chest curl with frustration, the truth was that Cassian could best me almost every time. I didn't need to admit it because he knew, and he spared no occasion to mock me for my inferior strength.

Cassian made a ridiculous face when he fought, where he pulled his lip in, and flared his nostrils. I'd never mentioned to him how odd he looked, but if he kept gloating about his skills, I was going to tell him.

If it wasn't for the fairy's gift of wisdom, I might have done it already, but I saw no benefit to the remark beyond the momentary hurt on his face, which wouldn't be worth the blow he'd deliver to my jaw in retaliation.

I groaned as I pulled myself to my feet and retrieved my fallen pole from the ground while Cassian waited, his sudden chivalry surprising me. No sooner had I laced my fingers around the wooden rod than Cassian swung his around and knocked mine free from my grip again.

"You're exceptionally weak today." Cassian laughed. "I'd beat you anyway, easily, but today it takes no effort."

I grabbed my polearm once more, this time making sure to grasp it tighter. "You're exceptionally arrogant today."

He chuckled again as his rod came down.

I blocked this move, and the one after that. In the moment it took for him to twist the pole back to a position to strike again, I swung mine hard against his thigh.

He grimaced but didn't give me the satisfaction of grunting.

The next blow was his hardest one yet, and it took all my strength to hold on. My right foot shifted back to stabilize myself while I pushed against him.

Cassian swung fiercely. Again. And again. His position showed no sign of relenting.

I peeked to the side of the arena where Gen stood, watching intently. Her eyes kept up with our actions. Her straw-colored hair fell to her cheeks, and she twisted the strands closest to her face and pinned it back.

The fiercest warrior this side of the mountains, that's what they'd called her, until a mountainside ambush left her without most of her left arm and a subtle limp in her left leg. Now the title belonged to Rivers, and Gen took on training new recruits.

Or in this case, training the future king and a girl she believes wished to be a knight. Someday she'd learn that she trained the future queen of Elenvérs.

Cassian let out a grunt, the first sign that he was struggling, but my triumph was short lived. As I prepared to slide down and overtake him, he pulled back his polearm and switched direction. I scrambled to block, but he continued swinging and the pole passed by a mere inch in front of me. For a moment I thought he'd missed, but he used the momentum to twist, bringing the opposite side down and around, knocking me from behind.

I didn't fall, but before I turned around, he'd attacked again, coiling the pole in a circle around me and sent me to the floor.

He dug the polearm into my back. "Yield."

I had no choice. "That wasn't a move Gen taught us." I spat dirt from my mouth.

Cassian shrugged. "I don't limit myself to her council." The other trainers aren't supposed to work with recruits. I narrowed my eyes, and he grinned. "You'd be surprised what being crown prince can get you."

He knew that comment would hurt. Those privileges should be mine.

Gen opened the door and came over with her arms crossed. "Where did you learn that?"

Cassian looked my direction before replying, "If you must know, my father taught me that himself."

That hurt more. King Olin never once offered to train me.

Gen looked impressed. "He's taught you well. Go ahead and put your weapons away; you need a rest." I knew that she wasn't talking about Cassian, who hardly looked winded. She left the training center for us to clean and promised she'd be back tomorrow.

The center consisted of twenty chambers each built with wooden posts in a circle and planks stacked high to form walls, so wayward weapons didn't escape the perimeter and strike unsuspecting knights practicing nearby.

Thanks to the creativity of the cave mages, each of the chambers took on a different season each day, so we got to practice in different environments. Today ours was spring, and little pink flowers bloomed along the railings. They'd be gone tomorrow, replaced by icicles or ivy vines. Along with changing seasons, some of the chambers were more intricate than others— with ledges to hide behind or targets to shoot at, but those were typically reserved for actual knights, while Cassian and I got stuck in a plain one. We'd sneak out after dinner sometimes to test our skills in one of the other chambers.

I suspected Cassian snuck out more often than he told me, and I wondered if any of those times were accompanied by King Olin.

I set my polearm against the wall, while Cassian knelt in the dirt. "What is this?"

When I turned around, my heart fell out of my chest. Cassian held my wish in his hand. I must not have noticed it slip from my pocket, and the gold color blended in with the vibrant flowers.

Though I was too far away to snatch it back, he tightened his fingers around it as if he could read my thoughts. "Magical, by the looks of it. Does it hold fire?"

"Yes," I answered without thinking.

Cassian's gaze bore into me, as if searching for the answers I wouldn't share. Then he smiled. "I was wondering if you would lie to me. Where did you get a wish from?"

My lips tightened, and I held out my hand. To my surprise, he dropped it in my palm. "I owe you nothing," I said. I didn't ask how he knew what a wish looked like. That was twice today he showed me knowledge that I hadn't thought he possessed. We took all our lessons and training together. Perhaps my father was giving him educational lessons as well.

"The fairies' gifts weren't enough for you?" he asked.

I scowled. "Am I still cursed?" He didn't reply. "Then no, they weren't enough for me." I started to walk off, but he called out after me.

"Will it break the curse? I know neither a fairy's gift, nor the cave mages magic, nor any sorcerer alive can break this curse. But can the wish?"

The crinkles in my nose deepened as he listed off all the people who couldn't save me from my long slumber. I wasn't aware he was so educated about my curse. "Have you been studying how to break my curse?"

He put his weapons away as I stared at him. The sun glistened off the metal bands on the weapons. Once he locked the rack in place, he strode toward me with hands planted on his hips. "You breaking your curse affects me too. I'd like to know the chances of that happening."

He wasn't rooting for me. If I broke this curse, Cassian lost the throne. He was the one person rooting for me to fall asleep, and I had no trouble believing he was counting down the days of this final year until we hit our nineteenth birthday and the throne was securely his.

One hundred and eighty-six days. I was counting down too.

Cassian wiped his forehead, pushing back his brown hair from his wild eyebrows. He took a few steps toward me while keeping his eyes on the wish in my hand. I slid it into my pocket, drawing Cassian's eyes back up to mine.

"It can't break curses," I told him. I didn't mention that it might stop one.

For a moment, he looked disappointed, but the expression passed to be replaced by a hardened one. "You won't ever be able to break it. You might as well enjoy what time you have left with your family."

My eyes squinted. "I'm closer than you think." False, but he didn't need to know that.

Now it was his turn to narrow his eyes. After a moment, he leaned forward. His warm breath hit my forehead.

I'd been threatened by Cassian before, but nothing compared to what he was about to say.

"You won't. If you break it, I'll kill you myself."

Color drained from my face. Despite his uncomfortable closeness, I didn't step back. "You think my parents will still put you on the throne if you kill their daughter?"

The wicked smile on Cassian's face turned my stomach to knots. "Maybe not. Perhaps I don't have to kill you. But thanks to the curse, your parents are going to lose you anyway. Being the next king is all I've ever trained for. I'm ready for it. If you break the curse, it'll come down to who they are fonder of, and if you think they love you more than me, you're even more blind than I thought."

He took a step back and straightened his tunic. "That throne is mine."

Chapter Seven

TWICE THIS WEEK, I'D been threatened for the throne—
first by Annon, then by Cassian.

Though he'd trained for it, I couldn't imagine Annon as
king. The years of watching his brother rule over what should
have been his had left bitterness where once was kindness. I
could relate to that.

I couldn't imagine Cassian on the throne because he
didn't deserve it; it wasn't his to take. It's as if the crown knew
it didn't belong on his head. Even the less glorious crown of a
prince looked foreign upon Cassian's brow. At least Annon
rightfully deserved the throne once, in the way that I did now.

Still, deserving or not, neither of them embodied the
values of Elenvérs: kindness, modesty, selflessness. They were
none of these things.

I couldn't claim to have mastered those virtues either. But someday I would. Once I found a way to be rid of this curse, the bitterness in my heart would melt away.

My hand tightened around the wish. I had to claim the throne; anyone else would ruin the kingdom. While smart, Annon had more ambition than was good for him, and within years he would march on ThornHigh. And Cassian wasn't strong enough to fend off an inevitable attack from ThornHigh. Either way, if I didn't break my curse, ThornHigh would come for my beautiful Elenvérs.

"Have you come up with anything?" Elis stepped into our small bedroom carrying two goblets filled with chocolate pudding, and I perked up at the sight.

"What are we celebrating?" I eagerly accepted the pudding and shoved a bite into my mouth, welcoming the delectable distraction from my own woes.

She dropped onto the bed across from mine and began eating hers with more grace than I showed. "Not celebrating, exactly. I thought you needed something to cheer you up after a rough couple of days."

I couldn't argue with that. The golden orb sat in my lap, taunting me that I still hadn't found a way to make it useful while my clock ticked closer to my nineteenth birthday.

"It's tough," I said with my mouth full, "to come up with a solution. This is great by the way. Thank you." I raised my cup to her before heaping another spoonful into my mouth. "I could wish all the spindles away." That was the best idea I'd come across yet, though I doubted its efficiency.

"Oh!" Elis's eyebrows shot up and for a moment she looked excited, but it didn't take long for her face to fall again. "Oh, wait. In just our kingdom? Because other people don't have caves mages to make clothes for them. That'd make things a lot more difficult for many people."

Her priorities didn't align with mine. "Yes, but I wouldn't die."

She rolled her eyes. "You won't die."

"I'll die." I poked my spoon back into the pudding and heaped another bite into my mouth. "The thing is, people can make more, and I don't trust that pricking my finger on any pointy thing won't do the trick. And I can't wish away all pointed things. So, I don't think I'd accomplish anything."

Elis bobbed her head as she looked to her pudding.

I didn't need her to weep heavy tears for me every time we talked about the curse, but over the years she'd lost interest in my plight, and I didn't see the concern that once lived in her eyes. Instead, I saw apathy.

That apathy separated us.

I loved my sister more than anyone. More than Lord and Lady Trelluse who raised me as their own, and more than my mother whose love for me was clear every time she looked my way. Elis was my dearest friend, but sometimes the friendship was difficult for me. In her compassion, she joined me on my futile quests to remove my curse: marching after dragons, seeking out fairies, calling on lost spirits, searching for magic stones, eating strange plants that put us both in the ward for a month—she joined me when it mattered.

But then she could step away from it and live her normal life; court an Elenvérs knight, pick an apprenticeship, plan a future. I couldn't. I may never.

Suppress it, Rowan. Jealousy is not an attractive trait. We've been working on this.

The part that pained me was that Elis didn't see why I hated my curse. She saw it as nothing more than a pause on my life. In her mind, I'd go to sleep, wake up to a handsome prince, and live the rest of my life content as my mother had.

I'm not my mother. I'd never stop mourning for my country. There was no guarantee a prince would wake me, let alone the crown prince to Elenvérs, let alone a prince who could love me. My mother was blessed by the Fates to awaken to my father and continue her life in Elenvérs, but I couldn't count on my awakener, whoever he might be. My country needed me now, not in a hundred years.

If I fell asleep, I lost everything.

"There are two directions this could go," I glanced at my wish. "Ideally, I use this to find a way to break the curse, but if not, then I use it to stop the curse."

Elis squinted. "I'll need you to explain that."

"Wishing all the spindles away would stop the curse, so the curse has no way to be fulfilled. Breaking the curse means I could prick my own finger on a spindle as many times as I want, it'd never put me to sleep. I could either wish away the conditions of the curse, put me inside a protective bubble of sorts, which would be easier to do but not reliable, or I could find a way to break the curse entirely."

Her brows drew in. "Break it entirely. Seems safest."

"Agreed. But do you have any idea how to do that?"

She shook her head.

"Me either. And the witch said this wasn't strong enough to do that anyway. Until I find another way to break it, I want to have a backup plan. A good backup plan that I can rely on. Something that ensures the curse can't reach my finger to prick it. I need to keep my hand safe from the spindle. I need..." I paused.

The curse. What were the precise words?

An unbreakable curse I place,
Dark as Stone, Strong as Ice.
Let a hundred-year sleep, lonely as winter
Fall once a spindle pricks her finger
On the last day of her eighteenth year
As snow beings to fall,
She will sleep
Until love's true kiss awakens her.

I knew these words by heart. They echoed through my mind before I went to sleep, and they haunted my thoughts during the day. For eighteen years I'd repeated these words over and over in my head as I fought to break their hold over me.

Now, I focused on the fourth line, *once a spindle pricks her finger*, and squeezed my own. I'd often wondered which it would hit, and since I'd acquired the wish, I've wondered how to keep the spindle from my finger. That seemed to be the key, if I couldn't break the curse, to instead stop the spindle from pricking my finger until my nineteenth birthday.

With the unpredictable nature of the curse, I didn't know how to do that. From what my mother told me, my grandmother burned every spindle in the kingdom to keep the curse away, but someone kept one anyway. On the last snowfall of her eighteenth year, she was mysteriously drawn to the spindle. I think the curse muddled her mind and had to assume the same would happen to me.

There was one sure way to keep a spindle from my finger, and I didn't need a wish to do it.

"I think I have an idea. It might do the trick..." I trailed off.

"What is it?"

"I can't be certain it will work, but it could solve the problem..."

A moment of silence. "Yes?"

My eyes narrowed in thought. "It would be messy, but I'd figure it out."

Elis dropped her spoon in her empty goblet. "Don't be coy about it. If you've thought of something, just tell me."

As far as ideas go, this might work. But I hated the thought of it.

Sacrifice. A ruler makes sacrifices for her kingdom. I could do that. This would be my greatest sacrifice for my kingdom, but it would assure me my throne.

I was willing to go this far for my country.

But how would I manage after? Would I still be fit to rule?

I'd still be the better choice over Cassian. The thought of Cassian on my throne could be my motivation in the moment to go through with my plan.

"If you're being like this on purpose, it's awfully mean."

I laughed, then laughed again. I couldn't tell if this was my gift of laughter surfacing or simply my own excitement at this new plan. It would still be the backup plan in case I couldn't break the curse, but this ought to stop my finger from getting pricked. This could work.

"I've solved it. If I get to the end and I haven't broken the curse, I'm going to use this wish to remove my hands. A spindle can't prick my finger if I don't have any hands. This will do it, Elis. This wish will save me."

Chapter Eight

"THAT IDEA IS SERIOUSLY the worst." It was days after her initial horrified response, and Elis wouldn't quiet about her concerns, no matter how many goblets of pudding I offered in return for her holding her tongue.

"You've mentioned that."

"Have I? Because you don't seem to hear me."

Elis followed behind me as we weaved through the crowd of people who'd come for the Full Moon Feast, a day of celebration in Elenvérs during each full moon starting with small performances, followed by a tournament, and finally a hearty feast. I usually skipped the performances, but I'd never miss a tournament or feast. Fighting, food, and honoring our beautiful country. These were the best days of each month.

Elis's mood did put a damper on my spirits, though.

I looked back to Elis and smirked. "Maybe if you say it again, I'll hear you this time."

She glared, the hazel in her eyes darkening. "I hate you."

"I can't imagine why, I'm delightful," I said under my breath.

She kicked my heel, implying I hadn't quite whispered low enough.

My hair was wrapped around my head and stood up like two red horns, leaving my ears exposed to the cold. A scarf of pure white feathers hung around my neck, and every so often my chin ducked down into them to savor the warmth. We walked south of the practice center where stands stood circling the tournament arena.

Light blue canopies shielded the stadium from snowfall. Intricate snowflakes made from glass hung from the banisters, and as the sun hit them, they'd throw the light against the fabric, illuminating their shapes.

A thin layer of snow covered the stone ground, revealing a large mass of footsteps that filled the area. If I followed each one by sight, I was certain most would venture up toward the same spot, where each would stop for a few moments before moving on, everyone eager to bid wishes to the king.

My feet didn't wander that direction. I had no desire to bow before my king today.

King Olin's seat was vacant, as was Cassian's, but Queen Marigold sat on her majestic chair with twinkling eyes as she spoke to a few of her subjects who'd wandered toward her pedestal to behold the beauty of their queen. A bead of pearls ran through her tight auburn curls, wrapping around her forehead and letting a small strand of tiny gems hang by her eyes.

My mother was truly breathtaking.

I spotted King Olin with Cassian to his right, both laughing as they spoke with some of the people. They could be talking about politics or their family; either way King Olin would know how to make them laugh. He was gifted in that way.

We always sat in the same place, three sections away from the king and close to the front so Elis and I didn't miss any of the action. Her parents waited for us there.

"Lady Rowan, your hair looks beautiful today." Annon stepped in front of my path with a smile that was more vicious than jolly. I knew his comment about my hair was to remind me that he knew which relative had given me my vibrant coloring. Next to me, Elis outright glared, causing Annon to chortle.

I hid my dislike behind a placid expression.

"Thank you, our mother taught us how to do our hair from a young age." I stressed the word mother as I slipped past him. The pain in my finger burned again where he'd pricked me, and I pressed it into my thumb to dull the sting.

As I stepped past, his hand grazed my arm. His breath found my ears as he spoke quietly, "You can pretend all you want. You can't hide the truth when you fall into an everlasting sleep. No one can save you then."

For the first time, I realized I would be vulnerable for a hundred years. My family would try to protect me, but the curse didn't save me if someone ran me through with a sword. Would Annon go so far as to kill me?

He could utilize his finely tuned skill set to sneak past my guards and locate me, asleep, helpless to save myself. He'd draw his sharpened blade from its sheath and plunge it into my chest without hesitation, leaving Cassian as his only barrier to the throne.

Perhaps before killing me, he'd drag me out before the kingdom to show how my parents lied. My parent's deception would be revealed, and his story would lead the advisors to appoint Annon as king in my father's place while they revoked Cassian of his title.

And I, in my peaceful slumber, would be unable to stop him from carrying out his plan.

In all my years of planning how to break the curse, I'd never considered someone might murder me while I slept.

If I were a less clever girl, I might be afraid, but I knew something Annon wouldn't predict. I would never fall asleep.

Elis dropped her glare and now chose the path of indifference, walking past Annon. I took up the glare in her stead. My hands gripped the collar of Annon's surcoat, and I whispered back, "Threaten me again and I'll run you through with a sword."

His smile faltered, only for a brief second, and he yanked himself out from my grip. "I see the fairies didn't give you a gentle spirit as they did your mother."

It unnerved me how much he knew.

I resisted reaching for the powerful wish in my pocket as I pushed past him and followed Elis.

Someday I would be free of him. Someday he wouldn't be able to hurt me.

I clung to that hope.

We pushed past the last group of people before finding our seats where Elis's parents waited.

They weren't alone.

A young man sat by Lord Trelluse's side with a suit as dark as his hair and his hand by his hip in a manner that suggested he was used to resting it on a sword's hilt. The tip of his sharp nose was red, and his mouth moved quickly as he spoke.

His hands mimicked his mouth, moving fast as he turned toward my parents. It was only when Lady Trelluse beamed at us that the stranger glanced our way. Now we got a better look at his face, where the skin was slightly darker than ours, and the birthmark by his jawline formed in the shape of a mountain.

"Meet my daughters, Rowan and Elis." Lord Trelluse stood to introduce us. He looked handsome this morning, and equally proud as he gestured to us. The man shook our hands with a tight grip.

"And you are?" Elis asked before I could.

"A diplomat's son who jumped at the chance to see this beautiful country." His voice carried a hint of accent to it, but the accent wasn't consistent, leaving me to guess if he was faking it or trying to cover it. He wore thick glasses over his face, and a slight fog from his breath made it difficult to see his eyes. If I was right, this man wasn't more than a few years older than me, surely young to be offered a diplomatic mission, which I didn't realize we'd extended to anyone.

Elis kissed her mother's cheeks, but I didn't move past the man. "What country are you visiting from?"

His smile carried a hint of nervousness with it in the way it lagged on the left side. "A small country, not an important one. Certainly not as beautiful as Elenvérs. We've heard so many tales of the splendor of your country nestled in the mountains, caught in winter."

His failure to answer my question didn't escape me. His suit coat was thin enough to see evidence of muscle underneath, which is what caught my eye, but that's not what held my gaze. Most visiting diplomats layered themselves in furs and feathers to protect from the cold, and what could be seen of their noses and ears was always bright pink.

But this man? He wore clothing no different than us, and he didn't even shiver. Either he hid it well, or he was used to the cold. My interest grew. "Which small country?"

The sign of unease grew as he pulled his lips tight.

Lord Trelluse stepped in. "You'll have to excuse my curious daughter. It was a pleasure to meet you."

I stayed silent and the man's stiff shoulders relaxed.

"Likewise, you have two beautiful daughters." I could have sworn his gaze hesitated on us, but then he ducked his head and moved on. I kept an eye on him until he'd slipped from sight.

"What a boring man," Elis said as soon as he'd gone, causing me to laugh. I could always count on her honest thoughts.

"Oh hush, I thought he was delightful," Lady Trelluse said, though she'd never admit to thinking a poor thought about anybody. I sometimes wondered if she truly only saw the good in people, or if she had mastered the art of speaking kindly. It was an art neither I nor Elis learned.

Lord Trelluse was usually more upfront about his opinions, but he appeared lost in thought as his glazed eyes slowly trailed the pages in striped vests while they set up the tournament arena for the jousting. After a long moment he spoke in a voice that would have floated away with the winder were it any softer. "He carried himself like a king."

Trumpets broke the air. Pages rushed to finish.

"Welcome, good people of Elenvérs," King Olin magnified his voice to the crowd through the magic of the cave mages. "We are here today to celebrate everyone who makes Elenvérs the glory that she is." Eager clapping followed.

Sometimes the speeches were longer, where he'd go on about the majesty of Elenvérs and what the monthly gathering stood for. He'd speak of the strength of the knights who were blessed to live longer than a normal man should, and of how they'd fight nobly for our honorable country. He'd speak of the vast riches in the heart of the mountains that kept us strong. He'd say that the celebration was to showcase the strength of the knights to offer the people a feeling of protection; then later we'd feed them in the same room in which we dined to show we are not above them.

We were together, one beautiful country.

Sometimes he'd tell the tale of Elenvérs, a kingdom that started out in the warm south where a few hardworking families planted seeds and built a kingdom from dirt. That small kingdom began to thrive, and the virtues of Elenvérs were created. But then a foolish king came upon the throne, and he allowed his heart to be swayed by a deceitful maiden. She used tricks to weaken him until her wicked men came through and destroyed the kingdom. The remaining people fled, running all the way to the north to be free.

We didn't know what became of our homeland. The last we'd heard, those wicked men had brought ruin to the land and other countries didn't dare touch it. That was hundreds of years ago.

Sometimes King Olin would tell us these tales. But other times, all he said was a simple sentence about Elenvérs. Either way was met with an applause from the crowds who clapped in such a manner that one would think they'd never heard something so beautiful.

Then King Olin would bow, raise his hand, and the tournament would start.

None of that took place this evening. There was no eloquent speech or deep bow. Instead, his arm stretched to the side.

"Please welcome our honorable visitors tonight: King Maven of ThornHigh and his son, Prince Tarion."

The applause that followed was delayed as a stunned silence befell us all, but somewhere, some smart lad picked up his hands and started clapping, and we all followed suit. Once we started, our cheers grew louder and louder so we didn't offend the visiting monarch from our neighbor country to the west.

An enemy stood in our land and we applauded him.

King Maven stood at the same height as King Olin. Snowflakes gathered in his patchy gray hair. He waved politely to the crowd and bowed his head a few times to each side. A thick coat hung over his shoulders and fell to his knees, but I could see a hint of a gut underneath.

Beside me, Elis gasped.

Prince Tarion nodded to the crowd, moving his head in our direction until I could see his face, and I instantly chastised myself for not recognizing him sooner.

"Your boring gentleman is a crown prince."

"Papa did say he carried himself like a king."

I could almost swear his smile deepened, pleased to have tricked us, and my hands stopped applauding so he could make no mistake where my loyalties lay.

That was why the cold hadn't bothered him—he comes from a country on the other side of the Northern Mountains, privy to the same eternal frost as we were. The longer he looked at me, the further the temperature plummeted as my arms shivered.

His gaze moved on and Elis nudged me, but I didn't raise my hands. If the monarchs of ThornHigh were here, then something was terribly wrong.

Chapter Nine

"I'M SORRY I LIED to you." Near the end of the feast, Prince Tarion sought me out in the banquet hall to offer his apologies, but I didn't sense any sincerity in his voice, which now dripped heavily with his rightful accent. A tall goblet, my mother's, if I wasn't mistaken, rested in his hand, almost blocking the small red stain on his shirt sleeve.

I'd been watching the king and prince all night, as most of the room had. I watched where they went, who they spoke to, and who they made a point to ignore. Cassian fell in the latter category, and while it was almost humorous how many times he tried to speak with them and they turned the other way, it made me wonder what sort of ruler didn't want to get to know the future king of their neighbor country.

Not a smart ruler, I knew that much.

They either weren't interested in being friends with our country, or they knew Cassian wouldn't be the one to rule it. They'd long been after our throne to secure the north entirely for themselves. Behind their congenial handshakes and wide smiles were the minds of monsters who would see this kingdom brought to ruin. They must be confident in their plans to not even feign pleasantries toward our crown prince.

Cassian took it in stride, but he frowned into his cup. He kept rubbing that bracelet on his wrist, until eventually he dumped his drink over the balcony and pushed out the doors. Guards raised an eyebrow at his early retirement, but he scowled at them.

Cassian was the only one to retire early. The rest of the castle remained in the festivities to push themselves closer to the king until his balding head could hardly be seen over the crowd. Almost all the caves must be empty as the people flooded to the castle.

They must not know the rumors of the neighbor king's wrath. They say his own people don't come from their homes to greet him.

He didn't show aggression tonight as he masterfully slid from the crowds to drift toward King Olin.

My breathing slowed as I shifted to get a clear image of the two of them. King Olin gave away nothing to the common onlooker, but I knew him better than they, and the tightness in his brow suggested the visit wasn't as merry as the smile pinned to his face.

From his lack of mentioning this to the council, it was likely this visit was a surprise even to him.

Our kingdoms were once sister countries; for a time we were even ruled by the same king. They shared in our virtues, but greed overtook ThornHigh's hearts and their armies turned to plunder on the weak and expand their small kingdom. Their kingdom did grow, but their friendships did not, and now they stood alone in this world—all other alliances burned away like the many bridges that once joined our countries in the mountains.

When they first began to plunder, we'd fought against them; we'd fought with almost our last breath. But that last breath we saved, and we used it to sort out a deal with ThornHigh that we would stay on our side of the Northern Mountains if they remained on theirs, and the uneasy agreement began from there.

They didn't appear to be on their side of the Northern Mountains now. Instead, they drank from my parent's goblets.

"You owe me no explanation," I said to Tarion, bowing my head. "I'm nothing but a noble's daughter."

A sharpness bit my chest as I belittled myself in such a way. This was the man I would fight one day, if my suspicions that they planned to attack were true. But first I must bow to him.

"Still, would you allow me a dance to make up for it?" He extended his arm and a smile charming enough to lure in any girl.

I bit the inside of my cheek as I spoke. "I shouldn't; I'm not worthy of dancing with a man such as yourself. You should be with someone who will inherit a crown." If my earlier words pained me, these ones killed me.

The last thing I needed was to be on Prince Tarion's radar. I didn't need him getting the same ideas that Annon had. Invisibility was one of my assets.

I looked up when he chuckled. "That leaves me with Cassian, and I don't fancy a dance with him."

"No one does. He's quite clumsy in truth," I said, acquiring a laugh from Prince Tarion. As soon as the words left my mouth, I wished for them back, because the feeling of sharing in a small joke with the enemy prince felt like betraying my country.

"I am curious why you are here though." I set my mouth in a straight line.

"Ah, you really are a curious one, aren't you?" He grinned but I didn't join in the gesture. The starlight came through the ice to brighten the darkness of his hair and flickered in his eyes as he stroked his chin. "Right. Would you believe me if I said we come offering friendship?"

Not even a little, but it didn't feel right to tell him that. When I was queen, I would. For now, I returned my gaze to the floor, where the ice glowed under my feet. "I hope it goes well. If you'll excuse me, I must go, but my sister Elis would make a delightful dancing companion."

He glanced back to find her through the crowds. The starlight seemed to settle in her hair as she leaned against the wall in conversation with the guard, Briggs. The fur of her cloak brushed the ground behind her boots. Her eye caught mine.

"I hope we meet again someday," Tarion said, bringing my hand to his lips. Elis gave me a look as he kissed it.

I took my hand back to point him toward my sister, who I hoped wouldn't mind being used in such a way. I stepped away as fast as I could, wishing I could remove my face from his memory. He'd know my face one day, and know it well, but now wasn't that moment.

Handing him off to Elis served a second purpose; if I wasn't mistaken, Elis would try to get information out of him, and something useful may come from that. She had a way of convincing people to trust her, something about her sweet eyes and gentle tone eased the minds of others and before they knew what was happening, they'd offered up their deepest secrets.

Tonight, I needed her to work her magic once more.

I searched for King Maven again. He stood still as he inspected the room. This was the largest room in the castle, with a bridge overtop that connected the sides of the upper floors, and balconies on either end that overlooked the caves of the people.

King Maven and Prince Tarion didn't deserve to see the beauty of Elenvérs, much less dance in the starlight with our people. I couldn't stay to watch them charm my kingdom. With high hopes placed on Elis's abilities, I left the feast behind while my enemies dined within.

Gen put up quite the fight, even with her missing limb and her limp that grew worse as we fought, until finally she leaned back against the wall with a heavy sigh and a remark about knowing when the fight wasn't worth fighting anymore. She pointed toward the straw filled dummy and watched with an occasional comment as I continued my training. I pictured the dummy as King Maven, and that image fueled my blows. One strike for his lopsided smile. One against his thick beard. One against his hand scarred by the blades of those he'd slaughtered.

Once he was properly ripped to bits, I replaced him in my mind and pictured Prince Tarion.

Though the visiting monarchs provided ample motivation during lessons, Cassian was the one I was training to beat. First Cassian, then one day I'd go after ThornHigh.

Gen lowered herself to the ground and massaged her leg. "You don't need to exert yourself so hard. General Domm is already eager for you to join the Elenvérs knights. You'll be little use to him if you work yourself to death."

I lowered my weapon and caught my breath.

If I was who she thought I was, the daughter of a Lord and Lady, this was the path I would choose for myself. Knighthood would suit me well, as next to the king himself, they were the most respected in our land, even above the nobles.

It was the path that Elis planned for herself. If the curse took me, I'd never see her satisfy those goals. She'd be dead before I woke.

I will keep Elenvérs safe until you return to claim it, she'd promised. She couldn't know that or hope to keep that promise if an attack came, but she made it, nonetheless. An effort to ease the bitterness of my curse, and perhaps stop my relentless pursuit of anything that might break the binds that hold me. She'd grown weary of chasing futile attempts over the years, though the kindness in her would never say so.

"You have nothing to worry about; you'll be one of the greatest knights we've had in years. Almost as strong as me if you keep training like you are."

Gen pulled a smile from me. "I'd like to beat Cassian just once first," I admitted.

Now it was her turn to chortle. "I may never understand the rivalry between the two of you, but he isn't your enemy. One day he will be your king, and the friendship between you will put you in a position to be a close general in his council."

I tossed my weapon to the side and joined Gen on the ground. "If it comes to it, I'd fight alongside Cassian. But that doesn't mean I don't want to beat him too."

Her hand, once done massaging her leg, instinctively moved to cover the stub of her other arm. "I can respect that. In my younger days I faced another trainee who I wanted to beat more than anything."

She paused and I raised an eyebrow. "Did you?"

"She died before I got the chance."

That quieted me. I wanted to beat Cassian, but I didn't want him dead. Gone, maybe, but not dead.

"Here's the truth: Cassian's stronger than you, so to beat him you'll have to be both smarter and faster than him."

"I'm already smarter than him."

"But not faster."

No, he was quicker than me. And he didn't need the fairies' gifts to get an advantage over me, a fact which he reminded me of constantly. For a moment, I imagined using my wish to make myself stronger than Cassian. The look on his face when I bested him again and again would be worth it, but only for a moment.

Besting him wasn't worth wasting my wish.

"To be smarter than him, you need to identify his weakness and use it against him, while identifying your own weakness and conquering it."

"Oh, is that all?"

She laughed. "It can be easier than you think, once you discover those weaknesses."

My head rested back against the wood and I wiped away sweat from my brow. Despite my clouded head, coming up with Cassian's weakness would be simple. "He doesn't do it for himself; he fights to please those around him and prove himself worthy of the crown. It's not a joy of fighting, but a strong desire to be accepted in his place. Though gifted, his lack of passion means he wouldn't do absolutely everything it took to win the fight. I'm willing to do whatever it takes."

Gen nodded. "It's true. Cassian has always displayed a strong desire to be liked by those around him, but any good king knows the importance of being loved. That's not a strong enough weakness to beat him."

I sighed. "He struggles with archery."

Her tongue clicked against the roof of her mouth. "Still not enough. Find internal weaknesses, and you can beat him. Now what about yours?"

I closed my eyes and crossed my arms. My list was long, and I didn't care to share them. Instead, I said, "I'm devilishly charming. I suppose that can be a hinderance at times."

"You're devilishly arrogant, that's for sure. And that can be one of your greatest downfalls." She shifted and softened her tone. "Rowan, I've been your mentor for years, so I'm not saying this to hurt you. But how often do you think of the people around you, and how often are your thoughts focused on yourself? Maybe arrogant isn't the right word, but perhaps self-absorbed."

Hurt vibrated through my chest, followed by a deep guilt. "I know," I whispered. "I'm working on it."

It was easy to blame the curse for my flaws. Easy to say that I was bitter because I'd been dealt a poor hand, jealous that others had a life I never could, and self-absorbed because of my determination to break this blasted curse.

But Gen couldn't see the curse. She only saw the manifestations of my pain.

Her hand lingered over mine, but she withdrew it before touching me. "Listen, confidence is a fine thing. But a lack of compassion for others? It can be detrimental on the battlefield to have someone who focuses on themselves and doesn't see the needs of their brother or sister. They depend on you, and you depend on them. Your isolation could be the thing that kills you."

I shook my head. "My determination to be the best will be my greatest asset. It's how I know I'll be great."

Her head tilted to the side as she brought her shoulders up in a little shrug. "Your motivation is unrivaled. But you must learn to see others instead of being so alone."

She had no idea how alone I was.

With a sigh, she pulled herself to her feet and offered me a hand. "It's something to think about. The warrior who sees their weaknesses can overcome them, and then there will be little to hold you back."

"Thank you, Gen. I'll think about it."

"Then my work today is done. Keep practicing; you may beat Cassian yet. But for what it's worth, I don't think you need to. I think you and Cassian could become powerful allies if you work together." With a slow limp she left the arena, sending in a blast of cool air as she opened the door. I stayed behind in the summer heat to clean up the mess and sort through the wisdom she'd left me with.

Chapter Ten

SOMEONE WAS HERE IN the dark of the night.

I listened as I slowed my steps. Every evening this week I visited the arena, sometimes with Gen, other times alone. I'd never practiced without Cassian before that week, but knowing he'd been practicing without me put a distance between us that was never there before.

Tonight, I'd stayed in the arena until the stars came out and the rest of the palace fell asleep. Only after my arms ached and my feet were like heavy stones did I pack up and tiptoe back inside the palace.

Unless I was mistaken, I wasn't the only one out at this hour. Another's feet moved besides mine.

My hand itched for my sword, but my sheath was empty. The starlight dimmed as it gleamed through the ice walls, offering little more than a soft blue glow to light the hallway littered with shadows, any one of them wide enough to conceal a lurker.

I'd think it was King Maven or Prince Tarion sneaking through the night, if I hadn't watched those same people leave that morning. I continued through the corridor at a slower pace. At the end stood the staircase that wound up to my quarters. The hairs on my arm stood on end, and I peeked over my shoulder.

I crept through the night with the grace of a winter owl. I could thank the fairy's gift for such gracefulness. No doubt this wasn't how she expected me to use it.

A small light caught my attention, so small that I hadn't noticed it before. It peeked from under a doorway in the soft orange of a candle lit from the other side.

My chest relaxed in relief that whoever stood inside must have made the noise. My next steps came with less worries.

A hand gripped my arm, yanking me to the side.

A scream built in my throat, but a hand covered my mouth and pulled my head into a set of wide shoulders, then whispered in my ear in a voice lower than a mountain's rumble, "You scream, and I swear I'll kill you."

My elbow prepared to jab backward until I recognized the voice.

I jabbed anyway. Hard.

Cassian grunted and released my mouth, then yanked on my arm until I spun to face him.

"Blast it, Rowan, there's spies in there. Calm down." His voice hissed through the darkness.

My mouth had hung open to ask him what he was doing, but I promptly shut it and stared back at the door, my eyes widening at the thought of spies in the castle. "How do you know?"

"I know, now be quiet." Cassian wore the clothes of the cave people, a simple overshirt tucked into pants, both of which were covered in what appeared to be paint. Other hints of paint dwelled on him: in his hair, on his arm, a small stroke under his bottom lip that almost reached his chin.

He stepped from the shadows and pressed himself against the wall adjacent to the door, twisting his head so he could listen to whatever lay within. Not wanting to be left out of the fun, I joined him.

There was nothing more than a hint of rustling inside to know that someone was in the small library, but it could be a late-night reader, someone studying, or the quiet man who organized the books from time to time.

Cassian cupped his hand against the door and twisted it in a strange motion. After peering closer, the dull shine of brass peeked through his fingers. He saw me looking and smiled. "A gift from the cave mages."

He didn't clarify, but from the focused look on his face, I guessed that particular gift allowed him to hear what went on behind the closed door. Quite a gift. I'd gotten nothing more than a pair of winter boots two years ago. No doubt they eagerly adorned the future king with as many gifts as they could to win his favor.

That was always one of the reasons I doubted the strength of their magic, because they didn't know Cassian was an imposter. Instead, they doted on him with magical gifts.

I waited as Cassian focused, wishing I could hear too.

He nodded once, then again, then his eyes grew wide and his lips stretched thin.

I'd seen that face before.

"What?"

He shook his head at me. After a few moments, his eyes bulged. "Run," he hissed. His long legs took off down the corridor.

Shoot. Someone must be coming.

After a moment of shock, I darted after him. He made it halfway up the stairs before I reached the bottom, just in time to hear the library door open behind me. Suppressing a yelp, I flew up the stairs with as much strength and grace as I could muster.

Cassian ducked into the doorway leading to his and Elis's parents' living quarters while I followed behind. He glanced back once, but by the way he looked behind me instead of at me suggested he was more concerned with someone following than my safety.

I eased the door shut as quietly as I could, then waited to hear if anyone followed us. If they did, they didn't stop at our door. We caught our breath inside.

Cassian plopped into one of the chairs around the living quarters and rested his feet against the indigo rug. The listening device rolled from his hands to his lap.

"Now will you tell me what that was all about?"

He ran his hand through his hair and looked up at me with weary eyes. "King Maven is planning to attack Elenvérs. Soon."

I couldn't say I was surprised. I knew better than to trust a man who hid most of his face behind a beard. But my mouth still dropped open and I staggered back. "But I watched him and his men leave this morning."

Cassian gave me a distressed look. "He came back."

I sat next to him on the couch and picked up the device from his hand. "What is this?"

A brass cylinder made up one side and a small ring fixed to the other, with etchings on the side so tiny that I couldn't tell if they were a design or another language. Perhaps a little bit of both, a language so beautiful that it decorated the sides with words that were both a phrase and a picture.

Cassian allowed me to examine it before he explained. "It helps me hear through walls. The cave mages felt it was a proper gift for a future king, so he could listen in on his enemies." I thought it was gloat that seeped through his tone, but when I met his eyes, I found a hint of apology.

I must have been wrong. Cassian never apologized for anything, especially when it came to me.

I handed the device back to him, though it ought to be mine. "I want that when I become queen."

His lips pulled tight again, reminding me of his threat to kill me before I could become queen. Of the other dangers I'd faced—Annon and now King Maven—I took Cassian's threat the lightest. He could best me in a sword fight, but he wasn't cold-blooded.

"We'll see." He rubbed his fingers across the worn-out leather of his band.

"Are you going to tell me what they said?" I asked, leaning forward.

"I have a plan." He said at almost the same time.

"Not yet." It didn't seem fair that because of a gift that should have been mine, he got to conceal information. If there were spies in my palace, I needed to know now. "My question first."

"Right." He pulled his hands away from his bracelet and started fiddling with the device again. "I saw the king as I was headed back to my room, which was a curious thing because he ought to be on his way home. So, I followed him. From the way he moved, he was clearly aiming for some level of secrecy about the whole ordeal, which only furthered my resolve to catch whatever he was up to. He led me to the library."

"Obvious spot for a midnight spy meetup."

"Naturally. But I couldn't hear him. It took me a minute to fetch my device. It's lucky that I did because his companion came later, and I might have been caught if I hadn't left."

"Who came?" I glanced toward the door as if someone might come through at any moment.

"This lets me hear, not see. I don't know who, but someone who knew the placement of our dispatched knights."

"Who would tell him that?" I asked, with wide eyes. "Whose head do I need to remove?"

"I'm not certain. The informant spoke too low for me to recognize the voice. But King Maven plans to wipe out our knights first, then come for us."

I leaned back against the chair. King Maven left no survivors in his battles, and Elenvérs was not prepared for a war.

"Do you know when?"

His eyes looked as dark as a storm as his brow wrinkled. "Probably soon since he knows the current placement of our knights. That information is only valuable for a short time until they move again." Cassian cursed and rubbed the edges of his nose. My father made that same gesture when he was upset. "I'll send word in the morning to move everyone, but it must be done quietly so whoever the spy is won't notice and report to the king. We will only tell my father before Briggs and I ride to warn the soldiers."

"I'm coming, too."

"No." I was prepared to fight over it, but he put up his hand. "No, I have a better idea for you. If they have a spy in our kingdom, I want one in theirs. You should go to ThornHigh for information of our own."

For the first time, I didn't know what to say. Did he trust me enough for that? Or was this all a ploy to put me in the belly of the beast?

"It makes sense," he continued as he tapped his chin. "If they sent us their monarchs as a sign of 'peace', it's only fair that we send someone in return."

"An emissary, maybe. Not me."

"It's perfect. Anyone else would appear too serious, but sending you shows we don't take them as a genuine threat. You're just a girl who loves to travel, has always wanted to see ThornHigh, and who swooned over their dreamy prince. Sending you is perfect."

My jaw clenched. "That doesn't describe me at all."

He leaned forward. "When you get there, that'll describe you perfectly. Besides, you haven't pledged yet. You can say you wish to pledge as an emissary."

I was due to pledge after my birthday. Cassian's pledge would simply be ritual where he would pledge himself to Elenvérs as the crown prince, but for everyone else, it was usual to pledge yourself in your nineteenth year to a field of study, an apprenticeship, or knighthood. For me, it wouldn't matter.

Either I'll sleep, or I'll become Queen.

Which did open the door for this to be a valid excuse to visit ThornHigh.

"So, I go to ThornHigh and the Court of Strength to find something that stops them from destroying Elenvérs."

"Yes." He leaned back and grinned triumphantly.

I studied him for a few moments, his casual stance and glinting eyes. "I don't know if I can trust you."

He chuckled. "I feel the same about you. But we both love Elenvérs. And if you plan to rule one day, this is how you help save your country."

A door opened and we both swung our heads in the direction. There were two doors that branched off from this main room, one for Elis's and my bedroom and another for her parents. It was the later that opened now. Cassian's mother stumbled out with bags under her eyes.

"Who—Cassian!" She held her arms out to her son, who hopped up to hug her. "What are you two doing up?"

"Sorry to wake you, Mama. Rowan and I are planning a little trip and we were going over the details. It's all quite last minute, I'm afraid."

She smiled at me over Cassian's shoulder. "Together? And no swords in sight I see. I'm glad to see you two getting along for a change."

It was a leap to make that assumption, but neither of us dared to correct her. Pleased, she trotted back into her bedchambers.

As soon as the door closed, I scowled at Cassian. "I guess we weren't going to consider the plan further? It's decided?"

Cassian sighed and placed his hands on his hips. "Unless you have a better idea, then it's decided—in the morning we leave. Briggs and I to save our knights, and you—"

"Tomorrow I travel alone to ThornHigh and the Court of Strength."

"Not alone. Take Elis with you, she is the more likable one of your duo anyway. She'll win them over, while you cut them from within."

Splendid. Now I had to tell Elis that I needed her to go on one more adventure with me. One of these days she was going to say no.

Chapter Eleven

"ROWAN, ONE OF THESE days, you'll be the death of me."
Elis tied a knot in her satchel and hung it over her horse
before strapping her sword to her side. She patted her horse
on the neck. "Isn't she? She's going to kill us, huh?" He grunted
happily at her.

"I'll do no such thing." I tended to my own horse, who
didn't nuzzle me with half the enthusiasm that Elis's horse
showed her. I woke Elis up early to tell her our plan, and she
agreed with little persuasion. Though she showed a suspicious
amount of eagerness to travel to ThornHigh, she also offered a
lot of complaints.

"If you don't watch out, she just might," Cassian said,
coming from the other side of the stable with Briggs in tow.

"If I die," Elis said to her brother. "Promise you'll kill her for me."

"With pleasure." Cassian promised. But he winked at me. I didn't wink back.

"But if he dies—" Elis approached Briggs and wrapped her arms around him. "Then I'll kill you myself."

Briggs buried his face in Elis's hair, the same auburn color as his own. His arms wrapped tight around her waist and pulled her in as close as his armor would allow. For a moment they paused there, and it was like all time stood still for the two of them while Cassian and I busied ourselves with our horses.

Briggs and Elis were an ideal match, and after their many months of courtship thus far, I suspected he'd ask for her hand soon. A part of me, so small that I didn't let myself focus on it, envied them. She had love and a promising future that she could rely on, whereas mine was complicated and uncertain.

If I focused on the joy she had, it would swallow me whole. I'd fade away. Instead, I kept it small, only visiting the pain to remind myself why I needed to break this curse.

I wouldn't find that happiness until this curse was gone.

Cassian led his stallion toward me while Elis and Briggs finished their goodbye. "There's a girl in the court at ThornHigh; her name is Mar. Find her. She has short black hair and a silver tattoo across her left arm. I've already sent a wind message to her." Cassian looked me directly in the eyes as he spoke. A wild strand of hair twisted down and blocked part of one eye. I thought I saw a smudge of paint in his hair, the same color as the paint on his arms last night, but the cuff of his sleeve covered it.

Had he taken up a new hobby? Advisor meetings, battle training, school lessons, and now painting? Crown prince duties weren't enough to keep him busy?

I swung my leg over my steed's side. "What did your message say?"

"Just that you are a friend and should be welcomed. But you can trust her, she's on our side."

On our side. I wouldn't consider myself to be on Cassian's side, but I suppose in this situation I was. We both wanted to protect our throne.

I picked up my reins. "I'll find her. If she's on our side, then is it necessary for us to go? She may be in a better position to gather intel than I could be."

Cassian frowned. "It'd be too dangerous to ask that of her. She wouldn't have our country's protection if things went awry."

He stroked his horse once before mounting, showing no concern for how equally dangerous this was for me. His gaze did linger on his sister, where he took a deep breath, but he pulled his horse away and made for the path outside.

As he passed them, Elis and Briggs separated to find their own horses. "We'll be back in four weeks. Stay safe," Briggs said. We told them to do the same, then waved as they rode off before us, turning east while we would travel west. It'd take a week of hard riding to reach the enemy kingdom.

"To ThornHigh we go," I said.

"Rowan."

I turned my head sharply, almost thinking I'd imagined the sound. At the other end of the stable stood King Olin, surrounded by rotting hay.

He took a few steps forward. I blinked before speaking. "Did Cassian tell you where we were going? He was supposed to, but it's just like him to forget."

King Olin shook his head. "He told me. Lady Elis, may I have a moment with my daughter?"

Daughter. He hadn't called me that in years. Thanks to the fairy's gift of memory, I recalled every single time he called me his daughter in comparison to every time his eyes glazed over me. I remembered it all.

I didn't remember him ever seeking me out in such a way.

Elis bowed her head and rode down the snow-covered path to wait.

King Olin fidgeted with his jacket as he inched forward. When he got to below my horse, he paused with his hands over his stomach and thumbs twitching.

He opened his mouth then closed it again. After a quick breath, he spoke. "You know Elenvérs is one of the most important things to me."

My chest sank. Foolish of me to think he was here as a father and not a king on behalf of his country. I shouldn't blame him—didn't I love Elenvérs more than I loved him? But for a moment, a tiny moment that warmed my heart, I thought he'd come to see off his child.

"ThornHigh is a dangerous court, filled with double-faced people who will weave lies faster than they claim the truth, and a pure heart like yours doesn't belong among them."

I pulled my eyes away. If only he knew that according to the White Bear my heart may not be as pure as he thought.

His hand flickered to my own, bringing my eyes back to him. He coughed as he stepped back and removed his hand from mine. Something in his eyes changed. He cast aside the softness in his voice, so it resembled the kingly tone I was so used to. "Be careful. I'll be waiting for a report when you get back. Send a wind message if you need help and I will come."

He turned abruptly and strode away while I tried to find the right response, but he left the stable before it came. I didn't know what I would say anyway, besides thank you. Anything less didn't feel right, and anything more sounded wrong in my mouth.

I turned my horse into a trot to find Elis, who raised her eyebrows at me.

"It was nothing more than a warning to be careful. Let's go."

She kept a questioning gaze on me for a few moments more before nodding, and together we rode west to infiltrate ThornHigh.

My hopes were high. I could find something to bring ThornHigh down, prove my value to both my father and our country, and maybe do enough good that my soul would be considered pure again. This trip could prove to Elenvérs that I was worthy of being her queen.

It was an ambitious hope. Fool-hearted, even. But perhaps this trip could change everything for me.

"Have you thought any more about your wish?" Elis asked me. "Or are we still chopping off your hands?"

I smiled. "I have thought some. But nothing better than that idea."

She frowned. "There must be something else."

I ran through the words again. 'An unbreakable curse I place, dark as stone, strong as ice. Let a hundred-year sleep, lonely as winter, fall once a spindle pricks her finger. As the last snow of her eighteenth year begins to fall, she will sleep. Until love's true kiss awakens her.'

Thanks to the witch, we knew this wish couldn't break the curse, but it might be able to stop it. I had to think of something the curse couldn't manipulate or break through. Something to stop the curse from happening.

"Can't you just wrap your hands? Then the spindle can't prick them."

It's a good idea, but I'd already thought of it. "I think the curse will play with my mind, and I don't want to risk unwrapping them, or the curse pushing a spindle through the wrapping. I need something stronger."

"Alright," she said. "What happens if you cut off your hands and the curse makes a spindle prick your lifeless fingers anyway? You fall asleep and wake up mutilated."

She had a point. "You'll just have to burn my hands as soon as I cut them off."

"Rowan!" She gasped, and I threw my head back to laugh. "You're insane."

We continued to ride as we pondered other ideas that didn't involve inhuman maiming as Elis put it. We had an easy path ahead as the snow was low and made it easy for the horses to ride through. A small snowflake landed on my nose, and I shook it off.

"What about the snow?" I gasped, pulling my horse to a quick stop. "The curse says it'll take place as the last snow falls on the last day of my eighteenth year. If I use this wish to stop all snow from here until my twentieth birthday, just to be safe, the terms of the curse can't take place."

Elis thought about it. "That might work."

"Might? The curse is clear. As the last snow begins to fall. It must be snowing. This wish can stop that, and no matter how much the curse dims my mind or senses that day, it can't make snow."

"Can it?"

I held up the wish. "This says it can't. And no one relies on the snow." I bounced giddily in the saddle. "If it starts to snow anyway, you take a sword and chop off my hands."

"I'm not doing that."

My head swiveled to look at her. "I really think this can work."

The hope that danced within me couldn't be bridled and I laughed. This would work. I would break the curse.

"Wait." Elis's held up her hand. I frowned at her tone. "It's too big of a thing to ask. Are you certain the wish can stop all snow for two years?"

No, I wasn't certain. My knowledge on the wish was limited. "What about for a week? I stop all snowfall for the last week of my eighteenth year. It snows every week, so there's no risk of the curse taking effect sooner, and pausing the flurries for a week isn't asking much."

She nodded. "I'd feel safer about that. Let's do it."

I grunted. "I can't yet. It can't be a future wish. Whatever I wish for has to be able to be fulfilled right then."

She shrugged. "Then let's do the year thing."

I breathed out as snow began to pick up from around us. "No, you are right. One week is safer. All I have to do is keep this wish safe for about six more months. To do that," I pointed at her in warning, "you can't tell anyone about this wish. Not our parents, not the king and queen, no one. No one can know. It's the best way to keep it safe."

Cassian knows, my mind reminded me. It seemed I was trusting him a lot this week. But if he could keep it a secret, then I was on my way to retaking my kingdom.

"Fine," she said. Then she looked at me and smiled. "I think we've done it, Rowan. I think you're safe."

I smiled too. "I think so. Now let's go save Elenvérs."

Chapter Twelve

SO, THIS WAS THORNHIGH. I'd crossed the Northern Mountains to peer at ThornHigh many times, but never been inside the walls. Never touched the floors with my feet, never slept in the beds at night, never eaten in the king's dining hall.

I did all those things now, and I did them with an innocent smile on my face and wonder in my eyes, hiding the wolf's snarl underneath. Elis's smile looked real enough that I almost thought she enjoyed her time here.

They'd given us a maid, a sweet girl who didn't talk much but worked hard, and it was difficult to dislike her. She didn't look at me as she worked and when she answered my questions, she kept her head turned so I couldn't read her face. She was well trained to keep her distance from emissaries.

She had bruises on her face. We'd heard that King Maven was strict with his staff. If she could survive him, she could survive my relentless questions.

I gave up pestering her and let her work in silence.

While not invited, Elis and I were welcomed into King Maven's court with much fanfare. The king himself had been there as the gates opened to welcome us in, though then he left the castle. They'd tucked us into a chamber in the corner of the massive building where someone came by often to greet us and suggest a tour. We took every tour offered, and by the end of the first day we knew the layout of the grounds fairly well.

The key differences between ThornHigh and Elenvérs were obvious. Their castle was made from stone while ours was built with ice. We saw no trace of cave mages to keep up the castle, only maids who bustled through the busy hallways. There was an attractive aesthetic to ThornHigh: the way the village and the castle blended into one magnificent city that centered around the keep, the tall battlements spaced around the side to guard the village—each with a lion's head painted on them, the brick clock tower that sat in the center of the town to stare toward the inner castle wall, the tunnels that ran through the mountain and met in small gathering rooms underneath—it was all beautiful. But it wasn't Elenvérs.

It was clear what this castle was built for. This was a war castle, and they well earned their name of the Court of Strength, as opposed to our Court of Valor.

But, as we stayed in ThornHigh, I bestowed a new name upon them: the Court of Parties.

While Elenvérs feasted once a month, they danced every other night, dressing up the room to befit the celebratory style and leaving the decorative gold on the walls long after the dancing stopped, so it was there when they started up again. Their castle was permanently dressed up for celebration.

We were more reserved in Elenvérs. We didn't make fools of ourselves by getting drunk on wine or eating more food than was good for us.

I stayed close to the back of the room while eyeing the lords and ladies of the court who'd given up trying to persuade a dance out of me. My hand stayed at my waist where I'd wrapped the sides of the dress around in a knot to conceal a dagger underneath. After two days of polite conversation and endless tours, I longed for a reason to use the dagger.

Tonight didn't look like it would provide me with such a reason.

Elis won their friendship first, unsurprisingly. She sat at a table surrounded by young maidens, listening to their stories and laughing in a way that had them all enthralled. Cassian had been right to send her along with me. I'd never charm them in the way that she did. She had a bit of queenliness in her, though she didn't see it.

As she interacted with the court, I focused on finding the girl Cassian told me about. It was our fourth day here and I'd yet to spot her.

Four days. Had we really been here four days already?

I'd gained no information to show for our time here, besides the layout of their castle and a description of the extravagant throne that King Maven sat on, neither of which could help Cassian. I'd yet to see any knights, which I thought was interesting until a casual conversation initiated by Elis taught us that the knights lived either on their own grounds not far to the west or with their families through the town. We did see castle guards, but only on duty. They never attended the dinners.

I'd think ThornHigh to be arrogant in keeping their warriors off grounds and their castle weak against attack, but in the mountains, there was little chance of being caught unaware. The terrain you'd have to cross before reaching the castle would provide little opportunity to sneak in undetected. Even from Elenvérs.

"So, you are the girl with the red hair that Cassian spoke of."

A girl moved from behind me. Her dark hair was twisted to the top of her head like a crown. She wore a silver dress with no jewelry, leaving her arms bare besides a tattoo.

"Mar?" I asked.

She nodded. Cassian failed to tell me how pretty she was.

"I assume you are here on less friendly terms than you led our king to believe?" She didn't lower her voice as she spoke, and if the group of ladies to our side stood any closer, they would have overheard.

"Hush." I lowered my eyebrows at her candor and motioned my head to the side. "I think we should talk."

She smiled innocently with a small tilt of her head. "I think so too. I know an ideal place. Follow me." She walked without checking to see if I followed. For a moment, I debated grabbing Elis in case Mar turned out to not be the friend I hoped she was, but Elis remained at the table surrounded by conversation, and any attempt to pull her away would certainly attract eyes.

I followed Mar alone through the crowd and out a side door to a silver balcony wrapped behind a red railing, circling sideways until it narrowed against the stone wall. Snow gathered on the balcony, and I drew my arms close to my side.

She led me to the edge where we wouldn't be seen through the windowed doors.

She placed a hand on her hip as her eyes raked over me. Her voice sounded cheerful and calculated at the same time. "Cassian told me you needed an ally at our court. I'm sorry I couldn't come sooner. How has your stay been so far?"

Without knowing how much information Cassian shared with her, I decided it best to keep my responses to a minimum. "We've been warmly received, though I'd love a proper tour of the castle sometime. There's a lot of underground tunnels I haven't figured out yet."

She leaned back against the railing. "Most emissaries don't need to be wandering the tunnels. Most prefer to keep their heads down and stay out of King Maven's way, not scope through dark passages."

That gave me pause. If she questioned my desire to scope out the tunnels, then Cassian told her even less than I thought. While I searched for a response that kept my cover, she pushed from the railing and began to pace around me.

"This is the story—two girls, both wanting to be emissaries, are granted a visit to ThornHigh, an enemy court, *without an invitation*, and then arrive without any guards. Yet, you're welcomed into our fold and given a comfortable place to sleep and a spot at our table."

As she circled behind me, my hands reached to the folds of my dress where my dagger lay.

She continued, "Perhaps a friendship between our two countries can be formed after all these years. It's a cute story. But here's the one I believe: you and your sister are spies hoping to uncover a weakness in our castle, and Cassian sent you to do it."

She paused in front of me, and I wished I'd brought Elis with me. Perhaps if I ran now, I could escape before she caught me.

Or perhaps she was testing if I would be honest with her.

I bit my tongue and waited for her to speak, itching for the comfort of my blade and prepped to retrieve it at the slightest hint of danger. My eye dropped to her waist in search of her own knife. If I hadn't, I never would have seen the subtle movement of her wrist flicking out and a blade sliding from her sleeve into her hand.

Her voice deepened into a low growl. "This is my kingdom, and you can't infiltrate it."

All subtleties were gone.

With a mighty cry, she swung at me just as I jumped out of her way, sending her weapon crashing into the stone wall behind me. Curses flew from her mouth and she spun around in time to grab my arm before I could leap away. A sharp scream dragged from my throat as she hauled me back. Someone would hear me. As I shouted, I drew out my own dagger in time to block her next attack.

I twisted my blade up to push hers away, but her blade slid across my hand, drawing a dark red line. Pain cleaved into me.

She smiled at the blood.

The exit lay behind her. I was trapped on a balcony with nothing below it but the side of a frozen mountain. Even if I survived the fall, I'd be too weak to move, and the cold would freeze my body as death took me. A shiver slivered over my skin.

I spoke though my teeth. "You kill me while I wear my king's livery, you bring war from Elenvérs onto your kingdom."

"War is coming anyway."

I could see death in Mar's eyes. She had me trapped—but not yet beaten. The balcony banister pushed against my back. She gloated over my fear with a snarl as wicked as the harshest winter.

The next thing I knew, she'd launched herself on top of me, throwing me to the ground. She brought her elbow down hard into my chest, and my breath escaped my lungs. Pain vibrated through my bones. Moonlight glinted off the pointed steel tip of her short blade as she raised it over her head.

Before she could strike, I summoned enough energy to tug my arm free and slice my blade at her side. It connected with skin.

She hissed and raised the blade again, slower this time as she winced. I used that moment to grab her hair and roll her downward. Snow smeared over the stone as we thrashed until I pushed myself up on top of her. Her blade hit the ground at an angle to tilt under her, pulling it from her hand.

The aggression in her eyes faltered. For a moment, I had the advantage, and I could use it to strike her down.

I could kill her.

I hesitated, and that hesitation was all she needed.

Her cold fingers grabbed my wrist with surprising strength, and she dug her nails in deep. The pain opened my hand and my dagger fell to her stomach. She snatched it.

I sprang to my feet, but she was faster, knocking me back down and fetching her other dagger.

My fingers curled over the snow as her boot met my chest. It pinned me down.

She wielded both daggers.

In a twist as surprising as the rest of the evening, the balcony door opened with a bang as a man charged in with his suit unbuttoned, his boots sliding through snow, and his sword in his fist. His face couldn't be seen as I struggled in the snow, but I had no friends at this court.

Death waited for me like a soft flurry, patient and slow, before it became a blizzard I couldn't avoid. I could almost feel its cold fingers around my neck.

I lurched against Mar's boot, but she didn't move. Who would kill me first?

But the stranger's blade didn't piece my skin. It poised before Mar's throat.

"Move, and I'll kill you."

She hissed at him, and the blade sunk further against her, threatening to spill blood. With malice in her expression, she backed off me, led by his blade. The stranger's frame positioned between her and I.

Mar glared. "You don't know what you're doing. She's a spy. You need to kill her."

I should run. But Elis was still in the dining hall. I couldn't leave her. Instead, I prepared myself, ready to react to whatever came my way.

The man didn't turn to look at me. "You don't give me orders; I assign them to you. Stand. Down."

After a few tense moments, she lowered her weapon.

A second man came from behind me, and together they took the daggers and pinned Mar's arms behind her waist.

"Attacking our emissary in the middle of a new friendship between our countries?" said the first man. "That doesn't reflect well on us. Take her to the cells; I'll deal with her later."

"Don't trust her. She's a spy!" Mar yelled again. She thrashed against the arms that held her and kicked at their feet, but he held tight. He dragged her through the doorway and away from the dinner party.

The first man faced me. I was prepared to defend myself against her claims, but instead I fell speechless.

Prince Tarion chuckled. The moonlight angled off his dark hair, creating silver tones within. "I assume one of these weapons is yours?" He picked up a bloodied blade from the pavement.

I didn't want to admit that I had been hiding a weapon in my dress, which would all but confirm Mar's accusations, so I shook my head. He smiled as if he knew anyway and pocketed the blade.

"The last time I saw you, you denied me a dance. Surely you wouldn't do so again?" He held a hand out to me.

I'd agree to anything that got me back to a crowd where I had a sliver of safety in their midst. I never should have trusted Mar enough to go where none could see us. I wouldn't allow myself to be trapped out here with the prince.

"Seeing as you saved my life, I can agree to a dance."

Chapter Thirteen

"EITHER YOU'VE DANCED THIS style before, or you are more modest about your talents than you let on," Prince Tarion said. We danced as servers weaved golden platters of wine flutes between us. The sharp scent of perfume burned heavier in the middle of the room, and the laughter of the people was louder.

Prince Tarion showed me through the first few steps, but with the fairies' gifts of gracefulness and wisdom, I picked up the rest of the moves on my own. I only turned the wrong way a few times, but Tarion's skill covered my mistakes and made them look like part of the dance.

His highness's presence had cleared the dance floor, but he beckoned everyone back to their places, so while we still drew many more eyes than I could say I enjoyed, we weren't alone in dancing to the brass instruments in the evening light.

"I've been gone a few days, and I've only just returned. They wouldn't clear it otherwise," he said.

He didn't offer up where exactly he'd been, perhaps battling the knights whose placements his father had acquired while visiting Elenvérs. There was no way to ask him without appearing suspicious, so I simply leaned my head back and smiled as if all the eyes on us didn't bother me.

So much for my plan of remaining inconspicuous.

He looked at me as one would look upon an old friend, a tactic I knew he'd learned to put emissaries and enemies at ease. I'd seen Cassian make the same face. Princes and princesses alike are taught how to appear friendly when their hearts are filled with schemes.

I didn't need lessons to fake a smile. "The dance isn't too complicated," I said to answer his question. Then I tilted my head. "Making friends at your court, however, has proved to be a far more challenging task than I'd hoped. Do your emissaries often end the night with a blade against their skin?" A playful grin remained on my lips.

"Mar isn't the type you'd want as a friend anyhow. There's a little too much fire in her eyes to be sane. Stick by my side, and you'll have more friends than you could ask for." His cheeks dimpled and a few lines appeared by the corners of his eyes where I noticed a small scar in the shape of an arc.

I glanced at my hand where Mar's blade cut me, hoping it wouldn't leave a scar of its own. "What's going to happen to her?"

His eyes glanced to the side. Two tall doors with golden trees carved into them.

"I'll deal with her; you don't have to worry about it." He twirled me.

I did worry. I worried more than he knew.

Mar hadn't given me a chance. She'd known right from the start that I was a spy, and she was prepared to kill me for it.

Not quite the ally Cassian promised me.

Now she sat somewhere, probably freely telling any who would listen that I was a spy. Someone would get curious and investigate her story, putting both myself and Elis at risk.

Why did Cassian trust her?

Unless.

A dark thought crossed my mind, but would Cassian do something like that? He swore to kill me before I broke my curse, and he knew I had a wish to help me.

The more I thought about it, the more it made sense, and I almost tripped in the dance. Prince Tarion's arms caught me.

"Careful," he whispered.

I was too lost in my thoughts to say anything back.

I didn't hear the spies whispering in the library that night. Only Cassian did. There was no way for me to know if the people inside were sharing kingdom secrets or innocent conversation, or if Cassian had planted them there himself to pretend to be spies.

He'd always been sneaky, so I should have known better than to trust him.

Disappointment and frustration equally filled me.

By the end of the song, I convinced myself Cassian sent me here for the sole purpose of finding Mar so she could kill me. I glanced at the doors again. He really would go that far to keep my throne for himself.

When we got home, I was going to kill him.

"Do you want to walk with me? You've had quite the night and based on our last meeting and the way you keep looking about the room, I'd guess being the focus of attention isn't what you want right now."

He guessed correctly. I'd rather be home with my hands around Cassian's neck.

I covered my anger with a sigh. "I could use a walk."

"Splendid." He offered his arm. I held mine back.

"Do you mind if my sister joins us? After my last walk with a member of your court, I wouldn't mind the extra company. I'd rather not be attacked twice in one night."

"Ah, but all the best nights start off that way." He scanned the room. "Very well, your beautiful sister can join us." He stopped by the edge of the room while I weaved through the mass of skirts to fetch my sister.

Within a few hours she'd managed to captivate half of the room with her face that was as warm as cider and her laugh that was as mesmerizing as starlight. She barely looked up when I squeezed my way through the crowd to her.

I placed my hand over hers. She continued to tell a tale that I recognized as the time she and I faced off against a cave troll.

"Can I see you for a moment?" I whispered in her ear.

She started to wave me off, but she caught sight of the cut on my palm. "What happened to you?"

I pulled my hand back and nodded at the people watching us. "Please?"

With great fanfare, she stood up and raised her arms. "It was lovely to meet you all, but I must go." I tried not to roll my eyes as she waved them farewell and pulled herself from their loving embrace.

"Seriously. What happened to you?" She asked as soon as we'd stepped away from her adoring crowd.

The cut hardly bled, and I wasn't eager to share my failures with Elis when it came to trusting her brother. "It seemed like a good idea at the time."

"Rowan, your ideas are never the best. I'm sorry to have to tell you."

"Well, this next one is. Prince Tarion wants to take us for a walk. It could be an opportunity to see parts of the castle we haven't gotten to yet."

She halted and pulled in her lips between her teeth to groan. "I don't want to. He's so boring." She drew out the last word for added effect.

"Don't be like that." I pinched her. "We aren't here to make friends, in case you've forgotten."

She rolled her eyes. "Yes, because people always share their country's secrets with strangers," Elis grumbled. We walked through the ballroom toward Prince Tarion.

My voice stayed low. "They won't share them anyway, and it's harder to betray friends." I pushed enthusiasm onto my face. "Prince Tarion. We are both very eager for our walk. Shall we?"

He smiled down at us, and I hoped he couldn't see the twitch in Elis's cheek or the strain in her hand as she held it out for him. If he saw, he possessed enough manners to keep quiet. "The first stop—" He motioned with his hands in an enthusiastic manner. "The kitchens. Let's see if the cook made any of her famous tartlets this week."

Though we'd both eaten already, when we smelled the apple tartlets, we made room for two. Prince Tarion cleared the room for us, and as we licked our fingers, he fetched us something to drink. "So," he said while handing us the glasses. "Two sisters from Elenvérs, both aspiring emissaries and both granted a trip to ThornHigh. That's impressive."

Blast. I knew these weren't friendship tartlets. He suspected something.

"Oh, I don't know about impressive. See, we enjoyed meeting you when you came to visit, and thought about how we'd never visited ThornHigh. Our king graciously allowed us this trip as a symbol of his interest in friendship."

"He'd send another emissary if something needed to be sorted out, but he thought, given our situations, we're harmless enough. It's good experience for us. I think we are handling it well so far, wouldn't you say so?" Elis looked to me.

I shrugged. "Decently well."

With a smirk, Prince Tarion traced his thumb around the edge of his silver goblet. "Well? Tell me Elis, does your sister often get attacked, or is this trip special in that way?"

A stiff silence cloaked the room that left only the crackle of the fire behind us and the slosh of wine as Prince Tarion twisted his cup in his hand.

Elis's eye twitched to my hand then up to my eyes where she glared a little. Make friends. That was all I'd asked her to do, and she'd worked incredibly hard to create allies among the Court of Strength, while I'd accomplished nothing more than almost getting myself killed.

The fairies hadn't gifted me with kindness or charisma. Both things that attracted friends. Both things that came naturally to Elis.

Elis gave long sigh, then forced a smile. "I've found the best times with Rowan happened when we were being attacked, so it's a good sign, really. Practically an honor."

Tarion set his cup down with a grin, making the scar by his eye twist into a deep arc. "Good to know what I can expect in the future. I'll keep my sword sharpened and eye alert for further incidents."

I set my own cup down with a little more force than intended. "Can we see the rest of the castle? I'd love to see a library."

Prince Tarion placed his goblet on the counter and wiped his lips. "Certainly. Are you a fan of books?"

I wasn't. "Tremendously." I presented my best smile, like the one that made Briggs fall in love with Elis, and offered my hand while he guided us through the remainder of the castle.

Elis chatted with him, but I'd all but given up on charming him.

Instead, I focused on anything that looked like a secret door or a hidden path that I could investigate later.

Cassian may have been lying about spies being in Elenvérs, but King Olin would still expect a report upon my return, and I was determined to have more to show for my trip than a cut across my hand.

It became apparent that Prince Tarion wouldn't show us anything more than the main parts of the castle. Every time we asked what was down this corridor or through that door, he'd give an eloquent answer of 'nothing you'd be interested in,' 'simply boring office things,' or 'more guest rooms.' They had an enormous amount of guest chambers for a kingdom with no friends.

After we walked through the great hall for the third time, I feigned a wide yawn that raised Elis's brow. "This evening has brought more excitement than I'd planned. I think I should retire if that's alright."

"Be my guest. Is it the end of the evening for you both?" He kept his hand over Elis's.

She hesitated for a moment before shaking her head. "I'll go back with you. Good night, Rowan."

I'd rather she retreated with me so we could talk, but I wouldn't fight her in front of the prince. Their heels clicked across the marble floor as they walked away, leaving me with their echoes and a determination to find something worth bringing home to Elenvérs.

I hadn't failed yet. I'd just begun.

I crossed the other end of the room and headed underground where I thought the dungeon would be. If I could find Mar and get her to admit that Cassian put her up to killing me, I could offer her passage to Elenvérs in return for her tale, and her testimony would force King Olin's hand into removing Cassian as crown prince. I'd reveal my wish and my plan to keep myself from the curse, and I'd be granted back my kingdom.

It was a better bet than hoping to find something here valid enough to undermine their kingdom and win favor with my king. I would undermine Cassian.

Trouble was, I had no idea where the dungeons were, and each turn I made left me feeling more lost than before. After another left turn down a familiar hallway, I accepted that I needed help.

"Excuse me, sir," I called to a guard with dull armor and twine holding back his hair. "Can you show me to where the dungeons are?"

His smile revealed large front teeth. "And why would you want to go down there?"

I raised my chin. "My business is my own."

He shrugged. "And the prisoners that the king keeps in these cells are his own business. Since he's the one who could have my head for disobeying, I think I'll follow his orders."

Ah, so he will listen to whoever spares his head. I could work with that. But first, I needed something. Without saying another word, I turned around and weaved my way through the maze of corridors to my room where I fetched my sword and changed from my dress into my riding pants, leather boots, and brown shirt. Then, I proudly walked with my sword through the halls and back to the guard with the long hair.

A loud clash filled the air as I threw my sword down at his feet. His eyebrows raised and he looked to both sides. We were alone in the hallway, and I didn't suspect someone else would come by any time soon.

"Would you fight me for it? I win and you escort me to the dungeon, where you can keep an eye on me the whole time. I only need five minutes."

"Who did you steal that from?" He gestured to the sword.

I pursed my lips, kicking at the sword again. "Will you fight me?"

He shifted on his feet. His hand rubbed his cheek, and he looked down the hallway again. "What if I win?"

I crossed my arms. "You win, and I don't tell everyone that an eighteen-year-old girl bested you with a blade."

He chuckled. "If I don't fight you, you can't say that anyway."

"I can if I want to. You fight me, and I promise I won't say a word."

He peeked at the sword, then back at me, wearing a mischievous smile. Another glance down the hallway, then a shrug. "I need something to liven up this night anyhow. First to disarm the other wins. No maiming."

"Sounds fair, if you want it to be boring."

He picked up my sword and tossed it to me. "Don't be too disappointed if I best you in under ten seconds."

I caught the sword and I held it up to cover my delight. "Don't cry if I beat you in five."

I didn't best him in five, but I did in twenty. His mouth gaped open as his sword slid across the floor and clanged into the stone wall. He blinked twice.

I wiped the edge of my sword against my hand as if cleaning it of blood. "I don't know what girls you're used to, but where I come from, we are warriors."

He snorted. "That would have been dandy to know before I accepted the duel."

He took it in good spirit though, reclaiming his sword and chuckling as he led me toward the dungeons. He waved as we passed other guards. No one questioned us.

"Here it is, just down these stairs. Mind the smell."

The stench hit me as the door opened, musty air and rotting bodies. I wouldn't be surprised if he told me this was their cemetery as well. My upper lip rolled up to push against my nostrils in attempt to block the dreadful smell from getting through, but it had little impact.

We didn't have more than two holding cells in Elenvérs. Our philosophy was the prisoner either deserved death, punishment, or to be freed. We didn't steal their time. Time was too important; my family knew that better than any.

Time clearly held little value here. From the stench, these quarters hadn't been tended to in ages. Behind me, the guard chuckled. "Onward. This is what you fought for, isn't it?"

I grunted with displeasure. I would make quick work of this. The wooden stairs creaked with each step and the thick stench grew worse as we descended into the dark. I avoided the eyes of prisoners as we walked the damp stone corridor. I scanned each one, looking for Mar. Hall after narrow hall. Eventually, we walked through the entire dungeon and she was nowhere to be seen.

"There must be more cells," I demanded.

"I don't know of any castle that has two separate dungeons," the guard replied in a dulled voice. He kept his hand over his mouth as we walked, and his eyes showed clear disgust.

"She must be here," I mumbled.

I made him lead me through again; this time I called out her name. There were a few replies, but she wasn't among them.

"If you're done?" The guard looked to the stairs.

I scowled. "Fine. We can go."

He practically leapt up the stairs and closed the door as soon as I'd exited. "Who was this Mar you were seeking?" he asked as he lowered his hand from his mouth.

I sighed. "Someone who tried to kill me."

He took a step back, and I turned to go my own way.

Where had they taken Mar? They could have taken her to a different holding room for questioning, though the guard said no such place existed, and while I had no reason to trust him, I suspected he told the truth. They might have killed her already, an idea that while I couldn't say I'd be disappointed to learn, sounded drastic.

The third idea was that Prince Tarion was on Mar's side. He was working alongside her, and she wasn't sent to the dungeons after all. Though if that was the case, then he would have let her run me through when she had the chance.

None of it made sense, but I knew my chance of getting her to testify against Cassian in front of King Olin was gone, and that infuriated me. I stomped back to my room where I rinsed the stench of prison out of my hair and started packing my things, throwing them in my bag with little care to how they were folded.

I wouldn't stay here any longer.

A sound passed my ear, the light noise of wind floating through the window. A message. A small wisp glided through the air with its tail curled behind it and a few snowflakes caught in its flurry. It positioned itself in front of me.

My bags dropped to the floor and I addressed the wind.

"Do you have a message for me?"

"Lady Rowan." The wind spoke in Cassian's voice. He'd sent me a message. Perhaps Mar sent him a wind message already detailing our encounter.

"Confirm."

The wind relayed Cassian's message. "I hope things are going well for you ladies there in ThornHigh. Remember, it's best to stay as hidden as you can, so don't draw attention to yourself. Have you found Mar yet? Briggs and I have located half of our troops and moved them, though it leaves several watch points defenseless. Briggs makes good company. I know we've been in a time of peace for many years now, but I fear a war will come during my reign, and I'll want Briggs by my side when it does. Best wishes, Cassian."

He'd never sent me a wind message before or said best wishes. While I thought we'd formed a sort of alliance over protecting Elenvérs, I now recognized his sudden friendliness as a ploy to lower my guard so he could strike.

Before the wind message could leave, I gave it a reply. "Find Prince Cassian of Elenvérs. This is my message. Mar is nowhere to be found."

It wasn't a lie. He could make of it what he'd like.

The message went off, and I finished packing my and Elis's things. The night was almost at an end when she came back to the room, whistling to herself. Her eyes widened at our bags in my hand. I threw one at her.

"Sleep. We leave at first light."

"What are you talking about?"

"We are going back to Elenvérs. I don't trust this place."

I crawled into bed while she looked over the things. "Fine," she said. "But just know that I'm not happy about this."

"We've stayed long enough."

Four hours later I was pushing her awake and ignoring her complaints. We saddled up before anyone of importance spotted us and rode from that wretched place.

Chapter Fourteen

"I HUMBLY BOW BEFORE my king."

The man lowered his head to the ground, one foot swept behind him in a wide circle while the other bent below him, just as one arm stretched out and the other held his hat in place. The red feather on the end of the hat brushed against the icy ground.

King Olin patted the seat next to him. "Rise, Thomas. Today, I work for you. How can I serve you?"

Elis and I arrived home shortly before People's Day, the day of the month that all the people are invited to the palace to seek out the king's service. He sat, not in his throne, but on the steps leading to it, where the beseeching visitors were welcome to sit beside him and converse freely.

No waiting lines. No stiff guards. No official rules.

Simply a king connecting with his people.

Queen Marigold lounged on the stairs further to the right of her husband, equally open to her subjects. While King Olin could dress down and blend in with the people, my mother always stood out. Even in the drabbest of dressed, her skin would still radiate like starlight and her eyes would still carry a sense of authority to them while maintaining their kindness. I'd never seen another like her. They say that while she slept, people would travel to look upon her beauty and be blessed because of it.

I wonder if they'd care enough to put me in a proper room while I slept. Surely no one would be travelling to see me. The kingdom wouldn't even know that I was asleep.

No. I wouldn't fall asleep. I would break the curse. I would make Cassian pay for trying to kill me first.

Cassian and Briggs had yet to return, a fact that made Elis bitter that we'd left so early. She showed a surprising amount of reluctance to leave ThornHigh, though I might have too if I had such an adoring crowd waiting upon me.

I, however, was grateful we'd left. The thought of roaming around ThornHigh like prey for Mar to attack from the shadows didn't appeal to me. I wouldn't give her another chance to strike.

But before I could worry about Mar, there was Cassian to deal with.

As my parents conversed with the crowds, I made my own polite conversation, but kept a watchful eye out for the return of Cassian and Briggs from a mission I couldn't be sure was real. It was likely that he'd made it up as part of his ploy to get me to ThornHigh where I would be killed, then he'd return a few days later in triumph.

I would savor the look on his face when he saw me still breathing.

"Oh Rowan, it's been too long." Plump arms embraced me, and eager lips kissed both my cheeks as they turned my face from watching the tall double doors. Miss Elizabeth fawned over me just as she had when I was a little girl and she'd come from her home in the caves to visit. "Look at you, you're all grown up!"

"Nearly." I teasingly rolled my eyes at the phrase she said every time she saw me, no matter if it'd been half a year or two weeks. In this case, she saw me three months ago.

"Nearly, nonsense. You're a grown woman now. Isn't she, Connor? Isn't she quite grown?" Beside her, Mister Carls, a tall man with a mustache that covered both his lips, grinned at his wife's enthusiasm.

"Quite, quite dear. She's quite grown. Not yet pledged though, am I right?"

I ducked my head. "Not yet, I'm still deciding."

Miss Elizabeth held tight to my hands. "You have time, darling. I didn't pledge until nineteen, though that's unheard of now," she exclaimed. "Say, you must come by some time. We've missed seeing you, and I've got some chocolate pudding fresh in a pot."

They knew my weakness.

As my mouth opened, so did the door. We heard a man's cries before we saw him, and even the cave mage near the dais stopped creating his music to watch the appearance of a wild man.

He came through the doorway, but he didn't walk—he ran, arms flailing and hair flying, mouth calling out for the king. "My lord, my lord!" his voice cracked with strain. Mud smeared across his face and his belt flapped as he ran, barely holding on to an empty sheath. He clung to a dented helmet, looking as if it'd been run through the dirt. His boots told the same story. He didn't seem to care—or notice—his ragged appearance as he ran through the room and threw himself at the feet of the king. The room silenced.

"What is it, Remir?" Worry flashed through King Olin's eyes. He clasped his hands over the Remir's to help him rise. As the king did so, Remir caught sight of his own filthy hands and he pulled them back.

He rubbed his hands on his clothes as he spoke. "My kind lord, RestingWater has fallen."

The hush that befell the room shattered into a thousand murmurs.

"How could this have happened?" Some whispered.

"What had he said?"

"Let's march now to reclaim the stronghold."

RestingWater was our last fortress between us and ThornHigh. Miss Elizabeth's hand tightened on mine. When King Olin raised his hand, the chatter ceased.

"How could this be?"

I squeezed Miss Elizabeth's hand before I crept closer to the stage. My mother's lips pulled tight and her cheeks sank in. Her hands rested over each other on her lap, appearing steady, but I knew that underneath the one, her other fingers drummed against her lap.

For a moment, as she looked past her husband, her eyes found me, and her expression relaxed. The moment was so short, such a tiny bit of peace in her moment of fear, but I cherished the fact that she could find comfort from looking at me.

Remir straightened himself and the previous composure of a madman was replaced by a gentleman who carried an important message for his king. Though his shoulders were pulled back, his hands still shook with the memory that he shared. "A cavalry rode through the night and wiped out the stronghold. They were faster than an avalanche and stronger than an ice storm. There were far too many to fight, especially with the women and little children in our midst, so our knights took them underground and they fled. I escaped on foot, and waited at the north tunnel exit for them, but they must have taken the south path, because they never showed up."

His hand steadied, but every so often his fingers still twitched and fumbled with the place where his sword should be.

King Olin's stroked the wispy strands of his beard. "They will be safe in the kingdom of Tullanti," he said. "They've been faithful trade partners for years and won't harm our men. But our people are trapped across the border until we can retake the stronghold."

He looked up, remembering the room full of nervous, watchful eyes and open mouths that would spread word of whatever happened here through the caves. He put on a smile and raised his hands.

"I'm afraid I must go attend to this dilemma," he continued, standing. "I know the matters you brought with you today are every bit as important, so I'll meet here again in one week's time to continue these discussions."

He lowered his voice and placed his hands on Remir's shoulders. "You go get food and a bath, my friend." The man bowed.

King Olin kissed his worried wife before leaving.

I knew which door he'd leave from, and I headed toward it. I waited in the hallway for him.

Cassian's story rang in my mind. Perhaps there was some truth to his tale of spies after all.

"We have to retaliate. ThornHigh can't go unchecked." I spoke as soon as he opened the door.

He sighed. "Violence shouldn't be our first answer. We will meet and discuss the situation. We don't know that this attack is ThornHigh's doing."

My brow raised. "Elenvérs has no other enemies."

The other advisors came through the door: Annon, Rivers, Carlene, Tristian, and Ebony, one after another. Annon looked between the two of us and smiled. I knew he thought this picture confirmed his suspicion about me being his brother's daughter. It did, but the grimace on my face told him to not bring the matter up now.

Though Annon's presence unnerved me, it was Rivers who managed to crush me with her words. "You shouldn't be here. Run home to your parents."

She looked at me, but it was as if her eyes saw through me before moving to King Olin. Likely, she didn't even know my name, or care to learn it. With that one sentence, she diminished me into a child of little importance, and I couldn't correct her.

Rivers was always my role model warrior. I wished to be more like her, and I looked forward to the day that she and I would strategize and fight together. To hear her dismiss me so easily stung more than I cared to admit.

She didn't know she spoke to her future queen. Someday she would.

Annon wore a smug smile as he waited for my reaction, while King Olin shifted in a passive action that hurt almost as much as Rivers' words.

I turned away just in time to see Cassian and Briggs turn the corner toward us. Cassian's faithful guard, Lance, was with them.

He was finally here.

"That's okay, I have something else to attend to," I mumbled, as I walked toward them. The hallway stretched long, and I willed the advisors to leave quickly.

"Cassian, join us," Rivers called from behind me before they slipped into a room. The door shut just as I reached Cassian. My fingers coiled around his wrist.

"With me now," I hissed. Lance raised a brow. Cassian looked past me to where the advisors had gone, but I held myself in front of him.

I stepped in front of him. "They will be there later. This is about Mar."

Cassian sighed and placed a hand on Briggs's shoulder. "I'll update my father later. You two get some rest."

Briggs and Lance glanced between the two of us with bent brows and frowns. I'd often wondered if ever Cassian told them the truth about his and my identity; those looks told me he hadn't.

"This will only take a moment." I pushed Cassian into a nearby room.

I wished I'd brought a dagger with me, but all I could do was pierce him with my glare and hold an arm against his neck. "Give me one good reason why I shouldn't kill you right now."

Chapter Fifteen

"IF I GIVE MORE than one, will that increase my odds of living? Let's see, my good looks for one. It would be a shame to ruin those. My humor is unrivaled; it'd be a bleak world without me. Hmm, losing my skill with the blade would be a waste—shall I give you more? Oh, yes. Your father would kill you if you harm me."

He pushed my arm away and straightened his brocade blue jacket. "What has gotten into you?"

My upper lip rolled back, and I sneered, "You tried to have me killed!"

His forehead wrinkled. "What in Elenvérs' name are you talking about?"

"Mar. I'm talking about Mar, the girl that you told me to find who tried to kill me within minutes of meeting me. She knew I was a spy, and I know who gave her that information."

He cursed and ran his hands through his hair. For the first time, I noticed the long tear in the sleeve of his shirt, and the blood stain that erupted from the cut and ran down the sleeve.

Cassian crossed his arms and hid the cut from my sight. "Why would I try to kill you?"

"You already told me you would try," I reminded him.

He threw his head back and sighed. "That? Rowan, I was upset. Can't you believe that I care more about the very real threat on Elenvérs than the slight possibility of you breaking your curse and taking my throne?"

I breathed deep. *One. Two.* The anger in my head cleared as I tried to rationalize the situation. *Three.*

Cassian continued, "Why would I send my only sister with you if I planned to have you killed? I wouldn't leave her alone in enemy territory to deal with your death."

My mouth remained closed as I inspected him, searching for some sign of whether he spoke the truth. I wished the fairies had given me the ability to know when someone was lying. It would have been much more useful than the gift of gracefulness.

"It's safe to say we don't trust each other." Cassian remained at a distance from me, leaned against the wall with his dark hair matted against his forehead. Deep circles rested under his eyes. "But we both love Elenvérs, and right now we need to unite under that bond to save her."

He stuck out his hand to me, and I eyed it.

"I'm not meeting any more of your friends."

He laughed. "Deal." My hand met his.

The narrow door scraped against the ice as it opened, and we both jumped. I pulled my hand quickly from Cassian's.

King Olin slid into the small office room with his head held down, displaying gray, thinning hairs. The deep wrinkles under his eye were impossible to ignore. Three too many for a man his age. One wrinkle for the stress of ruling Elenvérs. One for the trouble of ThornHigh. And one for the complication of his daughter and the curse that held her.

He studied us for a moment, Cassian first, then me. I shouldn't have noticed, but his eyes stayed on Cassian for several moments longer than he looked at me.

His eyes closed, and he took a deep breath.

Once he opened his eyes again, his face changed. It was as if that breath drew in energy for him, and now he was ready to face us. He crossed the small room to a mahogany desk with tiny ice sculptures lining the edge. He lowered himself into the tall-backed chair.

"Cassian first. What news do you bring from your mission to relocate the knights?" He folded his hands in his lap.

Panic settled in me as I recalled King Olin's parting words to me. *I expect a report when you return.*

Blast it. I had no report. I had nothing.

I sifted through what I'd seen at the court and wondered if there was anything I could stretch into helpful information.

Cassian, frustratingly, looked like the picture of calm as he faced the king with a hand in his pocket. "We went to the northern posts and shifted everyone inland until we can be sure the threat on them is invalid. We traveled south until we hit RestingWater, where I'm sure news has reached you that it has fallen."

"Only just."

Cassian nodded. "Upon seeing that, we rode right home to check on the castle, but we intend to ride out again to join the sentries in their watch for further attack."

"No," King Olin said as he shook his head. "Sir Briggs can go, but you must stay here. I can't afford to lose you."

I left the castle with only Elis, entered the enemy's court without invitation, utterly helpless, and King Olin merely asked for a report upon my return. Meanwhile, he wouldn't let Cassian ride a horse through our own lands because he couldn't lose him.

The hurt swelled within, but I wouldn't let it show.

Cassian nodded, but from my angle I could see the tightness in his lips at being asked to stay behind. Perhaps King Olin would send me in his place.

He turned to me. "Do you have a report from ThornHigh?"

I muttered in reply, earning a raised eyebrow.

"I know you are new to giving reports, Rowan, but they usually consist of more than just—" he mimicked my grunt and Cassian chuckled.

I folded my hands in front of me. "I have nothing to report."

The silence that followed, though brief, was sickening.

I watched King Olin squint for a moment, then blink twice as he searched for the words. "No report?"

I hated saying it again. "I have nothing to report. I learned no useful information."

"That is not for you to decide," King Olin said. "Tell me what you saw, and I will decide if it is useful."

My back straightened. "They dance each night as if they have no worries. But their maids keep their heads down to cover bruised faces, and King Maven was never seen. They kept their warriors off the castle grounds, likely because they were in the process of attacking Resting Water. Prince Tarion himself only joined at the last night of our stay, and we could get no information from him other than a polite tour of the basic rooms. I repeat, we learned nothing."

Though his voice stayed as calm as snowfall, King Olin stood up. His eyes were as piercing blue as the walls, and I swore the cave mages' magic failed for that moment because my heart turned icy.

"I sent you and your sister into enemy territory, risking an uneasy friendship, and you gained nothing from the experience?"

At the mention of Elis, I perked up. "Our presence was very well received, however. We'd be welcomed back, I'm certain of it." Though I wasn't keen on the idea of returning to

ThornHigh, I knew they'd welcome us, or at least Elis, with eager arms. She'd made quite the impression on the court, but I wouldn't admit to the king that it was her alone who charmed them. Some of my pride needed to be coddled.

Another long sigh. "Well, disappointing news on both accounts." His hand ran through his thin hair and settled against his arm. His fingers absentmindedly traced the long battle scar.

His stood up and crossed back to the door. "I don't want either of you to return."

He didn't say because he couldn't lose me.

"Cassian," he lowered his voice as his hand rested on the doorframe. His eyes asked a question that I didn't know, but Cassian did. He shook his head.

"The forest of Dunlirre offered us nothing."

I'd been to those forests once in search of vivid blue mushrooms that burst through the snow and stood three feet tall. They are said to heal ailments, but all they did was make me dizzy and weak for a month. They were helpless against my curse.

I didn't know what Cassian had searched for in those woods, but here was further proof of the secrets he shared with my father that I'd never know. The relationship that they had that I'd never get. My father shared no secrets with me.

King Olin left the room, leaving me to guess at how deep his disappointment ran.

His footsteps echoed down the hall, and I turned to Cassian to block out the noise. "That could have gone better."

He looked me right in the eye. "We have to go back."

My mouth dropped open. "You really are trying to kill me."

"No, I'm trying to save Elenvérs. I think we can do it together." He reached to shake my hand, but I stepped back.

"How?"

Cassian crossed his arms, and his smile looked too eager for my taste. "It's not a perfect plan, but you haven't pledged yet. So, pledge yourself as an emissary to ThornHigh. Stay there as my inside ear. We know they plan to attack and having one of our own within their walls would be more helpful than anything you could do back here."

Like break your curse, I could almost hear him say.

"What are we hoping for? That I accidentally overhear valuable information that can overthrow their entire kingdom?"

He chuckled. "No, you won't get that lucky. But I do expect you to put some work into this. I can teach you everything I know about how to be a spy later." His hand reached out to me again. "Are you in?"

When I didn't reply, he continued his persuasion. "It'll prove to our father that you are more valuable than he thought." Still silence. "Imagine bringing him the information and demonstrating that you are more capable than any of us realized." Still silent, but angrier. He lowered his head to my eyes. "I'll bring you chocolate pudding for a week."

I shook his hand.

"Good. Now you need to write a letter."

Chapter Sixteen

I FROWNED AT MY shoes: white heels with silk straps that circled my ankles and tied into a bow in the back. The ice blue tulle skirt of my dress filled most of the space between Elis's and my beds, and the high neckline allowed little opportunity for breathing. Delicate pearls the color of frost hung from my wrist.

"You can't be serious. I'm pledging as an emissary, not a fairy."

Elis refused to change from her riding pants and tunic, though frankly I didn't care what she wore to my pledging. I'd rather be wearing what she wore.

She stared at me. "Why are you doing this? You'll break your curse in five months. You should lay low until then. Not charge into enemy territory and form a friendship with the prince. It's not smart, and it's not safe."

Her remark was almost enough to throw me off my feet. Neither she nor I had ever been the type to lay low. Part of my zeal fell at the seriousness of her statement. The more high-profile I made myself, the more difficult it would be to keep my wish secured. If anyone found out I had a wish and took it from me, all my hope of breaking the curse would be lost.

Elis went on. "And our parents don't know you will break the curse. They think they only have five months with you."

I sighed and crossed to the door. "I've already saved myself, but Elenvérs is in trouble. I need to do this to help my kingdom. My parents will forgive me for leaving, especially when I break the curse, which we both know I will do." I squeezed the wish in my pocket.

Elis rose from the bed with her lips pinched together as she nodded. "If you say so. Here." She fetched a ring from her jewelry box, the one she planned to wear for her own pledging, and pushed the silver band onto my finger. Leaves twisted across the ring like a slow, methodical dance, and met at an emerald in the middle that they wrapped in their embrace. I'd always thought the leaves looked like they worshipped the emerald, but today I saw something different. Today, it looked like the leaves were shielding the emerald, protecting it from some unknown danger. Perhaps I saw that because I marched to ThornHigh tonight and was in need of a shield of my own.

Elis had always been my shield, and I'd been hers. But this time I would leave her behind.

"How do I look?" I wanted to cling to these last few moments with my sister.

Her arms crossed and she hardly looked me over. "Stuffy," she replied. "But you look the part."

We didn't hug, and in a way, I found myself grateful for that. It would have been strange to end the moment with her in such an uncharacteristic manner.

This moment felt big to me, larger than I'd expected it to when I'd thought about it yesterday.

In the place where we'd spent countless nights talking, my bed now lay empty with my bags sitting beside it, a change of riding clothes resting on the closed satchels.

Tears blurred my vision, and for a moment, I changed my mind and wished we'd had hugged, but Elis turned and left the room before I could embrace her. I didn't say anything as I followed behind.

Cassian stood in the sitting room with his parents as they waited for us. I'd told them I wanted to keep my pledging a secret, though they told me over and over that it wasn't necessary for me to pledge.

Because I had no future to offer. At least, not one here. That's what their eyes said.

After assuring them this was what I wanted to do and Cassian suggesting that it would be suspicious if I didn't pledge, they agreed. They hadn't pressed when I told them I didn't know what I would pledge to yet, and Cassian swung the conversation away before they could detect my lie.

Now, I hoped they wouldn't hate me for the position I was putting them in. It'd be too late to protest once I announced it publicly, and King Olin and Queen Marigold couldn't protest without claiming me.

Before we left, Cassian whispered in my ear. "He got your letter, and he came. It's all set."

Knowing he was here brought a small amount of fear curling through my chest and causing my finger to twitch. There was no turning back now.

"Perfect."

THE OFFICIANT CLEARED HIS voice.

"Lady Rowan Trulluse, daughter of Weston and Corrin Trelluse, are you prepared to pledge yourself to a position for Elenvérs?"

The ceremony wasn't large, it wouldn't be practical that way, but I didn't need a big crowd. I didn't need anyone other than the officiant and my invited guest, who waited behind the doors for Cassian to let him in. I needed to finish the ceremony before he revealed himself, because his presence would surely prohibit the ceremony. King Olin, for one, would never let me pledge if he knew my intentions.

I grinned innocently at the officiant in the large hat. "Yes."

A small crowd watched us: Elis's family, some friends of theirs, and the king and queen. Royalty didn't always attend pledgings, but Queen Marigold and Lady Trelluse were close friends, so no one raised a brow as they stood together and watched their daughter stand in the aisle to declare herself to the kingdom.

"And what position do you pledge yourself to?"

Now we were getting to it. "Emissary for Elenvérs."

He'd no doubt heard how my sister and I were sent to ThornHigh as emissaries in training, so while his mouth didn't drop open, several others did. Both my mothers', for example. Their hands found each other as they gawked at me. I avoided their gazes.

"And do you swear to uphold this position with the integrity and discipline befitting Elenvérs, doing everything for her glory?"

That was the easiest yes I'd ever said.

I risked peeking to the side. King Olin's jaw clenched while he watched me with a spark in his eyes that I knew would grow into a flame later when he confronted me. He'd be too late by then.

"Lady Rowan Trelluse, you are pledged."

Claps came from around the room, but instead of bowing to them, I turned to Cassian.

He grinned, and I knew he was enjoying this every bit as much as I was. His hand slowly opened the door beside him, and my visitor strode into the room.

A part of me hated to join forces with him, but in this moment all our interests were aligned.

Prince Tarion didn't stop walking until he stood next to me before the officiant who'd gone quite pale. Prince Tarion nodded once to him, then turned to the king.

"King Olin, there has long been tense relations between our two countries," Prince Tarion said. "When I take the throne, I plan to rule differently. To show you that, ThornHigh would like to officially invite Lady Rowan to join our court—the court of strength, I think you so charmingly call it—as an emissary from Elenvérs in the first step to join our kingdoms together in friendship."

Elis stared at Prince Tarion, but I couldn't read her face. I could read every other face, however. Cassian looked giddy with pleasure, though he masked it behind a tilted smile and a slight bounce in his leg. For the first time, he'd come through for me. Perhaps Gen had been right, and we could become allies of sorts. He winked at me, and I winked back.

Most of the other faces looked bewildered. The officiant was downright flabbergasted by the presence of Prince Tarion, whose focused hadn't strayed from King Olin.

King Olin's lips stretched tight. He glanced between Prince Tarion and me, no doubt wondering how close of a friendship this was and if I'd shared any other secrets with the prince, like about my curse. Thick eyebrows lowered over his eyes and his nostrils flared once.

Then his back abruptly straightened as if realizing something and his expression fell. When he looked at me again, he almost looked sad.

Realizing eyes were on him, he stepped from the small crowd and extended an arm toward Prince Tarion. "A friendship between our once sister countries would please me greatly. Allow me to send you a more experienced emissary as a token of my gratitude to you." His words sounded pretty as he spoke, an elegant maneuver to deny me this opportunity to save my country. When Prince Tarion replied, his words were far simpler.

"The offer is for Rowan alone."

The king's brow deepened. He glanced my direction, and I nodded to him, hoping to show my sincerity to Elenvérs. He could trust me.

He sighed. I'd heard him sigh a lot recently.

"So be it. Prove your dedication to our friendship."

Elis helped me pick up my bags with a cold frown. "That was cruel."

"What are you talking about?"

She dropped the bags on the floor and folded her arms. "Did it even occur to you to tell mother before announcing that you intend to leave? Did you think about how that'd hurt her? Every moment with you is precious to her, and you act like you don't care."

I picked up the bag she dropped. "I thought you knew I wanted it kept a surprise."

She scoffed. "If I knew, I would have told them myself. It was cruel for them to find out like that. But it's so like you to not think about anyone but yourself." She shook her head and crossed the small bedroom.

"I think about others. I care for Elenvérs and the people. I care for my family too, I just show it differently."

"I'd never be so heartless." She twisted the doorknob and yanked on the door.

"That's it? You aren't going to say goodbye?"

"Would you care?" she shot back, and I frowned.

Her shoulders relaxed. "I love you. But I'm not thrilled with you right now. Go and I'll come visit you, eventually." She placed a hand on the doorframe before glancing back to me. "Just, be gentle with mother. You have no idea how hard this all is for her."

Gen had warned me that my weakness was my inconsideration for others. I hadn't realized Elis saw it too. Perhaps that's why I couldn't see the White Bear—my inability to be considerate prohibited my soul from being pure.

Unlike Elis, who did see the bear.

Her words were sharp, and while we'd always been honest with each other, she'd never spoken to me in such a manner. We'd been harsh with other people—scallywags who had information we needed to find a secret flower, agitated trolls that lived in the mountains, and hopeful gentlemen who came on a little too strong—but never with each other.

I sighed and followed Elis with my bags in hand.

King Olin sat in the sitting room next to my mother, who wrapped her arms around her stomach as if she was holding in the hurt. The pain spilled out of her eyes in steady tears. Each one deepened the guilt within me.

How could I have been so heartless? Elis was right, it was cruel of me to do this to them. If I could save Elenvérs though, they'd understand. I dropped my bags as I embraced my mother who clung to me long after I was ready to let go.

"I don't want you to go. Stay here, with me."

I pulled myself back so I could see her eyes. "I promise, I will break this curse, and I will save Elenvérs. You aren't going to lose me. And I will write every week."

Her cheeks dimpled as she brought a hand to my hair, but her eyes still released a tear.

King Olin spoke over his wife's shoulder. His eyes were dry. "It's not too late for you to stay here where you'll remain safe."

Safe. If there was one thing I'd never been, it was safe. The threat of the curse hanging over me restricted my possibilities for a future. I was constantly reminded that one day I'd lose everything I loved.

And now, with the threat of ThornHigh to our west and Annon within these walls, I was in more danger than ever.

At least by going to ThornHigh to try to work against them from within, I could control some of the menaces that haunted me. Annon was a different beast that I would deal with in his own time.

"I'll be careful at ThornHigh; I won't get into trouble."

He kept his distance with his hands folded in front of him and only moved when Elis's parents came in to say their goodbyes. "Let me know if you need anything," King Olin said before brushing past Elis's parents and out the door.

I'd learned to not expect anything more from King Olin than short conversations and stiff nods, but disappointment still hit me like a block of ice, leaving a cold feeling behind.

The rest of the goodbyes consisted of tears and hugs and well-wishes, until my cheeks were fully kissed, and my arms squeezed countless times, and I could leave feeling loved. By the time I'd made it to the stables with my bags, the sun had begun its descent behind the mountains.

"You're late." Prince Tarion stood looking dapper in the stables with his back resting against the wooden support beam and a strand of straw in his mouth. The fur lining of his coat nestled into his neck, and the bottom of his sheath peeked from underneath the layers. He removed the straw while I loaded my horse and apologized.

"King Olin requested an additional emissary be sent. He was quite insistent on it. I say, he seems to care a great deal about protecting you." Prince Tarion swung a foot over his horse and settled back in the saddle.

I didn't have time to ask who the other emissary was, for as Prince Tarion spoke, Annon rode in.

"Are we ready?" His dark hair hid behind a wool hat, but his ever-present smile was visible. Behind him were a few packed bags, and his sword rested at his side.

"I think so." Prince Tarion looked back at me and nodded before riding from the stables, but Annon didn't follow him.

"You're the other emissary?" I asked. Even though I knew the answer, I prayed I was wrong.

"I've succeeded in obtaining many friendships before, perhaps even ThornHigh will be charmed by me. Your father thinks so." His casual reference to my parentage wasn't lost on me. He turned his horse after Prince Tarion as he finished speaking. "I suspect your father plans for me to protect you from the many dangers of ThornHigh, because Rowan," he peeked back at me, "there will be many dangers awaiting you at ThornHigh."

Neither of us pretended it was anything other than a threat, and for the first time that day, I feared I'd made a reckless mistake. With no other option, I clutched the wish in my pocket, a familiar habit of mine by now, and rode to what I prayed wouldn't be my death.

Chapter Seventeen

TARION, WHO INSISTED I call him that without the title, seemed genuinely interested in forming a friendship, not only with Elenvérs, but with me as well. Naïve prince. I didn't trust him by any measure, but I could accomplish more as a spy if I was known by all as Tarion's friend.

Even if he claimed to be a friend, I couldn't trust him when he offered to take first watch that night.

"I'll stay up, you sleep," I insisted as I combed my horse's mane. We'd made good distance in our first day of travel but had to stop for sleep eventually. The sun set and the last of the light left the sky. Annon put up the tent and spread a blanket across the bottom to shield us from the cold dirt.

I would rather die than sleep between Annon and Tarion. As soon as my eyes closed, either one of them could stab me.

Sleep wouldn't happen anyway, so I might as well be the one to keep watch.

"We can watch together," Tarion suggested. "If you don't trust me."

"I don't." His brow raised, and I sighed. *Friendship*, I reminded myself. *Be nice.* "At least, I don't trust you yet." That was better.

Snow had gathered at the tips of his hair and on the ends of his lashes, while the cold brought out color in his cheeks. He rubbed his hands together and blew heat into the thick mittens. "We have all night to talk and build that trust."

"I'll sleep." Annon stayed out of our way as he fetched some bread from his bag and chomped hungrily. He pulled out another item and tossed it to me. I caught the silver object in my hand, a small square box with a painting of flames on it.

"From the cave mages," he said.

The cave mages were giving everyone gifts but me, it seemed. I recognized the box and knew what to do with it. We'd need a few branches first. As soon as I began gathering some, Tarion jumped to help me, and we soon had a good pile. I arranged them in a small circle on the snow.

"Not much chance of getting a fire going out here. It's far too wet." Tarion nestled his cheeks into his fur coat.

I held up the silver box for him. "Not for this."

As Tarion watched, I placed the box in the middle of the circle and spoke. "Awaken fire."

A curl of smoke poured from the box with a hiss, then fire sprang to life. With a yelp, Tarion jumped back. The fire caught on the wood and began to burn, the magic from the box keeping the fire alive.

In the orange light, Tarion's face looked white, and Annon chuckled. "Not used to fire, boy? Or not used to magic?"

"Magic, sir." He settled onto a stone while staring at the hungry flames.

Annon chuckled again before closing himself in the tent while I folded my blanket and sat on the ground to warm my hands from the heat. Tarion watched for a few moments before inching closer, but he remained further back from the flame.

"It won't hurt you." I danced my fingers near the warmth.

"Why did we need the wood if the box can make fire?" He leaned forward.

I shrugged. "I don't make the rules. But we won't need to get more wood. This fire won't go out until we tell it to."

He stayed quiet as he watched the dancing flames, and I realized once again how handsome he was. His jaw was sharp and his eyes were a warm color of brown. His shoulders positioned outward with confidence. Except for now, when he practically trembled before the fire. His fingers kept rubbing the birthmark on his cheek. Finally, he spoke, "We don't use magic often in ThornHigh. My father doesn't trust it."

I hadn't known that. "We use it almost every day. The cave mages use it to keep the ice palace standing and fires running. We don't have maids, just the mages."

"You treat magic holders as maids?" He looked shocked.

"We don't treat them poorly, if that's what you are thinking. Far from it. They are respected and given fine rooms in the palace."

Tarion continued to stare into the fire. From the tent, Annon's shadow lay still on the blanket, but I doubted he was already asleep. Likely, he stayed awake to listen to our conversation. Darkness filled the sky now, but clouds blocked the stars from shining. At least there was no fierce wind, so the cold didn't feel so bad, especially next to this fire.

"Well," Tarion said softly. "I hope you can survive staying in a castle where we have to build our own flames."

I laughed. "I'll be fine."

We talked for a bit more as exhaustion set in. I rested my head in my hands as the fire warmed my nose and listened to

Tarion speak of ThornHigh. My lids grew heavy and I yawned. I closed my eyes briefly and took a deep breath.

The next thing I knew, Tarion was shaking me awake. Morning light filled the sky, and I sprang to my feet.

"You fell asleep," he explained. "We should start traveling again."

Annon had already taken the tent down and mounted his horse. The circle of charred wood and a few footprints were the only proof that we'd been here. I let Tarion help me to my feet and thanked him.

First night, and my enemy hadn't stabbed me in my sleep. That was something.

Elis would be proud of how well I formed a friendship with Tarion by the time we reached ThornHigh. I constantly had to remind myself to be nice, but by the end of the journey he chatted freely without pausing at the beginning of his sentences to check his words.

My own breaths came easier, and the nervous blood had stopped pounding in my cold ears, up until I pushed through the doors to ThornHigh with the crown prince at my side.

With the flood of heat came an instant swarm of nobles and maids alike, all eager to help us settle in after our journey, their bright skirts brushing against my ankles, their enthusiastic smiles stretching from cheek to cheek, and hundreds of eyes taking in every inch of me, until the floor swayed beneath my feet and my chest constricted again.

While we were flocked on every side, Annon slipped away relatively unnoticed, as if strolling into his own home. I marveled at his ability to blend in with the environment, though he'd had undoubtedly more practice at it than I had. Both my red hair, and the prince by my side, made me stand out in the mass. Usually, I enjoyed being noticed. But here, in the castle that'd always elicited fear from me, I wanted nothing more than to shrink into the walls until I'd properly come up with a plan.

Tarion sensed my unease and put up his hands. "Let's get her room prepped. Lady Rowan is tired from her trip."

A brave maid pushed through the crowd. "I have a room ready she can use. Right this way, miss." She hoisted some of my bags upon her shoulders that were half as large as she was and pushed back through the crowd with them. I mouthed thank you to Tarion before following her.

She peeked back after a while to be sure I followed, and when she saw me alone behind her, she fell back to walk by my side. We were the same height as each other, both with blue eyes, but the similarities stopped there. Under her hair cap she had dark braids with two curled pieces by her face. Her ears pointed slightly and her nose was almost as sharp as her ears. She didn't have bruises on her cheek like other maids had.

When she looked at me, there was a mischievous glint in her eyes. "It's been a while since Tarion had a lady friend."

The way she said that insinuated a closer relationship than Tarion and I had, and I shook my head violently. "I'm afraid we've given the wrong impression. In truth, we are hardly friends at all."

Her shoulders dropped. "Ah, for a moment I thought I might be serving the future queen." The disappointment on her face was clear. "I work for him occasionally, so I hear a lot of gossip about him. The most recent rumors suggested that Tarion fancied a girl from Elenvérs."

The corner of my brow raised. "That's news to me. It's probably nothing but rumors, but I can assure you that's not what this is. I'm an emissary from Elenvérs here to form a friendship."

Her eyes squinted as she peeked at me again. "You can't be older than me, too young for an emissary. Are you sure you aren't here to establish friendship through marriage?"

"Very sure."

She shrugged and dropped my bags in front of a door. "If you say so. Here's your room." Her voice raised with excitement.

I should have paid better attention to how we got here, but after looking around, it was the same hallway Elis and I stayed in when we visited, only a few doors down. I'd manage my way around just fine.

She opened the door, revealing a room much larger than I'd been given last time, and that was with Elis staying in the same room. The oversized wool blanket was soft as snow as I drew my hand across the mattress. Surely if I laid down sideways, I wouldn't reach both edges.

"Those pillows were just imported in," my maid said with a gesture to them. "Stuffed with bird feathers."

I couldn't imagine a kingdom rich enough in birds to spare their feathers.

I dropped my bags to the large, red rug that lay at the foot of the bed, stretching to the other side where two chairs sat in front of a dim fireplace.

"I'll light that up," my maid followed my eye.

"I don't mind," I told her. "Your kingdom is warmer than I'm accustomed to."

She whistled. "I imagine, coming from an ice palace."

My coat slid from my shoulders, then I removed my leather jacket as well. I stood in only my long-sleeved tunic and riding pants, yet it felt as hot as if my jacket was on. The castle was like a fire hot enough to lull you to sleep before it burned you alive.

I promised myself I'd stay on guard at this enemy court.

"Thank you for doing this, um, I'm sorry, I don't know your name."

Her eyes widened. I feared I'd done something wrong, but her voice was awed as she spoke. "No visiting emissary has ever asked me that before." She brushed her skirts before dipping into a curtsy. "Lindy. I'm one of the cook's daughters." Her chest puffed up at that.

"How long have you worked here?"

She shifted to mess with the fire as she worked, then brushed off the tops of the furniture—a small sofa and desk—making sure the room looked perfect for me. "I've worked for the castle all my life, though I started in the farms with my father growing food for mama to cook. I moved into the kitchens as I got older before receiving my position here."

She put her hands on her hips as she looked over the room. "Perfect. Modet is the maid that serves this hallway, so she will be by in the morning to start her duties. Can I help you with anything else?"

I recognized the maid's name. She was the one who helped Elis and I, though she hardly talked to us. I'd much rather have friendly Lindy, who would have a loose tongue if I was lucky, than stiff Modet.

"Is there any chance you can be my maid? I'll switch rooms if needed. If it's not too much work for you?"

She put a hand over her chest. "You are just too sweet. Yes, I would love to serve you. I'll let Modet know; she won't mind less work. Is there anything else you need?" She looked like I made her day by asking her to be my maid, and I was glad one person thought fondly of me after disappointing so many others back at Elenvérs.

My mouth opened to say no, but my stomach spoke first. "Do the kitchens have chocolate pudding? I'm quite obsessed with the stuff."

She giggled. "I'll bring some right up." She crossed to the door, but her feet hesitated at the threshold, tapping a few times before she twisted back.

"My lady? The king was not here the last time you were, but he is now." She licked her lips. "I'd suggest staying out of his way. He can be...moody at times. This time more than usual."

I stored that bit of information away. "Thank you, Lindy. I'll be careful."

She closed the door, leaving me in the crackling firelight with my life packed in bags around me and exhaustion settling in. Lindy returned shortly with a heaping bowl of pudding, then left me for the night to lounge in the chair with my dessert, which I finished quickly.

There was just one more thing to do before bed. I went to the window and called for a wind message. After several minutes, a quiet breeze floated through.

"You have a message?" Its essence floated around the room as a transparent, gray vapor.

"Yes." I checked that the door was closed. "Please find Prince Cassian of Elenvérs. This is my message: I've arrived safely and am eager to begin forming a friendship. Hope all is well with you."

Wind messages shouldn't be detected, but just in case, Cassian and I came up with a code for ours that would sound as if we really wanted a friendship with ThornHigh, while letting each other know if we needed help.

It's a strange thing, to have a secret code between Cassian and myself. For my entire life, I'd considered him to be the villain in my story—the boy who had what should have been mine, and I knew he thought of me the same way—the girl who threatened to take the throne he'd worked so hard for. Yet, there we were, banding together to fight a greater threat against Elenvérs.

The wind message took off into the night, carrying my secret with it.

I pulled myself from the bed and locked my door, just in case Annon came in the night to slay me.

Before falling asleep, I wrote a letter to Lady Trelluse and Queen Marigold, who'd prefer it to a wind message. Then I planned my next moves.

Make friends. Convince them I want an alliance with ThornHigh. Find a way to undermine them. Stay alive.

I can do this for Elenvérs. I am strong, and determined, and smart. I can do this.

I repeated these words over and over in my head, until even sleep couldn't take them from me. Before long, the sun came up and the handle of my door jiggled, and Lindy called out from the other side in a melodic voice.

I pulled myself from the chair and echoed the words Annon spoke to me last month when he cornered me in the hallway like prey. *Let the games begin.*

Chapter Eighteen

TARION MADE IT HIS personal mission to introduce me to the entire court. While I'd met most of them on my previous trip here, I vowed to remember their names this time. Most asked if my sister would be joining us again, so if there was ever any question who had won them over on our first trip, that was gone now. I politely informed them that no, it was only me. After seeing their disappointment I'd inform them that she would be visiting from time to time, to which they'd reply, "Jolly good. She's a delightful girl."

By the end of the first week, I'd shaken the hand of every courtier, cook, servant, tailor, groom. Everyone besides King Maven himself.

I was in no rush to meet him. I'd heard he murdered his own wife while she slept, and while the rumors had never been proven, it was enough to strike fear into my heart. A man who acted out of anger was not to be trusted.

Annon was a different foe. If Annon wanted me alive, even my best attempts at provoking his blade wouldn't cause him to strike me down.

Annon moved through the court with a confident smile and firm handshake, making almost as many friends as Elis had. My eye remained on him through every contact to catch any suspicious interaction, but so far, I'd only learned a great deal about communicating with others by watching him. I had to admit, he was an excellent emissary.

Sometimes he'd catch me looking and he'd grin, but the slight narrowing in the corner of his eye told me he'd be observing me just as often as I watched him.

Tarion watched us both, but there was a perception in Annon's eye that I didn't see in Tarion's, and it eased my worries about the prince.

"Are you enjoying your night so far?" Tarion was a difficult man to get alone. While none spoke of his father, they pressed themselves close to the prince. I could only hope to be as loved as him when I was queen one day. We sat at a table near the back as most of the room participated in a lively jig in the middle.

"I am, thank you." I ran my finger over the top of my wine glass.

He glanced at me. I wished one of the gifts the fairies gave me was great communication skills so I knew what to say. Instead, I took a sip of my wine.

Tarion's blue jacket reminded me of something I'd see at home. Most of the colors here were red, brown, or gold, as compared to the bright white, silver, and blue from Elenvérs. There were fewer windows and less natural sunlight, but they lit fires throughout the castle, keeping it warm from the mountain chill.

Tarion's brown hair spiked up in the front and a gold pin shone from his collar as he moved his arm. "Oh look, see that man there?" He pointed through the crowds. "The one with the curly hair and big hat?"

A tall, thin man with a wide smile stood beneath a pewter chandelier. "He's one of the funniest men I know. If you ever get a chance to talk with him, get him to tell the joke about the willow tree. I can't do it as funny as he can. And there—" his finger changed direction to the side. "The woman with the two braids and rosy ribbons? She is the subject of much scandal. People say only five minutes with her and she has you under a spell. She's the wife of one of our generals. And that man in black? He can fit two oranges in his mouth at the same time. It's truly remarkable."

I giggled at the thought. I enjoyed hearing his stories about the people and the weird ways he remembered them.

"And she's one of the girls who helps me feed the villagers every month."

The phrase confused me. At my expression, Tarion asked, "Have I not talked about that yet? It's a thing the castle does every month. A group of us goes out to one of the poorer villages and makes sure they have enough food. We leave next week if you'd like to join us."

I couldn't pass up an opportunity to get closer to Tarion and learn more about the layout of ThornHigh, so I nodded.

"Splendid," he said, then resumed pointing out people to me.

I listened for anyone who might know something that could be useful, but if there was someone here who could help me uncover secrets about ThornHigh, Tarion didn't reveal them to me. I knew he wouldn't, but I hadn't counted on how difficult snooping around would be.

Every day I walked through every hall and listened at every doorway, hoping to catch some important conversation. So far, I'd come up with nothing and I was positive a few of the guards were beginning to suspect me. My biggest chance still seemed to be winning over Tarion and prying secrets from him somehow, but wooing was not a strong suit of mine. I should have brought Elis.

Just then, someone walked in through the north doors and my heart dropped. Short, black hair and a silver dress. Just what Mar wore the night she attacked me. I shifted to the side to try to get a better look, but Tarion put his hand on my arm.

"It's not her."

"What?" I didn't take my eyes off the girl.

"That's not Mar," he said softly. "She's gone."

My head snapped toward him. "You killed her?" While a major part of me felt relief that there was one less person to keep an eye out for, a small part of me sickened at the thought of him killing her.

His head shook and leaned back, looking equally sick at the idea. "No, I didn't kill her. But she's no longer at this court. She's returned to her home kingdom of Osmelee."

Osmelee was several kingdoms away. As I breathed out in gratitude, he placed his glass down and glanced to the side. "However, that reminds me that I need to speak with you about a delicate matter."

Without giving me the chance to ask what, Tarion stood up and walked away, looking back once to nod for me to follow.

The last time I followed someone from this room, it ended with a blade against my skin, and I wasn't eager to repeat the situation.

A knife hid in the folded fabric belt of my gold dress, providing me with some level of comfort, and I'd surveyed Tarion earlier that night to be sure he had no weapon on him. His own eye had settled on my waist and hesitated over the knife for a few moments, but he hadn't said anything.

I'm here to make friends with the prince to extort information from him, I reminded myself. He must think I trust him.

A timid smile replaced my wary one, and I followed him out of the banquet hall, away from others eyes, and into the dark of a small back room.

A circular window let the moonlight through, illuminating a desk large enough to sit three people. A large cabinet sat along the back wall with a lock over the door, and a thin rug spread across the stone floors. Besides those meager decorations, the room sat eerily empty.

Tarion closed the door behind me, then locked it with a click. My hand flew to my waist, but he put up his hands. "I'm not here to hurt you, so you don't have to keep wearing that blade every night. It can't be comfortable."

It wasn't. I'd almost accidentally impaled myself on it the other night, but the safety it offered was worth more than my comfort. I'd keep wearing the dagger no matter how at ease I felt.

Tarion circled the desk, keeping one finger dragging against the wood as he did so. When he'd walked halfway around, he paused. "Mar told me you were a spy."

My hand itched for my blade again, keenly aware of what weapons might be hiding in secret compartments of the desk. The cabinet behind Tarion could hold a full-sized spear, and it'd take him only a few seconds to turn around and unlock it.

Silence would sentence me, so I risked speech. "I can see why it's hard to trust someone from Elenvérs."

Tarion's eyes stayed on mine. He paced again, his hollow footsteps echoing in the room until he'd finished his circle around the desk and stopped in front of me where he leaned back against the polished wood and crossed his arms.

A coy smile danced on his lips.

"I think you're a spy as well. In fact, I'm quite counting on it. You see, I need someone in the shadows to help fight against my father."

I'm certain no amount of emissary training would have prepared me for this.

I'd not seen Tarion interact with his father enough to know if their relationship was strained. But perhaps the fact that I'd been here a week and had yet to see them interact was enough to show it wasn't a tight bond.

Did Tarion hate his kingdom enough to fight against it? Nothing in his nature suggested anything other than pleasure with his position, and I found it hard to believe he wanted to jeopardize that. Fighting against his father would threaten his position as crown prince and put him at risk for banishment.

More importantly, I couldn't give myself away.

A calculating posture would reveal more of my cleverness than I wanted to, so I let myself stagger back and opened my eyes in wide innocence. "What are you talking about? I'm here to make a friendship, not fight against your king." The grin on his face told me he didn't fall for my act, but I kept at it. "I'm not a spy, I swear it."

A lie. Perhaps my ability to lie was why I couldn't see the White Bear. But surely aligning with the enemy crown prince in some deep plot would corrupt my soul more than a protective lie.

His shoulders raised. "That may be. Spy or emissary, your duty is to Elenvérs, so any plot to destroy your kingdom would alarm you, correct?"

A slow nod.

"Very good. Then I must tell you about my father's plot, and beseech you to work with me, *as a spy*, to fight against him."

With his round eyes and folded hands, he seemed as harmless as I hoped I looked. And here he was suggesting that he didn't care whether or not I was a spy when I walked into this room.

He just wanted to make sure I was one when I walked out.

You are here to make friends with the prince. Learn his secrets, exploit him. Work with him. I could play along with his game and still keep mine. I licked my lips with fake nerves and cleared my throat. "He plans to overthrow Elenvérs?"

"Demolish," Tarion corrected me. For a moment, my nerves turned real. "My father is prepared to launch a series of attacks that will obliterate your kingdom before the end of the year. He has enough soldiers to do it easily. Right now, evacuation is your kingdom's only hope."

"We could fight back." My feet shuffled.

Tarion laid his hands on the desk behind him, still looking at ease as he relaxed against it, despite the fact that we spoke of kingdoms falling. "By hitting us where? We have more soldiers than you can fathom, and no weak spots. Any attack you lead will end in our victory and weakened defense for you."

So, intimidation was his ploy. Little did he know how difficult it was to intimidate me. Still, I feigned a scared expression as I ran my hands through my hair. The corner of his mouth raised slightly as he watched me fret.

"What would you need me to do?"

He pushed from the table. "Now we get to the interesting stuff. As prince, it's hard for me to go about unnoticed, and even harder to find the time. But you, a girl with a small title, will be able to accomplish some things that I can't. I'll provide the resources and assignments, you sneak around—intercept letters, rummage through rooms, that sort of thing—and report back to me. Together, we stop my father from overthrowing Elenvérs."

It sounded simple. It also sounded like exactly what I planned to do anyhow. The possibility that he would put me in endangering locations crossed my mind, and I vowed to never go into a situation that I didn't think I could handle.

In addition to reporting to Tarion, I would report to Cassian, who would give the information to King Olin. They didn't need to know I was working with Tarion; I'd allow them to be impressed.

It still sounded like a trap. "Why would you want to work against your own father?"

"Because if Elenvérs falls at our hand, I don't believe ThornHigh will survive. The number of allies Elenvérs possesses, although too far away to save you in time now, would come after us and ThornHigh would be crippled. Our best bet of survival is to band together with Elenvérs as sister nations, like we once were."

"But your father doesn't agree?"

"My father thinks the opposite. He thinks with Elenvérs gone, we will have room to expand, and the other countries will respect us for our strength and align with us. Truthfully, he doesn't care whether other countries align with us or not, we don't need them."

I dropped my innocent, naive act by a little as I contemplated his words. "Why would Elenvérs want you as a sister nation? We don't need you."

"We will either destroy you or join you. There is no longer another option."

"Alright." I paced. There was always another option, and Elenvérs would find it without Tarion's help. Later, I'd relay every word of this conversation to Cassian, but for now I continued my stream of questions. "Who would you have as king over the two nations?"

He didn't hesitate. "We would keep two kings. One army, but two kings: myself and Cassian. It's the smallest change for everyone involved and will be best accepted by all the people."

One army, two kings. It would make us stronger, and if I trusted ThornHigh even a little I might consider it. But there was no trust between us, the fundamental core of friendship, so I knew it could never work. And unless Tarion was unwaveringly selfless, he wouldn't fight against his own father and kingdom to save Elenvérs, just to put Cassian on the throne. Our country would be saved, but it'd be under ThornHigh's control.

I remembered when Tarion first visited ThornHigh at the Full Moon feast with his father, and how they'd both ignored Cassian. Tarion didn't intend on any sort of friendship with him.

To save Elenvérs, I'd align with Tarion and intercept any plans ThornHigh developed, but I'd report to Cassian first. Together, we'd decide what to do with the information.

I would do whatever it took to save Elenvérs, and right now that meant working with Tarion.

I bowed my head and pledged myself as a spy to the crown prince of ThornHigh.

Chapter Nineteen

A BASKET SAT ON my bed with scarlet ribbon wrapped through the weave and sticky buns stacked high. Under the treats lay apples of many colors. I could almost hear Elis's mom as she insisted that I be sent something healthy along with the desserts. The only reason I wasn't plump was because of her, and a small part of me missed her constant pestering. It was good to be loved.

I missed that here. Though I'd made an uneasy alliance with Tarion, the relationship didn't give me the security of having someone who I knew was on my side.

This basket meant more to me than my family knew.

"That came this morning for you," Lindy said as she tidied up after me. Though I insisted she didn't need to clean every day, she still came in the mornings to pick up my things and dust off the surfaces, though I couldn't fathom they were dirty enough to warrant daily cleaning.

She reminded me of Elis as she worked, whistling to herself with a small smile.

"It's a beautiful basket," Lindy said, pausing from her work.

"Thank you. Oh, and I have a letter for my parents to be sent out with the post." I handed her the envelope.

She nodded at it and pocketed the note before closing the door behind her.

I tucked my hair behind my ears and sat next to the basket, pulling it into my lap. An envelope with my name poked from the side.

A few coins rolled out from the envelope along with two letters. I turned the coins in my hand for a moment as I wondered why they thought I'd need coppers here, though perhaps the letter would explain. The coins clinked together on the bed next to me while I opened the first note. Lady Trelluse's writing jumped out from the page.

To my strong daughter,

I miss you terribly, but I am so proud of you for your dedication to your country. Your strong spirit will take you far in life.

I noticed you left behind your thickest scarves. I hope you are not freezing while away. Please use this money to buy some while you are there.

Please eat the apples. They are good for you.

Lots of love,

Mama

My smile widened with each line. A small blotch in the bottom corner wrinkled the paper, and I rubbed my finger over it, imagining it as a tear she shed while writing the note.

To block my own tears, I quickly moved to the next note, this one from Elis.

There was no greeting.

Mama won't say it, but she wants you back for her birthday celebration next month. You know how she is about her birthday. Please be back in time.

I'll visit you soon,

Elis

I'd already planned to come back for Lady Trelluse's birthday next month since I knew how important it was to her. Each year we got together, the four of us and Cassian, to make dinner and spend the evening playing games until the fire went out. She'd talk about how excited she was for it a month beforehand, then about what a lovely time she had for a month afterward. That time together as a family was so scarce, and it meant the world to her. For that one night, Cassian and I pretended to be a family for her sake. I would never deprive her of that, on potentially her last birthday that I'm here for. Knowing Elis thought I would miss it reminded me of her poor opinion of me at the moment.

She should see me now, on my way to feed poor families in the village.

The coins jingled as they slid back into the note, which I placed in the basket while I fetched my parka.

My boots sat beside my bed, stacked together and sitting upright thanks to Lindy, and they warmed my feet as I put them on. Lindy had just come back in as I was leaving, and she wished me well before I took off, staying in the room while I closed the door behind me. Nerves swirled within me at leaving her in my bedchamber while I wasn't there, but nothing she could find would incriminate me as a spy. She didn't seem interested in snooping anyhow.

Out in the hallway, heels clicked against the floor, faster than the normal speed, drawing my eye behind me. With two more rushed steps, the lady at the other end darted behind the corner and vanished from my sight.

All I saw was auburn hair, but for a moment, I thought it was Elis.

Maybe it was the way Lindy whistled like Elis, or how I'd read her note only moments before, but I took it as a sign to write to her this evening and apologize for how we parted ways, so our strained relationship didn't taint my time here. I'd need to remain fully focused.

THOUGHTS OF ELIS GRADUALLY slipped from my mind as the village took over my focus. We traveled to the nearest town that wasn't connected to the castle, about ten of us on horseback each with large bundles strapped behind us carrying the food.

"Krivell is beautiful; you'll love it," Tarion said as he kept his horse near mine. "Here it comes."

Krivell looked like no village I'd ever seen. In Elenvérs, our people made their homes in the caves, spreading large rugs over the entrance to brighten the mountainside and distinguish their home from their neighbors. They took pride in displaying their rugs and changed them out whenever the sun faded their vibrant colors.

Here, in Krivell, they built homes from both wood and stone. Each home connected to the one beside it, so the entire village was a long road of homes, snaking through the wide mountain, absent from color except the occasional painted child's toy left in the frost-covered road.

Snow blanketed the roofs, only relenting around the chimneys as each puffed smoke into the air. A low bell rang as we neared, though I didn't see where the sound came from. As soon as the third ring echoed through the air, people started to file out of the homes, wrapping scarves around their necks and holding onto children's hands who pulled them toward the horses.

They came in a scramble of leather boots, muddied pants, and eager eyes, their voices clouding the air. Children wiped cold noses, and fathers struggled to keep their families in order.

It was chaos of the most beautiful kind.

They knew the drill well and formed a line on both sides of the street to wait, picking up conversations with those next to them and occasionally dashing to the other side to visit with those standing there. Some darted into houses only to return moments later with elder folk on their arm, who would beam at us as if we were their own children coming to visit. Little voices laughed while mamas hushed, but no one minded the noise. Everyone's eyes fixed on us as we hopped from the horses and pulled our bags open to hand out portions to each person as we passed.

Tarion led the group, though one by one we passed him as he stopped to chat with almost everyone he came across. They called him by name, without his title, and each hugged him tight before letting him continue.

Strange. I hadn't believed ThornHigh capable of goodness. Our people never looked this elated to see their own king pass. If King Maven himself showed up, I doubted the townsfolk could be more excited than this.

By the time we reached the end of the trail of houses, I had only five parcels left and a smaller, cloth sack which carried my meager lunch, all of which I folded into my bag as we returned through the town. Though we weren't passing out further portions, our horses trotted slower on the return trip, and the crowds seemed to grow in number, pressing me against the side of my horse as I walked beside it. The families' meals were tucked safely in their homes and now it seemed they cared as much about visiting with us as they did about the meal.

With each step they pulled me one direction to the next, showing off their shops or homemade trinkets or reaching to compliment my hair. I smiled through a cringe as they stroked the red locks, trying not to flinch when they pulled too hard.

"Such pale skin!" They compared their own arms with mine, making my coloring close to white in contrast. It took all my strength not to pull my arm back, but instead I laughed with them.

"Hello!" A tiny voice came from behind me, belonging to a small girl with dark braided hair and a patched-up dress. She stared up at my horse. "May I pet it?"

I picked her up in my arms so she could reach. "Of course. Here."

The smile on her face reached to her ears as she stroked the horse's muzzle. Her other hand, covered in dirt, clung to a piece of my hair.

"Poor thing," someone sighed behind me. "Losing her horse."

"That's not the main thing she lost," another pointed out. Murmurs of agreement followed. The girl didn't seem to notice the chatter.

"What do you mean?" I turned my head.

The few who'd whispered stepped back at my turn, but an older lady with twigs braided into her hair smacked her lips a few times. "Her father died not two months ago in a mountainside accident," she said. "They were lucky enough to own a horse, but her mother had to sell it to stay afloat."

"It was a nice horse too," someone else whispered, and they all nodded.

"That it was. That it was," the lady agreed.

The girl in my arms couldn't have been older than four. Too young to remember much of her father as she grew up.

"Allie, there you are, sweet girl." A woman pushed through the crowd, which parted at her entrance. One by one they ducked their heads and slipped away to see the other visitors from the castle, until we were the only ones around by the time the young woman reached me.

"Sorry if she's bothering you." The woman held out her arms and the girl jumped into them.

"Not at all. She's delightful."

The woman brightened. Her dress was patched up like her daughter's, and thin enough that she must be freezing. Her hair was in messy braids and her eyes carried dark bags under them. I couldn't imagine her pain at losing her husband or having to raise a child alone.

Without thinking, I grabbed my sack with the extra food, including my own lunch, and handed it to her. "Please, take this. It's extra portions that we don't need."

Her daughter grabbed the bag hungrily, but the mother looked resistant. "I can't take this."

"We have no use for it. You'd be doing me a favor."

She licked her lips again, giving the food a nervous glance, but I saw the way her hand tightened over the bag, so I pushed. "Please, it's yours."

Her eyes brightened. "Thank you so very much. Come along, Allie."

They wandered into a house, and others began to flock to me again.

An hour later, Tarion found me. We only made it a few houses before the crowd grew too thick for us to move any further. We'd talk for a few minutes to the eager faces around us, then continue two more houses.

The end of the town loomed ahead, and we got close before a hand grabbed mine.

"You know what would look good with your coloring?" A slender lady with wolf skin wrapped around her shoulders inspected me for a moment before pulling me toward her shop. I shot a look to Tarion, but he just grinned and gestured me forward.

Helpless, I let the black-haired lady lead me through the people to her little shop, where she shoved me inside.

Sudden warmth hit me, a pleasant feeling against my numb nose. Her shop crackled with the sounds of fire and the smell of lilacs, bursting with colors that I hadn't seen outside: red paint on the wall, pink scarves folded on yellow shelves, gold bracelets by the desk, and jewelry of every color hanging by the windows.

She crossed the room to the desk and beckoned me to follow.

"Welcome to my shop. Whiskers and belliberries, where did I put that...ah, yes. Yes, here it is. How pretty, yes?" From a bowl of links and chains she produced a bracelet and brought it toward me with a smile as wide as her face, laying it over my wrist with satisfaction. "There. It belongs there, yes?"

The design was simple, a flat circle of rose gold color with a blush pink strip in the middle. The gold color complimented me well.

Now that I thought of it, this would look beautiful on Lady Trelluse, and would be the perfect gift for her birthday next month.

The coins she sent me for a new scarf would be enough to pay for it. "I don't have the money on me now, but can I come back for this?"

Her eyes widened and her smile deepened. "Yes! Oh, lilies and lollies. Yes, yes. I will hold on to this until you come back." She took it back and danced back to the desk where she slid it in a drawer. The shop door creaked opened and Tarion poked his head inside.

"Good morning, Sanna." His chipper voice floated through the room. They exchanged a few pleasant words while I moved to wait by the door. As I did, a ring caught my attention.

A single rose blossomed from the center, with two intricate leaves blooming from the side and wrapping around, their tips meeting on the other side. From the center of the rose sat a single white gem. I leaned forward to inspect it better, which piqued Sanna's interest.

"See something else you like, darling?" In a heartbeat she stood next to me and picked up the ring. "Oh, yes. This one is one of my finest. Fit to be on the finger of a princess. Do you have someone special in your life? A special lad, eh? Men are always looking for jewelry to impress their lasses with. This ring would do nicely." She wiggled her brows at Tarion.

With the curse, romance was the one route I'd never pursued. It felt cruel, both to my heart and to someone else's, to make plans for a future that I didn't know if I'd get. I envied Elis in that way. She had Briggs. He'd buy something like this for her.

Now that I was confident that I'd break my curse, romance was an option for me.

But I didn't have anyone right now, so I shook my head and folded my hands in front of me. "No, nothing like that. We better be on our way."

Tarion thanked Sanna and led me out the door. The cruel cold hit us once more, and I sucked in a breath sharply.

"You're doing great; the people love you," Tarion whispered to me.

"They love you more," I pointed out. "Your people seem to adore you."

"I hope so. I want to be a good ruler for them." His eyes lit up as he looked over the village. Then he looked at me. "I think you'd be a good queen too, if you ever get the opportunity."

The way he said it made me wonder what he could know. But he couldn't possibly be aware of my real parentage. I bowed my head and grinned. "I'd hope so, but I'm destined for a mediocre life."

He chuckled. "I doubt that. I see great things in store for you."

Upon returning to the castle, I spent my afternoon training with some of ThornHigh's prospective knights, another attempt to grow closer to my enemies. While the other lords and ladies of the court shook my hand with fake simpers and spoke of friendships and bright futures, the trainees held no obligation to pointless pleasantries, so they hid their smiles and reserved their conversations with me. But by the end of the lesson, I received a few pats on the back and slow tips of the head in approval. My diplomatic skills wouldn't win these fighters over, but my skill with the blade could.

They might not have any secrets to share, but Tarion told me that generals occasionally came by to watch the trainees, and generals carried secrets that I very much wanted to know.

No generals visited today, but Tarion did show up for a few minutes, leaning against the railing to watch. As I walked by him, he whispered, "Wear the purple dress to dinner tonight."

I didn't have time to ask questions before he moved on.

A quick sweep of my room upon entering revealed it to be empty. I flung open my closet doors, scrambling through the fabric until I found the purple dress I'd worn my second night here, then plunged my hand into the pockets.

Sure enough, a folded piece of paper lay within. I remained in the privacy of the closet to unfold the note.

Tonight, after the first dance, meet me in the office room where we spoke yesterday.

My breathing quickened as I folded the note back up. In case of a trap, one where someone was ordered to kill the girl in the purple dress tonight, I wore a different dress, and tucked my dagger into the pocket. I'd nod to Tarion later, so he knew I got the message.

I had my first assignment from the prince.

Chapter Twenty

THE DOOR CLICKED BEHIND me. I'd come before the first dance started, so if a trap awaited me, I'd be prepared. The room sat empty. Once inside, I positioned myself by the window and took a deep breath. If anyone came in, I could claim I retreated for the fresh air and privacy, overwhelmed by the excitement of the night.

All there was to do now was wait.

My hand twiddled with the fabric wrapped around my dagger's hilt, openly free from its hiding place. It was only through my silence that I was able to hear the soft footsteps behind me and the handle as it twisted open.

"You didn't wear the purple dress." Tarion slipped in the room and closed the door behind him. My dagger stayed in my hand, but I turned to face him.

"I got the note."

"That, I see."

We hesitated for a moment, both watching the other. Finally, Tarion let his out in a large sigh. "It seems we are both on edge around each other."

"Better that than dead."

"Too true." He'd relaxed now and moved to the desk where he leaned against it in the same posture as last night. "Here is the task. My father hired a small army to fight for him who stay under the control of a man named General Valerie. Vicious man, any heart he once had has long frozen over."

"Sounds pleasant." I didn't move from my place near the window. If someone came into the room, I wanted enough space between Tarion and I that this couldn't be mistaken for a scandalous rendezvous.

"Hopefully you'll never have to meet him. He's sending my father a letter, which we will intercept. Then, we write two letters of our own, one a false reply to General Valerie, and another a decoy letter from General Valerie to my father."

"You want me to intercept it."

Tarion nodded. "When mail carriers come, we have a room for them to put their mail, get it arranged, and send it to the right people. If our letter came in that, it'd be an easier task. But General Valerie sends one of his own men to carry the letter and wait a day to bring back the reply. He only hands the letter to my father, so getting it will be tricky."

I twirled the dagger around in my hand as I thought through the situation. "Do you have a plan for that?"

Tarion pulled his lips tight and straightened his cravat. "The way I see it, we have two chances. The time between when the carrier arrives and he hands the letter to my father, or between my father receiving the letter and opening it. The trick is guessing which person will be easier to steal from."

"The mercenary," I said.

Tarion crossed his arms. "I think my father. The mercenary will have one job upon arriving, get that letter to

165

my father. Meanwhile, my father has multiple tasks to complete each day, so if we can give him an abundance of work, we can steal the letter for an hour, and he won't notice."

Now I crossed my arms. "As soon as your father gets that letter, he'll open it. The mercenary will be arriving from a long trip and can be persuaded into a room with a meal first."

"Have you ever persuaded a mercenary to do anything?" Tarion chuckled. "They are not weak-minded men."

The more I thought about it, the more nervous I got. Nothing about this plan sounded easy. I'd dealt with angry mountain trolls and baby dragons before, but never a mercenary. "He won't be convinced to give the letter to you instead of your father?"

For a moment, Tarion leaned forward and narrowed his eyes, but then he shook his head. "He'll only give it to my father. We'd arouse suspicion attempting to convince him otherwise."

"Alright, so what's your plan?"

"I'll be on the lookout for the mercenary. He always enters through the same back tunnel. As soon as I see him coming, I'll meet him at the end of the tunnel, escorting him to a small meeting room near the north bedchambers where he always meets my father. After he hands him the letter, I'll come up with an emergency that needs my father's immediate attention. He'll leave the letter behind and lock the door. But I have another key. You use the key, open the door, find the letter, and steal it, then lock the door without anyone spotting you."

There were so many ways this plan could fail. Someone could be in the corridor and spot me. Tarion would fail to convince King Maven to follow his emergency, or King Maven would bring the letter with him.

Or worse—Tarion could be setting this up to trap me.

If he wasn't trapping me, and if we managed to pull this off, one problem remained. "What if King Maven finds the letter missing before we return with a decoy?"

Tarion grunted. "That does seem to be the tricky bit." His hand stroked his chin. "The best I can come up with is for my distraction to keep my father at bay long enough for me to read the letter and write a decoy one. My father always gives me his reply to give to the mercenary, so the second bit shouldn't be a problem."

"Have you seen this mercenary's handwriting before?" I asked.

His brow creased. "Briefly, but yes. Why?"

"Simple, write a decoy letter first. If the handwriting matches, we only need to switch it out and my job is done."

"A bit difficult to know what to write in a decoy letter, without knowing what the original says." Tarion's head leaned to the side. "But it can't hurt to be prepared, just in case. Alright then, we have a plan." His eyes lit up.

I couldn't share in his enthusiasm, but instead bit at my lip until it warmed beneath my teeth. It wasn't a great plan, or even a good one, but we had a plan.

This letter had better be worth it. Whatever the note said, I intended to find out first, and report back to Cassian. Crossing the room, I put my hand on the wooden knob.

"Let me know if the plan changes. Or else I'll be ready. Don't follow me out right away." I left the room as casually as I could, with a blank expression and aimless step. It wouldn't have mattered. The corridor was empty outside and soaked with the fresh scent of sandalwood, while the chatter of nearby dinner guests echoed from the walls.

For a moment, I forgot the blade in my hand, but I slipped it in my pocket before pushing through to the banquet hall where I treaded along the back wall with slow steps as if I had nowhere important to be and nothing on my mind.

A few moments later, Tarion came through the same door, approaching the nearest nobles and striking up a conversation. His eye found me, and he risked a wink, but I looked away.

"Has the Crown Prince of ThornHigh become smitten with the heir of Elenvérs?" Annon's voice was sharp and dripping with mockery, and I almost wished to be back in the dark room with Tarion, risking being caught.

"Good evening, Annon." I didn't bother denying his claims on my true parentage anymore. He'd never believe me.

"I'd heard a rumor he'd taken a new fancy. Hmm. We could use this." Annon's hair, usually slicked back, now hung flat over his forehead with twists by his ears, matching the style of ThornHigh. He'd traded out his blue lapel for a red one, and the cuff links, usually ice silver, now shone gold. He'd become one with ThornHigh. He still wore the king's livery pinned to his jacket, but that was the only marker that he belonged to Elenvérs.

When I didn't reply, Annon stepped closer and leaned his head down. "This morning an important man, General Barrett, arrived at ThornHigh. I'm assuming you know the man?"

I did, because I'd snuck in on almost every advisory meeting at Elenvérs, but I shook my head.

Annon smirked. "Very well, keep your game. General Barrett is King Maven's most trusted man, who's led him in every victory during his reign. He's been stationed at a south point called Arcon, where they face pressure from Osmelee, but his presence here can only mean one thing. King Maven is planning an attack."

His eyes flickered up, and I followed his glance to a man in the back of the hall who watched the room. A black mustache clawed across his face until it tickled his ears, but that was the only facial feature I could make out at this distance.

"Don't let him catch you staring," Annon ordered, bringing my eyes back to him. "If he as much as catches you looking at him strange, he won't rest until he's uncovered your secrets."

I vowed to never look at General Barrett again.

Annon put on a smile for the sake of anyone watching, while he turned his back to the room. "If there is anyone worth spying on here, it'd be that man. His room is in the east wing, and he trains every morning when the sun rises, leaving his room open to be searched."

I shouldn't be surprised that Annon knew I was a spy. King Olin must have informed him that we were less interested in befriending ThornHigh and more interested in uncovering their weaknesses, but I didn't like Annon being privy to information which, if given to King Maven, would end my life.

"I'm not fool enough to search through his room where any maid could find me."

Annon laughed. "Haven't you learned anything about us military men? We don't trust anybody, least of all a maid whose allegiance could be turned at the sight of a pretty copper." His nostrils flared.

"Well then, I'm not fool enough to trust *you.*" I shifted on my feet.

"You're wondering why I would treat you as an ally in entrusting you with this information?" He clicks his tongue. "I forget no one else is as smart as me. You see, I don't trust you, and you don't trust me. But we both love Elenvérs, as it should be ours to rule. So, I expect that everything you do will be with Elenvérs' best interests in mind. Know this, I will expose your parents' deception once you fall asleep, but I don't mind using you to help me save Elenvérs in the process."

Elenvérs best interests were in my heart, but I didn't know if they were in Annon's. A strategic, cunning man like him—one could never be too certain of his motives. Perhaps he was the second king Tarion planned to put on the throne, though I doubted it—Annon was more calculating than Tarion, and far more experienced. If he worked against Elenvérs, he did so with King Maven at his side. Once Elenvérs fell, he'd find a way to rule ThornHigh.

Annon possessed the strength of a king but the mind of a pirate. And that made him dangerous.

Over his shoulder, I saw Tarion watching us with a thoughtful look, debating how close Annon and I were and how much information I would share with my fellow Elenvérs emissary. To keep his trust, I took a step back from Annon. Tarion's mouth raised in a half smile when he saw me looking at him, before his attention turned back to the people standing around him.

"Take my advice, or don't. But two pieces of advice I give you. Keep an eye out for General Barrett, because I guarantee you, he's keeping an eye on us." Annon peeked over his shoulder, but he didn't look at General Barrett. Instead, his eye wandered toward Tarion.

"And the second advice?"

His gaze swept back toward me. "Be wary of your young prince."

I glanced at Tarion, then back to Annon. "Be wary? That's it?"

Annon grunted. "Fine. Be very wary. A child of ThornHigh is not your friend. He's certainly no friend of Elenvérs."

Chapter Twenty-One

BEFORE THE SUN SPRANG over the mountain tops, I snuck out of bed for the eighth day in a row and crept down to the training arena where I waited to see if General Barrett came. Right as the first morning rays hit the rocks, he strode into the arena with his sword in hand. My feet were reluctant to move away. I swore I'd learned as much from watching him train as Gen could teach me in months.

But today called for a new task.

Today I was brave enough to go for it. I'd sneak into General Barrett's room.

Quiet as a snowflake, I retreated, only breathing when I reentered the castle, where I hurried to Tarion's chambers.

I knocked. My head stayed low within my hood to minimize the wandering maids who might see me and spread gossip about the emissary who visited the prince's room at the early hours of the morning. Maids weren't the only ones I had to worry about. Down the corridor to my left, a tall guard leaned against the wall and his head twitched forward when I glanced at him, pretending he hadn't been watching me a moment before. While I longed to pull the edges of my hood deeper around my face, I resisted the urge, certain that the action would do nothing but make me look more suspicious. If he'd recognized me already, there was nothing to do about it anyway.

Anticipation swelled within me, and I bounced on my heels, waiting for Tarion to open the door.

I knocked again, louder this time. The guard's head shifted again to watch me. As my hand raised to pound on the door for a third time, the handle turned and Tarion poked his head out and cursed.

"Rowan? What the blazes are you doing?"

By the state of his wrinkled shirt and the horrid smell of his breath, I guessed he'd been asleep. "Being a prince must not be as difficult as I presumed, if you're still in bed at this hour," I joked.

He moaned and ruffled his dark hair, which stuck out in every direction. "It's because I am such a great prince that I'm privileged to sleep in. How can I help you?"

I peeked down the corridor to the guard as he straightened his head again. My voice remained as low as wind rushing over a mountain. "Have you heard of General Barrett?"

Tarion groaned at the name. "Heard of him? The man sliced my leg in what was meant to be a friendly sparring match because I wasn't moving quickly enough." His hand grazed his leg as if the wound were fresh.

Good, if he disliked the general, he was more likely to participate in my plan. Or rather, Annon's plan. "Search his room with me."

Tarion's eyes grew wide and he poked his head out to glance around. "Are you mad?" he hissed. "The man will kill us if he finds out. *When* he finds out."

"He won't." I shrugged. "He just went to training; I saw him myself." Tarion sucked in his lip and drew down his eyebrows, looking ready to close the door on me and go back to bed. I needed to convince him quickly. "As your father's main general, he could have an abundance of information that we can use. There's no one I trust here more than you to do this with me."

It was a ploy, to make him think I trusted him, when in reality, I didn't want to get caught in that room alone. Tarion was my protection.

After a long pause, Tarion groaned and pulled back, shutting the door between us. Dumbly, I stared at it, but heard nothing from the other side.

When a few moments passed and the door didn't open again, I sighed and turned toward the kitchens. I wasn't foolish enough to do this on my own, so if Tarion wouldn't go with me, then I wouldn't go at all.

Hot tea sounded splendid right now.

Two steps toward the kitchens, and Tarion's door flew open. He stepped out, wearing the plainest outfit I'd seen him in yet.

"Where are you going?" He caught up to me. "His room is this way. Come on."

His steps were slow and hesitant while mine bounced with a combination of eagerness and fear at getting caught. The guard stared at us as we passed, and Tarion raised a hand in greeting.

Anyone could tell this was the royals' corridor without being told. The rug sank deeper beneath my shoes, the colors burned more vibrantly, and the looming walls were lined with oversized photos of past monarchs. Greatness seeped from the walls, each of the paintings staring down at Tarion, as if reminding him of the mighty leaders who came before, and of how easy it would be to fail. It was no wonder he devised a plan to make ThornHigh strong again; living in these walls, he wasn't allowed to be anything less than great.

I almost pitied him, knowing the burden on his shoulders. I wouldn't want to be next in line to ThornHigh's throne.

As we turned from his bedchamber's corridor into the next, a maid came out of one of the rooms. Her eyebrows lifted when she saw us, but she said nothing and scurried away. By now, the sky was half lit with the morning sun, but Tarion's hair suggested he wasn't fully prepared for the day.

General Barrett's room sat only two corridors from Tarion's, which made sense. If I were a prince, I'd want the greatest general sleeping nearby too, for extra security.

Unfortunately, it was the security that made this next step difficult. Two guards were posted in the corridor, and we waited behind the corner to figure out our plan.

"This was a bad idea," Tarion rubbed his tired eyes.

"Should we wait for the shift change?"

He scoffed. "That's not how it works. Guards will take their place before they leave. And the general will be done training by then." He thought for a few moments then grinned. His eyes searched the hallway, waiting until a maid came from one of the rooms to call her over. She hurried before her prince. "Please go inform the cook that I want them to make sticky buns for the guards today, to show our appreciation. Put them in the south wing meeting room."

She nodded eagerly and rushed off.

Before explaining his plan, he strolled into the hallway. "My good men," he addressed the guards, who snapped to attention. "There is a surprise for you both in the south wing meeting room. A special token of my gratitude."

They glanced at each other, then back to the prince. "But who will guard these rooms?"

Tarion pulled out a key ring from his pocket. "Let's lock them, and I can personally stand here until you return." He began locking the rooms, while the guards looked at each other again.

"Is anything the matter?" Tarion asked as he crossed the corridor, locking each door as he came to it. He threw them the key when he was finished.

"No, sire. Of course not. Thank you." They strode away.

I came from around the corner and crossed my arms.

"Well now they're gone, but we're locked out."

"I have more than one key." Tarion fished through his key ring until he found the one he wanted, unlocking a door and pushing it open. "Let's make this quick, shall we? You're going to get me in trouble one day."

General Barrett's room looked flawless, not a thing out of place. Against the back wall sat a bed with high pillars. A gray sheet wrapped around each pillar and swooped down between them. One large pillow rested against the backboard of the bed, and not a single wrinkle infiltrated the blankets.

No rug covered the stone floors, and a single chair sat by the fireplace with a single table in front of it. The message there was clear: guests were not welcome.

A few stairs led up to a landing, where a small table rested with a pot of flowers, the only color in the room. From this landing was the balcony, though I wouldn't risk stepping out and being seen.

To the side loomed two wide doors, far enough apart to lead to separate rooms. One must be a closet, because he didn't have a wardrobe in here. The other was, hopefully, an office.

Tarion let out a low whistle. "This makes it trickier. Everything you touch must be put back exactly where you found it, and not a hair off." With a nod, I took a step forward, but his hand shot out and grabbed mine. "Not even a tiny hair off," he repeated as if I were a child. I nodded again, this time more firmly.

"I know, I'll be careful."

"And quick."

"I'll be quicker if you stop lecturing me and let me go." I pulled my hand back while Tarion visibly swallowed. A bead of sweat had formed along his brow, and when I took off, he waited a few moments before following.

Something about this man instilled a deep fear in Tarion, and I appreciated that someone could make him afraid—it showed he was not invincible—but General Barrett couldn't be worse than Annon, and I knew how to deal with Annon.

While I figured the office held what I sought, I still searched his main room, dropping to my stomach to look under the bed, and lifting the pillow to look behind. Under the bed was bare, even from dust, and the pillowcase had been recently pressed. A strand of hair wouldn't be found in a room like this.

Lady Trelluse would be impressed. Frog's breath, even Lindy would be impressed.

Tarion watched me with obvious nerves that grew every time I touched something. He poked around the chair and little table, checking for a secret panel, but finding nothing. The fireplace looked normal, but if we didn't find anything in the office then I would come back to inspect that.

"Let's hurry up." Did Tarion's voice just tremble?

"He can't be past warming up yet. Every day this week I've watched him train to see how long he practiced for. We have time."

Tarion's eyebrows shot up and he looked at me in a new way. Since I didn't know his expressions very well, it took me a moment to place it. *Respect*, I named it. Maybe a bit of fear.

"Remind me to never become your enemy," he mumbled.

A smile crossed my face as I opened one of the doors. "Don't ever become my enemy."

Just as I'd guessed, this was only a closet. While still worth searching—since if I didn't keep my wish on me, it hid in my closet—the other room interested me more.

The office was even more meticulously organized than the bedroom. Two bookshelves sat bare against a wall with a single picture of a battle hanging over them. A man with a mustache stood near the front, and even from a distance I knew I was looking at General Barrett.

A dark oak desk paired with a high-backed chair looked toward the bookshelf. On the desk were three perfectly aligned stacks of papers, spread an exact distance from each other with no paper out of place. Again, no carpet on the floor, and no decorations besides the painting.

"Rowan—"

"I know, I'll be careful."

We both approached the desk and began looking at the papers. A part of me hoped for a table with a map of the mountainside and the exact location of their troops, along with a detailed report of how they planned to attack, but all I had were these papers. They better be enough.

Each stack held no more than ten papers, so I felt confident enough when picking them up that I could put them back as neatly as I'd found them. Tarion groaned when I grabbed them, but after hesitating for another moment he picked up a pile of his own.

It took me longer than I cared to admit to figure out what the papers said. "They're finance reports."

"You sound surprised."

I shrugged. "Not what I assumed a general would have."

Tarion didn't look up as he leafed through his pages. "A general hires his own mercenaries. He has an army that isn't tied to ThornHigh's." He glanced up. "Does Elenvérs not have any soldiers outside of their knights?"

With a blush, I lowered my eyes, aware that in my ignorance I'd given away more than I should have about Elenvérs. "I couldn't assume to know such a thing. I do know we have enough allies to defeat any foe," I sang, taking the moment to point out our advantage over ThornHigh.

"Not if they can't get there in time," Tarion sang back with a grin as he peeked at me. It felt nice to talk about it in a relaxed manner. I almost forgot the future of my kingdom was in jeopardy.

My experience with finance reports was minimal, but I didn't need Cassian to translate them for me. General Barrett had an army, a very large army. And not just one. Each stack belonged to a different mercenary group that he controlled.

My knees weakened beneath me, and my breath grew shallow. Tarion told me ThornHigh was strong enough to defeat us without our allies by our side, but seeing these numbers showed me the truth behind his claim. If these troops were stationed nearby and moved on Elenvérs tonight, we wouldn't be standing when the sun rose again.

Where were these armies stationed? I frantically searched the documents for some hint, but I found nothing.

Did General Barrett leave these reports here as a ploy to frighten anyone who snooped through his room? They sent a clear message—he was a powerful man. The painting over the desk stared down at me. While it first looked like General Barrett appeared in deep thought, the dark eyes now threatened me while his army fought behind him. His face taunted me with unspoken words. *I can see you. I can defeat you. I can kill everyone you love.*

With all my might, I pulled my eyes away. Cassian must be warned, and I must find something here to save my kingdom.

The papers fell back to the table, but I didn't restraighten them. "There's nothing here, I'm going to search the closet."

As I crossed the room, Tarion spoke out in a calm voice. "Rowan, we will stop the attack, and we will save both our kingdoms."

He nodded to me as he straightened my stack of papers.

The fate of my kingdom relied heavily on Tarion, and that terrified me almost as much as the strength of General Barrett's army.

Back in the main room, the yellow flowers on the shelf by the balcony stood out more than before. A moment away from turning the handle to the closet, an idea struck me like a sudden avalanche. I froze.

I scanned the rest of the room.

There wasn't a single decoration besides the flowers. We'd checked everything else that belonged to General Barrett—the bed, the plain desk, the simple chair, looking anywhere that he might have touched, but I'd never guessed the flowers were his doing instead of being put there by a maid. I'd not given the flowers a second thought, and hadn't seen Tarion touch them either.

In a room so plain and simple, the flowers were obviously not his. But that made them perfect. If an array of rugs and paintings and sculpted pieces loitered the room, we'd scan through each one of them. But the one vase of flowers had made itself invisible to our suspicions.

With a wild glace at the office door, which I'd left open, I sprinted toward the flowers. There was no time to be delicate, so I plunged my hands into the dirt and began to navigate through the mess. From where I stood, I could see the corner of the desk and on occasional sighting of Tarion's elbow. I'd have no more than a few seconds to react if he turned around.

The dirt was packed tightly, but as I felt along the back side, I found a patch where the soil separated easier. My hands plunged into the dirt.

Something thin cut my finger and I gasped. Paper.

As I yanked it out, soil went flying. My hands shook as they to open it quickly. Tarion had moved from sight. I couldn't see what he was up to, but he couldn't see me either. The paper opened and I began memorizing it.

It was a map. Nothing too complicated, but enough to recognize the locations. There was ThornHigh and Elenvérs, and the Northern Mountains that separated them. To the east were the Wandering Mountains.

And the markings of his armies.

Not just his, General Valerie's men were labeled at Yule Point, a town right inside the Wandering Mountains. The rest of the armies waited on the outside of the range. He marked them with large shields.

At a few points in the Northern Mountains, he wrote the word decoy.

Tarion told me Elenvérs was surrounded with armies. He was wrong, they were only in the west.

Liar.

I folded the paper and shoved it back into the dirt, then got to work cleaning up. I smoothed the top layer of soil over the hole I'd made one moment before Tarion came out of the office.

"Find anything?" He raised an eyebrow at the soil scattered across the floor and my hands. "You don't listen to instructions well, do you?"

"We needed to be thorough," I reminded him.

"That we do. Did you find anything?"

"No."

He sighed. "Let's clean up this mess then get out of here. It was a good try."

Tarion helped me clean up the mess and though he glanced at my pocket several times during the process, he didn't say a word. He suspected I found something.

I didn't say anything either, but when he bent down to scoop dirt from the floor, his pocket crinkled with the unmistakable sound of paper.

I wasn't the only one who found something.

We both kept our secrets though, cleaning the room to completion before shaking hands and going our separate ways. I itched to flee to my room and copy down the map, but my stomach complained of hunger and I took a detour to the kitchens.

The castle was awake now and the halls were a flurry of activity. My own maid, Lindy, passed by me with a curtsy and a chipper good morning. She didn't ask where I was that morning, or all the mornings before, when she'd come in and I was gone from my bed. Her discretion was appreciated. I'd set many traps throughout the room, placing clothes a certain way or folding the sheet just so, to see if she scavenged through my things while I was gone, but if she did, she never left a trace.

She continued while I took the last few turns toward the kitchens.

At the last turn, I stopped cold.

Elis—*Elis*—stood in the kitchens with a mug in hand, leaning against the counter as she chatted to the cook who worked around her. The cook's cheeks were wrinkled with her smile as she listened to Elis. She'd never smiled for me.

"Elis?"

Her head snapped up at my voice. Her elated expression dropped slightly before she plastered it back on.

"Rowan," she exclaimed. "I was just coming to find you."

"You know they don't make me sleep in the kitchens? They've given me a proper room." Because of how tense our last conversation was, I kept my distance, prepping myself for whatever response she would have. She set down her cup.

To say I was surprised to see her here was like saying the snow was cold, or avalanches were dangerous. Yet, she looked at me as if her being in the kitchens of ThornHigh, chatting with the bitter cook with the burns on her arm was the most natural thing in the world. Elis broke the silence and threw her arms open wide to embrace me.

"I've missed you. It's the longest we've ever been apart." Her voice was chipper.

I kept her at arm's length. "Where are your things?"

She flashed me a look. "I've already been settled into a room and refreshed from my journey. Now I'm eager to hear all about your time, if you are ready to move past our little disagreement."

"Disagreement?" As I recalled, she threw my honor to the ground and tore me to pieces, vividly telling me which parts of me she hated, then didn't speak to me for a month. That wasn't a disagreement. Coming from Elis, it was as good as a decree of war.

"The little one, yes."

"The one where you said—"

She brushed her auburn hair behind her ears. "I know what I said, I'd like to move past it."

My eyebrow raised. It couldn't be that simple.

She huffed, glancing at the few maids and cooks around us who pretended not to be listening to our every word, each of whom looked away from her gaze and picked up their paces.

"This is me apologizing. I want us to be sisters again."

Her words had hurt me, and I'd mulled over them repeatedly during the past month. I already knew I had flaws, but I was terrified that they were bigger than I'd seen and that no matter how many good deeds I did, my heart would never change. Was I no better than conniving Annon, or blood-thirsty King Maven? Maybe I didn't deserve the Elenvérs throne. How did I not see the magnitude of my flaws?

Was I less of a person than I ought to be?

She'd done that to me, she'd made me doubt myself.

And now, with meager words, she washed it all away.

My heart couldn't be so easily eased, but it also couldn't hold anything against her. I nodded slowly and let my sister's outstretched hand bridge the gap between us.

"Welcome back to ThornHigh. It's been a crazy month."

I spent the rest of the day at Elis's side, introducing her to the people I'd striven to befriend over the past month, and watching those same people fall in love with Elis by the end of the night. It almost wasn't fair how easily she charmed them, without even realizing the spell she cast.

Tarion saw us at dinner, but he only winked in our direction and walked away.

General Barrett was not at dinner that night. For as long as he'd been here, he'd never missed a dinner.

Chapter Twenty-Two

"YOU'RE SPRITE THIS MORNING," Elis said over the brim of her ivory teacup before blowing into it, sending a small pillar of steam flitting over her nose. Her morning dress wrapped around her crossed legs and her bare feet rested on top of her slippers as she watched the snow falling outside my window.

It all looked so tranquil that it was easy to forget we were in the enemy's court.

"Not chipper, exactly. More...hopeful." If the armies didn't surround us, we could better position our men to fight against them. We were still outnumbered, but we had a chance now.

The corner of her brow raised as she took another sip. "It's going well for me here. I think I can save Elenvérs from ThornHigh."

Elis tipped her head toward her cup and turned it about. "How can you be sure?"

"I've teamed up with Prince Tarion to do so."

She frowned. "Are you sure that's wise? How can you trust him?"

I glanced at the door to be certain it was shut. Lindy came by earlier but there was little for her to do, so after fetching us some tea she'd moved on to her other chores to give us one of our first moments alone together since Elis showed up yesterday. Now I could tell her about my workings with the prince. "Tarion is as eager to save his kingdom as I am mine, and he thinks we have a better shot at saving them both together. I think he's right—ThornHigh's best shot of survival is an alliance with us. They'll run out of resources soon enough. But I don't think we need them to survive."

"Tarion? Not *Prince* Tarion?" Her frown deepened.

"I'm trying to form a friendship here and learn their secrets. I can't do that while hiding behind stiff titles and formal pleasantries. I've had to get close to the prince." I shrugged and took a sip of tea.

"Not too close, I hope?"

"He is handsome, but I'm keeping my head about me. You know nothing means more to me than keeping my kingdom safe and breaking my curse. Love would only be a distraction."

"I hope so. I really do."

Her gaze turned back to the snow, every part of her frozen in thought as she studied the small flakes descending from the sky and piling on the balcony railing. Occasional clumps fell from the banister to the soft cushion of the landing, leaving tiny imprints in the sheet of white.

I'd sat beside my sister and watched the snow fall many times before, but never like this. Never with so much hanging in the air between us. Everything still felt tense.

After a long silence, Elis raised her cup back to her lips and took a gulp. Then she set it down on the desk beside her and rose.

"I should be going. I mostly came to remind you about Mama's birthday dinner in a few weeks to be sure you attend."

She only came for a day?

"I'll be there." I tried not to sound too disappointed that she was leaving so soon, and instead held myself back as if it didn't bother me. Instead of moving after her to the door, I went to the desk and quickly wrote out a note.

"Give this to Cassian for me. It's important." I handed her the note, and she shoved it into her pocket. Now Cassian would know the location of the armies, and we could pull forces back from the east side.

She turned to leave, but glanced back. "Be careful, okay?"

"I promise. This won't be like the time with the baby dragon."

That earned a small smile from her, but she didn't say more, leaving me with the feeling that so much went unsaid.

We'd attempted to restore our sisterhood, but there were walls up now that had never been there, and I didn't know how to climb over them. I didn't know if I wanted her to cross mine.

It would be better once I break the curse and save Elenvérs. Then I'd have my sister back along with my life.

I waited on the upstairs balcony, wrapped in my parka to watch my sister leave. Moments after I looked over the railing, I saw her red parka and brown horse speed from the castle. She waved behind her, not at me, but at someone down below. I leaned over as much as I could to see who she had waved to, but it was too far away to see. Probably only a stable boy who she'd managed to charm with a few sentences and tilt of the head.

She'd be a helpful ally to have here, and I would have asked her to stay if I had thought she would've said yes.

As coldness blanketed my skin, I wrapped my thick parka around my arms and nestled into it, retreating indoors.

The movement loosened a pin, and I freed an arm to replace it in my hair. The customs of the ladies here involved braided buns and twisted updos, neither of which I was skilled at styling, though I did enjoy the way the braids looked like a crown wrapped around my head. One day that crown would be real.

Just as I'd finished pushing the pin in place, Tarion came barreling around the corner. His suit jacket flapped at his waist and his dark hair bounced with his steps as he waved his arms wildly at me.

"He's here. The mercenary is here."

Any thoughts of Elis flew from my mind as nerves seeped in. "Is he in the castle?"

Tarion shook his head, bending over to pant. "No, I'm going to alert my father then lead the mercenary into the castle. Take this," he pushed a large key into my hands, "And go to the room to find the letter. Mind you, wait a few minutes so you aren't caught."

Just as fast as he'd come, he took off again back the way he'd come. I shoved the key deep into my pocket, letting it click against my wish.

Deep breath. Go to the room. Wait for King Maven. Unlock the door. Find the letter. Wait for Tarion. Switch the letter. Another deep breath.

Since my part of the plan relied on sneaking into the room after King Maven hid the note, I didn't need to rush to get there. In fact, rushing would make me look suspicious. I counted my slow steps as the long walk took me toward the upstairs office that overlooked the village below.

The walk took an eternity, and I shivered with more fear than I'd felt in the face of the baby dragon years ago.

This was where I'd find out if I could trust Tarion.

If we succeeded on this mission, he would earn a portion of my trust, though never my allegiance. If guards walk in a moment after I do to arrest me, then I'll know he was playing me all along.

Quite the gamble I was taking.

"Lady Rowan, did your lovely sister leave already?" Lindy came around the corner with a basket of folded clothes on her hip. Her hair was braided tightly over her shoulder, and she held one end of the braid as she walked.

"Yes, she just left." I crossed my hands as I slowed my walk, swaying from side to side as if I had nothing better to do than stroll the halls.

"Pity, Lady Elis is a sweet girl. Hmm. Well, I'm just headed to your room now to tend to the fire and put these away." She motioned to the basket of clothes.

"Ah, would you mind terribly taking my parka with you? It would save me the walk." The large coat would get in my way as I tried to move inconspicuously through the castle. She nodded and took the coat from me.

She gave me a funny look. "Are you alright? You're breathing rather quickly. Shall I fetch the doctor? The flu seems to be going around recently, got three of the maids this past week." She pressed her hand to my forehead and scrunched her brows.

I stepped back. "I'm alright, thank you though." Only worried about walking into a trap. Only worried about dying at the king's hand today.

She gave me another concerned look before trotting away. When I placed my hand to my chest, my heart pounded underneath. For a moment I chastised myself, both for putting myself in this situation and for allowing my worries to show, but I did this for Elenvérs. Tarion hadn't been honest about his armies surrounding Elenvérs. I shouldn't be trusting him now.

For Elenvérs.

I continued my slow walk to the upstairs office, stopping often to peer out windows and greet those I passed, biding my time. I paused at the top landing of the stairs and listened to the sounds around me. Distant voices drifted through the air, muffling as they hit the red tapestries on the wall. The thin, short corridors differed from the wide, long ones of downstairs, but more windows provided bright sunlight to flood the hallway.

I'd walked these floors each day this past week in preparation for the mercenary, save for yesterday when I entertained my sister. We knew which way Tarion would come in through and guessed which way King Maven would come and leave by. Both paths met at the office, where a third, narrower corridor intersected on its way to attic space.

There, in that thin corridor filled with dust, I sat in wait for the king and his mercenary.

Padded footsteps warned me of their arrival. I held my breath.

"Xavi." The king's voice broke the silence, deep with authority.

"Your Majesty," the mercenary replied. Footsteps grew closer to each other, and the muffled sound of fabric and paper mixed together.

"Thank you," said King Maven. "I'll have your reply by morning. Tarion, show him to his usual room."

Here is where he proved his loyalty to me.

"Actually, Father," Tarion spoke, "I have an urgent matter that needs your attending."

"Eh? What sort of matter is this? I hope you haven't gone and gotten yourself into any more trouble, have you?"

"No, Father."

More footsteps, then hushed voices. Soon, the king huffed loud enough that I could hear. "Alright. One moment." Just as Tarion predicted, he opened the office door.

A few moments later he exited and locked the door with a click.

"Show the mercenary to his room. I will attend to this on my own, since you've shown yourself utterly incapable of handling a little guard dispute." His voice dripped with annoyance as his heavy footsteps led him away.

Left behind, the mercenary mirrored the attitude of the king. "I know the way to my own room, boy," he scoffed. "I can see myself there."

Tarion didn't say anything more, and I waited until the mercenary's footsteps faded to emerge from my hiding place. Tarion stood outside the door with his hands in his pockets and his lips pulled in a straight line.

"What did you tell your father?" I asked him.

He shook his head as he reached out his hand for the key, which I passed to him. "It's nothing. It won't matter soon. Let's get this letter."

Tarion didn't struggle to unlock the door, and together we darted into the room to find General Valerie's note. Tarion found it within moments and brought it to the desk to open. He held the letter close and read it quickly.

"What does it say?"

"Their army sits outside Yule Point; he wants orders to march."

I wouldn't risk getting false information from him, so I snatched the paper away. Sure enough, the note stated that they were ready to attack at the king's orders.

"Yule Point? That's to the east of us." I'd just sent a letter with Elis telling Cassian to pull back from the east.

"They have you surrounded." Tarion didn't sound surprised. He lowered himself to a chair that sat behind a desk and got to work writing a letter. "We will write one from General Valerie to the king. Bring that closer so I can copy the handwriting. I'll say they've heard the plague hit Yule Point and they want to wait it out. Everyone is frightened by the plague. Then we will write one from my father to General Valerie ordering him to pull back and wait for his orders to attack. This is brilliant."

I retreated to the window while he wrote the letters, staring out over the village and wishing I could warn Yule Point of the army that sat outside their small town. Yule Point was a village made of retired warriors and their families, and it wasn't guarded. Very few western points were shielded from a potential attack, so with a small army they could get almost to the castle before being defeated. But if they attacked from both sides, we would be stretched too thin to defend properly without our allies.

We'd long suspected ThornHigh of desiring the riches of the Elenvérs mines, but we didn't think they would attack so soon. Annon had warned us they would, but our naivety now put our country in jeopardy.

Tarion finished both notes and slid one in the hidden compartment of the desk.

"There, he will find that later, and I will hand this to the mercenary." He picked up the real note. "We don't need this one anymore." He tore it and stuffed the pieces into his pockets. "Best be off now, don't want to get caught."

Quiet as could be, we slipped from the room, relocked it, and parted ways. I circled back to wait for King Maven after Tarion had left, and watched as the king returned to unlock the door, slip inside, and fetch the note.

I waited for a reaction from him to indicate our swap had failed. Based on how quickly he came back out of the room, he hadn't opened the note yet. His eyes scanned the halls before he returned downstairs, and I waited a few minutes before following behind.

At the top of the stairs, I froze, recognizing the king's voice. The wall dug into my back as I pushed against it, turning my head so I could hear but not be seen.

"Thank you for your friendship," he spoke. "It's been a valuable asset to us."

"Of course."

A shiver ran down my spine, and my fingers turned cold. I knew that voice. Annon. If I wanted any further proof that he was against Elenvérs, here it was. He was plotting against his own country.

They didn't speak again, and the stairway fell silent. After I'd taken a few deep breaths, I crossed the corridor and found a back stairwell.

Back in my room, I decided to do something Cassian and I had vowed not to do. I used the wind messages to tell him about the attack, and hoped the message wasn't intercepted.

Tarion had earned back a bit of my trust, but my kingdom came first and I couldn't rely on him to save it.

Chapter Twenty-Three

I COULDN'T BE DISTRACTED by the fancy evening gowns or the lively music or the sweet wine. My mind never left Yule Point and the people who lived there. I'd sent Cassian another wind message about the army's positions but there'd been no reply.

"Have you heard any news?" I asked Tarion, leaning close to him.

"It's been weeks and you haven't relaxed, Rowan." He raised his brows as he looked me in the eyes. "Everything is going to be fine." He took a sip of his drink and looked around the room while I tried not to be annoyed at his serenity.

It'd been weeks, *weeks*, since we heard anything. No word from the king on his troops, and no reply from General Valerie at the request to pull back.

"Rowan, really. Relax. You look ready to kill everyone here."

I loosened the tense muscles in my face, but nothing about this was enjoyable to me.

"I'll rest when Elenvérs is safe." I set down my glass. "Send word while I'm away if something happens."

THE RICH AROMAS OF the room hit me like a strong wind as soon as I stepped into the small shop. When I stomped on the rug to release snow from my boots, Sanna flew down the stairs. "Ah, m'lady. Back again I see. Here for the bracelet?" She danced behind the counter to fetch a small box and began tying a ribbon around it.

"I am, thank you."

I had brought food for some of the villagers, specifically Allie and her mother, and placed a parcel down on Sanna's front desk. Outside, my horse stomped his feet as strangers rubbed his mane. A few bags were secured to his side.

"Going on a trip, I see?" Sanna asked.

"It's my mother's birthday in a few days, so I'm on my way to see her." I trailed a finger over a glass case. Emerald earrings, a strand of pearls, and a diamond ring lay on velvet.

"Is the ring gone?" I asked, noticing the bare place beside the earrings. I'd debated purchasing the ring for Lady Trelluse as well, but the beautiful rose jewelry was no longer beside the window.

"A handsome fellow came in last week to buy it. Said it was for his lass. Quite the romantic sort, he went on and on about this girl—called her his queen."

"Lucky her."

In the end, I chose a simple necklace and paid Sanna for the pieces. She wrapped them together and asked me to tell my friends of her shop.

I tucked the small boxes into my horse's satchel next to my wish then mounted him.

"Ready, boy?" He neighed. "Good. Let's go home."

THE TRIP ACROSS THE mountains took eight long days, though we had to slow down for Wellinsway Path, where the windy trail was frozen over. Then we had to take a detour around Avalanche Crossing because, true to its name, an avalanche covered the way. I breathed a deep sigh of relief upon seeing the Northern Crossing and the familiar town of Harrowhut with their vibrant rugs covering their homes in the caves.

Harrowhut may one day turn to ThornHigh, but for now, we were home.

Beneath me, my horse relaxed. and his step quickened.

My joy deepened when a few hours later the tall turrets of the Elenvérs palace came into view, peeking over the side of the mountain, keeping watch over her towns as the sun set. As I drew closer, other features came into view: the thin balconies that wrapped along the upper hallways of the great hall, the wide barracks attached to the west point, and the caves of our people.

With the light almost gone from the sky, the palace shone deep blue, with the occasional twinkle from icicles clinging to the eaves.

By the time I'd put my horse away in the stables and climbed the stairs to the palace, the only light in the sky was the night stars, showing off their beauty.

As I entered the castle, three different urges tempted me. The first was to find Cassian and ask about Yule Point to be sure they were safe, and to inform King Olin of the armies that surrounded us.

The second urge was to find Elis and mend the broken bonds between us. Even as Cassian was proving himself a loyal ally, I yearned for a trusted friend.

The third urge, and a greatly compelling one, was to go to bed. Night had fallen over Elenvérs, promising a tomorrow full of many important conversations.

As I reached the doors to the palace, I took a moment to look out over the mountains and the home that I'd missed.

My gaze stretched further, across the endless mountains. Somewhere, over the range to the west, across the Wandering Mountains, an army lay, waiting to attack. Sharpening their blades, polishing their shields, preparing to bring death upon the mountainside.

That vision battled against my desire for sleep and turned me toward Cassian's room instead of my own.

My first steps into the castle were a sharp reminder of the differences between Elenvérs and ThornHigh, as my shoes clinked against glass floors and the corridor was bathed in an icy glow. I'd never felt unsafe in my home before, but it was a far cry from the fortified stone walls of ThornHigh with their ever-burning flames.

Ice can crack. If we didn't stop the attack, this ice would shatter.

One thing that was similar, however, was the guard that peeked at me curiously as I knocked on the door of the prince. While I'd ignored the guard outside Tarion's room, I gave this one an innocent smile. Cassian and I had spent our youth in each other's companionship, and even this late hour didn't feel scandalous to be at his door.

Still holding my bags, I used my foot to knock, then prayed he answered quickly so this guard would stop staring at me.

Tarion had proved he could be trusted to a small extent, but Cassian's loyalty was still in question. This would be my test for him, watching his initial reaction to finding me outside his door. If he looked nervous, even a little bit, I'd know not to trust him.

But when the door opened and he saw me, his face broke into a large smile. "You're here. You're safe," he breathed.

Despite my bags weighing down my arms, he pulled me into a hug.

That expression told me everything I needed to know. Cassian could be trusted. No one grins that big when their enemy shows up at their door unannounced.

"Hi, Cassian. The bags." I grunted under the pressure, and he set me down.

"Of course, let me take those. Come in. Did you just get here? I didn't know if you'd make it for Lady Trelluse's birthday." He used her formal title for the sake of the guard outside the room, who no doubt had confirmed his suspicions after Cassian's eager reaction to me.

"I wouldn't miss your mama's birthday," I said after I closed the door behind me. Once it was shut, I leaned against it and sighed, dropping my remaining bags to the floor.

Cassian wore a simple white tunic and black pants with black, wooly socks. His brown hair had grown out and was slightly wet. He picked up a bear-fur jacket from his bed and threaded his arms through it.

His room was as clean as General Barrett's, though far more decorated. One wall held so many paintings that I couldn't see the ice behind it. The paintings weren't any that I recognized and each depicted wildlife that I'd never seen. Bright flowers, endless fields of grass, lush forests, a rolling ocean, all vivid and alive so if I stood close enough, I'd feel like I was there. It was beautiful.

He saw me gazing at the paintings and coughed. "What have you learned from ThornHigh?"

All at once, I remembered why I'd come, and I gasped. "Yule Point! Are they safe?"

The darkness that fell over Cassian's face gripped my heart. He leaned against the side of the bed and crossed his arms.

"They were attacked a few weeks ago." He sat on the edge of the bed. "A small army has taken control. They sent a messenger offering peace if we surrender."

My knees wobbled and I slumped against the door. Either General Valerie ignored King Maven's request to stand down, or Tarion didn't send that letter. All trust I had in him diminished as I breathed out.

"They have us surrounded. We've greatly underestimated their numbers. We need to call on our allies *now*."

"Already have. We sent word as soon as the messenger came. In the meantime, we've started subtle evacuations. It'd be months before allies can get here though. Westfallen has had their own problems recently, and Vestalin is dealing with skirmishes on their southern borders." Cassian ran his hand through his loose hair.

"Blast. What about Osmelee?"

"Their army is small, but we've heard nothing back."

I moved from the ground to one of the chairs in his room that faced his paintings. I rubbed my temples to think. "General Valerie's men are on the western border. We hadn't expected that, but they still must either navigate the Wandering Mountains, or go around them. That gives us time. And I don't think they plan to march straight to the castle until they get word from King Maven. I'm disappointed though. Those soldiers weren't supposed to march on Yule Point. Didn't you get my wind message?"

Cassian's brows curved, then his face paled. "Rowan, I haven't gotten a message from you in a month. Have you gotten my messages?" My expression gave him my answer, and he groaned. "Have you sent anything that could incriminate you?"

Again, my expression gave myself away.

"It shouldn't be possible to steal wind messages." Cassian moved to the window where he pounded on the sill and yelled in frustration.

"Yet someone is. We can't send any more."

He cursed vividly. "No, we can't." He cursed again, then pointed at me. "You aren't returning to ThornHigh. Something is going on, and it's not safe there anymore." With another growl, he turned to stare out over the night. "Stealing wind messages...how are they doing that?"

I stood. "I can still help Elenvérs. I'm more useful at ThornHigh than I am here. Here I can do nothing."

He glanced back at me. "You're more alive here than you are there. I don't trust a place that can steal wind messages. If they can steal ours, they can steal others. We need to have the entire kingdom stop using wind messages. Blast."

"I understand you're frustrated, but you can't force me to remain here."

He turned with a huff. "Have you learned anything useful during your time at their court?"

"Yes. I knew that General Valerie's men were stationed there and planned to march on Yule Point. I read the letter from the general myself. King Maven intends to wipe out Elenvérs, and he has the numbers to do so without our allies' help. He won't wait long and risk them coming to save us. Tarion, however, wants to merge our two kingdoms into sister countries: one army but two kings."

Cassian's face remained blank, either expecting to hear more, or soaking in the information.

"I also learned that their large forces are located on the western side, waiting across the Wandering Mountains," I continued. "I realize they just attacked in the east, but it's the west I'm worried about. Didn't you get my note from Elis?"

His face scrunched. "Elis said she had a note from you, but she lost it. Are you certain of this information?"

How could she be so careless? "Yes, I'm certain. I snuck into General Barrett's room to uncover it."

His eyes bulged wide. "Do you know who that is? He's going to kill you. You definitely aren't going back now."

I smirked. "It was weeks ago, and he hasn't noticed anyone was in his room."

"He will."

I swallowed another piece of bread. "He won't know because I didn't take anything."

Cassian let out a dry laugh. "You're going to get killed." He drew nearer to me. "Tell me more about Tarion's plan?"

"Ah yes, it's quite interesting. He wants Elenvérs and ThornHigh to be united like they once were, under the same banner with two kings. He doesn't think either country is strong enough to survive the next hundred years on their own. ThornHigh is powerful, but they have no allies and no room to expand. Elenvérs is rich, but we are running out of resources to trade with, and ThornHigh can blockade us and starve us out. Really, there's many ways our two countries can destroy each other, but with their army and our wealth and allies, our countries have a better shot."

Cassian nodded. "And people won't protest, because we are keeping separate kings, so no one is really taking over the other."

"Exactly. It's not a bad idea, but with our allies, I don't think we need ThornHigh."

"No, he's right. I've already run through the situations in my mind. I'm surprised Tarion thought of it too, but I've been planning for the same thing—a merge between our countries."

My mouth dropped open. "Are we really so desperate?"

He nodded. "It's not something we like to broadcast to the people, but we are dangerously low on resources. ThornHigh doesn't have much either, but we have a better chance together. It opens trade routes for the both of us. What we really need is to move back to our homeland."

That wasn't an option. Our southern homeland was too far away for all the people to travel to. It'd take a year to migrate all the families, and there was no telling what state that land was in now, or if it was occupied.

"We can't trust ThornHigh. The plan sounds decent, but it can't work," I said.

Cassian tapped his chin. "Who does Tarion say he wants on the Elenvérs throne? He will rule ThornHigh himself, I'm guessing?"

I nodded. "He said he wants you on our throne. We both know it will be me, though, no matter what Tarion wants."

Cassian chuckled. "Perhaps. But Tarion would force his own man on the throne, just as I intend to put one of our own men on his throne."

"Who, Briggs?" I almost laughed at the idea of quiet, sensitive Briggs on the ThornHigh throne.

"Actually, yes. If you survive the curse, as you likely will with your wish, you'll get your kingdom. But if the curse takes you, I'll step back in as Elenvérs heir, and put Briggs on the ThornHigh throne."

Knowing I was his first choice brought a sliver of peace. A few months ago, he'd threatened to kill me if I broke the curse. Since then, we'd formed an uneasy alliance, but if he didn't need me dead to keep his throne, that opened room for further trust in him.

I sorted out what we knew. "So, you and Tarion both plan to unite the kingdoms, while King Maven plans to destroy ours. King Maven and his generals should be our first focus, along with Annon who is working alongside them."

Despite how simply I'd stated it, Cassian's jaw fell toward his chest.

"Annon wouldn't. He loves Elenvérs too much."

I shrugged, taking slight pleasure in knowing so much that he didn't. "Not as much as he loves planning and winning wars, and King Olin wasn't giving him that. He's working with King Maven, I'm sure of it."

A grunt escaped Cassian's lips. "I'll keep an eye on him. Anything else I need to know?"

The last bit of information brought me no joy to share. "Ah, yes. Annon knows I'm the true heir of Elenvérs." While I often forgot it, that bit affected Cassian as much as it did me and I held my breath to wait for his reaction.

He threw his hands in the air and groaned. "Things are in quite a mess, aren't they?"

"They've been better."

He stayed on the chair staring toward his feet and stroking his chin. "How in Elenvérs name did Annon find out?"

"He guessed."

He snorted as he leaned forward on his knees. "The biggest secret this kingdom has kept in...forever, and he just guessed?"

"Do you remember that day when we were three, and Annon, after seeing me with my mother, pricked my finger with a spindle to see if I'd fall asleep?" I asked Cassian, whose eyes widened. "He's suspected since that day, and then he found a painting of Mama's red-headed brothers, which furthered his resolve."

Cassian stared at me. "I've never heard of that before. He pricked you with a spindle? At merely three years old?"

A burning sensation pierced my finger, reminding me of the pain. I'd thought of that moment every day since, how Annon almost sent me into a deep sleep and my father gave him permission to do so. I almost lost everything that day, and they'd—both Cassian and my father—stood by to watch.

Each day since then, Cassian stood by while I fought for the life that ought to have been mine. Any traveling he did wasn't to forsaken swamps in search of a tiny flower, it was to other kingdoms to meet their kings. Those paintings on the wall, pictures of places I'd never been to, he'd probably seen them all.

"Yes, well," I said through a strained smile. "It failed to put me to sleep. But he's going to expose my parents as soon as the curse takes me."

Cassian sunk his head into his hands. "This would have been helpful to know much sooner."

"When would I have told you? Before or after you told me you would kill me if I broke the curse? Or have you forgotten about that?"

He chuckled, a light dancing in his eyes that was so different from the darkness of a few months ago.

"Fair point," he said. "Is it too late to apologize for that? Things have been stressful for me this year as all my time went to training to take the throne, which you'd just shown me I would lose. Forgive me if I overreacted." He smiled at the memory as if it were a joke now. As if I hadn't fretted many nights over Cassian slaying me once I broke my curse.

My brow raised at his serenity over the situation. "Overreacted? You threatened to kill me."

He shrugged "It's as I said, rough year. You've no idea the grueling training you're in for before becoming queen. Truthfully, now that I've had time to process that you'll break the curse, I think this could be great. As king I wouldn't have been allowed to travel like I've wanted or had time to paint." He gestured to the pictures on his wall. "You've freed me from a responsibility that I realized I didn't want. And I won't be removed from a position of power. I'll still remain on as an advisor."

While I ran through his words to find the lie within them, he smiled at me. "Looks like I don't need you to die after all."

I grunted, hoping he meant what he'd said. "I appreciate it. I trust that you want me alive more than I trust Annon or Tarion at this point."

My trust in Tarion was once again unsteady—a constant battle between moments where I was certain he meant well and times where I couldn't be certain of anything. I longed for a clarity that I worried he'd never give. There was no way to know if Yule Point got attacked because General Valerie ignored the king's request, or because Tarion never sent the order to retreat, but since I didn't know any respectable generals who didn't listen to their king's orders, I was led to believe Tarion changed out the notes as soon as I'd left.

He'd tricked me. For all I knew, he'd been working with his father all along, making my place at ThornHigh far more dangerous than I'd thought.

The matters with Tarion bothered me much more than my wind messages getting intercepted.

"Rowan," Cassian's tone lowered as he looked me in the eye. "I haven't always been the friend to you that you deserved. I know that. But I'm with you now, and I vow to protect you—from Tarion, ThornHigh, Annon, all of it. I'll do what I can to save you."

For the past few months, as threats came at me from each side, Cassian had proven himself to be a faithful ally and worthy of a portion of trust, but we hadn't fought for each other. We'd aligned for Elenvérs. Our love for our country and desire to control the throne bound us to the same cause. It was a similar bond that I had with Tarion, knowing he fought for his throne too.

But Cassian offered something more now—a loyalty, not out of love for Elenvérs, but for commitment to me. He offered a close friendship I'd only ever had with Elis.

Cassian's unrelenting love for Elis had always stirred an ugly jealousy within my heart. It made it easier to hate him, but I needed an ally now more than ever.

And here Cassian was, offering me his allegiance, not for Elenvérs, but for me.

Ironic that when my relationship with my sister was strained for the first time, another relationship should step up, ready to forge an alliance. The years had proven how strong the bond between sisters could be, perhaps the bond between Cassian and I could be equally powerful.

"Thank you," I said. "It'll be nice to have you on my side."

Chapter Twenty-Four

KING OLIN AND QUEEN Marigold spent most of the day neglecting their royal duties to celebrate Lady Trelluse's birthday with her. Her face tensed when they asked, but she couldn't say no once Queen Marigold begged her to grant these precious last memories with her daughter.

If I needed any further proof that my parents had given up trying to break the curse, here it was. They treated Lady Trelluse's birthday like a funeral for me.

My mother cried as she hugged me and spent most of the day attached to my side. When she asked about my time at ThornHigh, I told her of the prince's hospitality, leaving out the other bits so I didn't have to see her expression scrunch with worry.

King Olin kept his distance, but his gaze often rested on me. He'd visibly aged since I'd seen him last, though it'd only been a month. His gray hair was thinner, and the bags under his eyes sagged almost to the bottom of his nose. When he stood next to Lord Trelluse, a man with few wrinkles and lots of energy, they could be mistaken for father and son, not friends of the same age.

I wondered if Lady Trelluse ever hated my mother for asking so much from her. She'd given up her only son and gained a daughter that would never truly be hers.

Lady Trelluse's face stayed tight through my parents' visit until dinnertime when King Olin placed a hand on his wife's back. "We should let them have time together."

Her lip trembled, but one look at Lady Trelluse's pleading face kept her from arguing. "Do you return to ThornHigh tomorrow?" She looked at me with tears pooling on her lids, sending guilt coursing through me.

One day wouldn't give her anything more than this—hiding in Lord Trelluse's home, crying over a future she didn't believe I could achieve. Until I broke the curse, we'd never get more. She couldn't walk through the palace with me as a mother, or sit beside me at the Full Moon Feasts, or properly teach me how to be queen one day.

She was the only one that my heart called mother. But until I broke the curse, I couldn't fully be her daughter.

Her hurt was evident, and I could save her from it.

I'd kept the wish to myself as a safety precaution. If no one knew about it, no one could try to steal it. The witch had warned me of how valuable they were. I told myself I was being smart to keep the wish between myself and Elis, and Cassian who unfortunately found out, but now I realized it was also selfish. My parents didn't know I would break the curse. They didn't know I was free.

I could give up a little bit of my security to erase their pain.

So, I dipped my hand into my pocket.

I hoped I wasn't making a huge mistake.

"Before anyone goes, I want to show you something," I started. Elis eyed my pocket and slowly shook her head, but I didn't listen. This wasn't for me; this was for my parents. To soothe their worries and dry their tears.

I pulled out the wish.

"This is a wish. This is strong enough to break my curse. You don't have to worry about losing me."

The room stood still.

Then my mother fell to her knees and sobbed. King Olin's face went white, then he stumbled toward me.

"Where did you find this?" he asked in a raspy voice.

"Witch Marlogne gave it to me."

His glossy eyes widened. "She gave it to you? There are only a few of these in the world."

His hands closed over mine as he looked into my eyes. "You're saved. You saved yourself."

Then he collapsed into me with a tight embrace and cried into my shoulder. For a moment, I froze in shock, his scent that I remembered as a baby flooding my senses. His touch felt foreign to me, but that piney scent reminded me of a different time when he looked at me like I was his world.

As he held on, my arms squeezed him, thanking him for the affection I didn't think he'd give me again.

Any reservations I had about sharing my secret were gone. It was worth it to give them this.

With a coarse thumb he stroked my cheek, then pulled away, taking his warm scent with him.

Then everyone was around me with tears and hugs and excited plans about the future.

"Have you thought of how you'll use the wish?" my mother asked. I explained my plan to them.

"Why don't you use it now to stop the snow?" my mother pressed.

"It can't be a future request. I'll wait until the week before my birthday to stop the snow from falling."

Lady Trelluse continued to shake with sobs. Elis rolled her eyes.

"Must everyone cry?" Elis asked. She hadn't moved from the chair most of the day, where she sat with her legs crossed and twiddled with the strings of her tunic. Cassian sat in the chair next to her in his pointed brown boots, navy surcoat, and silver buckles. He, like Elis, hadn't spoken much today, likely thinking through the information I'd given him. I didn't know if he shared any of this information with King Olin.

Lady Trelluse dabbed under her eyes. "I can't help it. My daughter is saved." She and my mother squeezed each other's hands.

"She can be queen now," my mother exclaimed.

All at once, everyone remembered Cassian and shifted their gazes to look at him.

He laughed.

"I'm fine. I'll get to travel and paint, and once I get my fill of adventure, I'll take a place at the table of advisors and continue serving Elenvérs." He said it so casually, almost as if this is what he wanted the whole time.

King Olin clapped him on the back. "We can cancel that trip to the Tekmar Hills next week, son."

I almost asked what trip, but Lady Trelluse wrapped me in her arms too tightly for me to be able to speak.

"Besides," Cassian said. "Rowan still can't produce an heir, so there's a good chance it'll be my kids who take her place one day. My bloodline will still claim the throne."

For a moment I was offended that he thought that was up to him to decide, but I realized it didn't matter. Cassian and Elis's bloodline would be good rulers.

"We'll see," I said with a shrug.

"And if you marry Tarion." Cassian watched me closely. "Then my kids can rule both Elenvérs and ThornHigh."

For the second time that day, the room stood still.

Elis's face pinched as if she'd been struck by an arrow.

My mother clasped her hands over her mouth and squealed.

King Olin paled. "Is there something going on with the prince?" They all leaned closer.

"They are pretty close," Cassian added.

I shook my hands. "No, we're just friends."

"He doesn't seem like your type," Elis said from the couch.

I raised my brow. She'd met him twice. How would she know if he was my type?

"And how about Briggs?" Lady Trelluse took advantage of the moment to ask Elis. "Will you be getting married soon?"

Elis had never expressed a desire to marry young, at least not before she'd had her fill of adventure. She pursed her lips. "In good time."

Lady Trelluse looked pleased.

As soon as everyone had finished asking their questions and giving their hugs, King Olin and my mother took their leave. They looked much happier leaving now than they had earlier. I was glad to give that to them.

"Remember," I said before anyone left. "Don't tell a soul about this wish. Many people would try to steal it from me."

They all promised. Then my parents left, and birthday celebrations began. As the evening progressed, we morphed back into the family that we once were, laughing through the evening, playing games at the table, forgetting about the worries that surrounded us.

The few times Cassian glanced at me, I could tell his mind wasn't settled, but each time the look passed.

We stayed up until Lady Trelluse looked ready to fall asleep in her chair, elated but exhausted. "Come on, love. Let's go to bed." Lord Trelluse placed a hand on her back. With a soft look at us, he said, "Thank you all for the perfect evening."

As his door clicked shut, Cassian sighed as he rose. "Tomorrow we need to speak, Rowan. I don't think it's wise for you to return to ThornHigh."

Elis glanced between us.

"I still think I can be helpful," I said.

"Or you could die." He put up his hands before I could protest. "It's late. We'll talk tomorrow. Good night."

Then he left, leaving just me and Elis, who headed straight for our bedroom. "Can we speak?" She didn't turn around as I followed her. "Elis, it feels like something's wrong between us, and I don't know how to fix it."

She settled onto her bed and pulled the covers over her feet as she leaned against the headboard and thought for a few moments. I perched on my bed to wait.

"It's not you," she started. "It feels like our relationship is changing, and I think it needs to."

I frowned. "Because of the curse?"

"Partly." She nodded, pulling her hair back to fasten it. "The last day of your eighteenth year is coming, and once it does, things will be different. You'll be claimed by your parents and take your place as the future queen. Our relationship will never be what it once was. Two sisters who do everything together—that's not us anymore."

"It is different, but it doesn't have to be strained." I gripped the cotton sheets at my side.

She placed her hand against her forehead. "I know. I'm sorry, I don't know what's gotten into me recently. Things have been weird between us, but you and Cassian seem close now."

"Who would have guessed, right? Turns out he's a decent man." I released the blanket, wiggling my toes beneath it.

She smiled, turning to face me. Her hair wrinkled against the pillow. "What did he mean when he said you could die?"

"It's complicated."

Then I explained it all to her, King Maven's plan to destroy Elenvérs, Tarion's plan to bind our kingdoms together, and Cassian's plan to put himself, and either me or Briggs on the throne.

"And what's your ideal plan?" she asked when I'd finished.

It took me a few moments to answer. "Me breaking the curse, and our allies getting here in time to save us from ThornHigh. I'm not opposed to merging, but I think it'll be messy if we do. We are running low on resources though, so a merge might be smart."

"Hm." She stared at her blanket for a while as she thought. "And if we merged, who would you put on the ThornHigh throne?"

"Cassian." I didn't think before answering that time. She squinted in response. Suddenly, I realized if Briggs took the throne as Cassian wanted, it'd make Elis queen one day. I opened my mouth to ask her if she'd want that, but she spoke first.

"I think you should keep Tarion there."

"What?" I didn't think Briggs would be the best king, but I trusted him more than Tarion.

"You said it yourself, a merge will be messy, but not if they keep their king. Let Tarion remain their heir, and you eliminate an inevitable rebellion from ThornHigh."

If I trusted Tarion enough, I'd do it. But at this point, Cassian had earned my trust and Tarion had not. I wouldn't risk my future in the hands of an untrustworthy man.

"Right now, if Briggs isn't an option, Cassian and I don't have anyone else that we trust enough to sit on the throne. But I know this, I'd rather someone from Elenvérs than Tarion."

Her brows lowered as she shifted in the bed, twiddling with the ends of her cuffed sleeve. "So, if you can't put Cassian or Briggs on the throne, you still wouldn't pick Tarion? I thought you were starting to like him?"

As I replayed our conversations back through my head, I didn't remember saying such a thing. "I said I'm working with him," I clarified. "But I don't trust him. Many things must happen before we make the decision of who will be the two rulers, but I guarantee you that Tarion is planning for his own man on our throne, and King Maven and Annon are planning for there to be no Elenvérs throne to put someone on. Those are the pressing issues."

"And breaking your curse," she added.

With the wish in my pocket, breaking my curse no longer felt like a daunting task. It was more something I would do, and not something I had to worry about.

Together in silence, we shuffled under our warm covers, each left to our own thoughts. When Elis blew out the candle and didn't speak for a while, I thought she'd fallen asleep, but just when sleep almost claimed me, her voice reached through the dark. "Rowan?"

"Hmm?"

"Would you...would you be happy for me, no matter what happens?"

I propped myself up in bed. "What do you mean?"

Rustling came from her side. "I mean, whatever path I choose for my life—knighthood, a life here in Elenvérs, or somewhere else—whoever I marry or wherever I live, will you be happy for me?"

"Is something wrong with you and Briggs?"

She rolled to face me. "Of course not, I just want to know that you support me with whatever I choose."

Elis didn't care what anyone thought of her, that was part of her charm, so I'd never heard her ask if I'd support her, but my answer came swiftly. "Always."

"Thank you," she breathed. "You're the greatest sister I could ask for."

Chapter Twenty-Five

"I AGREE WITH CASSIAN," King Olin said as soon as Cassian and I finished filling him in. "It's too dangerous for you to return to ThornHigh." He leaned against the back of his tall chair at the meeting table, where I'd spent so many times hiding behind the curtains watching.

I wasn't behind the curtains now. My elbows leaned against the table as the other advisors surrounded me, all discussing the fate of Elenvérs.

Rivers looked at me with respect now, a spy who'd brought back information, and I soaked in the expression. I sat in the chair usually occupied by Annon, who we hadn't spoken of in this meeting. Cassian had warned that until I had proof—more proof than witnessing him speaking to their king, he'd pointed out once I'd protested—we couldn't bring it to the advisors.

The other advisors muttered their agreements with the King.

"I think I can still be of use at ThornHigh. I'd like to return."

"Will you go even if I say no?" King Olin's hand shook as he took a sip of water.

After a hesitation, I shook my head. "No, sire."

His shoulders relaxed, but they straightened again when Rivers spoke. "If she wants to go back, I think she should. Especially if she continues to learn their battle placements. If we don't have our people so spread out, we can fight them with larger numbers." She paused to curse. "We never should have let them get so strong."

"How does she know they are all on the western border?" Tristian asked with a voice that dripped in doubt.

"I searched his room."

All heads swiveled toward me.

"You went through General Barrett's room?" Rivers asked in a raised voice. The way she looked at me, I couldn't tell if it was awe at my bravery or my stupidity.

"Yes," I said meekly.

"Huh." She looked to the king. "She's brave. I like her. I say we send her back." Pride curled within me.

"We could send her with guards for protection," Cassian suggested. "I know the perfect man. Lance has been a companion since I was a boy and I trust him with my life. He'd protect her."

King Olin grunted at the idea. "Sending a guard will make it look like we don't trust ThornHigh."

"Isn't it obvious that we don't? We send two emissaries to forge a friendship, and they attack us?" Rivers twisted her knife in her hands as she sat back in her seat.

"That's precisely why she must stay here. It's clear that friendship between our countries won't occur, so her continued presence will be suspicious."

"But," I said. "Tarion personally invited me to join his court. If he plans to merge our kingdoms, then he needs my help. I won't be suspicious to him, King Maven doesn't pay me any mind, and their opinions are the only ones that matter. Besides—" I glanced at Cassian. "Annon is there. He can serve as protection." I hated putting Annon in that glorified position, but I didn't feel bad about using him. At my point, a few nodded their heads.

Rivers spoke, "At the least, she could provide us with a few opportunities we wouldn't otherwise have. In a war, opportunities are good."

All around the table, we looked to the king to wait for his reply. He looked between us all with a shrug and a helpless look on his face. It brought me no delight to band together against him, but returning to ThornHigh was the only way I could continue to fight for Elenvérs. Until our allies arrived, we needed another plan.

"Fine," he said at last with a sigh. "But I am sending you with Lance for protection and I need your word that you will keep him by your side."

"You have my word."

No sooner had I spoken than the doors flew open and Elis stormed into the room. Her hands were balled in fists and red splotches crept over her cheeks and stained her eyes. Her footsteps echoed as if she were pounding each step into the floor.

"Elis, we are in a meeting." Cassian stood with amazing speed, sending his chair crashing down with a boom that vibrated to my bones.

I blinked. In all my years of spying on the meetings, Elis never once came to hear conversations that she had no interest in. She was a soldier, and she would 'fight wherever they told her to fight, no need to participate in the boring discussions.' Something in the dangerous slit of her eyes told me this wouldn't be a boring discussion.

She slid her gaze across the room like a predator while her tight knuckles whitened. Pure rage dwelled in her eyes, and my muscle coiled.

Her eyes hardened at Cassian, and her voice was lethal. "I don't care."

"Sister." I stood with equal speed and shot Cassian a look to remind him that Elis was not his sister here. He righted his chair and eased himself back into it, gripping the armrest tight enough that the wood groaned.

Elis's eyes flickered to mine then back to the others. "I just heard that the soldiers sent to Brisburn perished. Our cousin, Hendrick, died."

Brisburn. I recognized the name of the place where men had gone missing in the night. We'd sent a small band of soldiers to find out why. From the grim look on the advisors' faces, this was not new information. Cassian hung his head, and Elis gave a dry laugh.

"Ah, so you all knew. When did you plan to tell me?" Thankfully, this time she looked at me instead of Cassian, but I could sense her pushing her anger through me to him.

"You'd be informed when it was the right time." King Olin stepped in before Elis could give anything away.

She shifted her glare from me to the king, pausing on Cassian where her lips tightened. His eyes begged for her to leave, but she didn't budge. Rivers and Ebony rose to their feet, but King Olin did not.

"Lady Elis, this is a private meeting," King Olin said.

"I told you to pull those soldiers out, but you didn't listen." Pain cleaved her tone.

King Olin's voice was laced with authority. "I made a decision, and it is not for you to question that."

She jabbed her finger in his direction. "My cousin died because you didn't listen to me.' Tears rolled down her cheeks.

Evidently, when Elis and I were speaking last night, she left out certain details of her time here. There was an important conversation that I'd missed, and I found myself lost between the two of them.

King Olin stood. "Sir Hendrick died protecting his kingdom. And I do not need to take the word of a young girl who has limited knowledge about these matters."

"Limited knowledge?" She was practically screaming now. Her hair hung wild around her shoulders, making her look like a fierce lion ready to face us all. She glanced at me again, and I prayed she didn't pull me into whatever this was. As subtly as I could manage, I shook my head.

With a breath deep enough for us all to hear, she stepped back and lowered her voice. "I know more than you think." She sighed again. "More than you think." Then she left, slamming the door behind her.

Rivers twirled her blade around her fingers, amusement dancing in the tilt of her smile. "The Trelluses raised strong-minded daughters. I fear that one's passion may get the better of her."

Though still confused by Elis's sudden outburst, I didn't want it to stain Rivers's opinion of me, so I lowered my head to show that I didn't possess the same recklessness as my sister. Around the room, the advisors shifted in their seats and stared between the door and the king.

"If it pleases Your Majesty, I'll return to ThornHigh today," I said.

King Olin ran his hand back and forth along his forehead. "You may go, Lady Rowan. But please, be careful. And visit Queen Marigold before you go, she's always been fond of you."

"Thank you sire."

I bowed my head and walked from the room. As soon as the door shut behind me, I sprinted after Elis. As I turned the corner, I spotted her at the end of the corridor and yelled out her name. She stopped but didn't turn.

"Elis, what was that?" I caught up to her and pulled her arm so she'd face me. Her eyes were as red as my hair and her brows were slammed together. Heavy tears rolled down her cheeks and her hands were balled in fists.

"Why didn't you defend me?" she shouted. Guards backed away from us.

"Defend you from what? What in Elenvérs' name was that?" I reached for her hand, but she yanked it away.

"That was your father—" She paused. She was moments away from giving away my secret.

She grabbed my hands and pulled me after her. When we'd reached a corridor free from guards, she hissed. "That was your father treating me like a child. I'm so sick of being treated like I don't get a voice!"

Her anger showed through the veins in her forehead. I'd rarely seen her this upset before.

"You're seventeen; you don't get a voice in these matters. You aren't even a knight of Elenvérs yet."

She huffed. "I'm not sure I ever want to be one with the way this king rules the country."

I took a step back, the shock clear on my face. She rolled her eyes and spun around. "I'm leaving, don't follow me."

"Elis."

"Leave me alone, Rowan." She stomped away, and this time I didn't follow.

What happened to her? Without her speaking to me, I couldn't hope to figure it out on my own. All I could do was pack for ThornHigh and hope to save Elenvérs. I'd find a way to help my sister later.

BEFORE I COULD LEAVE, Cassian found me in the Trelluse's living quarters, going over my things. He perched in the doorway with a shoulder against the frame. "Lance is getting ready. He'll meet you in the stables."

I'd met Lance a few times. He seemed like a good man, but I wasn't eager for someone to be stuck to my side the entire time at ThornHigh.

"Thanks. I'll try not to get him killed."

Cassian laughed. "I appreciate it."

Before he could leave, I remembered the weird interaction I wanted to ask him about. "What was that trip to Tekmar Hills that King Olin mentioned? I've been there once." I hoisted a bag over my shoulder.

Cassian helped me lift the other. "Let me guess. Looking for the purple stones that can heal people?"

I blinked.

He nodded. "That's what we were looking for, too."

My stomach knotted. "Is King Olin sick?" He had been looking tired recently.

Cassian shook his head and pushed off from the doorway. "You really don't see it, do you? We were going there for you. For the past several years, King Olin has been obsessed with chasing down anything that might break your curse. We've put countless of potions in your tea and leaves under your pillows at night and anything else that might break the curse."

My mouth opened but no words came out.

"He didn't want to give you false hope, so he didn't say anything. But of course he fought for you."

My heart expanded with a warmth that I'd been missing for years. The proof of my father's love.

Cassian glanced at my mouth hanging open. "He's at peace now that you've figured out how to break it yourself."

My words came at last. "Why in Elenvérs' name didn't you tell me? You knew how much it hurt me that he didn't care."

His hands found his pockets. "Bitterness, I suppose. I liked you believing that his love for me was stronger than any love for you, because that's what I think about you. It was torture to be dragged on all these trips for you as if he didn't think I was worthy of the throne."

Any pain he felt at thinking he was less loved by my parents than I, wouldn't get him pity from me. "You allowed me to live in that pain."

He winced. "I'm not saying it's the best decision I have made. The king doesn't show his true feelings often, so it was especially hard for him to show how much he loves you when he was terrified of losing you. I suspect things will change now."

I could be angry at Cassian for how he treated me. That anger might come later. But right now, one emotion pulsated through my veins with every heartbeat, swelling inside until I could cry.

He fought for me. My father fought for me.

My whole life had been spent with a wall of bitterness built up between us because my father hadn't acted like he cared. Each time I'd come back from some distant marsh having eaten a plant that nearly killed me or fought off some snappy troll or chanted spells into the night until I collapsed with exhaustion, I'd returned to a home where my father hardly looked at me, my sister didn't understand why I fought, and my parents told me it was pointless.

I never gave up, but it killed me that I fought alone. I'd been so, so alone. All I'd had was Elis, and her friendship was slipping through my fingers.

But with the idea that my father had fought for me, maybe I hadn't been as alone as I thought.

"Thank you," I said, my words tearing through a raspy throat.

He nodded, holding the door ajar. "Now go find Lance."

Chapter Twenty-Six

TARION CLAPPED. "AH, GOOD try, captain. I'll have a go at it, shall I?" he asked, picking up his mallet.

"Have a shot," said a guard, tossing him a red ball that fit in the palm of his hand.

Back at ThornHigh, there were no dramatic sisters, complicated fraud princes, or unusual family dynamics to navigate. Here, the people partied. The dining hall morphed into something unrecognizable as thick rugs had been rolled in, the tables were pushed out, and rows of chairs circled the room so the ladies of the court could sit and watch the game.

They called it rubber ball. Seven checkpoints were scattered around the floor, each of which they needed to hit in no particular order before directing the ball back to the start.

All of ThornHigh took the day off to come play. Even the staff were allotted time to play in the evening. I'd already given Lindy the evening off from any of my chores, so she'd have time to join in the activities.

Tarion hit the ball, striking the most difficult of the targets, one buried near the velvet curtains. "I'm coming to beat your record, Harold!" He lifted his mallet in the air, and the reigning guard laughed.

Gentlemen cheered him on while ladies clapped. One could almost forget we were on the brink of war.

It was a silent war, and I doubted most of the lords knew their king marched against Elenvérs. They'd know soon enough. Until then, I'd do all I could to extract information about their armies until the kingdom knew our countries were at war. Then I'd flee the court.

In the meantime, I had a guard from Elenvérs with me.

Lance stood fifteen paces to my right, hardly watching the game as he surveyed the room. Two women giggled as they glanced his direction, most likely because of his pale blonde hair and thin nose—unusual features in ThornHigh as most men held broad bone structure and dark hair. They caught me staring at looked away.

Lance peeked my way to wink.

He slept at the foot of the door and followed me through the day in a way that quickly became comforting, only because of his likable nature. Had he been less agreeable, I'd have sent him back by now. Two swords were strapped to his sides, and he chose a surcoat without sleeves to show off his muscle. By the looks of him, he could pick me up and throw me across the room with ease. I'd asked him to do it yesterday to see if he could, but he said throwing me was against his orders.

At the center of attention, Tarion navigated the ball back to the start in record time, and the room thundered with applause. With a smile that reached his ears, he dropped into three low bows before relinquishing the mallet to the next man in line, who didn't look pleased about going after the crown prince, much less the crowd's favorite.

Tarion slumped into the chair next to me. "He can't beat my time, I've seen his skill with the pole arms," he whispered. "He's not very good."

"He does his best, I'm sure," I replied politely, pulling up my white gloves.

Tarion glanced at me. "You alright?"

My hands sat in my lap, folded over my crossed legs as I watched the next guard hit the rubber ball across the rugs. I'd returned from Elenvérs yesterday and bid my time confronting Tarion to be certain I got my words right. There hadn't been a chance to speak to him anyway, since once I arrived, he spent the rest of the day avoiding me, claiming meetings and princely duties to attend to. The excuses, though possibly valid, fueled my distrust.

"Everything is fine; how were your meetings yesterday?" I pinned a pleasant grin to my face, and Tarion's chest rose.

"Your fake smile is quite unnerving. Is this about Yule Point?"

I dropped the charade. "It most certainly is."

He shifted toward me. "Rowan, I thought about it, and never once has my father asked General Valerie to pull his men back from a fight. Do you know how long it took us to get his men over there? Half a year. We spent half a year positioning them there without Elenvérs noticing—he wasn't going to ask them to back off now. If we sent that letter, the mercenary would no doubt have opened it before stepping foot out of the castle, and he'd know something was wrong. It would cue the king to our plan, and we'd be ruined. Yule Point's loss wasn't big enough to intervene."

My lips pulled tight. "It was big enough to me."

Tarion leaned back into his seat and watched the game with a thoughtful expression. Lance moved a few paces closer to us, but I waved to let him know everything was fine. The sun burst through the windows and warmed my legs. Tarion remained still.

"I have another assignment for you," he said. "It's a tad dangerous, so I wasn't sure about sending you, but it's your decision."

I shifted away from the sunlight. "I don't know if I can trust you."

"He beat me! Lucky shot. Sorry," Tarion pulled his eyes away from the game at my firm look.

"General Valerie's men will wait at Yule Point for our eastern armies to begin attacking. This gives us time, because those armies aren't in place yet. Trouble is that father doesn't trust me enough to tell me where those armies are. Funny, no one seems eager to trust me. Anyhow, I know who he does trust to tell, and one of those men is far too chatty for his own good. He also thinks he's funnier than it pleased the Fates to make him, but that's beside the point. That man will be on patrol tonight, out by the Fontelle Woods. If you spy on them, there's a good chance you'll hear this man, who goes by Bear, talking about the war plans to his patrol partner."

Lance straightened as a man came near us, but he passed by without a glance. Lance relaxed.

Once the man had moved on, I whispered, "No one is that dull." I didn't mention to Tarion that I'd discovered the placement of the soldiers while we snooped through General Barrett's room. Part of me believed that he knew their locations and just wasn't telling me.

"This fellow is. Why he's trusted with the information, I don't know. Think he saved my father's life from an assassin once, so my father keeps him around. Works out for us though, shouldn't be too difficult to overhear something important."

I tried to think of how he might be deceiving me now by leading me to a trap. Sneaking into the forest at night to spy on a chatty patrol guard didn't sound threatening.

"I thought you said it was dangerous?" I asked.

Tarion lowered his voice even further. "Spying on patrol guards is punishable by death. No trial, no hesitation. If they catch you, they will kill you on the spot."

My eyes widened and I glanced at Lance, who saw my worry and shifted closer. I held my hand up to pause him. I repeated the mission back to Tarion to be sure I had it straight. "At night, I sneak out to find the patrol guards, and hope to overhear something important."

"And don't get caught," Tarion added as he stared out over the game.

Lance would be there to keep me safe, along with a few blades of my own. A few chatty patrol men wouldn't scare me. "Sounds simple enough. I'll take the risk."

The corner of his mouth raised. "Good. That's it, Sir Signid! Straight on, you can't miss it! By the way," he leaned toward me. "My half birthday is in a few days and—"

"That's not a thing."

He pulled back and feigned an offended face. "How rude! It happens to be one of my favorite days of the year. I was going to ask you to spend the day in companionship with me, but if you aren't interested—" He straightened his velvet coat.

I peeked to Lance, desperate to escape with him and go over the information Tarion had given me, not remain and talk about celebrations for a made-up occasion. But I grinded my heels into the floor and feigned slight interest.

"It'll include chocolate pudding," he sang.

My eyes rolled. "I'm in. But I'm not getting you a gift. Or if I am, you're only getting half of one. A puzzle with half the pieces missing."

His cheeks dimpled with a grin. "Deal."

AFTER ACQUIRING THE PATROL guard's path, which weaved close to the castle walls then back out in the forest, Lance and I worked together to make our plan. We'd sneak out a few hours after sundown using the servant's entrance in the south-east wing that led into the frozen woods behind the village. Then, we'd find a hiding spot in the trees and wait until we saw the guards. Our plan from there was contingent on the guards' exact movement, but Lance made it clear that he preferred we stay in the pine trees until the guards passed.

"I must say, this is all against my better judgment. King Olin instructed me to protect you, not join you on such expeditions," Lance said. Still, he passed me my leather belt and glanced to the door of my bedchambers.

"These expeditions are the only reason I'm here," I reminded him as I tied the belt around my waist and strapped a few daggers to it. "Don't wear that, it'll be too loud."

With a frown, Lance put aside his metal armor and reached for his sword.

"Do you have to bring that? We'll be climbing trees. Can you maneuver well with that huge blade at your side?"

"I'm not going without it, 'less you want to be dead," he said. "If the king asks, I did try to stop you."

"If I die, I'll be sure he knows that you tried." That received a pinched look from Lance, but I laughed. "It'll be fine. We will stay in the trees until they get close, then if we don't hear anything, we follow them. We won't stay out for long, and we will be protected." I patted the daggers by my side, hidden under a white cloak.

"A few years ago, I caught a man spying on me during patrol, and I killed him on the spot. This feels like an ironic death waiting for me," Lance said. When my eyebrows shot up, he added, "Does that surprise you?"

I stumbled over my words. "I...I didn't know Elenvérs guards killed without a trial."

"We usually don't, but the man had a foul air about him. I stood trial for his death and was pardoned." He stretched on his black gloves and flexed his fingers. "But our guards aren't so different from ThornHigh's."

Outside our room, a hand tapped against the wooden door, then a gentle voice called out, "Lady Rowan? Sir Lance? I brought m'lady soup to ease her stomach."

We froze. Lance gestured to my bed, and I tiptoed over to it and climbed under the covers, hiding my face behind a pillow while he strode to the door.

"Ah, fair maiden. The lady thanks you for the soup. She's already asleep, but I'll keep the bowl here in case she wakes. No need to come fetch it later. The lady needs rest."

"Certainly," Lindy said. "Careful, it's hot. And there's pudding there, because I know how much she loves it."

"Thank you." Lance shut the door.

He carried a wooden tray to my bedside table. He set down a steaming bowl of a dark soup. It smelt of beef and saffron. The other, the smaller bowl, held—

"Pudding," I cheered, my mouth already watering.

Lance glanced out the window, where fresh moonlight bathed the stone balcony.

"Might as well eat," he said. "We've got time yet before we need to head out, and it wouldn't do well for you to lose your strength. Fates know you're going to need it. But m'lady?" He paused, turning toward me.

I held a spoon full of pudding before my lips. "Eat more than just that pudding. It's not healthy for you."

With my other hand, I scooted the obviously healthy beef and vegetable soup further away. Lance chuckled as I scooped more pudding, my silver spoon scratching the edges of the bowl.

Chapter Twenty-Seven

OUR BACKS PRESSED AGAINST the wall. A bit of snow found my wrist, and I brushed it away. My fingers wrapped around my white cloak and I pulled it over my frigid nose to blend with the snow.

Each time I stepped forward, Lance flicked his hand and I'd shift back again. Lance kept his sight fixated ahead, twitching his nose like a bloodhound and perking up at every sound. Cold wind nipped our cheeks and numbed our skin, but we didn't move. Over the sloped mountainside, an animal's cry rang out, a sharp sound that pierced the air and caused Lance's body to go still. The wild cry came again, further down the mountain.

Whatever beast lurked in the night, likely a wolf, didn't advance toward the castle or village.

A watchtower was posted a hundred paces to our left, built into the stone wall that circled the village and connected to the edge of the castle. It was too far away and too dark to tell if a man was stationed inside the tower, so we'd have to guess when it was safe to move. It was a short distance to the tree line, likely four of Lance's steps and six of mine, but for those few moments we'd be unprotected by the trellis's shield or the pines.

"We need to make for the trees," I said.

"There's not enough cover," Lance whispered back. He placed a hand in front of my body.

"If we don't get up a tree now, the patrol guards could be by any moment and see us."

Lance glanced at the watchtower. "I don't like this."

"Noted. Shall we go for it then?"

He grunted but nodded. "On my count. Ready? Hold it. One. Now." We darted across the ground, frozen over with ice, and slid into the trees' protection. There, we paused, waiting for a sound from the watchtower. After fifty counts, when no call came, Lance nodded. "Let's move in some, then up a tree. Maybe that one there?" He pointed across the way to a thick pine tree with branches sloped to the ground. "Should provide us with enough cover. Keep to the patches already beaten down so our footprints aren't seen in the snow."

"Let's split. You in one tree and me in another. That way if they spot and attack one of us, the other could come from behind." I mimicked a slicing motion with my hand, then drew my fingers across my throat.

The darkness hid much of his face, but his lips pulled tight. "Fine. You go to that one then, and I'll be there. But m'lady? Let's keep the," he mimicked my slicing motion, "to a minimum. And mind you, keep quiet."

I saluted, then took off. He sighed behind me. As he moved, his footsteps made no sound. Once I reached my tree, I used my foot to push aside the pine branches, wincing as snow fell and piled on the ground. The prickly needles encircled me as I slipped inside their cover and scaled the trunk. As I went, I broke off a few branches to hide behind. We'd agreed not to climb too high, which would shake the tree and practically wave to the guards, drawing them straight to us.

When the tree began to quiver and I could risk going no further, I stopped and strategically placed the branches around my body, then leaned against the trunk to wait. From where I sat, I could see Lance's tree, but not Lance, and with luck, the guards wouldn't either.

Time dripped by. Slow, cold, and silent.

My bent legs ached, and my back cried out from the rough bark piercing into my skin. If I twisted my body, it relieved some of the stress on my back, but exemplified the pain in my legs. In the same way, if I pushed up on my legs to free them from the pressure, it meant pressing my back further against the bark to hold my position. Neither option provided more than a sliver of relief, and I couldn't hold either for long.

Nothing I did could keep me from the cold. That bitter feeling was inevitable.

Periodically, a distant noise broke through the silence. A snap of a twig, a rustle of leaves as the wind blew, a distant cry of a child. All common noises, but nothing to tell us that the patrol guards were coming.

Perhaps Tarion had deceived me once again. I was a fool.

But then a new sound came, and I knew the patrol guards were near.

Their voices were distant and grew louder as they moved in our direction. With my hand, I wiped the tears from my eyes brought on by the cold and squinted into the trees. From my side, the voices continued, still soft enough to be indistinguishable.

Please come closer.

As if summoned by my desire, they broke out from the tree line and walked in the narrow strip between the trees and the castle wall, talking as they went.

No, I realized as they got closer. Only one man was talking. The other shoved his hands in his coat and kept his head low while the first went on.

"I would fancy moving, get myself a bigger place, perhaps closer to a stream. I don't mind the home I got now, but it's tight living with all of us in there, and I like having my own space. I hear they all live in caves over there, must be warm inside the mountain. I could get myself a nice, big cave." That must be Bear. Tarion had been right about his rambling.

"You've said all this before," the second man spoke.

"I know," Bear said. "I'm just checking if you are listening."

Now closer, I got a proper look at them and realized that Bear wasn't his name, it was a nickname. If someone told me he was descended from a bear, I'd believe them. He didn't wear a hat, but thick, dark hair covered his head and protected it better than any hat could. His burly hands swung eagerly by his sides and he towered over the man beside him. His voice rumbled as he spoke, deep enough that it sounded like it came from the heart of the mountain.

"We can't know that we will take Elenvérs," the second man grumbled.

"We will. You'll see. We will smash them to the ground." Bear pounded his fist into his palm, an action made scarier by the sheer size of his hands. "We're planning a covert attack soon."

The men stopped near the trellis where Lance and I had hidden, both looking in either direction as they stood watch. I couldn't see more than pieces of their bodies from where I hid. "How could you know of such things?"

"Because I'm important, that's how."

"Yeah? And what's so important that you get to know?"

Bear puffed up his chest. "There's going to be an ambush in their mines. We're stealing their money."

He spoke with no regard to volume, too proud to know something that his friend didn't, even as the other man shushed him. "You'll get us hanged if you keep talking so loud, then you won't get your big cave."

"I'll be fine, I've got friends," Bear boasted.

They were quiet for a few more moments, before the friend spoke again. "Are they really ambushing the mines?"

"In three weeks. Yes, sir. We're going to be rich." The excitement dripped in his voice. Three weeks: that gave me enough time to warn Cassian.

Both my back and my legs burned and my muscles shook. I pressed my hands into my legs to minimize the movement. I couldn't hold this position for long. I shouldn't have settled on such a small branch, without a second one nearby to steady myself against.

The patrol guards remained with their backs against the trellis as they watched each direction while thinking of the things they'd buy if they were rich. Soon enough, Bear suggested they move on, and they started walking away.

They only made it two steps before one paused. "What was that?"

"I didn't hear nothing," Bear's deep voice replied.

"No, shh. I heard something." His eyes prowled into the trees, searching along the distance. My breath caught in my throat, and for a moment the fear of being caught erased the pain in my body. My hand tingled for the dagger, but I didn't risk moving and making a sound.

"I'm sure it's just the wind, but I can check if you fancy," Bear said. The friend nodded while drawing his sword. "No need for that, can't do a thing against the wind. There's nothing else out on this cold night." Bear strutted out into the trees and began poking around. He moved between the trees that Lance and I hid in, keeping his eyes on the ground as he pushed at the frozen pines.

"See? What'd I tell ya?"

His eyes raised, and for a horrifying second, they settled on me.

I felt nothing. No pain in my legs, no breath in my lungs, no scream in my throat. Like a statue, I didn't move, terrified of what the large man would do to the spy in the woods.

It's too dark. He can't really see you.

"Anything there?" the other man asked.

He pried his eyes away from me and shook his head. "Nothing. Let's move on."

Together, they staggered away until they were too far to hear the deep breath that escaped my mouth as my head bowed. My hand shook and I pressed it between my legs.

I didn't move until I heard Lance call from below. "Are you coming, m'lady? 'Less you want to spend the night here?"

"I'm coming." My numb legs stretched out, enjoying the feeling for a bit before descending. At the bottom, Lance waited with his hand on his sword, scoping out the area.

"That was too easy," he said when my feet hit the ground.

"We were this close to dying." I showed him my fingers close together. "I can't feel my feet, and my whole body is tingling. And you're blue."

"It was too easy," Lance repeated. He sighed. "Let's get back inside before we talk further." He motioned for me to follow and held up his hand when we paused at the edge of the tree line. "Must be careful about that watchtower."

"I think it's empty, let's go for it." I darted across the clearing, eager to be back inside where it was warm and safe. Lance jumped after me, reaching the wall at the same time as me.

"Now I see why you need a guard," he whispered. "Follow me from here on out." He didn't speak again, but led me safely back into the kitchens, where we filled some cups with water to give us an excuse for wandering the halls at night. With our cups filled, we escaped to my room.

"Now," Lance said as he closed the door. "What did you hear?"

"There will be an attack in the mines in three weeks."

Lance nodded, tapping his chin. "I heard the same. Peculiar. There will be fewer guards at the mines, since almost all our fighters are stationed at the borders. But they'd be pulling their men from the lines, weakening themselves, simply to steal a bunch of rocks."

I warmed my feet under my blankets. "It makes sense to me. If our men aren't guarding the mines, now is the perfect time to steal some of our wealth."

"But," Lance said. "If they can beat us so easily in this war, that wealth will soon be theirs anyway. There's no value to taking it early unless they are short for money, or don't think they can beat us."

"Either way, we need to tell the king. We can't use wind messages right now, so you'll have to deliver the message yourself."

Lance frowned. "I can't leave my post here."

Since Lance started sleeping in my room, I'd snuck a small bag into my covers, which I put the wish in at night and kept under my pillow, just in case the wish slipped from my pocket while I slept. While he laid his blanket on the floor and set his sword beside it, I moved the wish to the bag.

"This is more important than my safety, and I'm both too tired and too cold to argue now. We'll go to sleep, and you'll leave in the morning."

Lance eased onto the floor. "We will go to sleep, and we'll *talk* in the morning."

My exhaustion told me nothing meant more right now than sleep, so I didn't argue further. Sleep didn't come, however. Instead, thoughts of Elenvérs falling consumed me, along with fears that we couldn't beat ThornHigh, and that death was near for us all. All the information I'd uncovered from ThornHigh came from Tarion, a man who'd yet to prove himself trustworthy. Lady Trelluse always told Elis and I not to trust a man with dimples in his smile and twinkles in his eye—she'd be disheartened to find I banked my kingdom on one.

Perhaps Lance was correct, that information today was too easy to acquire.

"M'Lady?" Lance whispered.

"Yes, Lance?"

"I'll go in the morning. This information is too important to not report right away."

I sighed. "Thank you. Lance? You don't suppose we are headed into a battle that we cannot win? Do you think Elenvérs is doomed?"

To his credit, he didn't answer right away. "No, I think nothing is certain. We have a kind king and a smart prince. Together they will save us."

He might be right. But more than the coming battle, the curse ticked closer, and if I couldn't find a way to save Elenvérs before my curse took hold, there might be nothing left to rule over.

I needed to save Elenvérs, and I needed to break the curse. Without both, I'd be doomed—either to a broken kingdom under ThornHigh's rule, or to wake up to nothing. I couldn't decide which was worse, but they both sent a chill up my spine that was colder than the wind I'd just endured outside. Colder than the coldest nights in the mountain.

That coldness wouldn't take me.

But my fears just might.

Chapter Twenty-Eight

LANCE LEFT AT FIRST light while I played sick a little longer to savor extra moments of sleep. Around midday I went in search of food, then looked for Tarion, who expected a report.

Instead, I found the king.

King Maven walked down the corridor with a few other men beside him, one of them Annon. Annon's outfit matched the king's in color but lacked the king's short cape and billowed sleeves. Annon's livery was the only indicator that he served King Olin.

They were halfway down the corridor as I turned the corner. My head lowered as I walked quickly, hoping to pass them without drawing attention to myself.

"Lady Rowan, how are you enjoying your stay at ThornHigh?" The king stopped walking to address me, crossing his hands over each other in front of his waist. He had the same eyes as his son, but his were clearly older, making him look wise. King Olin once said a wise mind and an evil heart make the most fearsome of foes, and he must have been speaking of King Maven. I stepped back to put some distance between us.

The other men, besides Annon, were Lord Hamptin and Sir Umphry. Both men were as tall as a horse, but Sir Umphry's belly took up twice as much space as Lord Hamptin's, and his nose was twice as long. He was a shy fellow, who I knew very little about. Lord Hamptin I knew some about, including that he possessed a loud voice and a deep laugh.

He didn't laugh now. They all stood silent beside their king.

King Maven waited for my answer. I bowed my head to him. "I feel very welcome here, thank you."

His attention swept over the wide corridor. "Your guard isn't with you, I notice."

Next to him, Annon's eye twitched.

"No sir, I don't feel threatened enough to need him as I walk through these halls."

Behind the king, sunlight flashed through a frosted windowpane, almost as bright as the gleam in his eye. "I see. He went home this morning, did he not? Perhaps my men were wrong when they said they saw him depart."

My surprise couldn't be hidden so quickly, so I bowed again to hide it. "I felt silly keeping him here with me, so I sent him back to Elenvérs," I replied.

King Maven glanced at the men beside him. "I must admit, I was surprised you had one. Makes me wonder what's so special about you that the king would send a guard to sleep by your bed." The way he said 'you' was unpleasant, like I was no more than the snow one kicks off their boots before warming their feet by a pleasant fire.

Annon stepped in for me before I could say a word. Again, his face couldn't be read as he turned it from mine. "My king is protective of all his people," he said. I searched for the trickery in his words.

"You don't have a guard," King Maven gestured to Annon, at which one of his companions chuckled.

"Yes, well, I can hold my own," Annon said, giving the chuckler a glance that quieted him. The king returned his gaze to me as he snickered, the sound falling stale upon my ears.

"Still, odd isn't it, that as our countries rest on the verge of war, while no talks of negotiation have commenced, that Olin should leave his emissary here in pursuit of friendship? Your role as emissary from Elenvérs seems irrelevant, don't you think? Does Olin really believe that friendship can come between us, or are you here on some other mission?"

"Annon is still here, so the threat must not be that great," I pointed out, gaining another laugh from King Maven and a scowl from Annon.

"Again, I can hold my own," he said.

"I'm sure you can, dear friend. I'm sure you can." The king clapped him on the back, his large white sleeves almost covering his hand. Annon straightened at his touch.

A sly smile played on King Maven's lips. "Maybe the lady is in pursuit of my son's hand? Saving herself from the war through a powerful marriage? I had heard my son fancied someone." He studied me in an unpleasant way, and my mouth drew in a line.

We'd ventured into conversation that made me almost as uncomfortable as the coy smile on King Maven's face.

"I must be off, Your Majesty." I stepped back as quickly as possible without being obviously rude.

"Be off then, on whatever mission you are here for." The king waved flippantly in my direction.

They moved on, and even though they exited the hallway from behind me before I'd reached my turn, I walked past it, uncomfortable with them guessing I was on my way to see

Tarion. This led me on a roundabout path toward his room, but it gave me time to think.

How naive of me to assume that King Maven hadn't noticed me. From now on when in his presence, I'd hold my head a little lower and glaze over my eyes to mimic the look of a helpless girl only here because she was stupid enough to fall in love with the prince. After all, he wasn't the first to assume a relationship had brewed between Tarion and me.

They were all mistaken, but I'd rather them think me a love-struck maiden than a cunning spy.

With these thoughts in mind, I knocked on Tarion's door. He opened it wearing nothing but loose, gray trousers tucked misshapenly into thin socks, and a chiffon undershirt with fur lining the sleeves.

After the king's remark about my interest in Tarion, the sight of him without his thick suits and high collars and in a fabric thin enough to practically see through brought heat to my cheeks, and I dropped my head. "Why in Elenvérs' name are you not dressed? It's half day already."

He left the door open as he laughed. The sound of his footsteps disappeared as his laugh grew quieter, then a muffled voice came, "I thought you were lunch."

"You let the maids see you like that? No wonder they like you so much." He laughed again, then his feet reappeared in the doorway.

"Are you appropriately clothed now?" I asked, keeping my head down to hide my blush.

"Yes, I am good and proper."

Timidly, I looked up. He'd put on a thick, red jacket with wide sleeves and silver buttons down the front.

I nodded in approval. "Right well, I wanted to give a report on my mission."

Tarion's head ducked into the hallway where one guard stood at the other end, too far to hear us. Still, his voice lowered. "It's all business with you. Alright, report away."

My face remained blank, with a slight apology to my tone. "I didn't learn anything. Bear wasn't as vocal as you thought him to be, and though I followed to my best ability, he never said anything useful." I bowed my head slightly then glanced up at him through my lashes to read his expression.

Tarion's fingers stroked the birthmark on his jaw, studying me for a moment. Then he dropped his hand. "You did your best. We will find another way to learn what they are up to." He didn't look bothered that I'd come up with nothing, in fact, he didn't even look surprised. He shrugged his shoulders and glanced back out in the hall. "Splendid. There's lunch."

I stepped to the side as a pretty maid with black hair passed Tarion a tray. Her eyes darted between the two of us and she smiled as if she'd caught us in the midst of a scandalous tryst, then scurried away.

"Maddie," Tarion called after her. "Can you bring Rowan's lunch here so we can eat together?"

The notion of scandal deepened in her eyes, and she nodded happily.

He nodded to the food. "Come join me."

I hesitated. "Are you sure that would be appropriate?"

He barked a laugh. "Rowan, you never smile for more than two seconds. No one can accuse you of anything close to flirtatious, or anything less than appropriate. But leave the door open if you'd like."

I tiptoed into the room. His chambers were split into two sections, one for sleeping and one for working. His bed was twice as large as mine, dressed in a black blanket and two black pillows. A few clothes lay on the ground and a pair of slippers, no, two pairs, sat beside the bed. Who needs two pairs of slippers?

The other half was a wall of bookshelves, almost like a library in his room. I'd never seen him read before. Some were brown, large, and dusty, but others boasted bright bindings and narrower spines.

A third pair of slippers sat by the bookshelves. He might have an obsession.

The maid came back with the food, stopping outside the door to glance in.

"Thank you. I can take that." I smiled innocently at her as I took the tray. Disappointed that she hadn't caught us in the middle of anything, she shuffled away.

I eyed our food. Tarion's portions were significantly larger than what I'd been getting and overall more delectable looking. His grapes were plumper, his meat thicker, and the wine smelled earthier than mine.

It wasn't worth complaining over though.

"I ran into your father today," I said as I popped a grape into my mouth.

Tarion grunted. "I'm sorry. He's not a pleasant man. What did he want?"

"Nothing, he just said hello," I lied, not eager to share how his father assumed Tarion and I were more than friends. "Is he always so...cold?"

I couldn't picture King Maven as a doting father, one who dressed his son in cute clothes or proudly showed him off to relatives. Even teaching his son to sword fight or ride horses seemed uncharacteristic. Most likely, Tarion was raised by a governess and saw his father about as often as I saw mine.

Kings are terrible fathers.

He nodded as he cut into his thick steak. "For as long as I can remember. How about you? What's your father like?"

I opened my mouth to say the same but caught myself. He's asking about Elis's father, not King Olin. Chastising myself for being forgetful, I answered, "Supportive. Growing up, Elis and I liked to go on adventures together. Instead of being terrified of us getting hurt, which I'm sure he was, he was always the first to help pack our bags and wish us luck. He's not like Mother, who would like to keep us safely by her side for our whole lives. He keeps his distance and encourages us with whatever we chose with our life."

Tarion grinned. "That sounds nice. You're lucky. That's the kind of father I want to be one day." He took a sip of wine. "You'll be a great mother one day."

Pain stabbed my heart. I'd never be able to conceive a child.

To hide my pain, I asked, "What was your mother like?"

As soon as I asked it, I regretted it, because grief crossed Tarion's face. "I'm so sorry, I shouldn't have said anything."

"No, it's okay. Mama was one of a kind. She was a skilled fighter with a sharp tongue but also so kind and generous. And she protected those around her. That's how she died. When an assassin broke through and aimed for my father, she stood in the way." He stared into his plate.

"She sounds like she was lovely."

"She was. I want to marry someone like her one day." He took another sip of wine while the comment led me to shift in my seat. In all the time we'd spent together, Tarion might have formed feelings for me. I studied him. He sat back in his seat, looking comfortable, leaning on the armrest closest to me. His foot stretched out near mine, close enough that if I stretched out my toes they would touch his. He winked as he caught me looking at him.

I was in trouble.

"I hope you find someone like her someday," I said as I eased my feet in closer to me.

He shrugged. "Maybe I already have."

I scarfed down the last bite of food and stood. "I promised Lindy my afternoon, so I should go now."

"Alright." He didn't look bothered or confused why a maid should have my afternoon. "And listen," he said before I left. "Don't worry about Bear. We'll beat my father yet. Everything will be fine."

The casualness of his voice concerned me, and the way he waved off the matter so easily, as if he didn't realize that the fate of our kingdoms rested on our ability to stop his father's advances upon Elenvérs. His dismissiveness irked me, but I masked it with a tender smile and nod of the head.

"I know we will. I'll see you this evening."

He closed the door and my smile dropped. Please, Lance, make it to Elenvérs safely.

If the ride went smoothly, he should reach the castle in a week, and King Olin could get protection to the mines with a week to spare before the attack. We'd save our men and our wealth from the clutches of ThornHigh, then find a way to beat them in the war that brewed on the horizon.

It would be a quick war, either an easy slaughter of our men or us finding some sneaky path to victory, but either fate would happen soon.

And yet, despite the looming chaos, Tarion acted nonchalant.

That was why I didn't trust him. It'd taken me this long to pinpoint what it was about him that made him difficult to trust, but that was it. He was far too casual for my taste. I didn't trust a man who didn't quake in the face of battle; it showed a lack of respect for the dangers a war brought.

It didn't help that he didn't save Yule Point from the attack. But if the information gotten from Bear turned out to be valid, Tarion would earn back a portion of my trust.

When my bedchamber door creaked open, my jaw fell to my chest.

From wall to wall, the room was torn apart.

The rug, now furled, blocked the door from meeting the wall. I glanced behind it to be sure no one waited there, then moved to the bed. My thick, gray blankets had been ripped from the bed and thrown across the floor, and the pillows halfway across the room looked like a melted snowman next to the fireplace. Each had an indent in them, as if stomped upon after being thrown to the floor.

I left them in their upheaval as I checked the rest of the room. The chairs were tipped over and the leg of one was broken, with splintered wood scattered across the stone floor. Glass crunched underfoot from broken paintings. My riding boots, dinner shoes, velvet slippers, and extra day shoes littered the floor with their buckles undone and insides pulled out. Ashes from the fireplace floated across the room, covering everything with black flakes.

The disaster didn't stop there. My closet was unrecognizable, with all the clothes dumped in a heap on the floor. This would take most of the day to put back together.

Whoever ransacked my room had found nothing—there was nothing to find—but their message read loud and clear: someone was watching me. Someone didn't trust me.

My toes hit a few bruised apples beneath the basket Lady Trelluse sent me, and I placed it on the empty desk. My hand slid in my pocket to where my wish lay safely.

This must be the work of the suspicious king or one of his advisors who didn't trust the girl from Elenvérs who ate from their table every night. The king who'd looked me in the eye this morning and questioned my motives.

I'd yet to see aggression from King Maven, but the tales I'd been told of him and his blood-thirsty sword were engrained in my mind. He was just as likely as General Barrett to remove my head if he thought me to be dangerous. My hope at this point was to make myself as little as possible to ease his suspicions, and if that meant charming Tarion, I would do it. The destruction before me proved that I needed to work harder to get what I came for.

For Elenvérs, I'd do anything.

Behind me, Lindy squeaked.

"My Lady, I sometimes wonder if you were raised in a barn."

Chapter Twenty-Nine

THOUGH I'D NOT ASKED Lance to return to ThornHigh after delivering his news to King Olin, I found myself hesitating at every window, staring out to the gates of the castle, hoping to see him riding in with his broadsword attached to his hip, ready to stand guard. As much as I wanted extra protection for myself, I also wanted news of Elenvérs.

It'd been three long weeks. The attack on the mines should have occurred by now if Lance hadn't gotten there in time.

Selfish, I reminded myself, to want to risk Lance's safety just so I could hear of home. Gen had warned me of my weakness, and while I sometimes thought I'd overcome it, other times my shortcomings radiated from me with such strength that I thought for sure they would take over.

The selfish parts of me had been speaking a lot recently. Leave ThornHigh, leave Elenvérs, take your wish and save yourself from the curse. Or, a more terrifying thought, use the wish to wipe out ThornHigh, saving Elenvérs. It tempted me further than I cared to admit, but I wouldn't be a merciless killer. Cassian had once told me that he didn't think I was capable of killing someone, and I often feared he was right. I hated the thought of killing someone, and I definitely couldn't kill a whole army.

Besides, if I used my wish on the army, then I had nothing to save myself from the curse.

My worry led me to the training grounds for hours a day, sparring with the few guards that remained at ThornHigh. With the nearing war, the number of guards at ThornHigh had lessened as one by one they were called to their posts. Today, it was only me and another guard who dueled in the training center.

"I see why Elenvérs allows women to fight alongside them," the guard wiped his brow, sweating despite the soft snow falling around us, and took a moment to catch his breath. When he'd straightened himself. "You are a force."

I beamed through my heaving and adjusted the polearm in my hands. The leather gloves over my fingers tore yesterday, exposing my palm. A bruise rested in the corner of my thumb and a tender pain coursed from the spot where the polearm pressed against it. A similar bruise marked my cheek, but I'd deserved that beating. I should have seen his move coming, but I'd allowed myself to be distracted by a distant figure who looked like Lance. It wasn't, but I got walloped before I figured that out.

I'd dealt a nasty blow to my opponent as well.

Short, rotting wood ran a perimeter around us, rising as tall as my shoulders to separate one chamber from another. As the snow fell it piled on the railings, occasionally spilling over and gathering on the ground. The rest of the arena was slick with trampled snow and periodic patches of ice that made the duel more interesting.

"I must say," he said as he raised his pole to spar again. "I thought it cruel of them to put women on the battlefield, when no man would ever kill them." He grunted as I blocked the swing. "But if I met you in battle, fighting the way you do, I don't think I'd hesitate on my blow."

I barked a laugh. I wanted to say the same, but I feared that despite my rough edges, I'd tremble at the sight of war.

He swung low, knocking me from my feet, but I scrambled back before he swung again.

"Have you been in battle before?" he asked me through gritted teeth.

"No," I admitted. "But my mentor told me all her stories. She's famous for her skill, or was, before she lost a hand in a fight."

His next blow threw me to the ground. I growled.

"Do you accept defeat?" He pinned me down with the end of his polearm.

I tapped the frozen dirt. "Accept."

As he helped me back up, another man entered the small arena. His boots sunk in the snow as he strode up, a furled parchment in his hands. His dark pants were tucked into muddy boots with scratched buttons.

"Benny," he addressed my opponent, handing him the parchment. Benny broke the seal and unraveled the paper.

I wiped the end of my polearm, looking busy while I watched him read. Finally, he looked up.

"I'm called to fight?" He dropped the letter.

The man nodded solemnly.

"But my wife is with child," he shouted. "I thought I was pardoned?" His brow creased. He picked up the parchment, wiped off the snow and read it again.

I lowered my gaze.

The other man waved his finger over the bottom of the paper. "But look here, it's just Morshug. You shouldn't be in danger there. You'll be home before Freya gives birth." He beamed, as if this were good news, but dropped the smile as soon as Benny cast him a dark look. "I'm sorry mate, I really am. We will deal with Elenvérs swiftly and get you back home."

I coughed, and he looked at me with wide eyes, remembering my place. "Rowan, I'm sorry. I forgot myself."

I waved my hand, not missing the tears brimming in Benny's eyes. The air grew thick with the situation, both him being called away from his family, and my loyalties to the kingdom that he'd fight against. If I were prone to betting, I'd say that was the last time I'd ever spar against Benny.

As I walked by him, I placed a hand on his shoulder. "I really am sorry. I wish I could help."

"Thank you," he whispered back. "Looks like I need to get packing." He shoved the note into the pocket of his tunic, kicked his polearm, and left the arena, leaving deep snow prints behind him.

His friend breathed in sharply and ran his hand back and forth over his curls, making them go wild. He shook his head as he watched his friend storm off. "Want a piece of advice?" He looked at me. "Stay at ThornHigh. You are liked here, and you'd be given the prince's protection. Don't return home."

I picked up Benny's polearm and tapped it against the ground to shake the snow off. "You're that confident ThornHigh will beat Elenvérs?"

He nodded. "And it won't be long. Remain here. Save yourself." He walked after Benny, leaving me alone in the arena.

Another guard called off to war. I shivered and pulled my coat closed.

If we could get our men here at the heart of the castle, we could easily take it, but we had no way to get over their lines. If we did, if I used my wish to get our men here, we'd take the castle, but they'd walk straight into ours, killing all the cave people.

The guard's words ran through my head. *Remain here. Save yourself.*

I couldn't save myself from this war. In a world where I ought to be queen, I was instead as powerless as a snowflake drifting in the wind, unable to command where it lands.

Just as I was putting back my polearm, a familiar voice called out.

"Need a partner?"

I turned to where Lance stood with a grin on his face and arms crossed, making his already large muscles appear enormous.

"You returned." I jogged toward him as the hopelessness of moments before began to dim.

He bowed. "The king was quite adamant that I return to your side." His eye twitched and his cheeks tightened. Under his eyes was darkness, and his shoulders didn't stand as tall as usual. I took a step back.

"What's wrong?"

From his pocket, he fished out an envelope and passed it to me. "This is from Prince Cassian. You'd better read it."

Chapter Thirty

THE WAY HIS FACE squinted, I guessed somebody died. My hands shook as I grabbed the letter. I eagerly slid a finger beneath the opening to yank it apart, but Lance placed a hand on my arm. "Might we head back to your room for privacy?"

"Lance, if someone died, I want to know right now. Please tell me everyone is okay. Is Cassian okay?" My voice came out sharper than intended.

Lance flicked one wrist up and patted the air a few times in a settling motion. "The prince did not make me privy to such information, but there was no talk of someone's death while I was there." He glanced at the letter. "All His Highness told me was he wanted you to read it right away."

I exhaled. "Fine, let's go quickly." The letter fit into my pocket above the wish. It took all my strength not to sprint back to my bedchambers with Lance at my side.

With the worst possible timing, King Maven spotted us walking through the halls, and raised an eyebrow at Lance while a sly smile danced on his lips. I didn't hold his gaze, but instead dropped my eyes to the ground and slowed my steps.

"Lady Rowan. I see your protection has returned." He whispered, his voice deep.

My head lifted just enough to meet his eyes, as I forced an innocent smile to my lips. "Yes sire. How are you today?"

His smile looked as fake as mine. "Quite well. On my way to an afternoon budget meeting. Seems the outer towns desire more money."

In the months that I'd been here, that was more information than he'd ever given me about his doings as king, but his forced pleasantries were not lost on me. He nodded once to me, then once to Lance, who bowed, before continuing with a low noise in his throat that I couldn't name. Before long, his footsteps faded behind us.

"He doesn't trust us," I mumbled to Lance as we walked down the hall

"Smart man."

I shoved an elbow into his side, and he laughed.

When we got closer to the quiet halls of the guest chambers, I told Lance how my room was ransacked.

"I wasn't hurt," I said to ease his concern, but his face remained tight.

"I never should have left."

"I'm glad you did, or else we wouldn't have gotten word to Elenvérs in time." I opened my door and peeked inside. The bed was made, fire crackling, and room was vacant.

"That's something we must talk about," Lance said as he stepped inside and began a much more thorough investigation of the room. He poked at every pillow, peeked under the bed, ruffled through the closet, and stared over the balcony railing for intruders before he relaxed.

His bag already sat inside the door, so I knew he'd come here before he found me. He motioned to one of the chairs by the fire for me to sit, but something he had said worried me. "What do you mean we have to talk about that? Did you not get to the mines in time?"

"Stand if you desire," he grunted, and dropped himself into the second chair. "Yes, we got to the mines in time. King Olin sent men right away to protect them, but they were never ambushed. I looked like a fool, sending a small army to stave off an attack that never came."

Now I sat in the chair. "There was never an attack?"

He shook his head.

"So, the information we got from Bear...?"

"Spoken for our sakes, I assume. Meant to throw us off a trail."

I buried my head into my hands. "Is there a chance they changed their minds?"

Lance watched the fire for a moment before replying, "Not likely. It's far more probable that Prince Tarion set us up to hear fake information, but I'm sure if you asked him about it, he'd say they altered their plans." Lance pulled off his black shoes and began to massage his feet while I shook my head, letting my red curls fall over my shoulders.

Tarion. He played me. He gave me fake assignments and fed me false information while prohibiting my ability to uncover anything useful. I didn't doubt that now.

I did doubt what to do next. Perhaps Cassian's letter would give me clarity.

Lance leaned back in the chair and continued massaging his feet while I read.

Rowan,

Lance told us how you uncovered news of the attack, but as there was no attack, I'm now certain we cannot trust Tarion. But do not let him know you don't believe him. Keep him close.

And if the moment comes, kill him.

I once told you I didn't believe you could take a life, but now I pray I was wrong. Kill him and flee home. Tarion is far more cunning than I'd assumed, and with their prince fallen, perhaps ThornHigh will be shaken enough for us to strike. If not, war is already imminent, and we have nothing left to lose.

Briggs has gone missing, and I fear something happened to him. The battles have not yet begun, and my comrades are falling. Keep yourself safe. Above all else, keep yourself safe. I don't know what I'd do if something happened to you.

Cassian

Lance studied his feet, pretending not to be interested in the note, but I saw the way he arched his brows and peered at the paper. I folded it softly. "Things are not right here."

His feet hit the floor and he straightened himself. "Best be on our way then, back to Elenvérs."

"We can't go," I said before he'd taken a step. "My job here isn't done."

Lance eased back in the seat and sighed. "With respect, I don't see what else you can do." The fire popped besides us, sending a few embers to the stone ground where Lance stomped them out. I wish our problems could be so easy to put out, but I feared this was a fire that couldn't be so easily squashed.

The sparks of this war were lit, and they wouldn't stop until they'd burned a kingdom to the ground.

I cursed. "I haven't done anything! The alliance I'd secured with Tarion that would protect both Elenvérs and myself is an illusion and every mission I've gone on while here has been at Tarion's bidding and never led to anything. Through my time here I've accomplished little more than meaningless friendships and pointless excursions." Cassian's note crumpled under my tight fingers.

"You have proved yourself to be brave and bold and determined. You have served your country well. If you desire, return home with me, suit up, and ride with us into battle. But in this enemy kingdom we can do no more."

My tension relaxed. I loosened my grip on the letter. From the corner, a few of Cassian's words could be read. *Kill him.*

Was it murder if I killed the prince during a time of war, or was it a heroic act for my kingdom? Was it heartless or was it courageous? Could I kill the man with dark hair and a dimpled smile who'd won my friendship during these past months?

The words echoed in my mind without prompting, a result of being repeated so many times throughout my life.

For Elenvérs, I'd do anything. Even kill the prince.

Scratch scratch. A paper slid under the door, flying a few paces before halting on the stone, and Lance flew to his feet. His hand waved to me without looking my way. "Get behind the bed."

"I'll get my blade, that's what I'll do." I said. We were both jumpy this evening, far too jumpy to be hiding behind a bed. I fetched my blade from the desk and held it as Lance read the note. His eyes squinted as he flipped it over a few times. "Do you have a idea what this means?"

He handed the paper to me, and the first thing I noticed was how nice the paper was. This wasn't cheap parchment, and the words had been written with a fine quill. Two sentences were scrawled across it.

You took something of mine. You have one week to return it. -General Barrett.

I cursed again. Vividly. Once I'd finished, Lance coughed. "Should I know what that means?"

I waved the paper at him. "Trouble. I didn't take something, but Tarion did. I can't return something I don't have." What did he take?

Lance closed his eyes and took a deep breath. "You are the hardest person I've ever had to keep alive. Pack up, we are returning home now."

I didn't pack, but instead threw General Barrett's note on the edge of my bed and put Cassian's in my pocket. "No, I have something to do first."

With a groan, Lance asked. "What could you possibly need to do?"

"I have a plan..."

"Yes?"

"It involves killing someone."

"No."

Fishing into my pocket, I retrieved Cassian's note and waved it above my head. "I'm merely following the crown prince's orders."

Lance's gaze followed, and his frown deepened. "And I'm merely following the king's orders. Keep. You. Alive."

My dagger clicked against the desk as I set it back down and smiled at my frustrated guard. "You can come with me. In fact, I'd prefer it."

In an act he'd never done before, Lance sat on my bed and folded his arms. The light from outside faded and the snow began to pick up. The time it took for a snowflake to fall from the sky and land on the soft blanket of snow covering the mountain was how long it took Lance to speak again. "How long would this adventure of yours take?"

"We could do it tomorrow."

"Then go home?" I nodded. He sighed. "Fine."

A knock from the door caused us both to jump, and a moment later Lindy walked in with a tray. "Dinner?"

She eyed Lance until he let go of his hilt and I beamed. "Lindy, oh good. I love poached quail eggs. And look, Lance," I exclaimed. "Pudding for the both of us. Marvelous."

She brought it to the edge of the bed to hand to us. Her eye caught the note before I could pull it away. She smiled as I snatched it up.

"I knew he fancied you."

"What?"

"The note?" She nodded to my hand. "I told you I work for Prince Tarion sometimes? That's his writing. I'd know it anywhere."

I looked at the note in my hand. "You're positive?"

She nodded. "Is it not a love letter?"

Lance laughed, and I shot him a look. "It is not. Thank you, Lindy, you've been quite helpful."

She smiled as if I made her day. "I'm glad. Let me know if there's ever anything I can do to assist you."

As she skipped from the room, I crumped Tarion's note. He wanted me to believe General Barrett was coming for me. Likely he took whatever he did from General Barrett's room to get him suspicious of me. Perhaps he was the one who ordered my room to be ransacked, too.

I would think on these things as I drove a blade through his unsuspecting heart.

Chapter Thirty-One

DESPITE THE COMFORTABLE BED, I'd slept poorly last night, often waking with chills at the thought of what I'd do. At the first hints of sun, Lance got up, his hair wild, and I rolled out of bed to greet him.

He took one look at me and laughed. "You look like death."

The irony of his comment was not lost on me. Today I would bring death upon another. It was valiant, I told myself. Tarion must be working alongside his father, and a countless number of my people would surely fall at his hand if I didn't strike him down first. The Fates would forgive me for what I would do.

I would forgive myself. Elenvérs would praise me for the deed.

Lindy would be in soon, so we began to pack. Most of my clothes would be left behind; only what fit in a small bag would return home with me. I'd be sorry to leave the fluffy pillows behind and the thick rug, both nicer than the ones I had back home. I didn't need a curse to sleep for a hundred years in that bed. It was soft enough to do that all on its own.

Unless I was plotting a murder. That proved to keep me up through the night.

"Why are you making the bed?" Lance tightened the drawstrings on his bag and looked at me.

"I try to make it every morning, I don't want this morning to look different." No sooner had I finished speaking, than a knock on the door made us stiffen, the corner of my blankets still in my hand.

"Do you always get such frequent visitors?" Lance whispered to me, not taking his eyes off the door.

"Perhaps it's Lindy?"

Lance crossed the room and pointed back. "Drop that. Pack, now."

As I scrambled around the bed, the door opened with a creak and Lindy ran into the room.

"Miss, you need to leave now!" Her face was white, and she bent over to catch her breath. "Leave," big breath, "now."

"What's happened?" I asked, taking her shaking hands in mine.

"Someone's been killed." Her eyes widened as she looked between the two of us, her face still the color of snow.

Lance as I exchanged glances. That wasn't me, right? I hadn't killed Tarion yet?

"Who?" Lance beat me to the question, putting a hand on Lindy's shoulder to lead her to a chair. With a stutter in her step, Lindy found the chair and slumped herself into it.

"Lindy, what's happened?" I stared at my maid.

"I like you, Lady Rowan. I've liked you since you got here. I've kept my ears open in case anyone from ThornHigh got any ideas about hurting you. I'm not dull, I knew our relationship with Elenvérs was on the brink of war. I wanted to protect you."

Her loyalty touched me.

Lance wasted no time. "Lindy, who's been killed?"

Remembering, she stood up quickly and almost knocked over the chair. "The king. King Maven is dead. They'll think one of you did it." Her eyes shot to me. "You're in danger. Lance, you must take Lady Rowan and flee to the west. Don't take her back to Elenvérs."

While I stood too stunned to answer, Lance darted to pick up his bag. "Why west?"

Lindy glanced at the door and spoke quicker, "West is the only safe way. A war is coming on Elenvérs, and you won't be safe there. Please go west."

"Pack," Lance reminded me.

I grabbed my bag and opened it on the bed while Lindy helped me throw things in it. I appreciated that she didn't ask if we had killed the king and wondered if part of her didn't want to know. King Maven wasn't a deeply loved man among the maids, so many might be grateful. "Hurry miss. There isn't much time to spare."

"Will you be safe here?" I asked Lindy.

She smiled. "No one needs to know I helped you escape. I'll be safe."

"You should go now, so you aren't caught with us."

She hesitated. "Are you certain you'll be alright?"

"We'll be fine. Thank you, Lindy. Your coming here means a lot to me." She smiled then picked up her skirts and ran to the door.

Before she left, I called after her, "If King Maven is dead, who is king now?"

"Tarion, of course. You can stay here and hope for the prince's protection, but I suggest you flee." Then she fled the room, leaving the door ajar. Her footsteps thumped down the halls.

"Pack!"

"Wait." I held up my hand as I sorted the chaos in my mind.

If Tarion was king, killing him would hurt ThornHigh more than if he was prince. Now, it'd leave them without a ruler. For Elenvérs, Tarion must die.

Where there'd been hesitation, I now felt resolve. My torn heart beat steadily and it chanted one thing: Save Elenvérs. To do that, I could kill Tarion—the man who'd deceived me time and time again, who'd plotted against Elenvérs, and who sent out a man to bring Elenvérs to its knees. That man deserved death.

"There's something I have to do first," I said as I dropped my bag. "I don't need to pack. Get the horses ready, and I'll be right there."

"I'm not leaving you, m'lady."

I hoped he'd say that. "Good, then we need to kill King Tarion."

Lance didn't need to curse out loud because his face gave away his thoughts. He didn't argue, but instead drew his mouth in a straight line, nodded once, and opened the door for me. "Then let's go."

We marched out of the room without a plan, but with a solid intention. To kill the new king.

All my focus went into putting one foot in front of the other. Slow. Calm. Don't appear frantic. My mind swirled with a plan on how to strike Tarion down without him suspecting. Most likely he'd be in his room to mourn the loss of his father, which gave me the opportunity to get close to him in comfort. I didn't linger on that thought, the idea of striking him down in his moment of sorrow, for if I thought about it too long, I might not be strong enough to do it.

The castle was unusually quiet. No lords or ladies gathered in the halls. Minimal guards standing post. No maids scurrying about. The whole castle held as still as a frozen night, waiting for what would happen next. We moved through the silent castle with our senses alert.

It was so quiet that when a maid did pass by, we both jumped. Her red, puffy eyes didn't meet ours as she ran past us.

"Let's get this over with, shall we?" Lance muttered.

"His room is in this hallway." We reached his door and knocked. Lance kept his hand by his sword, and I folded mine in front of me, my head lowered to join Tarion in his sorrow. No reply came.

I knocked again, then pushed the door open when he didn't come to answer.

The room was vacant.

"Guard?" I yelled to the man posted at the end of the hallway. "Where is Tarion?"

"His Majesty is in the throne room," he bellowed back with a small bow.

"Perhaps he's not in mourning?" I whispered to Lance as we changed our course for the large throne room that sat in the heart of the castle.

"Perhaps he doesn't know his father is dead," Lance whispered back, eyeing the guards as we passed. "I don't trust this."

His unease radiated off him and spread to me. As we walked, I reached into my pocket to find my dagger. I'd worn a thick dress today over my riding pants, one with deep pockets that concealed my objects nicely—the wish in my left pocket, the dagger in my right, giving me a sense of security as we ventured inward toward the lion's den. I could only hope grief dulled his senses and he wouldn't suspect my knife coming until it was embedded in his chest.

We turned into the throne room and entered through the tall, open doors to see Tarion sitting on the marble steps below his father's chair, the shining crown twisted in his hands.

There were no guards in the hallway or lining the side of the room. The only guards we'd seen that day were the ones who had directed us here. At the death of their king, ThornHigh should have been a flurry of movement and a rampage of guards in every corridor, but they'd sent all their men to war. And now the castle could only watch as their monarch died and another rose to take his place.

Tarion didn't wear black. He sat bedecked in red and yellow, the colors of ThornHigh, with pointed shoes and gold buckles, and frilly sleeves that draped over his knees as he held the crown between them.

The windows were positioned high on the walls to let sunlight come down in periodic square patterns on the floor. We stepped in and out of these patterns as we drew near to the throne. Our feet echoed in the open room, alerting Tarion to our entrance. He looked up and I prepared myself to see the face of a broken, mourning man. But his eyes weren't red and his cheeks weren't puffy. Instead, he smiled at me.

"You came."

"I heard about your father. I'm so sorry." I nodded to Lance to stay where he was, and though he winced, he nodded back. Then I timidly stepped toward the throne.

Then I made my mistake. I should have kept my focus, but I allowed it to slip long enough to look at his eyes. Tarion must be so broken inside. He'd lost his only remaining parent and now had to lead a country before he was ready, and in the midst of an approaching war. I could only imagine his deep pain.

And it was that thought that froze my feet.

Cassian had been right. I couldn't kill anyone.

"How kind of you to say." Tarion's attention slid. With both hands, Tarion raised the shining crown and placed it on his groomed head. Then, he pulled his shoulders back, lifted his sharp chin, and gestured at Lance. "You've been a faithful guard, both to your ward and to your kingdom. Tell me, do you love Elenvérs very much?"

Lance shifted uneasily.

"He didn't kill your father," I said. I tried to shake my head and Lance to signal that I'd changed my mind. We needed to leave as fast as possible. He looked only at the new king with a tight jaw.

Tarion bobbed his head. "I know this. Just answer this for me, you'd protect the Elenvérs people, correct?"

With hesitation, Lance replied, "Yes."

Tarion brightened. "Very good. Very good. You see, I'll need a loyal guard to protect my Elenvérs bride."

His words caused my face to pale as Lance's eyes widened. For a moment, no one knew what to say. Tarion snickered at our confusion.

"I'll never be your bride," I said. I backed up. "I should go."

The smile that stretched across his face was sickening, but nothing compared to the feeling in my stomach when a figure stepped out from behind the throne. Her hair was braided, and her lips painted, and the dress that billowed to the floor was unlike anything I'd ever seen her in, filled with colors of flowers that didn't bloom in these mountains. A sash hung across her body, and her hand grazed its fabric. Heels clicked across the floor as she stood by Tarion's side. She hated heels.

I'd been shocked before, but not like this. She chuckled softly, pure joy radiating from her eyes.

"Not you," Elis said. "Me."

Chapter Thirty-Two

A DAGGER TO THE heart wouldn't hurt as much as this betrayal. An unforgiving smile played on Elis's lips as her hand settled on Tarion's shoulder, and a ring on her finger caught a ray of sunlight—the same ring from Sanna's shop in the village that I'd admired before she said it'd been sold.

This wasn't new. They'd hidden this from me for a long time.

Things began to make sense now: Elis showing up at ThornHigh unannounced, her distance from me, her attitude toward Briggs, the remarks about Tarion fancying an Elenvérs lady—it was always her.

Though my mouth hung open, no words formed. The thoughts in my head were far too jumbled to create coherent sentences.

"It's not often someone makes her speechless," Elis said with a giggle. Tarion smiled back and his gaze lingered on her as if she was his whole world. The softness in his eyes was unrecognizable to me.

"Tell me, sister," Elis carried on, unaware of Tarion's eyes on her. "Are you surprised?"

Lance stepped to my side and I found my voice, but it wasn't for Elis. "Tarion, you still have time. Call off this war, unite our kingdoms."

His hand found Elis's, but his eyes returned to me. "I *have* united our kingdoms. But instead of two kings, there will be just one. A King from ThornHigh and a Queen from Elenvérs. My men march to Elenvérs now to get your king to surrender. Or should I say your father, if we are finally being honest with each other."

The betrayal hit me again, almost knocking me off my feet. Elis showed no remorse at sharing my secret with Tarion.

Beside me, Lance didn't react. Either he hid surprise well, or Cassian had told him the truth. I'd be fine if it were the later.

Tarion continued, "My father wasn't strong enough to handle two kingdoms or loved enough to fend off a revolution. But I'm strong enough, and my queen," his gaze returned to Elis, "she is loved enough. Together we will make ThornHigh greater than it has ever been."

His thumb traced along the back of Elis's hand, and I noticed a ring on his finger. At some point, likely the moment his father died, he'd gotten a priest and made Elis his bride. From his lack of tears in this time of loss, I didn't doubt he'd been the one to drive the dagger through his father's heart.

Tarion was right that Elis was beloved by all—she needed only five minutes with someone and they'd love her forever. Except me—right now I hated her. I hated them both.

But now, killing Tarion meant I was killing my sister's beau, and that took a new level of darkness. One that I wasn't sure I could summon.

"Your men will kill hundreds of my people before you reach the palace. That won't earn their love. And King Olin will never surrender."

Tarion didn't hesitate. "Then we kill him and take Elenvérs ourselves."

Next to him, Elis didn't flinch. Her stone eyes looked at me, and all hints of compassion or kindness were lost from within them. If there was any care in her heart for her home country, she could turn Tarion's ear and save Elenvérs.

"That is your home," I pleaded with her. "The country you were ready to swear yourself to fight for. Our family lives there. You'd bring it to the ground?" I searched for the emotion within, but the sister I'd once known so well was now closed off.

She scowled down at me and her nostrils flared with anger. "My parents are safe. Your parents are foolish. When you weren't there, the way they treated me was completely different. They didn't see me, they didn't respect me, they didn't value my opinion. And when I told them to get their men out of Brisburn, they didn't listen, and those men died."

For months, her heart had been turning cold toward Elenvérs, and none of us had seen it.

I came closer. "Who told you to get those men out? Tarion? How could King Olin have trusted that information? Elis, you were merely a lady asking him to pull men out of a village he's sworn to protect! He couldn't have known."

"He should have listened to me," she yelled as she sucked in her chest and drew her brows down. "I am more than a lady. I am smart, and respected, and loved." She took her hand from Tarion's and descended the dais. With her movement, she stepped from a shadow and into sunlight, where I saw a fire in her eyes that I recognized, one I'd seen many times when we'd fought next to each other. She'd never used that fire on me.

She continued, "I am a warrior. And I am a queen." She stopped at the lowest step so she could still look down on me as she spoke. "But you? You will never be queen."

My face didn't show the pain her words brought me. Lance's hand found mine and squeezed it.

In that dress, standing next to the throne, Elis did look like a queen—all she was missing was a crown, but there couldn't have been a coronation already. She wasn't queen yet.

She repeated her words. "You will never be queen."

She crossed to my side. "Rowan, stay here." Her tone softened. "Use your wish and break the curse. You'll have our protection, and the promise of a new life here with us."

Behind her, Tarion's expression was unreadable.

The idea of leaving Elenvérs in the midst of their darkest hour was unfathomable. This coming battle was too big for me to help much, but I wouldn't abandon my people. "I can't leave them to fight for themselves."

I expected her to get mad, but Elis sighed and lowered her voice. "Can we talk for a moment?"

I nodded, and she began to pull me away but Tarion called out. "Check her for a blade. She always carries one."

Elis's laughter floated through the room. "She wouldn't kill me. We've always known Rowan doesn't have the stomach to kill someone."

My teeth clenched. If only she knew.

Lance mumbled, "I could." Elis and I both shot him a look and he took his hand away from his hilt. His gaze flicked to Tarion who narrowed his eyes.

"We'll only be a moment," Elis promised. She pulled me a few paces to the side where she leaned against a pillar. Her shoulders relaxed, and for a moment she looked like the girl I remembered.

Just four months ago we'd been in this room together as we were welcomed into ThornHigh's court. It felt like an eternity ago.

We'd changed so much. Elis had evolved from a girl pursuing a life of knighthood and courting a fellow Elenvérs knight to a woman in love with the king of ThornHigh and willing to betray her home kingdom.

I had changed from a girl who pushed everyone away in my obsession to break my curse and save myself to someone who had hope for the future and was finally letting people into my heart.

Elis had undeniably changed more than me.

"I'm in love, Rowan." She smiled as if it was the happiest occasion of her life, to be in love with the enemy prince.

I brought my hands to my head and rubbed my temples. "How? When?"

Her eyes glazed over. "Do you remember that day when you and I were pretending to be emissaries visiting ThornHigh, and Tarion gave us a tour of the castle? You left early. We spent the rest of the night together and I swear I fell in love that night. Though perhaps I started to fall in love the night he and his father visited Elenvérs."

My heart pinched. I'd been the one to point Tarion to Elis that night.

She continued. "It was so easy with him. We're so similar. He kissed me that night here at ThornHigh, and it was different than with Briggs. I couldn't stop thinking about him."

She grinned, and I had to stare. I'd never seen her like this before.

"He wanted to keep seeing me, but you made us leave early. When he came for your pledging, he asked me to come back to ThornHigh with you, but I wasn't ready to tell anyone yet. So I snuck back. Most of the time you were here, I was here too. And we fell in love."

She'd been here? She'd only spent one day with me. One day out of the months that I was here, and I had to catch her at the castle for her to spend time with me.

She'd hurt Briggs too, when he was such a good guy. Suddenly our conversation made sense, when I told her Cassian wanted Briggs to be the second king and she begged me to let Tarion keep his throne. I should have seen it then.

A dark thought crept into my mind. Cassian told me Briggs went missing. Did Elis... My stomach turned at the thought. "Elis, did you kill Briggs?"

She tilted her head to one side and arched a brow. "How highly you think of me, sister. No, I didn't kill him. I told him if he wanted my heart, he needed to go on a mission to find the fabled flower of Chiaraz in southern Zindell. It's a year-long journey to find a flower that doesn't exist."

My jaw dropped open. That's crueler than killing him. Though she saved him from the coming battle.

"And the king? Who killed King Maven?" I glanced back at Lance who shifted on his feet. Tarion appeared at ease as he rested against the arm of the throne.

Elis's lips tightened and darkness fell over her eyes. "Tarion wanted to, but I knew it'd weigh on his soul forever if he killed his own father. I did it."

I took a step back. I'd been mistaken; this person before me was not the sister I thought I knew. This figure was unrecognizable to me.

She held her hands out to me. "I did what needed to be done for my kingdom. The king was responsible for my cousin's death at Brisburn. Now his death is avenged."

Tarion was also responsible for that, I wanted to point out. But she was in love with him, and that love made her blind.

She clasped my hands in hers. "Rowan, stay with us. We can have a good life here."

Tarion and Lance still eyed each other. My chance of killing Tarion was gone now. My only goal was to get me and Lance out of ThornHigh alive, and perhaps convince Elis to join us.

With luck, a piece of Elenvérs' spirit remained in her.

"Together, we can try to save Elenvérs. Use your position with Tarion to stop his men from attacking. We just need to buy a bit of time before our allies get here."

She pulled back from me. "I'm not using Tarion. And Elenvérs can't win. We already control several points within your boundaries. Harrowhut, Yule Point, Brisburn, they are all taken. Harrowhut has been sworn to ThornHigh for years now and your king didn't notice. Elenvérs is not smart enough or strong enough to fend off our men."

Ah. So that's why Harrowhut stopped paying the king's taxes.

My head shook. "You already speak of ThornHigh as your own, and of Elenvérs as the enemy."

"You don't have to be the enemy," she said.

"It's too late for that now."

And now, that divide of mountains between our two countries felt like the divide between us, icy and cold and vast. Our relationship was broken shards of land that we couldn't unite, and she was ready to let my kingdom fall.

I couldn't convince Elis to leave. But I wouldn't stay.

I absorbed one last sight of my beloved sister before turning to Lance. My voice cracked with a deeply etched sorrow. "We are going home." He exhaled and strode toward me.

"Rowan," Elis called from behind me. "It's no use. Elenvérs is doomed."

"No!" I swung around to her. "I'm not giving up like you did. There are good people there that need to be protected. My people. My family." The first tears fell down my cheeks as anger bubbled inside.

She raised her voice, spreading her arms out across the large room. "We will protect any who come to us. We will be stronger once the lands are united."

My heart burned with her betrayal. "The army already marches."

Lance joined my side and together we began to walk from the room, but Tarion stopped us.

"I can't let you leave when you know so much." He stood. His eyes narrowed, threatening us to defy him. His hands were balled into fists on the throne.

He was not my king. I did not take orders from him. "If you don't want us to leave, you'll have to kill us."

"Rowan," Lance warned.

Tarion grinned, though the expression was far from kind. "I was hoping you'd say that." With a swift flick of his wrist, Tarion threw a dagger at me. I dropped to the floor before it hit me. Elis cried out for him to stop, the first sign that she still cared for me, but he reached to the side of the throne and pulled at a ribbon, unravelling another dagger.

I plunged my hand into my pocket and pulled out my own dagger, but I didn't throw it. Instead, I looked at my sister.

We'd gone through everything in this life together. She'd been more than a sister or a close friend, she'd been my strength. But as I pulled out my dagger, she threw herself in front of Tarion to protect him.

I'd never understand how he won her heart so quickly, but she wasn't loyal to me anymore. She was his.

It was too late to win her back now. I turned and ran.

Together, Lance and I bolted from the room while Elis called after us. Lance drew his sword midrun and glanced behind us. A moment later he spun around, and the sword deflected the blade that Tarion had thrown. It clattered with a hollow sound.

Tarion roared.

We turned the corner, but we didn't slow our pace. We continued as fast as our feet could take us away from ThornHigh and my deceitful sister. We only slowed when we reached the stables to strap a saddle on our horses, cling to their manes, then ride hard from the castle.

"What if he shoots us with arrows?" Lance glanced behind him at the castle wall as we rode across the bridge.

I resisted looking. "I'll have to hope that my sister will protect me one last time," I said.

My back flexed at every noise, but no arrows followed us out of ThornHigh. Perhaps it was the persuasion of Elis, or perhaps Tarion simply didn't care enough about us to follow. He was king now, and he had a war to lead.

The castle and village faded behind us as the snowy mountain surrounded us. We had a harsh few days of riding ahead of us with no provisions, but my fury at Elis would drive me.

We needed to get back to Elenvérs and to Cassian. I glanced back once, but ThornHigh was far behind us by then.

Goodbye, Elis.

Chapter Thirty-Three

"SO, YOU'RE KING OLIN'S daughter, then?" It took Lance almost the entire trip—which we made in a record five days— back to Elenvérs to ask me, and I laughed.

"Yes. Please don't tell anyone. At least, not yet. In a few months it will be announced once I break the curse."

"The sleeping curse," Lance placed. He glanced at me. His cheeks were sunken in from lack of food, and his eyes were red with exhaustion. It took all our strength to sit up on our horses, and our stomachs rumbled with hunger.

We were almost home.

The Elenvérs palace was still standing, and that was a good sign. How much longer did we have until General Barrett's army was upon us?

My mind tried to focus on a way to win the war, but thoughts of Elis continued to plague me and sent surges of anger and sadness coursing through my veins. How could she do this to us? How could she turn her back on Elenvérs?

What was I going to tell her parents?

I wondered if Elis and Tarion were suiting up for battle, or if they would stay at the castle while their men fought.

Lance tapped his chin. "So that must be why Cassian begged me to take care of you. You're his sister. I've never seen him talk about someone the way he talks of you."

I blushed. "I'm not his sister. He's not the true heir."

I could see his mind working to process that. "Ah. When will you fall asleep?"

I patted my pocket. "I won't."

Lance fell silent as he continued thinking. A post guard spotted us as we rode in, and we waved to him. Soon after, we were riding up toward the Elenvérs' gate.

As we neared the stables, Cassian ran from the side of the palace to meet us. I swung off my horse just as he crashed into me.

As soon as his arms were around me, I was filled with a sense of safety. All my worries for the future of Elenvérs, all my fears of what Tarion might do, all my frustrations at Elis, it all drifted away as he held me tight.

"Not his sister indeed," Lance muttered.

"You're safe." He breathed into my hair, crushing me in his embrace.

"We came back to help fight," I mumbled into his chest.

He pulled back and nodded to Lance. "I'm so glad you've returned. One day later and you would have missed us. We ride out tomorrow to battle in the Wandering Mountains. Have you heard any updates on their locations?"

Guilt filled me as I shook my head. My time at ThornHigh had been informative, but I knew no more about the armies other than what my search in General Barrett's room told me.

"I've learned some more information, but it's not about their men. It's about Elis."

The way his face tightened told me he already knew. "Yes, unfortunate business there. She left behind a note. Mama and Papa are beside themselves. Nothing to be done about that now." He shook the pain off his face, but a sliver remained. "Come, you must be cold."

"And hungry," Lance said as he rubbed the side of his horse.

We handed our steeds to the groom, who got to work brushing them down.

Cassian led us through to the kitchens where we ate everything in sight. As we did, Cassian filled us in. Scouts had been sent out three weeks ago to see where their armies were placed, and none found more than a small company of soldiers to the east. Upon their return, the king sent out a few riders to meet small pockets of our knights and relocate them to the Wandering Mountains. All of our fighters would be moved there in order to fight the bulk of their army. Tomorrow, the remaining warriors at Elenvérs would ride to meet them.

In two weeks, our armies should converge, and then we'd fight.

In three weeks, it would be my birthday.

My hand slid to my pocket where I rubbed my wish.

"Here's the interesting bit," Cassian continued, sitting on the table next to me. "Annon is helping us."

"No," I cried out. "Don't trust him. Any information he gives us has to be false."

Lance raised a brow at my outburst. His cheeks bulged with honey bread. Cassian shook his head. "I thought so too, but so far it has turned out to be real. Valuable, even. He's known when the armies planned to attack which towns, and we were able to save Reffiel thanks to him. It's because of him that we know where they will be in two weeks."

"Is he here?" I spoke through a mouthful of dried meat.

Cassian refilled my glass of spiced wine. "He returned two weeks ago."

Fear curled in my chest. I'd hoped to leave him behind with ThornHigh. I didn't trust him to be anywhere near me when my curse was due. When I didn't fall asleep, he might take matters into his own hands.

"We will deal with him later," I said as I wiped my mouth with a cloth napkin. My eyelids ached with exhaustion. I could barely focus on Cassian's words.

"If you're finished stuffing yourself, your parents will be eager to see you." Cassian clapped his hands. "Lance, thank you so much for keeping her safe. Will you be riding out with us tomorrow?"

Lance took another gulp of water. "It'll be my honor. Now if you excuse me, my bed calls." He set down his cup and bowed to us both.

He'd been the most loyal guard I could have asked for, even amidst my wild antics at ThornHigh. Whether it was sneaking out at night to spy on Bear or planning to kill Tarion, he'd stood by me through everything. When I was queen one day, he'd be the ideal guard.

If I became queen. To do that, we needed to defeat ThornHigh.

"C'mon. Let's see your parents. Then you need a bath. Desperately."

THE NEXT DAY, ALL the Elenvérs knights suited up to ride toward the mysterious Wandering Mountains and face the ThornHigh army. I kissed my mothers' cheeks and promised them I'd see them both soon, then tied my satchel to my horse's side and swung my leg over.

Cassian mounted next to me, and we took our place next to King Olin's side. Annon was behind us, the first time I'd seen him in weeks. He didn't look at me but nodded to King Olin as we all took off.

I kept one eye firmly planted on Annon the entire time. Every time he spoke with someone, every time he coughed into his shoulder, every time he patted his horse's neck, I watched him.

We rode until the last of the light left the sky, then we set up tents for the night. The Wandering Mountains sat in front of us and Elenvérs behind us. So far, we'd traveled the same way that Elis and I came in search of the White Bear. If we passed by that stream now, maybe I'd see the bear this time.

All around me, people made fires and settled down to eat their small portions. We had six more days until we reached the mountainside where we planned to wait for the enemy. They shouldn't know we were coming, so we'd have the element of surprise, but they had the numbers. It'd be a tough battle.

Having Annon here just made it trickier because he took half of my attention.

"He won't hurt you," Cassian whispered next to me as we sat beside the fire. "'Least, not yet. He'll fight for Elenvérs first."

I muttered under my breath, "I'm not so sure about that. I don't trust the man. We should have left him behind."

"Your father would never have agreed to that. We need everybody we can get if we hope to win this battle."

There was no merriment as we ate our dinners, no men toasting or clapping around the fire. Spirits were as low as the food supply, and the battle ahead was uncertain. Many of us would not return. What few of us did return would need to pray our allies got here soon to save us from the attack that would surely follow. Tarion wouldn't give up easily.

And even if we won this war, we were still dangerously low on resources. Elenvérs would need a miracle to survive.

"Do you have your wish on you?" Cassian leaned close to ask. I nodded. "Good. I've been reading about them, and apparently there are only three in the world. Once you use it, the wish takes fifty years before the magic inside is strong enough to be used again."

My hand slipped into my pocket to the pouch where I'd put my wish. "I wonder what makes the knowledge of my fairies' gifts powerful enough that Witch Marlogne would trade a wish for it."

Cassian's brow's crunched together.

My hand tightened on the wish. "That witch is a strange lady. I had to tell her what my gifts from the fairies were, then she handed over the wish."

He stared at me. "I would have told her that in a heartbeat. You got that wish easily. Men have died trying to acquire one of those."

King Olin walked by at that moment and gave us a look. "You two should get some rest. We have another long day ahead of us, and there's no telling what dangers await." He paused like he might say more, but then continued his rounds. His red nose dripped from the cold. All around us, hundreds of small tents were pitched and fires were burning. The white mountainside was now filled with antsy soldiers, tired horses, and black smoke.

Annon already had his tent made and had closed himself inside. I'd sleep better with Lance at my side but I hadn't spotted him today. I'd been too busy watching Annon.

Cassian stood to find his tent. "Sleep, Rowan. He won't harm you tonight."

I couldn't be so sure. While my body begged me for rest, my mind wouldn't let me sleep, keeping me awake with worries. I tossed and turned inside my small tent, until hours later I pulled myself from the tent and sat beside the fire.

The camp was mostly asleep, but a few patrol guards remained awake as they paced around the camp. It was all quiet, besides the crackling of fires, footsteps, and the occasional horse neigh. I stared into the bright fire as I tried to push gruesome thoughts of the coming battle out of my restless mind. How many Elenvérs people would die this week? How could we beat an army of their size?

A sharp noise startled me, and my father sat down at my side. "Can't sleep?" He set down his blade.

I shook my head.

"Me either." He stared into the dying fire, and I wondered what thoughts plagued his mind.

I peeked at Annon's quiet tent.

"He worries you." My father didn't say it as a question, but a statement. "Why?"

"Annon?" I whispered. How much did he want to know? Should I tell him how his brother plans to show me off to the kingdom once I'm asleep and take back the throne that ought to have been his? Or should I tell him how he worked alongside King Maven at ThornHigh?

Would he believe me if I did?

Finally, I shrugged. "I have a bad feeling about him."

My father nodded. "Is it because of how close he was with King Maven?"

My jaw dropped open, and my father smiled. "That was a necessary part of my plan. Annon helped delay this battle so we could get as many people to safety as possible. He also uncovered invaluable information from ThornHigh, but to do that he needed everyone to believe that he was working with King Maven. Even you."

Cassian told me how useful Annon was to them. But it still didn't make me trust the man. "Did you know he knows I'm your daughter?"

I waited for the look of shock, but what came out of King Olin's mouth was a snort. "I suspected he did. But when you break your curse in a few weeks, we will tell everyone anyway. Annon will be managed." He ran his fingers down his blade. "I don't want you to worry about him. I'll keep you safe from anything he might have planned."

The fire cast shadows across Annon's tent and melted the surrounding snow. My father shook his head and sighed as he leaned his hands against the log to watch the flames dance.

Moments like these were rare, and a feeling lingered between us that I struggled to properly name. Calm.

Comfortable. There were no walls up or bitterness clouding the relationship that we ought to have, only understanding and the start of what I could call love.

The curse and our unique ways of handling it had robbed us of a lifetime of moments like these. But once I broke the curse and we beat this army, we would have a lifetime of opportunities to build our relationship.

I wasn't the only one feeling the change in our relationship. My father's hand found mine and he squeezed it. "I'm so proud of the young woman you've become. You got the best parts of your mother and none of my weaknesses. I'll be so proud to introduce you to Elenvérs as my daughter."

A warmth tingled through my body despite the cold, and I squeezed his hand back. "Thank you. I hope to be half the ruler you are."

He wiped a tear from his cheek. "You'll be twice as great. I believe in you."

He'd never know how much those words meant to me. Even as he returned to watching the flames, I repeated his kind words in my mind.

Soon my head grew heavy and my eyelids drooped, so I waddled off to bed. The cold tent and lumpy ground made it difficult to get comfortable and I tossed a few times before finding a good position. My sword nestled into my side and I buried my face into my thin blanket as I closed my eyes, falling asleep to the sounds of footsteps in snow and fire crackling.

All too soon Cassian was shaking me awake. "It's time to get moving. We don't want to waste the light."

Chapter Thirty-Four

I FOUND LANCE THE second day and invited him to ride with me and Cassian. He made for pleasant company, though it was hard to forget that we rode to battle. Each gallop forward brought us closer to ThornHigh's men and a fight that many of us would not survive. As we rode, we met up with other groups of our warriors that were stationed along the way, until finally, as the sun rose on the sixth day, we had a few thousand fighters ready to fight.

Then we waited.

Be brave. You're prepared for this. Still, it was difficult to keep visions of the coming battle from haunting my mind.

We snuck into the valley during the cover of night and prepared ourselves for battle. Tomorrow, we'd cross the last mountain and ride to the men that should be waiting on the other side.

Early in the morning while the others rested, Cassian, Lance, and I rode up the side of the mountain to see the army we faced. We left our horses behind, taking only a few stale pieces of bread with us and canteens of water that needed to be filled. I wore my wish in a small bag on a chain around my neck, then tucked into my shirt so no one would see it.

"How many soldiers do you suppose they have?" Lance asked through heavy breaths.

"I don't know. I'd guess a few thousand," Cassian said.

I laughed as I climbed higher. "I'd say more than that."

Cassian frowned. "We can't handle many more than that."

A shimmering stream trickled beside us, and we stopped to fill our water. The perfectly-rounded stones reminded me of the stream where Elis and I had spotted the bear all those months ago. How the times had changed.

"I think I see some of their army now. Annon was right—they are in this valley," Cassian said, pointing between drooping branches.

He was right. Black tents spotted the foothills of the mountain. Smoke rose to the sky, and flashes of light showed their fires.

As we crept up our side of the mountain, their full army came into view.

It sat on the bottom half of the two mountains and across the valley between them. Soldiers moved through camp on horseback. It wouldn't take them long to spot us on the other side, especially if they sent scouts, but they hadn't planned to advance for another few weeks.

That thought made me shiver. They were still waiting on soldiers to arrive before attacking. Their army wasn't complete.

We stood at the mouth of the stream and stared down at the men. Fear filled my chest and my knees trembled. Their army didn't just fill the valley or the sides of the mountain, they filled the mountain behind that one, and the one behind that. Their dark tents spread for as far as we could see.

The Wandering Mountains once looked so beautiful. Now they were deadly. They didn't have a couple thousand men. They had many, many more.

Slowly, we looked at each other and gulped.

"For Elenvérs," Lance said. Cassian nodded.

"We will be slaughtered." My voice rang in my ears.

"We won't run like cowards. We will fight with all our strength to protect our country." Cassian spoke in a daze.

I shook him. "We won't have a kingdom left after this. They will kill us all, and march to the weak back home. Nothing will survive."

He looked back over the men. Perhaps we could kill half of them, but there were too many for us to kill them all. I didn't like the idea of running from a fight, but we weren't strong enough to win.

My hope began to sink, and I clutched my wish for strength.

It was then, in my hopeless state, that a new idea took root. I pulled my wish from around my neck and opened the bag. The golden orb glowed for me, reminding me of its power.

I glanced at Cassian who shook his head at me. "Don't do it. You need that."

Lance looked at the wish with a puzzled expression. It appeared golden against the rest of the white mountain, and bright enough to illuminate my jacket. "What is it?"

"A wish. It can save our people."

Lance brightened. "Then what did we have to ride all the way out here for? Use the wish."

"No," Cassian said again. "If she uses the wish, she can't save herself from her curse. It's your only hope, Rowan."

Once, I thought that was what I cared about the most. Breaking my curse. Nothing meant more to me than that.

Then I'd found this wish. I thought I'd done it. I thought I'd solved my dilemma.

I could still save myself, but this wish might be the only thing that could save Elenvérs.

And surely my life wasn't worth the lives of my people.

This wish could destroy the whole army. But then I'd be responsible for killing all those beings, and Elenvérs would still be in a land that was running out of resources. I couldn't solve both problems with only one wish.

"Don't do this." Cassian's hands fell to my shoulders.

I remained lost in thought. How could I save my people? Our land?

Our homeland.

For so long people had passed down tales of our homeland in the south, the land we had to leave after a foolish king let a girl deceive him and the land was destroyed. It might not be livable now. But hopefully it wasn't under attack.

This wish didn't have to kill anyone. It could evacuate everyone out of Elenvérs and back to our homeland.

"What if I send everyone home," I said. "Back to our homeland? The one in the south?"

"No," Cassian said without thinking. Lance cast a look to the army.

"Cassian, this would save everyone. No one would die."

"We'd be in a land we know nothing about," he said. "And you'll fall asleep. You won't be able to stop the curse. This is what you've worked for."

He couldn't change my mind. One more look at the army was all I needed to know this was the right decision.

"I have to do it. It's the only way we survive this."

Lance gulped as he looked over the army. "Is there any other way to stop your curse? Perhaps if we went to the southern homeland, they might have something there that is strong enough." His voice faded.

I smiled sadly. "It's not a nice victory, but it saves every life and offers a new hope."

That hope didn't extend to me. I knew nothing could save me from my curse. No matter where I was, as soon as snow began to fall somewhere in the world on the last day of my eighteenth year, I would fall asleep.

I didn't want to sleep in a country that wasn't my own. "I won't be going with you. I want to stay with Elenvérs."

Cassian's hands picked up my own. His finger rubbed over the wish. "Rowan, you don't have to do this. Come with us. There's nothing left for you here." His honey brown eyes looked into mine from beneath short lashes. A snowflake landed on his cheek, turning into a small drop of water, and he wiped at it with his shoulder. His face was so familiar to me, I'd seen it all my life almost every day, but this would be the last time I looked upon it. The last time he looked upon mine.

"I'll fall asleep soon anyway." I looked over my shoulder. "I'd rather sleep with my kingdom. I'll settle in the back cupboards of the kitchens where I used to hide from you as a child, and perhaps the same magic that keeps me safe while I sleep will protect Elenvérs."

Lance stayed quiet as Cassian wrapped his arms around me. "I'll keep a journal for you, with pictures of the family and letters from them to you."

Again, tears pricked my eyes. "Thank you," I exhaled.

He pulled back and nodded his head. "And I always knew you hid in that cupboard, but the cook never let me in."

A laugh escaped me, and he joined in. The last time I'd hear him laugh.

Sadness threatened to overwhelm me as I looked into Cassian's eyes, and a tear slid down his cheek.

With a thick voice, he said, "I wanted a life with you."

A pain vibrated through my heart. I should have trusted Cassian sooner. Now I'd never know what future we might have had together.

A tear slid down my cheek. "That would have been a beautiful life."

Lance coughed. "I don't have a deep sentiment to share, but I'll miss you too."

I laughed through my tears. "Thank you, Lance. Keep Cassian safe."

He smiled back. "You're doing that all on your own." He nodded to my wish.

I wanted to go back down and say goodbye to my father, but there wasn't time. Cassian would tell him for me. He'd be sure everyone knew how much I loved them all. If I waited too long, my resolve might shake.

So, with one hand in Cassian's and another on the wish, I breathed my desires into it. The warmth of the wish tingled over my lips, almost like a warning. Use the wish wisely, the witch had said. I only get this one chance.

"I wish for my people be taken safely back to our southern homeland." Cassian squeezed my hand. I clenched the wish. A cold tear dripped down my chin. "Except for me. Leave me here."

For a terrifying moment, nothing happened. I'd wished for too much.

Then their forms shimmered before me. Slowly, Cassian and Lance turned to vapors of gold that caught in the wind and disappeared.

Lance bowed deeply before his form drifted away.

Cassian didn't look frightened, or fascinated, or sad. His stoic face nodded to me, the edges becoming blurry, and he spoke his last words. "You are the strongest queen Elenvérs could have asked for."

Then the feeling of his hand was gone from mine, and he was gone.

The large army in front of me remained. But when I turned around, the Elenvérs camp had faded away. Gold mist loomed behind, but soon that too drifted away.

I could only imagine their confusion. But they were safe.

For the first time in months, I didn't feel afraid. My people would be safe outside of these cold mountains and could start a new kingdom back in our homeland. The palace of Elenvérs might fall, but the kingdom would live on. And it'd be waiting for me when I woke.

The wish in my hand turned black and lightweight as the power had seeped from it. I placed it back in the bag and tied it around my neck. I better start my return home.

A movement came from the corner of my eye. My head snapped up and my hand flew to the sword at my side.

But it wasn't a soldier. Standing at the edge of the stream was the White Bear.

I could see him.

The White Bear didn't move. Every muscle in my body tensed but he didn't charge at me.

We stared at each other until he nodded. He was the same as I remembered him: the thick white hair, the striking blue eyes, the sense that he knew more than a bear normally knew. There was something different though.

This time, approval dwelled in his gaze in the way his eyelids turned downward and his snout smiled. I'd done it. I'd made my heart pure. Five months ago, I wouldn't have given up my one shot at breaking the curse to protect the knights from a battle. But today, I'd given up my only hope in order to save those around me.

He bowed low to me, and I bowed back.

"I've appeared before many," his voice spoke clear in my mind. I startled. It was deep and rich like the stream that he stood beside. "Some have seen me, and some have not."

He took a small step toward me. "But you are the first to return and see me when you previously did not."

A smile tugged at my lips. I'd been so worried when Elis saw the bear and I didn't. It felt silly now how often I'd worried about it. Then again, maybe it was because I cared so much that I fixed the bitterness in my heart.

My heart had healed during these past few months, while Elis's heart had changed.

"White Bear," I said. "Do you remember the girl that I came with the first time?"

His head dropped. "I do."

I licked my cold lips. "Will she be okay?"

His whole body expanded with breath. "There is no way to know. Her future is uncertain."

I frowned. "Is there anything I can do for her?"

"She's no longer yours to worry about. If the queen of ThornHigh wishes to restore her pure heart, she will need to do it herself."

I hated that I couldn't do anything to help her. She'd always been there for me, so it didn't feel right that now there was nothing I could do for her.

"But you have your own problems to worry about." He glanced back at the ThornHigh army. "I've already summoned a friend to help you."

He bowed again, and his voice began to fade in my mind. "Well done, Princess Rowan. Well done."

Then he ran away.

What friend had he meant? Did I need to wait for them?

I decided to wait, but one more look at the army changed my mind. I turned and started back toward the castle.

I only got ten paces in before a crackly voice chortled. "You'll freeze before you make it back."

Where the White Bear stood a moment before, now Witch Marlogne waited by the stream. She wore a purple dress and her dragon shoes, with the little creature curled around her ankle. Her hair was piled on her head and made her twice as tall as she ought to have been.

She grinned at me. "Surprised to see me? I've been watching you closely. This is not how I expected your tale to go."

"And how did you expect it?" I placed a hand over the wish around my neck.

She shrugged, brushing the fur on the shoulders of her dress. "I thought you'd kill Tarion. He almost cost you everything. But I must say, I am impressed with how much chocolate pudding you can consume."

I almost laughed. "It's a gift."

"That it is. Now what do you say I get you back home? The soldiers will still march on Elenvérs, so you're not safe yet. But I can bring you to the Elenvérs palace."

"Yes, please." I nodded. Anything to save me from this long journey home.

No sooner had I agreed than the world began to fade away. As the snow and the stream began to drift away, the tall, ice walls of Elenvérs came into view, along with the long bridge over the Grand Hall and the high ceilings. The snow beneath my feet turned to hard floors and the cold wind died.

Witch Marlogne wasn't here, and the wish was gone from my neck. Her voice echoed in my mind. "Be careful here. You aren't safe yet. The army will still come."

Then it was silent. I was home. And I was alone.

Chapter Thirty-Five

EVERY SOUND STARTLED ME, and I didn't often wander too far from windows where my watchful eye kept to the paths. By nightfall, there was still no sign of an approaching army, only white sheets of snow across the horizon.

I clad myself in armor in case a spy came first to scope out the palace. By now, the armies must realize something had happened as they found each of the caves empty.

An unnerving silence filled the halls, along with a bitter cold to remind me that the magic from the cave mages was gone. As the moon and stars appeared, their glow didn't illuminate the palace as it once had, and the snowflakes didn't shine in the walls like they used to. Instead, the halls turned to a dark gray color and frost began to take over the furniture, starting in the corner of windows and moving inward.

Soon, this palace would be nothing but a frozen remain of its former glory.

All the personal possessions were gone. The only things that remained were the furniture and plates and food. I left most of the rooms alone but hesitated outside my parent's chambers. Finally, I pushed the doors open and wandered in.

It was empty, except for a single picture on the desk of their faces. One last gift from either the wish or the witch for me to hold on to. I folded the picture and slid it into my pocket. Then I left their room in peace.

As dusk turned to night, the darkness grew thicker. If I didn't hide in the kitchens soon, I risked being caught by a spy sneaking in with the cover of night. I first headed to my bedchambers to find blankets and a pillow to stuff in the small compartment with me.

As soon as I stepped into my old chambers, regret filled me.

This place reminded me so clearly of the sister that I'd lost. Memories rushed me, each one featuring her, and so many of them in this little room. Our most recent time together was here where she'd asked me to let Tarion be king once the kingdoms merged. She'd loved him then, and I'd been unable to see it.

I'd been unable to see a lot.

The pain of this room and the betrayal of Elis gripped my heart, and with the darkness and quiet surrounding me, the room tasted of pure sadness.

Three breaths, that's how long it took to decide I couldn't stay in that room, and I slammed the door behind me. I'd use some of Lord and Lady Trelluse's blankets instead.

I grabbed the thickest blanket and softest pillow and practically ran from the room and the memories that came with it.

Tears weren't allowed to come, not yet.

The kitchens smelled like spiced meat, reminding my stomach of hunger. Before I feasted on whatever could be found, I cleared out the back-corner cabinet and made up my bed within. There was hardly enough room to stretch my legs, but if I bent them, I could lean my head back a bit on the pillow and be halfway comfortable, while still able to push open the crack of the cabinet to see the doors.

Fear began to set back in, but I pushed it away like the tears. Both could wait.

Cooking the meat would require fire, and the smoke would send a clear signal to ThornHigh's armies that someone remained at the castle. The bulk of the army wouldn't be close enough to see it, but I didn't know what other men lurked in the mountains. I couldn't risk a fire.

I found some bread and cheese to munch on. The cheese block was like ice in my hand, as the entire castle began to freeze. It would have been smart to grab a second blanket, but it was too late for that now. Tomorrow I'd fetch another one. For now, I gobbled down the food and some water, then eased myself back into the small cabinet where I curled up and prepared myself for a long night of restless sleep.

SLEEP DIDN'T COME UNTIL first light, when I drifted into an uncomfortable slumber.

A door breaking down awakened me, and I almost cried out. I sat up straight and pulled my knees into my chest.

Somewhere, someone moved.

Not someone, I realized. Multiple people. Heavy footsteps, loud doors, and the clanging of metal rang through the halls of the palace.

They shouldn't have had to search too hard to realize that no one was here. They should leave soon. I repeated these hopes in my mind as the sounds grew.

From the light seeping through the crack in the cupboard, I guessed it was midday. My legs cramped badly, but it was nothing compared to the worry that caused my heart to beat out of my chest.

With a slow hand, I found my sword and clung to it. For an hour the sounds of soldiers barging through my home continued. Soon, however, they grew quieter, and I allowed myself to breathe easier.

Then, to my horror and dismay, the door to the kitchen opened.

My heart would never beat normally again.

My breath filled my cheeks, but it didn't release. My eyes closed and my ears perked up. A pot fell to the floor, sending a jolt through me.

"Watch it, will ya?" a man with a soft voice said.

"Sorry." The pan made a noise again, lighter this time, like he'd put it back on the counter. "Look, elk meat."

The first man snorted. "It'd be rotten by now. I'm not eating that."

"See how frosted over it is? The cold has preserved it. It's waste to leave good meat behind."

Their footsteps moved dangerously close to my hiding place. Through the tiny crack I saw outlines of two men clad in armor as they scoped out the kitchen. A few times they stopped to open cupboard doors and rummage inside.

"Let's grab the meat and be gone, we don't want to be left behind."

"Not in this cursed place. Here, grab that knife. We'll hide the meat in this sack and cook it tonight when everyone else is sleeping."

"Good idea, more for us."

They cut it along the bone and chopped it into pieces before shoving it into their bag, then marched back out with their contraband. They left the door open behind them.

Every muscle in my body stayed taunt, and only when my head felt dizzy did I realize that I was hardly breathing. I took a large gulp of air. The sounds around me were rare and distant, nothing but echoes of savage men leaving my precious home. I cringed at what destruction they must have left behind.

But Elenvérs still stood, and my people still lived. We did not fall today.

When hours passed with no further noises, and I could stay in that small cupboard no longer, I quietly opened the door and sprawled onto the floor.

"Ugh," I groaned through the aches. The cold ground licked my face, but the relief in my legs was too great to care about the ice against my cheek.

"Food, I need food." My arms ached as I lifted my tired body to a sitting position, and that's when I saw it. The cupboard next to mine was open.

They'd opened several cupboards, but I hadn't realized they'd gotten so close. If they had opened one more, they'd have found me, and I'd be dead right now.

Deep breath.

Suddenly I wasn't as hungry anymore. I grabbed my sword and went to inspect the damage.

The soldiers had torn apart the castle at random, shredding some rooms and leaving others untouched. The throne room got the brunt of it. They'd slashed the throne cushions and pulled out the stuffing, then tore the dark blue curtains in half. The room looked haunted with the empty seats and scattered pieces of fabric strewn across the floor like a frozen sea.

I'd never be able to guess that a week ago, a king sat on that chair.

This was more than looking for hidden people. This room was savaged in malice.

My fingers ran over the ridges of my father's throne, then my mother's. It wouldn't be right to leave it this way.

I fetched a needle and some thread, stopped at every window to look outside for more soldiers, then got to work patching up the throne room. I worked until my fingers hurt from the activity that I wasn't used to doing, took a break for food, then worked some more. As the sun began to set, I found another blanket and curled into the cabinet again to be safe.

Thus began my quiet, last days in this lifetime. Fixing what had been torn, eating the last of the food in the kitchen that could be prepped without a fire, and keeping watch over the mountain side. Each day the palace grew colder, and each day my fear for what would happen when I fell asleep grew stronger.

I could only hope that the magic that put me to sleep would protect me if ThornHigh found me. Elis certainly wouldn't.

Tomorrow might be my birthday. Or was it the next day? Somehow, I'd lost track of a day and couldn't be certain.

Clouds gathered in the sky outside, but snow didn't fall. I tried to distract myself from the curse with my work in the throne room. Besides a slight overlay in the fabric's pattern, my father and mother's thrones were put together once more, and they looked magnificent. The curtains proved a more difficult task, but I did what I could.

I'd just wound the needle up with the leftover thread after finishing the last of the stitching when a sound came from behind me.

Footsteps.

Someone was here.

I whirled around, prepared to leave, but I was too late.

Tarion stood with his hands folded as he watched me like a hunter eyeing its prey already ensnared. My blood boiled within, and heat flooded my face. In my week alone I'd grown too comfortable and left my sword on the floor next to my father's throne. It'd take several bounds to reach it, and he'd get there first.

Shoot.

He had his own sword drawn, a blade as long as the smile on his face and as sharp as the expression in his eyes. He didn't lunge, but allowed me a moment of shock where he gloated over my helplessness. He wore the same outfit he'd worn when

I pledged myself as his spy, the first time I'd teamed up with him.

There was no doubt that he was the enemy now.

"Tarion."

"You can call me Your Highness," he sneered. "I'm not surprised to find you in the throne room where you always thought you belonged. Though, I was expecting to find you whimpering in the back cupboard of the kitchens."

"How did you—" I stopped. Elis. There was no end to her betrayal.

"My wife suspected you used your wish when we couldn't find anyone. She also suspected that you stayed behind. You'd never leave your precious country. She wasn't strong enough to come check for herself; this place holds bad memories for her, but I couldn't leave you here alone." He took a small step toward me, and I eyed his blade.

I moved back. "I'm defenseless, and the curse will take me soon anyway. You don't have to kill me. My sister would never forgive you for that."

As subtly as I could manage, I maneuvered the thread from the needle, giving me a small weapon. It wouldn't do much, but if I could get it into his eye or his neck, I could achieve some damage.

"Tell me," I said—both to buy time and because I was curious. "How did you steal wind messages?"

Tarion moved closer to the throne where my sword sat, though his eye stayed on me. "I didn't." His lips curled in a cruel grin. "Mar did. Turns out she was helpful for more than just getting you to trust me."

I turned still as ice.

That was before I'd known I was returning to ThornHigh. That was before Tarion could have known who I was. That was before I even suspected him of working against Elenvérs. He'd played me before I even knew I was playing.

I'd kept an eye on his father, due to the stories I'd heard of him. But I hadn't looked at Tarion closely enough, and he'd deceived me.

I pinched the needle between my fingers as my blood boiled.

"You're thinking about where you could stab me with that, aren't you?" He nodded to my hand. "See, you think you're so clever, but I've always been ahead of you. And now I'm here to be sure you fall asleep." He sheathed his sword. I glanced at mine once more, and he laughed. "Think you're faster than me?"

Without warning he darted to the sword and plucked it from the seat of the throne. "You're helpless against me." He threw it. Steel clanged against the ice floor. "Nothing can save you now."

I dropped the thread and lunged at him.

He smiled as if he anticipated it, but I crashed into him with such force that it sent him rolling on the floor underneath me.

My knee pinned him down, pressing my weight into his chest. My hand flew to his hilt. From this angle, I couldn't pull the blade out, but I could block him from grabbing it. He squirmed and shoved at me, but nothing he did could budge me. His lips tightened as he strained to loosen himself.

"You were never smarter than me," I said as I dug my knee in deeper towards his lungs. He choked out a grunt and used a hand to shove my knee, then brought his other hand to the hilt to push at mine.

He rolled, taking me with him.

I continued the motion, pulling him down hard against the floor where he heaved. This time, I drove my knee into his hip harder, and he grunted. If I'd known it'd be this easy to wrestle him, I'd have done it in the throne room of ThornHigh.

"I'm," he heaved. "Always...ahead of you."

A sharp point pressed against my finger, and I looked down.

With his hand, he'd pulled a gold spindle from his pocket, and while I thought he'd been attempting to remove my hand from his sword, he'd been searching for my finger.

He'd pricked me.

My hand flew backward, and I staggered away. The spindle dropped to the floor with a hollow clank as Tarion brought himself to a sitting position, clutching his side. He didn't take his eyes off me.

A small red dot formed under my skin, then a drop of blood trickled out. Despite the cold room, heat flooded my body and I squeezed the finger, willing the wound to go away. My breaths came shallow and raspy as tears clouded my eyes.

Tarion stood up. "For my wife, I won't kill you. But you'll never be queen here."

"You." I tried to speak, but my mind spun like a chariot's wheel.

Darkness creeped in from the corners of my eyes, fighting against the light. My legs grew weak and my finger tingled. One by one, my senses began to drift away, first the feeling of cold and the heat, then the sound. Next, the darkness overtook the light, and my legs fell out from under me.

Tarion smiled and began to walk away, leaving me alone.

Outside, the clouds released their snow.

"As the last snow of her eighteenth year begins to fall..." A lyrical voice sang in my mind.

Then it was silent, and a heavy sleep set in.

Chapter Thirty-Six

DARK. COLD. ALONE.
So tired.

Chapter Thirty-Seven

"WHAT WILL IT BE like?" I once asked Mother. "When I sleep?"

"Do not fret, dear child. Sleep will be the start of a great adventure for you."

But I needed to know, and when she looked in my eyes, she saw this. She stroked my hair and held me close. "Peaceful. And it'll go by quickly. Before you know it, you'll wake up to a handsome man."

Chapter Thirty-Eight

His Story

HE WAS A KIND lad, many said. Though perhaps a bit too ambitious for his own good.

Oh hush, others would say. He's just got a sense of adventure. All good lads do. He'll be just fine.

Perhaps he was too adventurous. There was a light in his eyes that only lit up as old knights told tales of days gone by. And there was a hunger in his belly for a tale of his own. He was being trained in swordplay and archery and jousting and chess, and would one day save kingdoms with his skill. That was what he wanted the most of all, to help the people around him. He got that trait from his grandmother, who was a healer.

The boy didn't want to be a healer. Blood made him woozy.

There were many things to know about that lad. The first, was that his name was Sir Nicolas Earnest Zapallis, and the second was that he was third in line for the Thames throne. But he didn't want it, he'd be quick to say. Just in case the others were ever assassinated, he didn't want any to assume he did it. He was smart like that, for a six-year-old boy.

Another important thing to know about him was that he was very brave.

There were other things to know, like his love for poached eggs or his three-year long fascination with insects, or his stutter when he got nervous, but none of those things mattered.

The last important thing to know, was that on this particular day, on this particular month, the lad was getting ready to go to a ball. He did not want to go; the lad wanted that to be known. Even if the two countries had worked hard to come up with this alliance, and now were throwing this ball to celebrate, he didn't see what that had to do with him.

"Will there be dragons?" he asked.

His father sighed. "No."

"Will there be jousting?"

Another sigh. "Not likely."

"Will there be knights?"

Now his father's eyes lit up, happy to give his son a good answer. "Yes."

Nicolas brightened. "Will they fight?"

Now a frown. "No."

He crossed his arms. "Then I don't want to go." His father pulled his son into his side as they rode in the carriage. It was far too late to turn around now. They had this conversation often, and Nicolas always agreed in the end.

"There will be cakes there," his father said. "And I'm sure some of the Elenvérs knights will tell you their tales. Tonight is important for the friendship between Thames and Elenvérs, and as third in line for the Thames throne, you ought to be there."

Nicolas didn't see why it mattered. Prince Gunther would be there, and Sir Holland. Both were older and far more interested in these social gatherings than Nicolas.

But he went. And he would like it noted that he did not complain one more time. Instead, he heaped his plate full of goodies and sat at a back table near an older man with kind, brown eyes, a cheerful smile, and wispy hair.

"Enjoying yourself?" the man asked as Nicolas sat down.

He bounced in his seat. "I'm hoping to meet some knights."

The man laughed. "Well you know, I was a knight once. And a king."

Nicolas's eyes sparkled as he looked over the frail man. "King of where?"

The man leaned in. "Elenvérs."

As the boy's eyes grew, the man settled back. "I'm not king anymore, though. My son has taken over for me. Soon his son will take over for him. There are more important matters for me to see to."

The boy pushed away his plate and turned in his chair. "What could be more important than being king?"

"I'm also a knight, remember? I have important, knightly duties."

The boy nodded. He remembered. But the man before him had stark white hair and a back that couldn't be fully straightened. He didn't look like a fearless knight. He certainly couldn't face any dragons.

"How old are you?"

The man chuckled again. "Not old enough. I'd hoped the last of the cave mages magic could keep me alive long enough, but I'm a few years too short."

The boy sat back in his chair. This man must be mad, he thought. He wasn't making sense. Nicolas picked a cookie off the plate and bit into it as he watched the finely dressed figures dance around the room. His father spotted him and gave him a nod, and Nicolas waved back.

"What do you think is the most important part of being a knight?" The old man spoke again. "The glory? The honor? The ladies?" He nudged Nicolas.

Nicolas wrinkled his nose. None of those answers were right. He thought for a moment as he recalled what his grandmother had taught him. "The most important part is helping others. That's what really matters."

For a moment, the old man didn't say anything. Then he smiled. "I've asked many lads that question. You are the only one to give such an answer."

Nicolas beamed at having impressed him. "My grandmother taught me to help people."

"She sounds very nice." He leaned forward again and whispered to Nicolas. "Do you want to hear a tale?"

Nicolas nodded, for he loved knights' tales best of all. The man cleared his throat. "There once was a girl. A beautiful, beautiful girl."

Nicolas scrunched his nose. He was hoping for a tale about a knight, not a girl. But he didn't interrupt the man.

"That girl loved her kingdom very much. One day, her kingdom needed her help. She sacrificed herself to save it. Then, she fell into a deep sleep. All time is frozen for her as she waits for someone to wake her from this sleep."

"Is she dead?" the boy asked. "Because when my grandmother died, they told me she was sleeping, but I knew better."

The old man grinned. "She's not dead. She's alive. But she must remain asleep for exactly one hundred years, waiting for a brave man to wake her. Are you brave?"

Nicolas nodded.

"Good." The man smiled. "In fifteen years, this maiden will be ready. And she needs someone to wake her from her sleep. Will you do it Nicolas? I can't be the one to wake her, and I don't want her to be alone."

Nicolas straightened his back. His first assignment. "Yes, I will do it. I will wake her for you."

Tension visibly released from the man as he slumped back in his chair. "Very good. This is your mission then. Wake the sleeping princess. When she wakes up, I have a journal to give her. Will you do that for me?"

The boy nodded. The old man pulled a folded piece of paper from his pocket. "I carry this with me just in case. You never know who you'll meet. I want you to have it."

He passed the paper to Nicolas who opened it. "It's a map," he said in awe.

"Yes, a map to find the princess. Fifteen years from next month, find the princess in the mountains and wake her."

Nicolas clutched the paper and nodded firmly. "I will. I will find the princess."

The boy put the paper in his pocket and patted it. Then he remembered to ask her name.

"Rowan," the man answered, and Nicolas had never heard a more beautiful name.

"And what's your name?"

He smiled again. "I am Cassian. I'm a friend of the princess."

And that is how the young boy first learned of the sleeping beauty in the northern mountains. And from that day on, he kept the map safe, and he didn't forget his promise.

One day, he often thought at night. One day I will find Rowan and wake her.

Chapter Thirty-Nine

The Princess, many years before the lad.

MAMA WAS RIGHT, IT'S peaceful. But she forgot to tell me how lonely it is. Or perhaps she left this out on purpose.

I don't dream. I sense things around me, but I can't see them or touch them or hear them. Something tells me I'm in a bed, but it isn't mine. It takes me a while—minutes or days, I don't know—to place whose bed it is. Cassian's.

A bed or the ice floor, it makes no difference to me. I can't feel anything anyway.

Time continues.

Sometimes I think I sense Tarion, but I can't be sure. Several times I'm sure I sense Elis, but she never comes to the room. Her presence shifts around Elenvérs, but she keeps her distance. Whether there's magic keeping her out, or her own guilt, I don't know. I sleep on, undisturbed.

There is no hunger in this sleep world, or pain or sadness or joy. I don't feel the loss of my family or my kingdom. I don't feel scared at the thought of the unknown.

I just am.

And it is like this, in the vast darkness of my mind, that I sleep on.

Chapter Forty

The lad, many years later

WHEN SIR NICOLAS EARNEST Zapallis was thirteen years old, Prince Gunther and his parents died in a carriage ride when his carriage slipped on ice and rolled down a mountain. Now, Nicolas was second in line for the throne. But he still didn't want it.

He was quite skilled by now and mature far beyond his years. He and his father worked hard until they'd acquired a fair amount of money through sea merchant trades.

Now Nicolas had time to travel. The first place he went? North.

He sought out the sleeping princess, clinging to the yellowed map. It wasn't time to wake her. He was nine years too early. But he wanted to find her. He had to see her.

Nicolas wasn't used to the cold or the way it made his nose numb. He didn't know how easy it was to get lost in a blizzard. It was during one of these blizzards that he lost his way and stumbled to the doorstep of a kind woodcutter.

The woodcutter lived alone in this cabin in the woods. He was also very sick. Nicolas stayed with him for the next few months as he nursed him into the grave. Before he died, Nicolas asked him about the sleeping princess. The man told Nicolas the same tale Cassian had told him. He said he'd heard the story many times while living in these mountains.

He was the only other person Nicolas had met who knew the story. So it wasn't just a mad man's tale, after all.

After the woodcutter died, Nicolas continued his search for the princess.

It was too early, he told himself. And that's why he couldn't find her. But he fixed up the woodcutter's home and turned it into a shelter for when he would come back. Because the lad planned to come back. He wouldn't leave the princess to sleep forever.

Chapter Forty-One

The Princess, who lost track of time

I FELT CASSIAN. I'M sure of it. Now accustomed to the feeling, I'm able to find a slight sense of my parents in the distance, reassuring me that they are safe. Though I try, I never learn more than that. They are okay. That is all I need.

But one day Cassian comes, his presence stronger than ever. Like Elis, his aura moves about Elenvérs but never inside. Now I am sure of it, no one can get within the walls.

This should bring me joy, I think. I am safe here. But I don't feel it. I don't feel anything but tired.

Sleep drags on.

Chapter Forty-Two

The lad

WHEN SIR NICOLAS EARNEST Zapallis was nineteen years old, Crown Prince Holland died in a jousting accident.

Now, Sir Nicolas Earnest Zapallis was renamed Prince Nicolas Earnest Zapallis. The mourning king adopted him as his son and began training him to take the throne one day. Again, the lad didn't want this. But he didn't say so. It was his duty to help people in whatever role he was given.

The next year was hardly his own. Every moment of his life was spent in ruthless preparation to be king of Thames. The current king wanted to retire, and Nicolas had to be ready.

He served his country well, and quickly became loved by the people. But a year and a half into his time there, he begged the king for time. His request was granted. Nicolas had one year to find the princess and wake her.

She ought to wake soon.

He set off toward the north.

Chapter Forty-Three

The Princess

TIME IS PASSING BY outside; I am sure of it. But how much time, I cannot know. Perhaps years. Enough that my life has played on repeat through my mind several times, reminding me of every moment that brought me here.

Sometimes I think of those events, other times I don't think at all.

Then I feel something new. The presence of my parents wanders close to home. I feel them outside the walls. They look in but they cannot enter. They call my name, but I cannot answer.

Cassian is with them. I recognize his presence easiest of all. Their presence stays for days, weeks, months. I'm uncertain. Elis does not join them. Then, one day, my parents are gone. First my father, then my mother. Their presence didn't drift away, it simply stopped. I search but cannot find it. Cassian's presence stayed, but he pulled away.

My parents are dead. I'm sure of it.

This tells me one vital piece of information: more time has passed than I thought. Even if someone found a way to break the curse now, free me early, I'd still be waking to an unknown world. A world where all those I knew are aged or gone. A world without my parents.

Cassian must be older now, perhaps with a wife and children, but he never brings them. He is always alone.

After my parents die, Cassian only visits once more. Then, I can no longer feel him either. Just like my parents, his presence in this world suddenly ends. Gone, while I'm left behind.

I remember what sadness is, but I don't feel it. I do feel alone.

Cold. Dark. Alone.

I sleep on.

Chapter Forty-Four

Nicolas

ACCORDING TO THE MAP, the castle should have been here, he thought.

Nicolas wandered through the frozen mountains in search of the sleeping princess. He'd lost track of the days, but it was almost time. He had to find her.

He licked his cracked lips. He hadn't eaten all day, and he took his last sip of water a few hours ago.

A glittering stream ran down the mountain. Clear water. Nicolas ran to its side and drank. Though it might have been the extreme thirst speaking, he swore it was the freshest water he'd ever tasted, and he eagerly filled his canteen. A few apples and bread and dried meat rested in his worn-out pack on his shoulder, but he was saving it to give to Rowan. She must be hungry after sleeping so long.

Nicolas pulled out the map again and gave it a long look. The writing was faded by now and the lettering hard to read, but he should be in the right spot. How big was this palace he ought to find? He couldn't see anything nestled among the bitterly cold mountains.

Just as his spirits were getting low, Nicolas spotted a bear. Its white fur blended with the snow, but its blue eyes gave it away.

At least I'll have a full belly, he thought, as he slowly reached for his bow. The bear ran at the movement. But he didn't run fast enough. Nicolas could catch him if he tried.

He took off after the bear.

All morning, Nicolas chased the bear. Just when he thought he was close enough to hit him with an arrow, the bear would pull ahead and duck through trees, and Nicolas would have to catch up to him again. Sometimes he thought he'd lost him, but the bear always reappeared.

After one such time, the beast appeared on a mountain crag and roared. Nicolas pulled out his bow and took aim.

The bear ran away.

Nicolas's bow lowered. Where the bear stood, he now saw something else. A blue spire, rising above the pines.

Could that be it? He looked closer. It was the top of an ice palace.

He'd found her.

It took Nicolas almost the rest of the day to reach the palace, and by then he was so tired that he could hardly move another muscle. The castle was more beautiful than any he'd ever seen. He'd expect nothing less from a mysterious palace in the abandoned Northern Mountains. Something about it called to him, drawing him in closer. He tried to get in, but the door held tight.

No matter how much force he used, it wouldn't budge.

Perhaps he was too early, he decided. So he waited. He was so close to her; he could almost sense her waiting inside.

I'm coming, he whispered. *I'm coming to help you.*

Chapter Forty-Five

The Princess, who is quite rested

SOMEONE ELSE COMES. HE carries an emotion I haven't felt in years. I struggle to name it. Curiosity?

He doesn't get inside the palace, but he doesn't leave. His presence lingers around Elenvérs, circling it like a wolf.

I don't fear him. I'm not sure I can feel fear anymore.

He tries to enter; time and time again. But I don't sense frustration from him. I sense patience. Patience and curiosity.

I think I'm curious too. It's the first emotion to return to me.

My entire world was black, but today it's grey. The darkness starts to drift away.

He pulls again at the door, but it doesn't open.

Still, he doesn't leave.

I can feel the soft pillow beneath my head. My hair around my neck. Things I haven't felt in so long. But I don't wake.

Breathing. I can feel my lungs taking breaths. Have they only started doing that again, or have they always been breathing? I don't know the answer, but I can feel myself breathe in. Breathe out. It feels familiar.

The man tries again.

This time is different. His presence gets closer. I think he's inside. He doesn't come to me right away. He goes through the palace, searching. I try to call to him, but my voice says nothing. My tongue feels heavy in my mouth and my hands and feet begin to tingle. They must feel him too. He's coming.

I try to call out again, but still no sound. I try to move, but my body won't respond.

New emotions come to me. Anticipation. Eagerness. Hope. They swell within my heart and make me feel alive. His presence strengthens.

A door opens near me. It's the first sound I've heard in a hundred years. Then footsteps, slow and careful.

They stop, and he takes a sharp breath. After a few moments of silence, his footsteps come closer. He's beside me now. A gentle hand strokes my arm, and his hand takes ahold of mine.

"Wow."

The first voice I've heard in a hundred years. It's a gentle and quiet sound that sends his breath dancing across my forehead. It's warm. I'd forgotten what warmth felt like.

"You are the most beautiful thing I've ever seen," he says. Now my arms and legs shiver. They are coming awake.

The gray turns into a soft light that I wait behind, ready to wake.

His nose brushes mine. I try to lean forward into him, but I'm still paralyzed. Eager, I wait for his lips.

They find mine. A soft, simple kiss is placed upon my lips. He lingers there, and I feel his breath on my cheek before he pulls back.

My eyelids flutter, letting in the first light in a hundred years.

I'm awake.

Chapter Forty-Six

MY MOTHER WAS RIGHT, he was handsome. Oval eyes stared at me through long lashes. He had long hair the color of honey, bronzed skin, a slender face, and a wide mouth that hung slightly open as I stared back. For years I'd imagined the face of the man who'd awaken me. Sometimes I pictured him with dark skin and friendly eyes. Other times, he was pale and reserved. Sometimes he had red hair, like mine.

I hadn't expected him to be so warm.

A calmness drifted within me, though I couldn't know if it was from him or a lingering effect of sleep. I tried to sit up, but he still held my hand, and I didn't want to appear cold by pulling it away. Without speaking, he knew what I wanted, and tugged to help me sit. His hands were rough like stone, with little callouses at the tips of his fingers.

There was a sword at his side. It was the first real detail I noticed about him that gave me a hint about who he was. A bear's head was engraved in the hilt. The bear is the kingdom of Thames's marker. What was a man from Thames doing here? Was he a knight who got lost on a mission and happened to stumble upon Elenvérs? Or had he known to find me? The way he'd waited patiently outside the walls then searched for me told me he knew what he was looking for.

With his steady guidance, I threw my legs over the side of the bed and allowed my head time to stop spinning.

"Are you alright?" He spoke no louder than a whisper, and kept a firm hold on my hand. His grip was the only thing keeping me grounded to this room; without it I feared I would float away.

I nodded to him.

My senses continued coming back to me: the navy of his jacket was vibrant, the softness of my own fur dress more noticeable, and his smell, a mix of forest pine and apples, was strong.

"Who are you?" I tested my voice. My words came out raspy, and I cleared my throat.

He sat on the bed beside me, still holding my hand. "My name is Prince Nicolas of Thames." He stuttered over his title.

"How did a prince from Thames end up in Elenvérs?" I asked. No one besides Cassian and my parents had come close to the palace in a hundred years.

Had it really been a hundred years?

His lips pursed. "The king graciously allowed me to travel here in search of you." I didn't fail to notice how he called his father by his title rather than his name. His eyes showed no animosity there, however.

He looked into my eyes so deeply that I had to look away. He cleared his throat. "Do you need anything? I don't have much food, but you can have anything that I have."

I shook my head. "I'm okay, I think. I could stretch my legs though." The fog in my mind continued to clear. A hundred years.

He slid off the bed and took hold of my other hand, gently pulling me to my feet.

"Rowan."

My mind woke up when he said my name. It sounded nice on his tongue as the slight accent made his words longer and put the accent on the first syllable of my name, instead of the second.

"Do you understand what happened?" he asked.

I looked around the empty room. It felt like just yesterday that Cassian and I were in these chambers, talking about how we would save Elenvérs from ThornHigh. He'd leaned against this bed, while I told him of Tarion's plans.

If I closed my eyes, I could almost imagine that Cassian would burst through the doors at any minute. But he wouldn't. Cassian was gone. My family was gone.

Sadness crept in, but I breathed through it, gulping in as much air as I could fill my lungs with. The armor I wore when Tarion put me to sleep had been replaced by a brown fur dress with long sleeves, which would struggle to protect me from the coming cold.

The cave mages' magic was gone. The curse kept me alive through the eternal winters, but I'd need to find my own heat soon.

Outside the window, everything looked the same. The same mountains, the same snow, the same caves. Time had frozen for me and the palace while the world moved on.

Nicolas stayed by my side, waiting for my answer.

With a slow tear falling down my cheek, I nodded. "I've been asleep for a hundred years."

Saying it out loud made it feel true. I'd been asleep, and everyone was gone.

He took my cheeks in his hands and wiped away the tears. To my surprise, I didn't pull away. Before, I would have yanked away at someone's touch, but his hands were comforting. He felt familiar to me, like someone I'd known my whole life. And right now, he was the only thing keeping me sane.

His gentle eyes looked into my own. "I am right here for you. Anything you need, I'm here. If you'd like, I'll take you back to Elenvérs—the one in the south, that is. It's a thriving country."

My eyes lit up. I'd love to see the kingdom that Cassian and my parents built. But there was no one there who knew me, and no one there was waiting for me. I breathed out deeply. "I don't know. I'm unsure what to do now."

He smiled. "We'll figure it out together."

I nodded. I had no other options but to trust this stranger.

Had my mother trusted my father when she woke?

She said she fell in love with father as soon as she opened her eyes. Father said he fell in love before she opened her eyes. Someday I might say that too, just to make a good story. But right now, I wasn't in love—not truly.

However, I was smitten with this kind man and his charming accent. Was it because he was the one who woke me? Would I feel this way toward any chap who found me? Was my mind awake enough to make sense of all this?

What did he think of me?

The steady hand in mine told me he wasn't leaving any time soon.

"Is your father needing you back in Thames soon?"

He adjusted the pack on his shoulder as he shifted back against Cassian's bed, bringing him closer to eye level with me. His cheeks were pink, and he rubbed his hand against his thigh as if cold. "In a few months. But the king isn't my father. I'm not even a true prince." I drew my brows down, and he flustered. "I am heir of Thames, but I wasn't born a prince. The real prince died, then the next fellow did too, and now the king made me prince in their place. It's an honorary title, it's not even necessary. I'm originally just Sir. But now some call me Prince. And someday I'll be King."

He stumbled over his words, and I suspected there was a bit of a tale to how he had acquired his new title. He was cute as he stammered.

"It's strange, I know. I think the king missed his son and wanted someone in his place to fill the vacancy in the palace. He's a kind man." Nicolas coughed. "Well, now that I've made a fool of myself, do you want something to eat? You must be starving. I can go to the kitchens to see if there's anything I can prepare."

I nodded. "Okay."

He smiled. He had a kind smile.

"I'll go look for something. I'll give you a moment." He hesitated before leaving, glancing at me as if he worried that I'd disappear the moment he walked away. In truth, I feared I would too. It all felt so fragile, like one moment I might drift away and be lost in the wind.

Then he moved down the hallway and out of my sight, leaving me alone.

Without his warmth beside me, cold gripped me. My skin prickled and my arms shivered. This was the strangest feeling I'd ever experienced, almost like waking from a dream just to find I was in another. It didn't feel real. This time, *this era*, it wasn't mine. I was an imposter in someone else's timeline, and I didn't belong here.

My mother must have felt so alone when she woke up too. I wish I could have asked her more about how she got through this.

The cold feeling didn't go away, and I realized it wasn't just because Nicolas left. The room was growing noticeably colder as I stood there.

The magic was fading fast. Soon this palace and all the furniture inside would freeze over.

I moved through the room in a daze. As I walked, I felt something in my pocket and reached for it. A picture of my parents was folded inside. I stared at their faces. My mother looked ravishing, and my father looked so in love with her. This is the way I wanted to remember them: happy and in love. My heart ached. If only we'd had a little more time.

This room was too much for me suddenly. I needed air.

The dark, narrow corridor outside echoed my footsteps as I left Cassian's room. Here, everything looked exactly as it had before I'd fallen asleep. I might have preferred it to look different.

"A hundred years," I breathed as I looked both ways down the hallway. It felt like just yesterday that I hid in these halls, watching for ThornHigh's army. I wondered if ThornHigh still stood or what became of Tarion and Elis. There was a lot for me to learn about the world now.

I journeyed toward the great hall and the top balcony overlooking what had once been the true splendor of Elenvérs: balconies on either side letting in sheets of sunlight, a blue glow in the air, a diamond chandelier in the sky, tall ceilings, twisted columns lining the floor where we once danced under lights and snowflakes.

Now it was abandoned. An empty, unfamiliar sight.

Tears threatened to spill. Nicolas's words repeated in my mind to keep it from breaking. *They are a thriving kingdom.* The weight on my chest lightened. Elenvérs was okay. That alone made everything else worth it, even waking up a hundred years later in a time where my family didn't exist.

From below the balcony, I saw Nicolas enter the great hall with a platter. There must have been food in the kitchens after all, though I couldn't fathom how. If I squinted, I thought I spotted a silver bowl with some chocolate pudding inside, along with a large loaf of bread and a bowl of fruit. The magic of the curse must have provided food for us. It was a small consolidation for all I'd lost.

As Nicolas moved up the steps back toward me, he saw me. His smile was enough to melt my heart.

"Is it getting colder in here?" he asked with a shiver.

"I'm afraid so," I said as I reached for the pudding. "I know where we can get some blankets."

He held the platter as I took my first bite. The familiar flavor settled on my tongue, and I closed my eyes for a moment to revel in the taste. At least pudding still tasted the same.

"Do you want to go back to your room?" Nicolas asked as I took my second bite. My room. He meant Cassian's room. No, I didn't want to return to the room with all the memories.

"Let's find some blankets, and we can sit here for a bit." With my pudding in hand, I led him toward the nearest bedroom and stole the blankets. As I did, Nicolas told me about the blankets he saw in the kitchen cupboard and how he'd found that peculiar. I laughed as I explained how I'd hidden for several days from ThornHigh's soldiers.

"You slept in that cupboard?" Astonishment and awe filled his face.

"I figured a spy or looters wouldn't be checking the back cupboard. So yes."

He grinned. "Resourceful. You know, I used to hide in the kitchen cupboards as a kid." A piece of me brightened at finding our first similarity. The discovery felt momentous somehow.

We brought the thick blankets back to the top of the stairs where we sat to overlook the grand hall below. This was always the most beautiful spot in Elenvérs, and I was glad to show it to Nicolas. The room continued to grow colder and ice groaned around us.

The palace was sending a message. With my awakening, it no longer had a purpose. This palace wouldn't stand forever.

Nicolas covered our shoulders with blankets as he sat beside me and wrapped his arm around my body with a closeness that made my heart quicken.

"This is so beautiful," he whispered as he looked over the enormous grand hall. He turned his gaze to me. "What was it like to live here?"

His honey eyes watched mine as I hummed with the memory. "It was lovely. At its height, Elenvérs was glorious." And I told him tales of time spent here. I told him of the Full Moon Feasts and the tournaments that were held. I told him of the way Elenvérs came alive as the moon came out, and how the starlight sparkled through the ice. I told him of my father's kindness and how he served his people loyally. I told him of the White Bear and the best ways that knights brought the paw before the king.

I didn't tell him of Elis or Tarion or Cassian. That pain was still too great to share. The loss stung too deep.

But then Nicolas asked, "Did you ever know a man by the name of Cassian?" My jaw dropped.

My heavy voice clawed up from my throat. "Do you know him? I thought he was dead?"

At the hope in my eyes, Nicolas apologized. "I'm so sorry. He is. He died several years ago. But I met him when I was a boy, and he told me to find you."

An unexpected joy filled my heart knowing that Cassian handpicked Nicolas to come find me. It made me trust him a little more. Cassian had watched out for me in more ways than I knew.

Nicolas squeezed my hand. "He sent this for you. It's from your loved ones." He drew out a thick journal from his satchel and passed it to me. It settled heavily in my hands.

I could keep them back no longer. Tears flowed down my cheeks, and Nicolas repositioned himself so he could wrap his strong arms around me. I sobbed into his chest as he stroked my hair.

He whispered into my ear, "I'm so sorry. I'm so sorry."

I pulled back and wiped my eyes. As far as first impressions go, Nicolas was making a much better one than I.

He looked at me with kindness, even when I must look like a mess. I hadn't brushed my hair in a hundred years. To distract myself from my own sadness, I ran my fingers down the spine of the journal, yearning to open it now. I'd find time soon.

My cheeks chilled with wet tears. "Can you tell me more about yourself?" I longed for a distraction.

He straightened. "Where to start?"

Before he could say anything, the front doors flew open and two people stormed in, bringing the raging snow with them. One moved faster while the other stopped to close the door against the howling wind.

I jumped up, knocking the food everywhere, and positioned myself in front of Nicolas before realizing I had no weapon. He put his hand on my shoulder and stepped from behind me with a small smile.

Nicolas bent over the balcony and squinted at the man and woman. "Christopher? Anika? Is that you? What in the blazes are you doing here?"

They threw their heads back to look at us. "Nicolas." The girl wagged her finger up at us. "What mess have you gotten yourself into?"

The girl, Anika, looked about my age with shoulder length caramel hair, tall brown boots fastened over tight pants, an embroidered brown tunic, and a dagger at her waist. The other was a man with brown hair and a chuckle on his face as he followed the girl across the hall. He examined the palace with an eager bounce, but I didn't fail to note the sword at his hip or the bow over his shoulder.

"It's okay," Nicolas turned and whispered over his shoulder. "These are some of my friends. They've had quite the adventure of their own."

The girl shouted again. "Who is that with you? A witch? We don't need more witches."

Nicolas called back, "Let us come down so we can talk as civilized beings." She humphed but stopped shouting.

"Is she usually so loud?" I whispered to Nicolas as he led us down the stairs.

"Yes." He chuckled. "You'll find she's quite different than normal ladies."

When we reached the bottom of the stairs, he asked them, "How did you get here?"

He moved forward to shake Christopher's hand. Anika stayed back with her arms crossed, watching me. After shaking hands, the other man pulled his arms across his chest and shivered.

"Grandfather's magic. We'd heard of some power that stirred up here," Christopher said as he looked around.

"Not surprised to find you in the thick of it," the girl added. She wasn't upset, I realized, despite her posture. There was pleasure in her eyes. "Thought it might be a dragon." Was that hope in her voice?

"I've faced a dragon, they aren't that scary," I said for some unknown reason. They each stared at me, impressed. They didn't need to know Elis and I faced a tiny, baby dragon, or that we only lasted a few moments before irritated knights pulled us away.

I shifted and my arm grazed Nicolas's. Anika eyed our closeness. Her nose tilted toward me. "So, do you have a name?"

I cleared my throat. "I'm Rowan Sordwill," I said, claiming my rightful parent's name as my own. "And I've been asleep for a hundred years."

Her eyebrows shot up, while recognition flashed across Christopher's face. "I've heard stories of you," Christopher said. "I didn't think they were real! Incredible. And this is the fabled ice palace of Elenvérs. It's truly extraordinary."

Pride welled within me. I was glad others could see Elenvérs' beauty, too.

The ice moaned again. Another warning. I couldn't place how I was so certain, but I knew what the palace was trying to tell us—it was built with magic, and without that magic, it couldn't survive.

"It's pretty, but is it safe?" Anika asked as her eyes shifted. Somewhere, a crack vibrated the floors, and I placed a hand on Nicolas's arm.

They each looked on edge as the ice cracked again.

You must leave. My mother's voice said, clear as day. My body froze, but beside me Nicolas continued to stare at the floor as if it might give out. He gave no indication of hearing the voice. *You cannot stay here. The life of the castle is dying in your wake. It holds no purpose anymore.*

No, I spoke back in my thoughts. *I can't leave here.*

In reply, the ice groaned once more, and a crack followed. My home was falling, the glory of Elenvérs crumbling to the ground. No more would it rule over the mountains or shine like a beacon in the moonlight. No more would it hold great kings or fierce princesses. Soon, very soon, it would be nothing but shattered ice.

"Rowan." Nicolas's hand brushed mine. "I think we should leave."

My words were difficult to get out. I wasn't ready to leave. Even with a hundred years of preparation, I wasn't ready for anything that came next.

But I held my chin up, even as my lip trembled. "You're right. We can't stay here; the ice is going to break."

With a heart full of sorrow, I stole one final look at my forgotten home. The images of people long gone floated about the room, my mind allowing me to see them one final time. This was the room I thought I'd dance in once I became queen. This was the palace I ought to have ruled over. This was the home I'd fought to protect. These frozen mountains were all I'd ever known.

My mother's words sang in my mind. The last time I'd hear them. Do not fret, dear one. Sleep will be the start of a great adventure for you.

With a lump in my throat, I took a last look at my home. "It's time for me to leave Elenvérs."

Discover the rest of Rowan's journey in my next book, *Heir of Roses*

"We will find a girl fit enough to rule. Pure, strong, and enchanting. A queen of roses."

Rowan's sleeping curse is broken by a stranger's kiss. Their happily ever after should begin, but they aren't in love. They struggle to develop feelings as plots of betrayal, mysterious deaths, and a sword-wielding mother-in-law challenge them.

When the king sets up a Queen's Competition as an attempt to settle unrest, Rowan's place is threatened. She must fight for the prince she ought to love to secure his position at court, while competing in challenges that seek to unravel her, bit by bit. For though they can force her to compete, she's the only competitor who knows she can never truly win.

Just as Rowan finds her place, a poison apple could destroy it all.

The conclusion to The Storyteller's Series is here.

A note to my readers

Greetings from this side of my laptop! *excited wave* Thanks for reading the third book in my Storyteller's Series! I consumed way too much hot chocolate while writing about an icy kingdom, but it was worth it.

If you want more from Rowan, I have good news! The next book picks up where this one leaves off, and we get to watch Nicolas and Rowan navigate the complexities that come when a stranger awakens you with true love's kiss. They aren't in love, but she's meant to be his true love, and right away she's asked to help him fight for his claim to the throne while deciding if she wants to stay or find what happened to her beloved Elenvérs. It takes a twist on the Snow White and Princess and the Pea tales.

As an indie author, for a book to be successful, reviews mean EVERYTHING. If you could take a moment to leave a review on Goodreads or Amazon, it would help my career immensely. I'll read every review posted so I can hear your thoughts on my book! I love hearing from readers and am grateful for your time. You are also welcome to find me on social media (Instagram: victoria_mccombs) to connect further! My inbox is always open to readers!

Thank you! Your support means the world to me.
-VM

Other books by Victoria McCombs

Acknowledgments

First, thank you to my kids for somehow understanding, "mommy needs to write." And thank you to my husband who makes this possible for me.

I owe a huge thanks to all those I've met in the writing community who encourage me every day. You are all so amazing and I'm so grateful for your friendship! Ruth Wilson, you are a particular gem. Danielle Harrington, Stephen McClellan, and Caitlin Lambert: you have been wells of knowledge for me to draw from and I can never repay you for that! For everyone else who has reached out on Instagram to encourage me or talk about my books, I appreciate you all so much! The support and love from you all warms my heart.

Oma, this book is dedicated to you for all the phone calls, texts, emails, and conversations we had about this story. It made the writing process so much easier to have someone to think through the plot with me, and who encouraged me through it all. This might have been a very different story if it wasn't for you!

Next, thank you to the editors who have worked on this story, Gretchen and Sophie. And a huge thanks to Lindsay Rankin! I can't thank you enough for the work you put into my story. Without your help, I wouldn't feel prepared to send this into the world.

Thank you to my family for being supportive, for listening to all my crazy ideas, and for reading through the story. You've believed in me for a long time, and I couldn't have done it without your encouragement. And of course, thank you to Jesus for being my savior.

About the Author

Some of the things I love most in this world are peppermint hot chocolate, peanut butter ice cream, golfing dates, Jesus, and game nights with family. And of course, books.

Fairytales were my first love. I became obsessed with the idea that if one was brave enough, they could defeat dragons, and that true love was real. I met my true love in college, and together we raise our boys. I have my dad to thank for my love of writing, and my mom to thank for allowing us to keep a wall of medieval weapons in the house, which cultivated my love for that time period. My dream is to write vivid worlds and charming characters that will leave an imprint on my readers hearts, the way that so many books have done for me.